The Fool's Errand

The Fool's Errand

R. Charles McLravy

Arbutus Press ~ Traverse City, Michigan

ISBN 978-1-933926-27-8

This is a work of fiction. All incidents and dialogue, and all characters are the products of the author's imagination and are not to be construed as real. Any resemblance to actual events or persons, living or dead, is entirely coincidental.

Library of Congress Cataloging-in-Publication Data

McLravy, R. Charles.
The Fool's Errand / R. Charles McLravy.
p. cm.
ISBN 978-1-933926-27-8
1. Attorneys--Michigan--Detroit--Fiction. 2. Man-woman relationships--fiction. 3. Murder--Investigation--Fiction.
4. Detroit
(Mich.)--Fiction. I. Title.
PS3613.A2719F77 2011
813'.6--dc22

Printed In the United States of America

Arbutus Press
Traverse City, Michigan

FOR

CHRISTI

ACKNOWLEDGEMENTS

While my name is appended as author, *The Fool's Errand* simply could not have been written without the invaluable assistance and unflagging aid of those who follow.

Thanks to my wife, Christi, for her encouragement, support, tolerance, patience, and most of all, her love.

Thanks also to my three children -Charlie, Tom, and Kathryn- for their love and support. Also to Charlie for his encouragement and his research. Also to Tom and Kathryn for putting up with my commandeering of the breakfast table on Saturday and Sunday mornings and their recurring question: when is it going to be done?

To my parents, Bob and Yvonne McLravy, for their love and support and especially for passing on their love of the written word.

To Lynne Kohon for her countless hours of typing, her printer, and especially for her infuriating attention to detail.

To writer Pat MacEnulty for her thoughtful editing and advice.

To Deb Hansen for her ability to help me do what comes next.

To Steve Pruett, Bob Larson, Frank Shumway, and Steve Spencer for reading early versions of the book Also to Frank Shumway, Steve Spencer and Julie Spencer for their sage advice.

To Jim Lozier and Bob Stocker for legal advice. Also to Bob Stocker for his wise counsel.

To Tom Hitch for his knowledge of criminal procedure.

To Joe Ross for his help in promotion and public relations.

Finally, to Susan Bays for her daring spirit and firm hand in seeing to it that *The Fool's Errand* was actually published.

PROLOGUE

THE GRAVE'S A FINE AND PRIVATE PLACE,
BUT, NONE I THINK, DO THERE EMBRACE.

TO HIS COY MISTRESS
— ANDREW MARVELL

PROLOGUE

Saturday, December 18, 1982

Frank stood in his shirtsleeves and watched his house from the sidewalk across the street. The picture window in the living room framed the Christmas tree, a freshly cut white pine. Snow had started falling again, and it softened the light in the picture window, blurring the edges of the Christmas tree lights, the old fashioned kind. Big bulbs—red, blue, green, yellow, orange, and white. The kind that didn't blink.

Two hours ago, the three of them, Claudia, Jason, and Frank, had cut the tree twenty miles to the north. After Frank stood the tree up in the Christmas tree stand and centered it in the picture window, they strung the lights, wrapped the garland, and hung the ornaments, but they hadn't put the angel on top. It was the garland that had started the argument. That was why the angel wasn't on top of the tree. The argument about the garland had stopped everything.

Frank had retreated to the basement, and that's where he'd left Claudia, lying at the bottom of the stairs.

Outside, the snow, light and powdery, melted on Frank's head and drifted onto his shoes. He studied the Christmas tree. It began to teeter, swaying back and forth. Once, twice, three times. Then it tipped over out of sight.

Frank thought that the paramedics must have knocked it over with the stretcher.

Then Mrs. Larsen, the next door neighbor, came out the side door of the garage with Jason. She had her arm around his waist, but she had to reach up to do it because Jason was at least a head taller than she was. She walked him over to her house, onto her front porch, and inside.

Rollie Gustafson, the Petoskey cop, and the first to arrive, came out of the house. He opened up the door of his cruiser and turned off the flashers. He waved at Frank and motioned him to come back across the street.

Frank started across the street just as Van Arkel, the coroner, came out. The paramedics came out right behind him, wheeling the stretcher. A body bag, zipped shut, lay on top of the stretcher, Claudia inside.

PART ONE
THE INDICTMENT

Is this a dagger which I see before me,
The handle toward my hand?

MacBeth, Act II, Scene One
—*William S. Shakespeare*

CHAPTER ONE

MONDAY, DECEMBER 12, 1988

The wind had backed around to the southwest and blew about thirty. A chop bucked the current in the Johnston on the way out. The wave tops broke off and sprayed them both in the face. When Burr saw one coming, he turned his head, but Zeke, his yellow Lab, took them head on and didn't seem to care. The old moon glowed behind the overcast and lit the wave tops, lighting the spindrift as it blew off the waves, the shore a silhouette in the moon shadow.

He knew the wind had shifted last night when the shutter on his house, a cabin really, had started banging. It only talked to him when the wind blew hard from the southwest. He'd never fixed that shutter because a strong southwest wind brought him good news—big waves on Lake St. Clair blew the ducks off the lake and into the marsh. They rafted out in the lake by the thousands, tens of thousands, mallards, blacks, redheads, cans, bluebills, but mostly mallards, and when the southwest wind kicked up the waves they blew off the lake and swarmed into the marsh for cover.

In the darkness, half an hour out, he cut left at the break in the cattails. He could barely see the cut and he flashed his light and picked up the channel marker—a stick jutting five feet out of the water. He turned off the light, throttled the outboard back and eased his way out of the Johnston and into the Swift. He slid through the cattails rising on each side of the boat, well over his head. The wind bent them, but there was no chop in the Swift, underneath the wind. He lit a cigarette and motored through the channel. He could see yellow in the east now and the waves again, breaking hard as the cut opened on to the lake. He gunned the engine at the end of the channel and took one head on. He veered left again now running broadside with the waves. They lifted him as they rolled underneath. If he could run this quarter mile without swamping, he'd go left one more time up into the Hourglass.

Zeke, sitting in the bow, looked back at him and shook the spray from his head, ears flapping. The dog turned back, nose into the wind. In the gusts, his ears lifted like the wings of a bird.

The boat washed toward the cattails with each roller, and he had to stick the bow into the wind every chance he got. A wave lifted the boat and swept underneath. The boat rolled. Above the noise of the wind, and the waves breaking and then crashing into the cattails, he could hear the decoys shifting in the bottom of the boat. Zeke turned his head and looked back at him again.

The lake shoaled at the mouth of the Hourglass. In the darkness Burr couldn't see the bottom, but he knew a sandbar at the mouth would be exposed between waves. He'd have to time his approach to avoid grounding, and if he did ground, the next wave would swamp the boat. The nearest house was a cabin five miles upriver through the marsh.

Burr saw what he took as the mouth of the channel, a white line where the waves broke. No sunrise today. This would be a day when it never got light, just a measured grayness until dark. A December like all the others where the only bright lights would be man made. At the mouth now, he needed to rush in on a wave, timing his charge. The boat yawed on top a wave, then sagged. He turned downwind toward the cut. Another wave lifted them. Then he gunned the engine. Its roar drowned the sound of the surf, wind, and rattle of the cattails. The boat raced to the crest of the wave. He cut the engine back, stayed on top of the foam, gunned it again, and surfed his way over the sandbar into the cut.

The roar of the wind and the waves gave way to the cracking of the cattails scraping against each other. He motored slowly and the wind that found its way up behind him blew the exhaust back into the boat. He sucked in a breath and remembered every other time he'd smelled that smell.

The water in the channel shoaled. He shut off the outboard, lifted the prop and untangled the punt from the decoys. The iridescent film, gas and oil, swirled on top of the water sloshing in the boat. He pushed the blade of the twelve-foot push pole into the muck and squeezed up the channel. A twelve foot white ash plank —one piece —carved not turned—the base splayed out like a canoe paddle—the end fitted with an iron jaw, now rusted, to grip the bottom. He felt the edges of the wood where they had been carved and sanded almost round. It had been rough sanded and oiled once. A crosspiece snugged on the end helped him push. He could buy a push pole, but Victor had carved this for him, and he counted it as one of his most valued possessions. A splinter sliced into his hand.

The boat nosed into the Hourglass, a two-acre pond, three hundred yards from the lake. Another channel opened at the far end and edged a mile further up then petered out, leading nowhere.

He poled the boat around the edge of the pond. When he was halfway to the blind, the ducks went up, about two hundred of them. The cattails reached over his head even when he stood in the boat. He felt trapped and safe at the same time. He set the decoys in front of the blind—twenty-three—always an odd number Victor said —in a hook shape with the pocket ten yards in front.

Zeke jumped into the blind, a six by three platform, cattails lashed to the handrails. He hid the boat in the weeds and climbed into the water, knee deep, but he sank to his waist in the muck. Then he slogged to the blind and pulled himself out of the ooze. He sat in a rusty, folding chair and lit another cigarette. The season ended in a week and with it his smoking, a seasonal indulgence, and then only when he hunted. Almost light now, a mallard circled the decoys, cupped and came in. A hen. He didn't shoot.

The wind built behind him. Ducks all around now. He blew his greeting call: five burry quacks, each descending, and each shorter than the one before. No response. He called again. Three buzzed the pond. He chuckled the feeding call. He looked down, hiding his face, saw the mud on his waders, then turned his head and tried to see out of the corner of his eye, careful not to spook them. Two mallards and a black. They circled downwind. He quacked a greeting call. Back again then another circle. More quacks from him. Now they cupped their wings, heads up into the wind, rocking back and forth, spilling the wind from their wings, like a maple leaf falling in October.

"Mark" he said. Then he rose from the chair and swung the shotgun through the lead duck, a drake mallard. He pulled the trigger just as the barrel passed the duck's head. At that precise moment, he felt connected to the bird by the shot string—two living creatures tied together for an instant in time. The duck faltered. He pumped, fired again and splashed the duck.

"Fetch it back."

Zeke launched himself from the blind and hit the water eight feet in front of the blind and twenty yards from the bird. The duck dove when Zeke closed in. The yellow lab pirouetted on his hind legs. The duck surfaced and Zeke lunged. Another lunge and he caught the bird. The dog swam back to the blind, climbed up the dog ladder, sat in front of him.

"Zeke, give." The dog released the orange-legged mallard. He spit out feathers and shook off the water, head to tail.

"Good dog," Burr said.

He wrung the duck's neck, made sure it was dead. Then he lit another cigarette and looked across the pond, towards Detroit. The cattails shrunk his view to this pond, but Detroit was just across Lake St. Clair, twenty miles to the southwest. Here though, in Ontario, a ferry ride across the St. Clair River, it was a different world. Not really Canada but Walpole Marsh, at the edge of Walpole Island, the largest freshwater marsh on the Great Lakes. The unceded land of the Council of Three Fires—the Ojibwe, the Odawa, and the Pottawotomie —at least that's what the sign said when he drove off the ferry.

More ducks blew in off the lake, a full gale now. Burr couldn't seem to turn them into the Hourglass. They sought shelter further in the marsh. The wind had stirred up the pond and he saw a little corn floating on top. Ontario prohibited baiting but that didn't stop Victor.

From the lake, more ducks blew downwind for cover. This time his hail call peeled off a flock of seven. He sat down, scrunched into a corner of the blind and worked his call. They circled him twice. He lost track of them. Zeke looked up and whined softly. Burr looked at Zeke and saw the ducks in the dog's eyes. They circled again, now right overhead. He clucked. They started to settle in. He clicked off the safety.

Then they were gone.

He looked around. What went wrong? A boat nosed out of the cut into the pond. Damn. Who would possibly come in here today? The boat push poled its way into the Hourglass. It was Victor. Damn that Indian.

"How's the hunting?"

"Improving, until you scared off the ducks," Burr said.

"There will be more ducks," Victor said. He climbed into the blind. Victor Haymarsh was fifty-five and looked it, short, stocky, leathery, with a black ponytail streaked with gray. Burr reached into his pack and handed the Indian a pack of Players, the traditional ceremonial gift to a chief. Victor, too, only smoked during duck season.

"Why'd you come all the way out here," Burr said, not really asking.

"Not my idea," Victor said.

"Oh," Burr said, not really wanting to hear what might come next.

"You got a phone call," Victor said.

"I don't have a phone."

A pair of mallards landed in the decoys. Zeke twitched, did not move. Burr ignored them.

"On my line," Victor said.

"Nobody's got that number," Burr said.

"Somebody does," Victor said

"What's the message?" Burr said.

"No message." A man of few words, Victor had a gift for mystery.

"Who was it?"

"I don't know," Victor said.

"You came all the way out here to tell me that" Burr said, again not asking.

"No," Victor said. "She said she'd hold."

"It was an accident," Suzanne said on the phone.

"I don't care if it was an accident," Burr said. "I don't care what it was."

He had run the boat back to Victor's house on the Johnston River, half a mile downstream from his own cabin, which (purposely) had no phone. Somehow he had known it would be Suzanne. Suzanne, Jacob, and Eve were the only ones who had Victor's number, but only Suzanne would hold for two hours. He looked out and saw Zeke, still sitting in the boat. He wouldn't run the risk of being left behind.

"Yes, Suzanne," he said into the telephone, "it is coincidental that I'm just across Lake St. Clair, but I'm a world away, and you know I don't do criminal work."

"You could, and this is easy," Suzanne said. "It's just some mistake.

"Suzanne," Burr said, "let's go back to the beginning. It is wonderful to hear your voice. How long has it been?"

"Two and a half years," she said. "And that's not really the beginning."

"No, of course not," Burr said. "I never thought I'd hear from you again."

"You wouldn't have," she said, "except I need your help."

"You should get a criminal lawyer."

"Please do this for me," Suzanne said.

"I don't think it wise," Burr said.

"A. Burr Lafayette," Suzanne said, dragging out the 'A'. "I really need your help."

"Suzanne, together we lost my marriage and my law practice."

"As I recall, you quit. As I further recall, you started it," Suzanne said. "And you lied to me about Grace. And about the other thing."

This is not going well, Burr thought. He certainly hadn't forgotten what happened. "I did leave Grace," Burr said.

"After she found out," Suzanne said. "And you never did explain the other thing. Not that I would have believed you."

Actually, thought Burr, he had left Grace before she found out, but that was probably a small point, especially considering the "other thing" for which, after all this time, he still had no satisfactory explanation.

"Mea Culpa," he said, delighted that Suzanne had apparently not chosen to pursue the further reason for their demise.

"Burr, I really need your help," Suzanne said.

"I don't do criminal work. I've never done criminal work," he said. "More importantly, there's a gale from the southwest. It's blowing all the ducks off the lake and into Walpole Marsh, and that's where I'm going." He hung up and walked out the door. The phone rang again on the way out. Victor followed and shut the door behind him. The wind cycloned underneath the bill of Burr's hat and twisted it sideways on his head. They took two boats and made for the Holiday pond.

Hearing Suzanne's voice without seeing her, Burr remembered how musical it could be. She had a rich alto voice, melodious, not husky, that ranged up and down the scale. Burr thought it softened her tongue and the bite she could have. He remembered how much he had liked listening to her, no matter what she said.

An hour later, decoys set, Burr and Victor sat in a stake blind on the Holiday Pond, tucked well into Walpole Marsh.

"That one, she's a beauty," Victor said. "But I think she's trouble."

"Be quiet," Burr said in a whisper.

Overhead, a half-dozen widgeon whistled at the decoys. Burr took his dog whistle and blew softly, trilling at them, his finger on and off the end of the whistle. The ducks circled back.

"How old were you then, forty-six, forty-seven?"

The ducks cupped their wings into the wind.

Burr killed a duck on the second shot. On command, Zeke leapt into the pond.

"Midlife crisis, I guess," Victor said.

"What would you know about a midlife crisis?"

"That's right. Indians don't have that. We're too emotionally healthy. We just drink ourselves to death."

The dog climbed back into the blind and shook himself off, mostly on Victor.

"Good dog, Zeke. Give." The dog let go of the bird.

"Nice soft mouth on that one," Victor said.

"Forty-seven. I was forty-seven then," Burr said.

"Two years ago. That's about right," Victor said. "Was it worth it?"

"No." Burr bit his lower lip. "Yes, it was," he said. "No. No, I guess not."

"I guess it wasn't about money," Victor said.

"No," Burr said, "that was one thing that wasn't about money."

They smoked and waited for the next flight. Half an hour later a single flew right in. Burr knocked the bird down at the end of the pond, but it swam into the cattails. Zeke looked for it. After twenty minutes, Burr called him off.

A hundred yards off, a marsh hawk lifted up and flew low, flat circles, fast downwind, fighting upwind.

"Hawk will get your cripple," Victor said.

By three the wind had clocked to the northwest. When it swings back around to the northeast, it could blow me right across the lake to Detroit, Burr thought.

Zeke's head jerked up. Burr looked across the pond and saw someone in his boat, poling over to the blind. It was Suzanne.

"Damn," Burr said.

She hid the boat and climbed into the blind. Her neoprene waders hid the curves in her legs. From the waist up, the camouflage parka covered up the rest, but Burr remembered it all. She was just shy of six feet, a head taller than Victor.

Victor nodded at her, stood, and left.

Burr watched him slog through the marsh to the boat. As Victor's feet sunk into the ooze, the wind blew the rotten egg, sulfur smell down on Burr. Victor hitched himself into his boat, stiff legged. His hip must be out again, thought Burr.

"Why did Victor leave?" Suzanne said.

"Because you came," Burr said.

"I didn't mean to chase him away," she said.

"Well, you did," Burr said.

She had her hair in a ponytail, shorter than Victor's, and jet black. Pouty wine-red lips, her only makeup out here in the marsh.

"How did you find us?" Burr said.

"It's too rough to get out to the lake," Suzanne said. She sat in Victor's chair and loaded her over/under, a ported Weatherby twelve gauge and locked the barrels into the stock. Burr saw that she'd clicked on the safety.

"At least let me tell you what happened," Suzanne said.

"I don't want to know what happened," Burr said.

"There's been a terrible injustice," Suzanne said.

Burr pretended to ignore her, but his interest was pricked, which he knew that she knew.

"A man has been arrested for murder," Suzanne said.

"Suzanne, that may not be an injustice, especially if he did it," Burr said.

"Please let me finish, " Suzanne said. "There was an accident in Petoskey six years ago. An accident. And now this man has been arrested for murder and hauled off to jail."

"Would this man have a name?" Burr said.

"Frank," Suzanne said. "His name is Frank. The police broke into his house in Grosse Pointe and hauled him off."

"I thought you said Petoskey," Burr said.

"The accident happened in Petoskey, but now he lives in Grosse Pointe," Suzanne said.

"I'm not a criminal lawyer," Burr said. He wondered how many times he had already said so.

"You're a trial lawyer," she said. "You know how to do it."

"Not anymore," Burr said. "I am not competent to do this for you."

"You are perfectly competent to do this," Suzanne said.

Burr looked over the tops of the cattails. The brown tops had dried out and faded. The wind melted them away and the seeds scattered across the marsh, sideways like snow on a day when it was too cold for anything but flurries.

"Burr, you practically grew up in Petoskey."

"Summers only," he said. "It was Harbor Springs, not Petoskey."

"Same thing," Suzanne said.

"Not really," he said.

"As a favor to me, then," Suzanne said.

"I'm all out of favors," he said.

Four years ago, when first they met, Burr was looking northeast twenty miles across Lake St. Clair to the First Nation and Walpole Marsh—northeast from the 35th Floor of Tower 100 of the Renaissance Center at Jefferson Avenue and the Detroit River - the great hope for downtown Detroit. Floor to ceiling windows, but through the haze, he could barely see the green border of Grosse Pointe and the blue of Lake St. Clair. The marshes of the First Nation lay out of sight, beyond the commerce of the Detroit River and Lake St. Clair.

Her scent reached him before he knew she was there. Rose. It had been rose, but musky underneath. He turned, saw her framed in the doorway to his office. Striking, not beautiful, but striking. Tall, narrow waist, very black ponytail, and full, pouty lips, painted red. Not beautiful, not yet thirty, perhaps not pretty, but she took his breath away.

She had arrived unannounced, which Burr would learn was how Suzanne always arrived. She simply walked in, his new client. A copywriter for a big Detroit ad agency. She worked on a car account and was sent to Detroit (which she hated) from New York (which she didn't hate). She had written the copy, which had gotten the agency sued, and the agency hired Burr to handle its defense. She was sent to meet with Burr who was stunned by her appearance.

"Suzanne Fairchild," she said, thrusting her hand towards him.

He had totally lost his place standing there by the window. Speechless, which for him, a litigator, was nothing if not unusual.

"Are you Mr. Lafayette?"

"Yes. Yes, I am," he said, still standing next to his window.

"For some reason someone at the agency thinks you need to talk to me," Suzanne said, "Although you don't seem like you're very talkative."

"Yes. Yes, of course," he said. "Here, please sit down." She started to sit down at one of the side chairs, facing his desk.

"No, not there. Please sit on the couch." He pointed to a leather couch fronted by a glass coffee table flanked by a matching leather chair.

As she sat down, Burr tried to look up her skirt, but she was too quick for him. Years of practice with long legs and inquiring eyes.

"Are you all right, Mr. Lafayette?"

Burr absolutely could not concentrate with her in the room. His partners protested duck season as it was, but Suzanne Fairchild would be taking things too far. Not to mention Grace.

~

Suzanne knocked down a black duck with a shot directly behind them over the cattails. Burr gave Zeke a line and sent him.

"He's a great dog, even at eleven, but I would never name my only son after a dog," Suzanne said.

"You don't have a son," Burr said, "and he's not eleven. He's ten."

After a quick foray into the marsh, Zeke-the-dog, splayed his front legs on the floor of the blind, his back legs in the ooze. He presented the duck to Burr.

"There is no greater honor than to be Zeke's namesake," Burr said. "Besides, Zeke-the-boy likes it."

"What a way to go through life: as Zeke-the-boy because there already is a Zeke-the- dog."

"Suzanne, I can't help you. Jacob and Eve wouldn't hear of it."

"Frank's going to be charged with murder," she said. "By now, he probably has been. His wife is hysterical."

"Frank has a wife," Burr said.

"Yes, he has a wife, and she needs someone to help her." Suzanne reached into her parka and took out a cigarette. She pulled the parka up around her head and lit the cigarette inside her coat, out of the wind.

~

When the wind blew around to the northeast and the snow came, the ducks quit flying. The blowing snow stung Burr's face like sand. Suzanne left the blind right after he told her no (again), but she had been waiting for him at the dock. He knew he would have to tell her no again, but now he was intrigued, and he was more intrigued by what he knew she hadn't said.

His Jeep skidded along the road on the way back to the ferry, fishtailing on the icy spots. A Grand Wagoneer, the kind they didn't make any more, blue with fake wood sides, and a rear window that didn't work right, now fogged up as Zeke dried off in the back. Burr didn't like to admit to himself that he cared about things, possessions, but he was afraid that he loved his Jeep (and his sailboat).

Suzanne followed him, surefooted in an Explorer, rented he thought.

He reached the paved road on Walpole Island, the speed limit marked in kilometers and turned north along the St. Clair River. Suzanne followed him. They drove onto the ferry —a ten car with diesels and painted over rust. He saw the ice, big chunks for December, drifting down river in the current.

They had to wait on the Walpole side, the Canadian side, half an hour, for the ice to clear. When the ferry finally left for Algonac, across the River on the Michigan side, Suzanne climbed in beside him. She always wore her hair in a ponytail, accenting her high cheekbones and aquiline nose.

"We're only half an hour from Grosse Pointe," she said. "Just help me get the bail posted. That's all," she said.

"Can't do it, Suzanne."

All the windows had fogged now. Suzanne rubbed a porthole on the windshield and looked out.

"Please, Burr. What's the harm?"

"Two choices. I'd say you have two choices. One, hire someone, a real criminal lawyer. Two, a public defender."

"Frank's wife is scared to death. She hasn't heard from him since Saturday night," Suzanne said.

"Almost two days," Burr said.

"Just help me get him out, then get back to your esoteric appellate practice. Please."

"I don't have time," Burr said.

"You can't be that busy if you've got time to hunt on a Monday," Suzanne said

Who would pay?" Burr asked.

"Frank would," Suzanne said. "Over time."

"Ah," Burr said, "it's not my scintillating mind you want. It's my fee schedule."

"No, that's not it at all," Suzanne said. "They have money. Well, some money."

"Suzanne, I don't work for free."

"So, it's just the money then," she said.

"No, it's not just the money," Burr said.

"It sounds like it to me," Suzanne said. "There's someone who's been jerked out of his life and all you can think about is money."

"Suzanne, why do you care about this so much?"

At that Suzanne removed herself from the Jeep and got back into the Explorer. Burr watched her in the rear view mirror. She hadn't told him quite everything, and he had some experience with that.

The ferry docked at Algonac on the Michigan side of the St. Clair River. After they cleared customs, Suzanne climbed back in the Jeep.

"Please help me," she said. "This one thing."

"Just this one thing," Burr said. "Suzanne, I thought you moved back to Manhattan."

"I did," she said. "I wouldn't be here if it weren't for Frank and his wife."

"When are you leaving?" Burr asked."

"As soon as you get Frank out of jail," Suzanne said.

"Just who is Frank's wife?" Burr asked.

"My sister," Suzanne said. "And you owe me."

Burr wasn't so sure he did owe her. He had certainly been in the wrong, but she had left him.

CHAPTER TWO

Burr heard a woman's voice shrieking inside as they walked up the sidewalk to the Grosse Pointe Police Station.

He's not here," said a man's voice.

"Well, then, where is he?" screamed the woman.

"Sarah got here before we did," Suzanne said.

"Obviously," Burr said.

Burr opened the door for Suzanne. Sarah's voice echoed through the first floor, bouncing off the brick walls. "You took him, kidnapped him, Saturday night. Now it's Monday afternoon."

Shoulder length hair, honey blond, and a small turned up pug nose. Short. Maybe, five two. Plump, that's what she was, not fat, plump, a little plump. Late twenties or early thirties. Suzanne's younger sister, but she didn't look like Suzanne. Attractive, now. Pretty, twenty pounds ago.

"Where have you been?" Sarah said.

"I couldn't find him," Suzanne said.

"Here's my lawyer," Sarah said to the cop at the desk. To Burr: "Help me find Frank."

"I'm not your . . ."

Suzanne cut him off. "Where is Frank Tavohnen?" she said.

"And who may I ask are you?" said the cop.

"Co-counsel," Suzanne said.

Burr grimaced, fairly certain that Suzanne had not gone to law school since she had left Detroit.

"I was here yesterday," Sarah said. "You can't arrest someone and lose them for two days."

"Day and a half," said the cop. He shuffled through a pile of manila folders. Burr looked around the room. For all the time he'd lived in Grosse Pointe, he had never been here.

Suzanne bumped him with her hip. "Pay attention," she said.

The cop kept shuffling. The shuffling blew the smell of dead cigarettes into Burr's face. It made him sick to his stomach. How could the smell sicken him. He remembered again. He only smoked outside. That's how. With no ashtrays. And only during duck season. Burr looked at the cop's hands—fat and puffy and red, and saw the ash tray next to the folders. He picked up the phone, said something Burr couldn't hear, and hung up. More shuffling.

A gray-haired cop came in from the bowels of the building carrying a file. "Mr. Tavohnen is not here," he said.

"Did you let him go?" Sarah asked.

"We never booked him," said the gray-haired cop.

"You arrested him. Now where is he?" Suzanne said.

Burr felt decidedly useless at this point. He couldn't see why they needed him. He thought about Zeke in the back of the Jeep and wondered if he was getting cold. Then he thought about Zeke-the-boy, now eight, and only about five streets away. Maybe he should stop by. No, Grace wouldn't like that. He'd better call first.

"Well, the chief didn't want a murderer here. The paperwork didn't get filed because it was Sunday. Mostly though, there was no room," said the cop with the gray hair.

"He didn't murder anyone," Sarah said. She stopped twirling her hair, curling it around her forefinger. "Where is he?" Sarah asked again.

"We released him to the Detroit Police," said the gray-haired cop.

The three of them rode in silence. Not an awkward silence. A stony silence. Burr knew Suzanne had led him on. If she had come right out and said that it was Sarah's husband who had been arrested, he never would have helped her. Sarah (Suzanne's younger sister by two or three years, Burr didn't know which), along with just about everyone else, didn't approve of Burr at first because he was almost twenty years older than Suzanne. It had gotten worse when the Grace part had come to light.

They were on the way to the Fifth Precinct, but none of them knew exactly how to get there. Burr looked in the rear view mirror: the back of the Jeep fogged up except for the four lines of the rear defroster that still worked. The Jeep smelled like a wet dog, which was fine with Burr.

Too proper for a murderer, he thought. That was just like Grosse Pointe. Drugs and drunks, yes, as long as they were residents. No murderers though.

"What do you mean, gone?" Sarah said to yet another duty officer, this one at the Fifth Precinct. Burr saw Sarah's rage dissolve, and now she started to cry.

"Somebody picked him up a couple hours ago," said the cop on duty.

"Who?" Suzanne said.

He read from a file. "Says here, Emmet County Sheriff." He looked up. "File says he was released to a deputy who said he was taking him to Petoskey."

"You arrested this poor man two days ago," Suzanne said. "No one has heard from him, and now he's gone."

"Before my shift," said the cop.

Suzanne jerked the file from him.

"He didn't murder her," Sarah said.

Burr looked over her shoulder. The People of the State of Michigan had charged Frank Tavohnen with the murder of Claudia Tavohnen. Open murder. That could be anything from negligent homicide to first-degree murder.

"Who's Claudia Tavohnen?" Burr asked.

"Never mind," Suzanne said. "We have to go to Petoskey."

A light, dry snow fell straight down in Saginaw, just as the wind died. By the time they got to Standish, the left lane traffic on I-75 had slowed to twenty-five. The Jeep ground through the left lane in four wheel drive. He could see the woods becoming white like in Frost's poem. At this point, Burr felt that his continued presence depended on the Jeep and not on his lawyering. Which was fine with him. He'd drop them off and leave. Mission accomplished.

"Burr, for the fifth time, Frank didn't kill anybody," Suzanne said.

"Well, yes. It happened," Sarah said, "But he didn't mean to kill her." She scowled and rubbed her left eyebrow. "It was an accident."

The Jeep jumped out of the ruts dug into the snow. Burr jerked the wheel and the Jeep bounced back in. Two tracks carved into I-75. The snow blew sideways —dry and powdery now that the front had blown through. The wind had backed to the northwest and the temperature dropped.

"Is she, or is she not dead?" Burr asked.

"She's deceased," Sarah said.

"And did Frank kill her?" Burr said.

"No," Suzanne said.

"It was an accident," Sarah said.

Burr looked at Suzanne through the rear view mirror. The two of them sitting back there and I'm the chauffeur, he thought.

"First of all," she said, "it was six years ago. Second, Sarah wasn't there. No one was there but Frank and Claudia. Third, it was an accident. He was cleaning his deer rifle in the basement. Claudia, his wife, came downstairs to talk to him. The gun went off accidentally. The bullet killed her. The sheriff thought it was an accident. So did the coroner. No charges were ever brought."

"Some mistake," Burr said. The Jeep lurched again. Burr let the Jeep slide. When the wheels grabbed again, he eased it back into the ruts. The left lane was impassible. The afternoon light had faded and everything looked two dimensional. The snow blurred his sense of depth. They were just past Saginaw, halfway.

Lights flashed at the next exit. The state police had shut down the freeway. "We're going to have to stop for the night," he said.

"No, we're not," Suzanne said.

The state police closed I-75 Monday night and kept it closed all day Tuesday. Burr, Suzanne, and Sarah had ground their way to the Wayfarer on US-23, a longish gray motel left behind when the freeway opened. Burr, ever hopeful despite what happened between them, had left the room arrangements to Suzanne who took two rooms, which he thought a good sign. He knew he should have known better, as the sisters Fairchild took the double. Mercifully, there was a tavern across the street.

They spent Tuesday snowbound, could not reach Frank. Burr thought Frank was no doubt snowbound himself, a bit further north.

Wednesday, December 14, 1988

The freeway reopened on Wednesday morning, and the three of them arrived in Petoskey—three hundred miles north of Detroit and right on the 45th parallel, exactly halfway to the North Pole—just as Frank was being charged. They had been half a step behind from the start, and this latest half step hadn't really surprised Burr.

Petoskey was on the south side of Little Traverse Bay, on Lake Michigan, twenty miles south of the Straits of Mackinac and the Mackinac Bridge. Harbor Springs, where Burr had spent his summers growing up, was five miles across Little Traverse Bay to the north. The courthouse had been built, Victorian style architecture, in the late 1800's, just as the loggers finished clearcutting the white pine. The oak paneled courtroom had seen its share of murders in the logging days, but now the chambers heard divorce and zoning cases as both families and land subdivided.

Before that, Petoskey had belonged to the Odawas. (Victor was half Odawa.) Petoskey, Odawa for "rising sun," was named after an ancient Odawa chief, as was the Petoskey stone, a fossilized crustacean, with a pattern like a rising sun.

Burr, Suzanne, and Sarah sat in the gallery immediately behind Frank and a sincere looking young man who Burr presumed to be a public defender hired by the county on short notice. Sarah hugged Frank over the railing that separated the gallery from the litigants. He seemed, at the very least, disoriented. Calvin Truax, the county prosecutor, sat across the aisle. He was tall, about six-three. His eyes bulged in their sockets and his Adam's apple stuck out, almost as far as his nose, which Burr thought looked like a beak on which his rimless glasses perched. Mid fifties. Burr thought that he did not look like a pleasant person.

Promptly at 1:00 p.m., a uniformed man, entered from the side door. He was a smallish man with a full head of blond hair, a disappearing nose, and a pleasant but crooked smile, with matching crooked teeth.

"All rise," he said with perhaps the most watery lisp Burr had ever heard.

Immediately thereafter, a fat, bald, sixtyish judge called the court in session. His slightly tarnished nameplate read "Honorable Benjamin R. Gillis." "Thank you, Swede," said the judge. Then to the prosecutor, "Calvin, what is going on here?"

The prosecutor rose, his suit hanging on him. "Your Honor, the People of the State of Michigan are here to charge Franklin X. Tavohnen with the murder of Claudia Tavohnen."

Gillis banged down his gavel, apparently for no reason other than he was annoyed (there being no disturbance in the courtroom other than Calvin Truax). "That was six years ago and ruled an accident at the time. Now, what's got into you?"

"Your Honor, the people have new evidence that will prove that the shooting could not have been an accident."

"Which people would they be, Calvin?"

"Your Honor, at my request, the state police forensic laboratory has done a laser study that conclusively demonstrates the gun was picked up and fired."

The judge thumped his forehead. "Calvin, I did not sign a warrant for this."

"Judge Chambers did, Your Honor. You were grouse hunting," Truax said.

"Calvin, you better have something here. How do you plead, Frank?" Apparently the judge knew him. Frank sat there, dazed, as if he'd barely heard the charges. "Frank, what do you say?"

The sincere looking young man got to his feet.

Burr got a good look at Frank for the first time. At least six feet. He stood erect, straight in the back, but his stomach stuck out beyond his chest. Short, sandy hair, thinning in back, retreating in the front. Gray eyes, broad nose, straight, slightly yellow teeth, square jaw, red faced, but Burr thought the red face might be situational. Handsome, Burr thought, at least formerly handsome, the extra weight, not confined to his waist, had rounded and softened his square features. An aging athlete. He looks like an aging athlete, thought Burr.

"What is the plea?" said the judge.

Frank mumbled something.

"Your Honor, the defense requests a ten minute recess," said the public defender.

Gillis thumped his forehead again. "No recess. The court notes that the defendant does not respond and determines that he stands mute. Therefore, a plea of not guilty is entered." The judge shuffled through some papers. "The preliminary exam set for February 6, 1989." Gillis banged his gavel. "Adjourned."

"Your Honor?" said the prosecutor.

"We're adjourned, Calvin."

"What about the bail?" asked the prosecutor.

"What about the bail?" asked Gillis.

"Your Honor, this is a capital crime," said Truax.

"So it is," said the judge.

"I request, given the gravity of the charge, a one million dollar bond," said the prosecutor.

Judge Gillis cocked his head like a bird dog on point. A pause. "Hearing no objection, bail is set at one million dollars." Judge Gillis looked down at Frank over the top of his reading glasses. "Frank, that means you need $100,000 to get out."

The four of them—Burr, Suzanne, Frank and Sarah —sat around a beat up table in the first floor visitor's room of the courthouse, a dreary affair with formerly white walls and dingy gray tile. There were no bars on the windows. Burr thought Emmet County had a more casual approach to murder suspects than Detroit. They probably didn't have much experience with it. Burr, sitting between Suzanne and Sarah, who sat next to Frank, watched the domestic scene unfold. Burr drummed the fingers of his left hand on the table.

Sarah squeezed Frank's hand. "Why didn't you call? We looked all over for you."

"They only gave me one call before we drove up here," Frank said, "and the line was busy."

"Baby, I'm so sorry," Sarah said. "Have you slept at all?"

"No, not really," Frank said.

"You look terrible," Sarah said.

"I feel terrible," he said.

"Burr's going to get you out," Sarah said.

"I have a lawyer," Frank said.

"Burr's going to get the bail reduced," Suzanne said.

"I thought you hated Burr," Frank said.

"He's going to get you out of jail," Sarah said.

"When?" Frank asked.

"Now," Sarah said. "As soon as he can get in to see the judge."

Burr continued drumming the fingers of his left hand on the conference table.

"Would you please stop that," Suzanne said.

"Burr gave Suzanne an icy glare, but he stopped the drumming. "Frank," he said, "tell me what happened."

"It happened a long time ago," Frank said. "Six, maybe seven years ago."

"No, not that. I don't care how you killed Claudia," Burr said. "Tell me about your arrest."

CHAPTER THREE

Saturday, December 10, 1988

The Christmas tree blew off the roof on the way home. The wind lifted the tree from behind and it somersaulted over the hood. Frank swerved and missed most of the tree, but he squashed the very top where the angel was supposed to go. Becky screamed from the backseat. Sarah scowled at him as he got out.

The wind screamed down Lake St. Clair from the northeast and jammed the brash ice against the shore. The waves crashed in towards Lake Shore Drive, but the ice absorbed their power and they washed toward the beach, spent.

Frank turned his head away from the wind and crabbed his way back to the tree. After almost six years, he still wasn't used to buying a Christmas tree. Up north, he always went out and chopped his own. Bird's Christmas Tree Farm in Clarkston wasn't the same, no matter what Sarah said. They cut their own tree, but the scotch pines all stood up in rows. He knew that Becky liked the ride on the hay wagon, even if it was pulled by a tractor. She liked the cider even if it tasted like a plastic jug, and she liked the doughnuts even if they chewed like rubber.

Frank shook his head at the wounded tree and then shook the slush off it. He jumped when the red lights started to flash but when he spun around, he saw that Sarah had turned on the emergency flashers. He lashed the tree back on the roof of the Suburban, and the wind whipped into his face again. It carried the wetness of early December and a dead fish smell. All the cars had their lights on now. It wasn't quite five o'clock, but the light was almost gone. The darkness sank in on him this time of year, and when it was overcast, like today, it never really got light. No boundary between the lake and the sky. The cars honked as they splashed by, reminding him of his tree-tieing mistake. There wasn't much traffic on Saturday. Between cars, he heard the wind rattling in the trees.

Frank looked over the roof of the car at the trees and below them the mansions. They had just passed the Grosse Pointe Yacht Club when the Christmas tree disaster struck. He expected the Grosse Pointe Shores police any moment, moving him along to keep the narrow strip of Grosse Pointe Shores secure from whomever might dare interfere with the lives of the upper class. Frank was sure they would have much preferred closing Lake Shore Drive altogether, making it into a private road and rerouting the traffic along Mack Avenue.

He finished lashing the tree back on the roof and climbed back in the Suburban. They continued slushing down Lake Shore towards Detroit. At Seven Mile the land bumped out to the east and houses appeared on the other side of the road. Somehow, Lake Shore became Jefferson and would stay that way all the way downtown.

"Nice work on the tree, love," Sarah said.

"I always threw it in the back of the pickup," Frank said.

"Who would have a pickup in Grosse Pointe?" this from Sarah.

"Did the tree get hurt, Daddy?"

"No, baby, it's fine," Frank said.

They splashed through Grosse Pointe Farms, the City of Grosse Pointe, and were half way through Grosse Pointe Park, the oldest of the old money.

The tree started to wiggle again. Frank looked up.

"Frank, watch where you're going," Sarah said.

Grosse Pointe Park, is the oldest of the five Grosse Pointe suburbs: five small, old brick enclaves, appended to Detroit, on the shores of St. Clair. Mostly the rich, very rich, and the somewhat rich lived in the Grosse Pointes, but, just inside Grosse Pointe Park there were a few blocks where the not so rich lived (or in Frank's case, the slightly struggling) and sold things to the various rich. Two blocks into Grosse Pointe Park, he turned onto Collingwood, a suburban, tree-lined, unassuming, dream-come-true street. Not his dream, but surely someone's.

At 505 Collingwood, they pulled into the driveway of their smallish, two-story colonial, vintage 1940. The house was about as big as the lot, but that was city life and all they could afford.

"No, Daddy. First you have to light the fire. Then you bring in the tree."

Frank nodded, turning his attention from the Christmas tree to the red brick fireplace on the west wall of the living room, relieved to delay the reckoning with the Christmas tree stand. In his entire life, he had never had an easy time with a Christmas tree stand. Inevitably, the trunk would be too big for the stand and needed shaving, and, in spite of the botanical rationale for growing straight, a tree that looked perfectly straight in the woods and more recently on a lot, inevitably had a crook at the base of the trunk. More surgery, and then those damned screws that held it in place but always pushed it off plumb. Not to mention the crawling underneath and the pricking needles. The mounting usually ended with a paperback, usually about two hundred fifty pages jammed under one leg to straighten it the way nature had intended.

All that considered, lighting the fire first seemed like the right thing to do.

Frank got down on his hands and knees and blew on the fire. Becky kneeled beside him and blew ashes in his face. He coughed violently.

Sarah rushed in. "Are you all right?" she asked.

Frank's face had turned to cherry and his eyes bulged. He looked all of fifty, his scalp red underneath his thinning hair.

Sarah clapped him on the back and his stomach jiggled.

He stood up, gasping.

The fire staggered to life. Frank chased down the ashes with a Stroh's. He'd quit drinking it when they closed the Detroit brewery. Later he'd reconsidered, and he'd made his own long distance peace with the Stroh family and started drinking it again.

"Now it's time for the tree, Daddy."

"Right. Right," he said.

"I'll bring it in," Sarah said. "Your father needs to rest a minute."

"No, Daddy does it. That's how we always do it."

"How long is always to a five-year old?" Frank said.

"About five years," Sarah said. She brought the tree in the house. "Don't die on me now," she said.

Frank gave her a blank stare. He had gray eyes, not steely, but a soft gray, like the light at dusk He impaled the tree into the three prongs in the bowl of the stand, screwed in the screws, and leveled it, finally using a paperback book from the bookshelf. This year it was a thin mystery by an author he didn't know. Frank strung the Italian lights. Then the three of them hung the ornaments. After much debate, they decided against tinsel. Sarah found the box that kept the angel safe eleven months of the year.

"We can't put the angel up yet," said Becky. "We have to have our snack first."

"It's got to be just so, doesn't it?" Frank said.

"Like we always do it," Becky said.

Out came the Christmas cookies. The Christmas tree smell carried through the room on the current of the fire and mixed with the smoke. He took a deep breath.

"Now we can do the angel," Becky said.

Sarah opened the box that kept the angel safe eleven months a year. She handed it to Becky. In keeping with tradition, Frank bent over and picked up Becky. His back cracked, but no one seemed to notice. Becky stretched to plant the angel on the top of the tree. His left leg buckled. Becky teetered. Frank locked his leg, righted them both.

"Watch out for your knee, Frank."

Frank looked at Sarah, almost twenty years younger and wondered if he still looked good to her.

"The angel's crooked, Daddy."

The angel did indeed cant off to the side, the top of the tree bent from the collision with the Suburban. Frank put Becky down and handed her the angel. She had Frank's gray eyes and sandy hair. He went to the garage to find the pruning shears. The damp and the dark hit him squarely in the face when he entered the garage. He fumbled for the light switch.

Frank looked out the garage window and saw a shiny Grosse Pointe police car cruise by. He found the shears hanging on a nail. The blades squeaked, rust against rust, as he worked them back and forth. He lumbered back in, sluggish from the beer and not at all fresh from the cold air. He stood on a stool and began clipping the wounded spire.

"Not too much, Daddy."

Enough so the angel wouldn't tilt like a sinner but not so much that she couldn't stand straight on her perch.

Becky picked up the angel.

"Be careful, Frank," Sarah said.

At that instant, the front door crashed open. Two of Grosse Pointe's finest, pistols drawn, burst through. The first one through had a mustache that hung over his upper lip. The second one was tall and skinny.

Frank teetered on the stool with his clippers. His mouth fell open. Becky started to cry. Sarah spoke first.

"What are you doing?"

The cop with the mustache pointed his gun at Frank.

"Are you Frank X. Tavohnen, 505 Collingwood, Grosse Pointe Park?"

"What?" he asked.

"You're under arrest," said the cop with the mustache.

"He's what?" Sarah asked.

"Drop those shears and come down, hands up." The cop spit the words through his mustache.

"There must be some mistake," Sarah said.

"No mistake, lady, not if he's Frank Tavohnen," said the tall cop.

"Get out of this house this minute," she said.

The cop with the mustache ignored her. "Down off that stool."

Frank lost his balance and stumbled toward the cop with the mustache, clippers first. The tall cop hit Frank in the head with the barrel of his pistol. Frank fell to his hands and knees.

Becky screamed. The tall cop smashed Frank's face to the floor with his boot. He jerked Frank's hands behind his back and tried to lock the handcuffs around his wrists.

Sarah screamed at them, "Get out of here. You have no right to be here."

"We got a warrant for this man," said the cop with the mustache.

"Warrant? For what?" Sarah said.

Frank rolled to his side and the tall cop lost his grip. "Don't move or I'll shoot," said the tall cop. He pointed his pistol at Frank.

The cop with the mustache pulled a crumpled paper from his pocket. "Says here, murder. Open murder. That's what it says."

Frank twisted himself to his hands and knees and pulled himself in like a turtle. He saw blood dripping onto the carpet, felt the cut on his face. It ran down his left cheek and he tried to squeeze it shut with his fingers. The blood will stain the carpet, he thought. He had no idea why, after all this time, he was being arrested. It was so long ago. He pulled himself to his feet.

"Don't move or I'll shoot," said the tall cop.

Somehow he didn't think the cop would shoot, but then he also thought it was over. It had been six years.

Sarah shrieked at the cops. "What in God's name are you doing?"

The cop with the mustache cuffed Frank's hands behind his back and jerked him through the door. The tall cop pulled Frank down the sidewalk by the crook in his elbow. Frank skidded along behind him, sideways. Blood dripped down his face. Becky screamed in the doorway. Sarah hung Frank's coat over his shoulders. Then she ran in front of the cops and tried to stop them.

"What are you doing?" she shrieked.

"This man is being arrested for murder," he said. "Now get out of the way."

Sarah stood her ground. The procession stopped.

"Madame, all we're doing is fulfilling the obligations of the warrant," said the cop with the mustache.

"You can't just break into a house and take someone," Sarah said.

"When we have a warrant for murder, we execute it with extreme care," said the mustache cop.

"He's bleeding." She ran to Frank and wiped his face with her hand. He stood there, stunned. "You can't do this. It's wrong," she said.

"She's right," said the tall cop. "You haven't read this guy his rights," said the tall cop.

In the cold of the twilight, the cop with the mustache, who apparently was at least nominally in charge, read Frank his rights. Frank didn't say a word. His coat had fallen off his shoulders and he shivered in the cold. Sarah draped it over his shoulders again. They started off to the patrol car again.

"I'm going with you," she said.

Sarah ran to the patrol car. Becky screamed louder. She turned back to the house.

The tall cop politely ducked Frank's head into the police cruiser.

The police car pulled out. Frank craned his head backward to look for her.

"Sit in your seat," said the cop with the mustache.

Still in shock, he had no words to tell them to wait. At the corner of Jefferson, they stopped. He looked back again. He thought he saw the Suburban pulling out of the alley, but he wasn't sure.

The cruiser turned left on Jefferson. It was only six blocks to the Grosse Pointe Park Police Station.

When the tall cop got Frank out of the car, he stepped in a slushy puddle. The slush ran over the top of his shoe. They hauled him to the front desk.

"Here he is Sarge," said the cop with the mustache.

"Well, now we got no room," said the Sergeant.

"What?" said the tall cop.

"Just booked the last room," he said.

"Stick him in the drunk tank," said the cop with the mustache.

"I can't stick a murderer in there with guys wearin' lime green pants with pink whales on them," said the Sergeant.

"Why not?" said the cop with the mustache.

"Hell to pay when their fancy lawyers come bail 'em out," said the Sergeant. "Two choices: Wayne County or Fifth Precinct."

"Wayne County's an hour from here," said the tall cop. "Fifth it is. Then I'm outta here."

"I'm a Grosse Pointe resident. I'll stay in this jail," Frank said.

"The boys from up north are comin' tomorrow," said the Sergeant.

They trundled Frank back to the police car and took Jefferson four more blocks into Detroit. He was really getting scared now.

"They'll like you at the Fifth, white boy," said the cop with the mustache.

The two cops took Jefferson past Alter Road, the Detroit cop cars following. Of the buildings that were still standing in the Fifth Precinct, at least half were boarded up or caged in.

"I didn't murder anyone," Frank said. "There must be some mistake."

The two cops ignored him.

"I said I didn't murder anyone," he said. "You must have the wrong guy."

The tall cop looked back at him. "Frank Tavohnen, that's you, right?"

"Right name, wrong guy."

"505 Collingwood, right?" said the cop with the mustache, looking over his shoulder at Frank.

"Well, something's wrong," Frank said. "Let me go."

"What kind of name is that? Tavohnen," said the cop with the mustache.

"Finnish," he said.

"Yeah, you probably are finished." He laughed. The cop with the mustache sneered at the tall cop.

They stopped in front of the Fifth Precinct which was now nothing more than an outpost with nothing left to protect. Bars on everything. Two story concrete the color of the sky. Frank's other foot got soaked getting out.

"You'll like it here, Mr. Finished."

At the front desk, a white cop close to his pension didn't look up.

"A single please," said the cop with the mustache.

"I need to make a phone call," Frank said.

"Any vacancies?" said the cop with the mustache. "I believe we have a reservation."

The old cop peered over his reading glasses.

"Officer, there's been a terrible mistake here," Frank said. "These policemen arrested me, and I haven't done anything."

The cop with the mustache fished a wrinkled paper from his pocket. He handed it to the old cop.

"Are you Frank X. Tavohnen?" The old cop dug a little wax out of his ear. "Is that Finnish?"

"Yes," Frank said.

"Says here you're wanted for murder," said the old cop on duty.

"I didn't kill anyone," Frank said.

"Says here, Claudia Tavohnen. December 18, 1982. That's a while ago. You been hiding out?" asked the old cop.

"Nobody hides out in Grosse Pointe," said the cop with the mustache.

"I didn't murder her," Frank said.

"That's not what it says here," said the old cop. "Says here, Emmet County. That's up north. Lots of Finns up there. So who'd you kill?" asked the old cop.

"No one," Frank said.

"Who's Claudia Tavohnen?" asked the cop with the mustache.

"You read him his rights?" asked Old Cop.

"Already did," said the tall cop.

"Who was the blonde? The one who screamed at us," one of the cops asked Frank. "Your daughter?"

Frank stared at the floor.

"He don't look so good to me," said the tall cop. "Don't look so young either. Kinda bald."

The cop with the mustache pushed Frank's stomach with his shoe. His stomach rolled over his belt. "Kinda flabby," he said.

"Leave him alone," said the old cop. "I'd say he's got enough trouble."

Frank looked down at his shirt, wet where the cop with the mustache toed him. How could this be happening, after all this time?

The old cop studied the warrant again. "Doesn't say who she was. But she must have been a relative."

"Maybe she was his mother," said the cop with the mustache.

"Did you kill your mother?" asked the tall cop.

"No."

"Well, Emmet County's gonna come get you," said the old cop.

"When?" Frank said.

"Roads don't look too good. You may be here awhile," said the cop with the mustache.

The old cop read the warrant one more time. "Open murder, December 18, 1982."

"There's been a mistake," Frank said, pleading. "Please let me call my wife."

"Who'd you say Claudia was?" said the old cop.

"I didn't," Frank said. "If this is an interrogation, I have a right to an attorney."

"Well, it ain't," said the cop with the mustache. "Just a little twenty questions."

The tall cop looked at his watch. "Come on, let's go. Our shift's over."

"I want to know what's going on," said the tall cop." I never arrested anyone for murder in Grosse Pointe."

The old cop finished the paperwork. "Open murder, almost six years ago. Long time," he said. He led Frank through a door down a hall with cells on each side. The two Grosse Pointe cops followed. Frank's fellow inmates heckled him as they went by.

"My phone call," Frank said.

"For a story," said the old cop.

"It was an accident," Frank said.

They stopped in front of an empty cell. Four by eight, maybe: a bunk, a sink, and toilet with no seat. The old cop took off the handcuffs and shoved Frank in the cell. He heard the cell door slam behind him.

CHAPTER FOUR

Wednesday, December 14, 1988

Burr started drumming his fingers again. He still hadn't agreed to take the case—Jacob would be furious, not to mention Eve. Frank had clearly been abused by the police. Burr thought, he may as well help as long as he was here.

"I'm going to enter an appearance and try to get the bail reduced. That's all." He pushed his chair back, winced as it squeaked on the floor. Then he stood and left the room. In the hall, he took four steps to his right.

Suzanne appeared, silently on his left. She smiled sweetly at him. "First the bail," she said. "Then we'll get him acquitted."

"Not me," Burr said. "I get him out, I'm done," Burr said.

"We'll worry about that later," she said.

"No, we won't. Get yourself a criminal lawyer. I do this and I'm done," he said.

"Burr, Please."

"I drove you up here because the roads were bad. I'll do this and I'm done." Burr looked out the window, noted that it had no bars. He saw the waves rolling into Little Traverse Bay and felt the wind leaking in through the windows. He felt like a fool for letting it get this far. "If what Sarah said is true, anybody can get him off," Burr said.

"If anybody can get him off, why not do it?" Suzanne turned on her heel.

Burr retrieved Zeke from the Jeep, and retired to a visiting attorney's conference room on the fifth and final floor of the courthouse. The radiator at his feet leaked, puddling water on the floor. Burr pressed the palm of his hand on the window and melted the frost away. He wiped it off the pane with his shirtsleeve and peered over the rooftops, north across the bay to Harbor Springs where he still kept a boat. The sky had cleared but the wind kept blowing, piling up eight-foot waves on the beach rolling in from Beaver Island, thirty miles west northwest. Zeke looked up at him from the floor and Burr wondered if the dog had any hard feelings about the duck hunt being cut short.

Suzanne entered without knocking. "How'd he get in here?" Suzanne asked. Somehow she had found somewhere to change into a black skirt with a matching black jacket. Burr thought the knee-length skirt did not do justice to her legs.

"I pretended I was blind," he said.

"You did not," Suzanne said. "You're the big city lawyer whose supposed to get Frank out on bail and you've got a dog up here."

Her eyes flashed at him. Green eyes. The right one had gold flecks. He had forgotten her eyes. How could he have forgotten? Full lips, painted crimson. Lips with a pout. Maybe it was her lips that made him forget he was married. More likely it was her legs. He had been stupid to woo her, stupid to let her get away.

"It's too cold for him to stay in the Jeep," he said.

Burr watched Suzanne sit down and cross her legs. "When was Frank arrested?"

"I don't know," she said. "Where's your tie? We're on in an hour."

"I didn't bring one," Burr said.

"You can't go before the judge without a tie," Suzanne said.

"I don't usually wear one duck hunting," Burr said.

"I'll go get you one," she said. "And a shirt. Suzanne stood on her toes and peered at the label inside Burr's collar. Burr felt slightly aroused by Suzanne's touch, then felt slightly ridiculous for feeling slightly aroused. "Are you still a 15 ½- 34?"

"What?"

"Shirt."

"Oh, yes," he said. "What day is it?"

"Wednesday," Suzanne said.

"When was Frank arrested?"

"I don't know. Who cares. Saturday, I think," she said.

"He's just now being charged. That's four days. I might be able to get the whole thing dismissed," Burr said.

Suzanne stood up and lit a cigarette. "Please, Burr. Nothing cute. Just the bail. Sarah just got her Visa limit up to ten thousand. So get the bail down to a hundred thousand and we're done."

"Where are the court rules?"

"Please, Burr," Suzanne said again. "Nothing cute. I'll get you a shirt and tie. You take Zeke back to the car."

She gave Burr a domestic kiss on the cheek and left.

~

"Your Honor," said Burr, standing next to the seated Frank on his left, Suzanne seated to Burr's right, "My name is Burr Lafayette and I would like to enter an appearance for the defendant."

"Granted," Gillis said.

Burr pushed his hair back with his fingers. It curled as it broke over his collar. He knew it was thinner in back, but Eve told him it wasn't.

"Yes, anything else?" said the judge.

"Your Honor, I move that the charges against Frank Tavohnen be dismissed," Burr said.

"This court set the bail at one million dollars based on the nature of the crime and the defendant's distant residence. There was no protest at the time I set it," said the judge.

"Your Honor, I'm not asking for the bail to be reduced," Burr said.

"Why should I reduce it?" Gillis said.

"I'm asking you to dismiss the case," Burr said.

"What?" Judge Gillis rubbed his right eyebrow with his forefinger.

"I said, Your Honor, I move to have the case dismissed."

The prosecutor, leapt to his feet and elbowed Burr out of the way. "Your Honor, I object," said Truax.

"It's not your turn yet," Burr said.

"I'm the judge," Gillis said.

Suzanne grimaced. Frank gave Burr a blank look.

"Your Honor," Truax said, "the defendant has been charged. Those charges stand, at least until the preliminary exam."

Suzanne hissed at him. "What are you doing?"

Burr pushed his hair back again. At one time he had been six feet, but with time and gravity, no more. Still lean. His hair was still the color of an acorn in early October but now had a few hints of gray. Tan complexion. Hawk nose, straight teeth, strong jaw. His eyebrows arched when he spoke. Blue eyes, cerulean. Long eyelashes. He picked up a book from the defendant's table.

"Your Honor," Burr said, "according to MCLA 28.51, a defendant must be charged within forty-eight hours of his arrest.

"So what?" Truax said. A vein running across his forehead bulged. Burr thought it might burst.

"My client was arrested on Saturday. It's now Wednesday," Burr said.

"Give me that book," Gillis said. He thumped his forehead with the palm of his hand. Then he put on his reading glasses. "What is the purpose of this rule?"

"It's habeas corpus, Your Honor," Burr said.

"It doesn't apply here," the prosecutor said.

"It most certainly does," Burr said.

"Be quiet," said the judge to Burr. "Yes, Calvin? You have something of importance to say?"

"Deputy Brubaker got stuck in the blizzard on the way back. He made every effort to bring the defendant back in a timely fashion to the jurisdiction from which he fled."

"I wouldn't exactly call moving to Grosse Pointe six years ago fleeing," Burr said.

"Your Honor," Truax said, "there must be a rule of reason applied here. The State did everything reasonable —beyond reasonable. The deputy said it was very slippery. Then they got snowed in."

The judge looked over his glasses at Truax, who nodded back at him.

"Your Honor, there is no rule of reason when it comes to habeas corpus," Burr said. "This is a fourth amendment right, designed to protect against the tyranny of the state. It is a constitutional right further codified by this statute."

"Your Honor," Truax said, "it was snowing. What could they do?"

"There are Wayne County judges on call twenty four hours a day, seven days a week to protect against this very situation," Burr said.

"What tyranny?" Gillis peered at Burr, looking down his nose, over his reading glasses.

"The power of the state, when brought to bear against an individual is formidable indeed." Burr began to feel that this would turn out badly.

Suzanne stood up. "Your Honor, may I have a moment with my co-counsel?"

The judge nodded. "Calvin, come on up here a minute," he said.

Burr turned to face Suzanne's glare, thought it was mildly amusing that she referred to herself as co-counsel. He removed the tin of Altoids from his pocket, opened it, and carefully examined its contents, knowing full well that they all looked alike, were alike. He selected four and placed them in his cheek.

Suzanne now stood. Leaning towards him, she hissed at him again. "Burr, we're here to get Frank out on bail. The judge doesn't care about habeas corpus."

"Suzanne, I've got him. They waited way too long to charge him."

"We only need the bail reduced," she said. "No one here even knows what habeas corpus is."

"I'm going to get the charges dismissed."

"Counsel, are you ready?" Gillis said.

"Yes, Your Honor," Burr said.

Gillis stared at Burr's feet. "Young man, as much as I admire your hunting boots, do not, I repeat, do not ever wear them in my courtroom again." Gillis had a round face, but the skin was still tight, with a fringe of hair around his ears.

"Yes, Your Honor," Burr said.

"Mr. Truax has told me that he would consent to a bail reduction to obviate the other question," Judge Gillis said.

Burr slicked his hair back again. "Your Honor, the State has clearly violated my client's constitutional rights. The charges should be dismissed."

"Don't be stubborn, young man," Gillis said.

"I'll just charge him again," Truax said.

"You do that," Burr said.

"Calvin, are you sure about this?" Gillis asked.

Burr watched Calvin's Adam's apple bob on his neck. He was sweating and Burr smelled Old Spice. "Yes, Your Honor," he said.

Burr turned to Calvin. "Why are you doing this anyway? Leave the poor guy alone. You got a grudge or something?"

"Hush, young man." Judge Gillis thumped his forehead again. "Well, what'll it be? You going to let him go Calvin?"

"No, your Honor."

"All right then," Gillis said. "The court rules that the snowstorm made it impossible to charge the defendant any quicker and that the State acted as soon as it could. Motion denied."

Burr turned and walked back to the defense table. He opened his briefcase and threw the papers back in.

"Counsel, you are still in my courtroom," Gillis said.

"I am aware of that," Burr said.

He tossed the statute book in his briefcase.

"Counsel, would you like to spend the night next to your client?" Gillis said.

"I would like some justice," Burr said.

"One more smart remark and you will spend the holidays as the guest of the people of Emmet County."

Burr still had his back to the judge.

"If that book is from the court's library, I expect you to return it on your way out," Gillis said.

"I'm sure you'd never miss it," Burr said.

"What was that?" Gillis said.

"Nothing, Your Honor," Suzanne said. "Burr, be quiet. You've done enough damage for one day. You were just supposed to get the bail reduced. That's all you were supposed to do." She turned to Frank. "I'm sorry."

"Very well, then. Court is dismissed," Gillis said. He banged his gavel and left.

"Just the bail, Burr. That's all you were supposed to do," Suzanne said.

Burr picked up his briefcase. He could smell Suzanne's perfume mixed with a hint of sweat.

"What's going to happen now?" Frank said. He looked confused, but mostly tired. Burr didn't think Frank understood the enormity of his miscalculation.

"All we needed was the bail reduced," Suzanne said. "We had the money. You did not have to get cute."

The bailiff came over to the table. Burr saw that he had a tick that jerked his head about two inches to the right about every thirty seconds. "Mr. Tavohnen, please come with me," he said.

"What?" Frank said.

"Come with me. I don't think we'll use the cuffs." Burr saw him twitch again.

"What?" Frank said.

Sarah took Frank's arm. "We'll try again tomorrow, honey."

"Back to jail?" Frank must really be exhausted, thought Burr.

"Burr, I can't believe you did this," Suzanne said.

"Come with me, Mr. Tavohnen," said the bailiff.

"Frank, I'm sorry," Burr said. "The law is clearly on our side. It's clear. Not gray at all."

Frank looked away from him. He shuffled off with the bailiff. Sarah held his other hand. When the three of them were about halfway across the courtroom, Frank stopped. The other two each took another step, one on each side of Frank. The procession stood there in a "V." Frank turned back toward Suzanne and Burr. Burr thought Frank looked like he would pass out any minute.

Frank raised his arm and pointed at Burr. "You're fired," he said.

Burr walked ever so slowly to the visitor's room. This was not a meeting he was looking forward to, but hopefully, Frank would have calmed down in the last two hours. Burr had been right in that amateur hour of a court. Criminal lawyer or not, Burr knew enough about habeas corpus and had read the court rules. Frank had not been charged within forty-eight hours of his arrest. It had taken almost four days. He should have been released. Judge Gillis had been wrong, but Frank was still in jail, and Burr now thought that perhaps he should have just gone for the bail reduction. His ego had gotten the better of him. Now he was going to have to eat his words and try to make it right with Frank. Nevertheless, the judge had been wrong.

Burr peered through the window of the door to the visitor's room. Frank sat across from Sarah and Suzanne. Frank, hunched over (in defeat, Burr thought), held Sarah's hand. Burr's eyes fixed on Frank's bald spot.

Frank looked up and caught Burr peeping at them. Burr popped in, posted himself just inside the door. "Hello, Frank." Burr offered his hand to Frank who did not move.

Frank had on the same blue shirt he had on at the abortive habeas corpus hearing two hours ago. You could wear what you came in with, at least for awhile. Burr thought Frank had ripened a little even since then.

"It's been four days now. When do I get a shower?" Frank said.

"As soon as we get you out," Suzanne said.

"I thought that's what you were supposed to do," Frank said, pointing at Burr.

"There's just one thing," Suzanne said.

Burr looked at his feet. He wiggled his toes inside his boots. His left boot had a dent in the steel toe where he had dropped his duck boat on it.

"What's that?" asked Frank.

"Burr can't get you out until you rehire him," she said.

Frank's back cracked when he stood up. He turned his head from Suzanne to Burr. "He's done a great job so far."

"The judge was wrong," Burr said.

"He may be wrong, but I'm still here. I didn't murder anyone." Frank stood up and Burr thought it might get ugly now.

"For some reason, the prosecutor thinks so," Burr said.

"Here's what happened," Frank said.

"I don't care what happened," Burr said.

"What do you mean, you don't care what happened?" Frank asked.

"It doesn't matter what happened," Burr said.

"If it doesn't matter, then why am I here?" he asked.

"What Burr means is that it doesn't matter right now." Suzanne at her most sincere, Burr thought.

"None of this makes any sense," Frank said.

"That's right," Burr said. "The law is an ass."

"What?" Frank said.

"Dickens," Burr said.

Suzanne gave Burr perhaps the nastiest look he'd ever seen.

"The issue is your due process was violated," Burr said. "You shouldn't be here."

"I didn't murder my wife. It was an accident. I want to be home with my family."

"We'll appeal this, Frank. That's all we came for," Suzanne said.

"Why can't you just get the bail reduced?" Frank asked.

"I'm afraid it's a bit late for that," Burr said.

Burr felt that Frank was easing up. Maybe this wouldn't be ugly, not that he didn't deserve it. He walked over to the table, stationed himself at the end of the table between Frank and Sarah.

"Frank, we'll get you out," she said.

Burr looked up from his boots. "However, you should be a free man now. You were not charged promptly, and you should be released. Bail should not even be the issue. The judge erred," Burr said, erred rhyming with heard.

"He erred? He erred? How dare you say he erred?" Sarah said. "This isn't the Supreme Court. My husband has been in jail for almost a week. The last time his daughter saw him, the police were dragging him away. He's been charged with murder. Christmas is in a week. You totally screwed up the bail hearing. And you have the nerve to say the judge erred." She glared at Burr who met her stare. He thought this would be a poor time to flinch. He immediately dismissed those thoughts when Sarah jumped to her feet. Burr was about to flee, but Sarah scooted past him and hugged Frank. She began to cry. "Please," she said, looking at Burr. "I really don't care about your theories. Please get my husband home by Christmas."

CHAPTER FIVE

Burr and Zeke climbed the six floors to the top of the building. Burr refused to take the elevator. Past the Italian restaurant on the first floor, past the atrium shops on two and three, only half of them rented. Past the offices on four and five, mostly not rented. To his office (next door to his living quarters) on the sixth, top and final, penthouse floor. He saw the Christmas tree in the corner of the waiting room, a white spruce. He quite liked it except that the angel on top refused to stand straight. He straightened her for at least the twentieth time. Eve, missing in action at the moment, had said they were one box of ornaments short. Burr had told her not to decorate behind the tree.

Within thirty seconds of sitting down at his desk, his partner, Jacob Wertheim, walked into his office, a cherry-paneled affair. (Burr knew it was a cliché, but he liked it anyway.)

"There's a court rule and pages of case law. Why didn't you cite one?"

"The judge wouldn't let me," Burr said.

"Why not?" asked Jacob.

"He didn't want to hear it. He offered to reduce the bail," Burr said.

"So why didn't you take it?" asked Jacob.

"The judge was wrong," Burr said.

"The judge was wrong and what's his name…

"Frank," Burr said.

"And Frank is still in jail," Jacob said.

"That's right," Burr said.

"Why didn't you apologize and accept his offer?" Jacob said.

"I thought we could appeal it," Burr said.

"Appeal it? It's almost Christmas," Jacob said.

"You don't celebrate Christmas," Burr said.

"The Court of Appeals does," Jacob said.

"They will have to hear this immediately. It's habeas corpus," Burr said.

"I don't think we should push the Court of Appeals," Jacob said. "I am sure you realize that is where we earn our living."

"Then we'll do it after the Christmas recess," Burr said. Although Burr thought Sarah might be arrested for his murder if they waited. There was also the matter of Christmas with Zeke-the-boy. Burr thought it might be best to temper his constitutional outrage with matters economic and familial.

Jacob sneezed, came around the corner of Burr's desk and looked underneath in the kneehole. Zeke barked once at him. "Damn that dog."

Burr had moved to East Lansing three years ago, after he had resigned from Fisher and Allen. Two hundred lawyers in the firm. He had been head of the litigation department. Jacob had told him not to resign. Maybe he shouldn't have. Maybe he shouldn't have left Grace either. Jacob, also a partner at Fisher and Allen at the time, had quit, too, although Burr told him not to.

Jacob said he needed a change, so they opened up an appellate practice (state and federal, mostly state; Court of Appeals and Supreme Court, mostly Court of Appeals). Jacob did the research and the writing. Burr did the oral arguments and held the client's hands.

Jacob reached into his shirt pocket, took out a cigarette and lit it. He twirled one of the curls on the side of his head. Like steel wool, Burr thought. Jacob Wertheim and steel wool. Short, wiry, like his hair. Olive skin. Prominent nose, not big. Prominent. Very well dressed. Natty, Burr thought. Jacob's natty.

Burr smelled the sweet smoke. "Do not smoke a joint in my office."

It's not a joint. It's a clove cigarette."

"Right," Burr said. Zeke barked again. "He knows a joint when he smells one."

"I got it at the café where the students hang out," Jacob said.

"You can't do appellate work stoned," Burr said.

"It's good for my allergies," Jacob said.

"There's no way you're allergic to dogs," Burr said.

"I'm not allergic to all dogs. Just one dog." Jacob pointed, "that one."

"Put it out," Burr said.

"It helps my research," he said, looked Burr in the eyes, "How much does it pay?"

"Pay?" Burr asked. Perhaps Jacob is having a change of heart, Burr thought.

"As in money," Jacob said.

"It will pay enough for your next fishing trip," Burr said.

"I am absolutely not working for free," Jacob said.

"We get paid, just not right away," Burr said. Jacob spent a small fortune on clothes, but not as much as he spent on fly fishing. Since Jacob had neither wife nor children, Burr supposed Jacob could spend his money any way he wanted.

Two knocks on the door. Eve McGinty, an extremely attractive woman in her late forties, who also happened to be Burr's long-time and long-suffering legal assistant, followed the knocks into his office. "Jacob, put out that joint," she said.

He clipped off the end with scissors from Burr's desk and dropped the cigarette in his shirt pocket. "It's not a joint. It's a clove cigarette. And if it were marijuana, which it's not, it is a $100 misdemeanor in the city of East Lansing."

"You are a forty-five year-old substance abuser," Eve said.

"I am a decorated Vietnam veteran," he said. "And just how old did you say you were?"

A hint of crow's feet around her eyes. The beginnings of wrinkles near the corners of her mouth, which was large and full of white teeth. Short brown hair. No roots. Gold hoops. Classy, Burr thought. She is classy. He couldn't understand why she ran their office, bothered with them, especially him, especially after she had rejected each and every one of his well-intentioned but misguided advances.

Burr saw the color rise to Eve's cheeks. He didn't know when she would turn fifty, but he knew she didn't want to. And he knew she didn't like being older than he was. She had been his assistant at Fisher and Allen for fifteen years. He had begged her not to quit, but she insisted. She had divorced well and said she wanted a house close to work with a yard with full sun so she could have a proper flower garden.

"Eve, please," Jacob said. "Burr and I have pressing work. We have things to do."

"You two don't have any pressing work. At the moment, you have no work," Eve said. She marched out, followed by Jacob who never marched.

After Eve and Jacob left, Burr sat at his desk, stared out the window, saw nothing but the impending darkness. Zeke snored softly now sleeping on the couch. It was four o'clock and almost dark. The winter solstice was tomorrow. In the winter he got up in the dark and went home in the dark. With the clouds in December, some days it never really got light. The black faded to gray and then to black, over and over and over again.

Burr walked into the walk-in closet. Some time ago, he had diagnosed himself with Seasonal Affective Disorder. (He thought it made a wonderful acronym.) "Now," he said to himself, "it's time to find the lights." By Spring, he wouldn't need them, but now he did and he couldn't find them.

The banging noises in the closet brought Eve back into Burr's office and Burr back to the present. He poked his head out of the closet.

"If you're looking for those stupid lights, they're in the basement," Eve said. "And don't take this case."

Burr sniffed the cedar paneling in the closet. It reminded him of his house (more of a combination cabin and shack) on Walpole Island.

"Yes, I like the smell," she said. "No, I've never been to Walpole Island. And yes, Jacob is already doing the research."

Burr stumbled over his old waders on the way out of the closet. He bent over to see if the hole in them had perhaps fixed itself.

Eve peered into the closet. "If you're thinking about fixing something, you should get the elevator fixed," she said.

"I don't take the elevator," Burr said.

Still in the cedar walk-in closet, Burr drifted back to thoughts of elevators when he was practicing law in Detroit. He had work then, perhaps too much work, which, upon reflection, he thought was either a cause or an effect of his marital troubles, perhaps both.

The elevators at the Renaissance Center ran up and down on the outside of the building. He watched Lake St. Clair disappear as the elevator dropped and thought about Walpole Marsh out of sight and a world away from the Detroit River at this end of the lake. He was on his way to a motion hearing, Suzanne in tow. Burr had an uneasy feeling as they stepped out of the elevator. Perhaps, it was from the elevator. He had seen riders on the outside elevator vomit on the way up as they left Detroit below them, but more often as they dropped down. Maybe that was it.

He had let Suzanne exit the elevator before him, manners notwithstanding, the real reason lying in the opportunity to look at her from behind. She wore a dark blue suit with a cream blouse, an accommodating slit up the back of her skirt. Her hips swayed courtesy of her black pumps.

The lobby of the Renaissance Center, dim even at midday, spread out before them like a cavern. In the half light, the blank, damp concrete walls seemed as if they could grow mushrooms. The maze of the four outside towers, surrounding the fifth, center tower, which held the hotel, twisted his sense of direction.

Burr had met with Suzanne three times since she had first appeared, twice at her office, once more at his. None of these sessions was necessary. The lawsuit was not complicated and should have been delegated to a more junior attorney. He took it on himself, giving a flimsy reason that probably no one believed. The truth was he was smitten. He knew it. He was afraid that Suzanne knew it as well.

Further, there was absolutely no reason for Suzanne to attend the motion hearing. His motion was perfunctory, would certainly be granted, but would give him another chance to be with Suzanne, and a chance to show off.

~

Standing in the closet, Burr watched Eve as she reached up her skirt and pulled up her nylons.

She looked straight at him. "Please," she said, "it is so annoying the way you gape at me. No, not me, my legs."

"I didn't think you saw me," he said.

"That's my point," Eve said.

"Well, then, let's go have dinner," Burr said, stumbling over his waders on his way out of the closet.

"Fraternizing with the help is frowned on," she said.

"Please," he said, emerging from the closet.

"I'm sorry. I have plans," said Eve, who left again.

He had asked her to dinner a thousand times, and a thousand times she had said no. Probably good judgment on her part, he thought. He drifted back to the motion hearing.

~

He and Suzanne had returned victorious from the motion hearing, as he knew they would. Suzanne congratulated him all the way back to the office. (He worried whether she had known it was a set up.)

She had laughed at his imitation of the judge, a musical laugh he thought and a big smile, a slightly too big smile, framed by those full lips, at the moment, not pouty. He had no idea she had a laugh like that, the law of course not really given to bringing out one's sense of humor.

Suzanne was not quite twenty years his junior, almost young enough to be his daughter. She had grown up in Lake Forest on Chicago's old money North Shore (not unlike Grosse Pointe). Her mother walked out when she was fifteen, and, but for an occasional birthday card, had virtually disappeared. Her father sent her to boarding school and then Vanderbilt, and she (and Sarah) became, more or less, stray cats.

Suzanne graduated in English, moved to New York, and had gone to work as a copywriter on a package goods account (a detergent of some kind). She had a dagger-like wit and a mastery of the English language, not to mention legs that stretched up to her (modest) breasts.

The advertising agency had transferred her to Detroit to work on a car account that needed a boost. Suzanne said she couldn't decide what she hated more: Detroit or cars. Burr believed the two so intertwined as to be impossible to separate. The only compensation to what Suzanne hoped to be purgatory rather than hell was that her sister Sarah lived in Grosse Pointe.

In any event, Burr had been elated that Suzanne's written words had gotten her and the agency in trouble. The Federal Trade Commission was of the belief that her copy had gone beyond permissible puffery.

Now she stood arms outstretched, hands pressed against his office window staring at the river below them. The light framed her silhouette, long and slim, in the window. Burr locked the door and approached her from behind and put a hand on her hip, cautiously. She didn't move. Burr felt he had done something terribly wrong. He quivered, pulled his hand away. She turned and he kissed her full on the mouth.

"I was hoping you wouldn't do that," Suzanne said. Then she left.

Burr, resigned to his own company, looked out from a window booth at Michelangelo's, the restaurant on the first floor of his building. East Lansing had emptied out when the students had gone home for break and with forty thousand fewer people, he could have shot his twelve gauge across the street and not hit anyone.

Buying the Masonic Temple, circa 1927, had seemed like a good idea at the time. It wasn't big, even by East Lansing standards, six brick stories and narrow, very narrow. He'd taken the top floor for himself—offices and living quarters. But the renovations, especially the new elevator, which apparently was broken (again), had nearly broken him.

As much as he loved pasta, Burr could never eat enough to cover the rent Scooter, the would-be restaurateur, owed him. Zeke sucked in a number twelve angel hair and smacked his lips. Burr ordered the Castello Della Paneretta, which Scooter stocked solely for him.

"How is it, Mr. Lafayette?" Scooter asked.

"Fine Scooter. It's fine."

"No dogs allowed, Mr. Lafayette."

"He's a seeing eye dog, Scooter."

"He may be, but you're not blind," said Scooter.

"I'm also not six months behind in the rent," Burr said. "That's nine grand."

"More pasta?" Scooter asked.

"No. More money," Burr said.

"The kids all went home," said Scooter.

Scooter, all Wasp, not a drop of Italian in him as far as Burr could tell. Pasty complexion, droopy, straight dirty blond hair. Great Italian food but not much of a tenant, at least as far as paying the rent was concerned.

"They were just here for four months. I need some money or I'll have to evict you," Burr said.

"Then how will I pay you?" asked Scooter who scurried away, apparently not interested in Burr's reply.

Suzanne waltzed in wearing a full-length coat, fox. Burr knew it well. She stomped the snow off her boots. Burr watched the snow, white on the reddish fur, sparkle in the light and then melt.

"There you are," she said. She seemed glad to see him, but Burr believed she had other plans for him.

"Hello, Suzanne," he said. "Will you join me for dinner?"

Suzanne had on black leather boots that disappeared into her coat and Burr wondered what took over where the boots left off. She opened her coat as she sat. Blue jeans. Black ponytail partway down the back of a white turtleneck.

"Disappointed?" she asked.

Burr felt silence was the best response at this point, not a good idea to rekindle the events of the night when he first saw her in the fur coat, however erotic that had been for him. "I thought you had to go back to New York," he said.

"I've taken a leave of absence until this is over," Suzanne said.

"I see," Burr said, who didn't know how he felt about Suzanne's continued proximity. Actually, he thought, I do know. I'm delighted that Suzanne is staying, but I fear things will turn out badly. Again.

"How do you propose to get Frank out?" she asked.

"We'll file the motion and the brief right after the Christmas recess," Burr said.

"After Christmas," she said.

"The Court of Appeals is on Christmas recess until January third."

"Frank has to be home for Christmas," Suzanne said.

"So do I," Burr said.

"There's no reason you can't get the brief done right away," she said.

"My dear Suzanne, four days from now is Christmas Eve. And I would prefer not to annoy the Court of Appeals."

"That's just enough time to get Frank out for Christmas," she said.

"Suzanne, tomorrow I'm going to pick up my son."

"So it's all about you," she said.

"Who else would it be about?" Burr asked.

Scooter reappeared with a wine glass for Suzanne. She ordered linguini with red clam sauce.

"Jacob can finish the brief by Christmas Eve," Suzanne said, getting right to the point.

"I'm going to pick up Zeke-the-boy tomorrow morning," Burr said.

"Can't he wait? Just for a little while," Suzanne said.

"Little boys do not understand time. Late is like not coming," Burr said.

"You have made a career of being late," Suzanne said.

"Not for Zeke," Burr said. "We're going sledding. And grouse hunting," Burr said.

"I'm sure he doesn't want to go grouse hunting," Suzanne said.

"How would you know?" Burr asked.

"I know he likes sledding. I know he likes his namesake, Zeke-the-dog, I know he loves you," Suzanne said. "But I'm also sure he doesn't want to go grouse hunting. He's humoring you."

"How would you know?" Burr asked.

"I have spent some time with him," Suzanne said.

Burr knew that Zeke-the-boy did not understand wait. Burr was to pick him up tomorrow at three o'clock in the afternoon in Grosse Pointe Woods, where Grace and Zeke and he had lived on the corner of Sunningdale and Wedgewood, a brick Tudor with three fireplaces. Zeke asked his father why he had left; why if it was so bad being married, did the three of them still have dinner together sometimes; and if his dad didn't love his mother, who did he love? Burr had no answers for any of those questions. Burr had borrowed a cabin on the Manistee River near the headwaters. That's where he and the two Zekes were headed for the next four days for their Christmas. Zeke-the-boy wanted to sled on the big hill next to the cabin, and Burr had bribed him with that. There was a cedar swamp nearby that held grouse (the last legal bird of the year) when the snow was deep.

"Burr, are you quite done with your reverie?" Suzanne asked.

"My reverie?"

"What you need to do is quit moping and get on with your life," Suzanne said.

"I am on with my life," Burr said.

"You appear to have quit life, except for bird hunting," Suzanne said.

"And fishing," he said. "And sailing."

Suzanne gave him a look that he could only describe as withering. Burr grew uneasy.

"I have a prominent appellate practice and a large office development," he said.

"It looks to me that you have a less than thriving practice with a pothead and an empty building that smells like spaghetti sauce," Suzanne said.

"Spaghetti is one of my three favorite foods," Burr said without hesitation.

Suzanne reached across the table, laid her hand on Burr's, looked at their hands, then into Burr's eyes. "Do this one thing for me. Please."

"Suzanne," Burr said. "That was perhaps the most melodramatic cliche I've ever heard."

"It was, wasn't it?"

"But I liked it," Burr said.

"I thought you might," Suzanne said and squeezed his hand.

~

The next morning Burr looked out the window of Jacob's office, down the street over the tops of the houses, mostly student rentals with a few fraternity and sorority houses mixed in. He redecided he liked his building but it did smell like spaghetti sauce.

"I said we'd get Frank out, and we might as well do it before Christmas," he said.

"That's only three days," Jacob said, natty in a camel sport coat and charcoal slacks.

"Jacob, you know as well as I do that habeas corpus issues are heard right away."

"We don't want to upset vacationing appellate judges if we don't have to," Jacob said.

Eve marched in. "Who's we?"

"Jacob and me," Burr said. "Not you."

"Haven't you learned anything?" Eve said.

"This is a constitutional issue," Burr said.

"Suzanne Fairchild is certainly not a constitutional issue," Eve said.

"Actually, had Burr simply asked for bail reduction this wouldn't have occurred," Jacob said. "He's put himself in a spot."

"Jacob, I can't, for the life of me, understand why you are a litigator if you can't stand conflict," Eve said. "We don't need you as a peacemaker," she said.

"I do the writing," Jacob said. "Burr does the fighting."

"Frank needs help," Burr said.

"What about Zeke?" Eve asked.

"I'll bring him back early and trade for a couple days between Christmas and New Year's."

~

Burr and the two Zekes sledded (but did not hunt) while Jacob finished the brief. Burr then delivered Zeke-the-boy to the beautiful Grace in Grosse Pointe at noon on Thursday, December 23rd. While his fatherly duty had been satisfactorily completed, he wished he had not had cut their Christmas short. Burr asked Grace if he could have Christmas dinner with the two of them, a request she had taken under advisement.

CHAPTER SIX

SATURDAY, DECEMBER 24, 1988, CHRISTMAS EVE

"Your Honor," Truax said in the courtroom of the Michigan Court of Appeals, "it is altogether fitting and proper that the defendant, Frank X. Tavohnen, is in jail awaiting trial. He killed his wife. He has admitted as much. He should have been charged with murder six years ago. My predecessor should have done that. In addition …"

"Stop right there, Mr. Truax," said the Judge.

Burr felt Jacob jump in his chair to his right. He still smelled of marijuana. Maybe he had dozed off, not uncommon for Jacob, who said he learned how to sleep anytime, anywhere, after he was drafted and sent to Vietnam, where he became a lieutenant in the quartermaster corps, which was where his fondness for marijuana (nurtured in college) became what Burr considered an addiction. Suzanne, to his left, had insisted on sitting at the lawyer's table. Sarah, stationed in the gallery behind him, had refused to acknowledge his presence. Eve, under protest, waited at his office with Becky.

Burr turned his gaze to the source of the blast, Chief Judge Miriam Florentine, a petite, attractive, white-haired woman in her sixties (who obviously refused to color her hair), who Burr had argued before many times, and whose intellect he respected.

"Mr. Truax, we will not discuss the merits of the case. Frankly, the defendant's culpability is beyond the purview of this emergency hearing. If, as county prosecutor, you believe the People of the State of Michigan have reasonable cause to charge the defendant with murder, you may do so. I don't care. But I expect anything further you may care to say to address the procedural issue before us. Not the underlying issue."

The judge pushed her glasses back up to the large dent in the bridge of her nose, which Burr speculated had been caused by the gravitational pull of her glasses on her nose over the last who knew how long.

"Now, as for you, Mr. Lafayette, while I do appreciate the constitutional aspects of your plea, off the record . . ." The court reporter stopped in mid-sentence. "For my entire adult life, I have wrapped Christmas presents on December 24, which is today. And a Saturday to boot. And as I treasure my free time, I expect this interruption to be brief. Is that clear?"

"Yes, Your Honor." Burr looked sideways at the other two judges. The older of the two men looked sleepy, and the younger looked like he wanted to be somewhere else. Both judges were clearly overfed. Based on his personal experience, Burr knew that each of them had an intellect uncommonly unremarkable. His prospects for victory would rest solely on the intellect of Judge Florentine.

The chambers were on the second floor of the Pruden building in downtown Lansing, in an oak-paneled courtroom (the varnish old enough to have turned almost black, obscuring all but the brightest of the oak grain) one of Burr's most familiar battlegrounds.

"May it please the court," Burr said rising. He brushed against Suzanne's leg and felt her nylons through his pants. This distracted him for a moment.

"Yes?" Judge Florentine said.

"MCLA 28.51, clearly states that a person accused of a crime must be charged within forty eight hours of his arrest," Burr said. "This is a codification of the Fourth Amendment's constitutional protection known as habeas corpus."

"I am aware of the concept," Judge Florentine said. Tweedledum and Tweedledee nodded in unison.

"Of course, Your Honor. In fact, the legislature believed this protection so vitally important that it provides for judges to be available on weekends and holidays to ensure compliance with this legislative and constitutional safeguard.

"Mr. Lafayette, as you must undoubtedly be aware, we are here today, Christmas Eve, because of that very reason."

To Burr's right, Truax popped up like toast in a toaster.

"Mr. Truax," said the Judge, "Do you have something further to say?"

"Your Honor, " Burr continued to stand.

"Sit down, counselor," said Judge Florentine. Burr sat "Mr. Truax?" she asked.

Burr saw the vein on Truax's forehead bulge and pulse. Burr thought he looked like a mean spirited Ichabod Crane. "Your Honor, the State did everything in its power to arraign the defendant in a timely fashion. Unfortunately, the jail situation and the inclement weather precluded strict compliance with the statute. The State, however, made more than reasonable efforts to ensure statutory compliance, and in any event, charged the defendant less than twenty-four hours after the prescribed time period."

"For the record, it was two days too late," Burr said.

"Whatever," Truax said.

"Stop it. Both of you," said Florentine. "Mr. Lafayette, you of all people should be aware of the deportment in this court."

"Yes, your Honor," Burr said.

Calvin Truax took a deep breath and swallowed. His Adam's apple stuck out and Burr felt Truax might feel better if somehow it could be pushed into his neck. "Your Honor," Truax said, "in People v Hitch, a blizzard, as in this case, prevented the defendant from being charged for a full week. In that case, the court held that a reasonable test should be used in interpreting rights of habeas corpus.

Burr jabbed Jacob. Jacob jumped in his seat. He shook his head like a wet dog, scribbled a note and handed it to Burr.

"Mr. Lafayette, are you familiar with this case?"

Burr opened the tin of Altoids, sucked on four and studied the note.

"Mr. Lafayette?" Burr had dropped his pen and reached down under the table to pick it up. "Mr. Lafayette, where are you?"

Burr appeared. "Your Honor, the case cited by counsel is from Wyoming and has no direct bearing on Michigan law."

Truax bent at the neck as if his Adam's apple pulled his head forward. "Your Honor, in People v Stocker, a Michigan court of appeals held that when a defendant could not be charged in a timely fashion, again because of a snowstorm, a rule of reasonableness should apply."

Burr leaned toward Jacob who whispered something in his ear. "Your Honor, with all due respect, the case cited by counsel is a Court of Appeals case and not…"

"Stop right there, Mr. Lafayette. I am well aware of the jurisdiction and would remind you that we make good law on the Court of Appeals. Off the record …" The court reporter jumped. "Unless I am mistaken, you make your living here, do you not?"

"Yes, Your Honor," Burr said.

"Then you would be well advised not to criticize those whose favor you must curry."

"Your Honor," Burr said, "my complete thought was that the legislature enacted this statute subsequent to the Court of Appeals decision. The statute would seem to supersede the prior decision of the court."

"Not at all, Your Honor," Truax said. "Judicial precedent is always useful in interpreting statutes. In fact, there are no cases subsequent to the statute that overrule the reasonableness test we seek to uphold. We must, therefore, assume that the legislature intended to codify a constitutional right along with its common law precedents."

Another conference with Jacob. "Your Honor," Burr said, "the legislative committee notes directly contradict Mr. Truax. They state that the statute is to have a strict interpretation and that the forty-eight hour provision is purposely designed to be inflexible: any arraignment within that time period is not a violation and any arraignment over forty-eight hours is invalid."

"Where did you find that?" The chief judge barked at him. Tweedledum and Tweedledee showed some interest.

"We have the legislative hearing records in our law library, Your Honor," Burr said.

"May I see that please?" she said. Burr handed her the document. "Why wasn't this included in the brief?"

"It's in the footnote, Your Honor," Burr said.

"I see."

"Your Honor, the People have not had access to this material," Truax said. "We request a twenty four adjournment to review the material and prepare a response."

"Your Honor, the whole purpose of the statute is to prevent citizens from being imprisoned and left to languish in jail without being charged with a crime. It is one of the pillars of our judicial system," Burr said.

"Spare me the rhetoric, counselor," said Judge Florentine. "Approach the bench." The judge spoke in a harsh whisper: "You are ruining my Christmas, Mr. Lafayette. Now, if I grant your motion, what do you suppose will happen?"

"My client will be released immediately," Burr said.

The judge arched her eyebrows. They rose up over the frames of her glasses. Carefully tweezed, he thought.

"What will happen is this, Your Honor," Truax said. "I will immediately ask that a new warrant be issued, and the defendant will be charged before he leaves the jail."

"Assuming you can find Judge Gillis," Burr said, mostly to himself, but loud enough for Truax to hear it, who did, and flushed, and soft enough so Judge Florentine could not, who didn't.

"That's what I thought, you'd do, Mr. Truax, and I assume you are aware of that as well, Mr. Lafayette." She stared directly into Burr's eyes. "So, what's the point?"

"The point, Your Honor, is that my client's statutory and constitutional rights have been violated," Burr said.

"No," Truax said. "The point is you should have just asked for a bail reduction without getting cute."

"Really?" said the judge.

"Your Honor, I apologize for the inconvenience. Frankly, I would like my client to be home for Christmas," Burr said.

"I, too, would like to be home for Christmas," Judge Florentine said.

"Your client murdered his wife," Truax said.

"My client killed his wife, but it was an accident. That's not murder," Burr said.

"It will be when I'm done," Truax said.

"When I'm done, you'll be lucky to have a license," Burr said.

"Sit down, both of you," Judge Florentine said. She huddled with Tweedledum and Tweedledee. They looked like a sandlot football team trying to decide whose turn it was to get the ball. They whispered together for about ten minutes.

"Gentlemen," Judge Florentine said. Her voice boomed through the chamber and echoed off the back wall. "We find that the constitutional underpinnings of the statute are of the utmost importance in preserving the individual freedoms of our democracy. We find that the people of the State of Michigan have a duty to charge defendant's promptly and that MCLA 28.51 should be strictly interpreted. Therefore, we further find that the defendant was not charged within the prescribed forty-eight hour period and that the charges against him should be dismissed, without prejudice."

Burr exhaled, slowly letting all his breath out. The appellate judges filed out

"What now?" Suzanne poked him in the ribs with her finger. He felt the nail, knew it was painted red and knew it wasn't her forefinger. She painted that one too, of course, but Suzanne kept her trigger finger trimmed.

"Now we get a true copy of the order and the two of you drive to Petoskey and get Frank out of jail," he said. "Merry Christmas."

Sarah walked around the table and offered her hand to Burr. "Thank you, Mr. Lafayette. I'm not at all sure what happened, but thank you."

"You're quite welcome, Mrs. Tavohnen. Now if you'll excuse me."

"Where are you off to?" asked Suzanne.

"Actually, I've been invited to Christmas dinner with Zeke," Burr said diffidently.

"Don't you think it a bit odd to have Christmas dinner with the woman you divorced?" Suzanne asked.

"Not if Zeke is involved," Burr said. They looked at each other for a silent moment before Suzanne turned away.

Burr saw Truax writing furiously on the other side of the courtroom. The prosecutor stuffed his papers in his briefcase and rushed out.

"Ladies," Burr said, "We need a new plan."

Burr, Jacob, Suzanne, and Sarah had all met at Burr's office after the victory in the Court of Appeals. Becky, Frank and Sarah's daughter, had been typing away on Eve's Selectric when they arrived and seemed somewhat annoyed to see her mother. She had her mother's blond hair and her father's gray eyes. She was just a bit chubby, shorter than Zeke-the-boy, but not all that much shorter.

When Burr saw Truax writing so furiously, he knew that Truax would have a new warrant issued before Suzanne and Sarah could make the four-hour drive from Lansing to Petoskey with the true copy of the court order dismissing the murder charge. To thwart his not altogether incompetent foe, Burr had faxed the order to his aunt who lived in Harbor Springs, and she had gotten Frank released before Truax could have a new warrant issued. Burr then sent Suzanne, Sarah, and Becky to Petoskey to fetch Frank and take him to Burr's cabin on Walpole Island for Christmas.

After they had all left his office, Burr looked out from his window, down on the city of East Lansing's Christmas tree. It stood perched on a brick walkway off the intersection of Albert and MAC. The lights from the tree twinkled at him. A white spruce, twenty feet tall. Tall as Christmas trees go, but shorter than the one at the state capitol just down Michigan Avenue which, of course, was shorter than the one in Washington, all in keeping with Christmas tree protocol. This one had silver lights and was topped with a silver star. The angel had been lost in a lawsuit brought by a Michigan State University student against the city of East Lansing and which Burr had lost on appeal.

He thought he'd bought, rented might be a better word, Frank a little time—until after Christmas—before he'd be charged again. Maybe Truax won't charge him. Maybe Truax will just forget it.

Why did Truax charge Frank in the first place? It happened a long time ago. Why would anyone care after all this time?

Burr smelled spaghetti sauce. It stuck in his nostrils. Scooter must be making a powerful batch of marinara with the stairwell door open. The smell must have drifted up the stairs and into his offices. I must smell like a meatball, he thought.

Calvin Truax blew in just behind the smell of the spaghetti sauce "Where is he?" Truax asked. A hint of Old Spice hung in the air, just under the spaghetti sauce.

"Did you take the stairs?" Burr asked.

"What?" Truax asked.

"The stairs. Did you take the stairs?"

"I don't trust elevators," Truax said.

"I don't either," Burr said. "It doesn't work anyway. That explains the smell."

"What?" Truax asked.

"Never mind," he said..

"Where's Tavohnen?" Truax asked.

"I assume he's home with his family for Christmas. It is Christmas Eve. Merry Christmas to you, Calvin. It is Calvin, isn't it?" The blood vessel on Truax's forehead pulsed and Burr could see he was out of breath. Six flights is a hike, Burr thought. "Please, sit down," Burr said.

Truax slammed a one-page document on Burr's desk. "Here's a new warrant. Where's your boy?"

Burr glared at Truax who, standing this close, smelled distinctly of Old Spice. Burr refused to look at the warrant. "That didn't take long, Burr said. "If Frank's not at home with his family, I don't know where he is."

"You've got him stashed somewhere. Now, where is he?" Truax said.

"How did you find the judge?" Burr asked.

"I know where the grouse winter," Truax said.

"Where do they winter?" Burr asked.

"In the cedars. I expect you know that," Truax said. "Now, where's Tavohnen?"

"Why don't you just give it up? Burr said. "What's the guy done to you?"

"He murdered someone in my county," Truax said.

"I thought it was an accident," Burr said.

"Well, it wasn't," Truax said. "And it doesn't matter what you think."

Zeke crawled out from the kneehole under Burr's desk. He walked over to Truax, sniffed his leg and then his crotch. Truax did not pet the dog.

"Give the guy a break," Burr said. "It's Christmas Eve."

"Do you even know what happened?" Truax asked.

This took Burr back a bit. Actually, he had no idea what really happened. "At this point," Burr said, "it makes no difference if Frank Tavohnen was the husbandly version of Lizzie Borden."

"It most certainly does matter. I have a warrant for his arrest, and if he doesn't turn himself in by tomorrow, he will be a fugitive." Truax pointed his long, bony finger at Burr. "And I'll have you arrested for contempt." Truax then pointed at Zeke. "And, please, get this dog away from me."

"Here, Zeke." The dog wagged his tail and shuffled over to Burr. Burr felt a small depression setting in, which he attributed more to the seasonal lack of sunlight than to the presence of Calvin Truax. Burr was sure he could handle Truax. Burr then removed himself to his closet, and with the assistance of Zeke, he rummaged through it. "I know I have them in here," Burr said.

"What?" Truax said.

"They're in here somewhere. I didn't need them until the Solstice, and I know I put them in here. Eve said they were in the basement, but they're not." Burr disappeared from sight, deep in the bowels of the closet. It had been built to Burr's specifications, the size of a small office, complete with a window and lined with shelves. Burr's specifications, however, did not call for lights, and he stumbled over who knew what.

"Lafayette, your client is in serious trouble, and so are you. Do you realize that? What in God's name are you doing? I'm talking to you. Where are you?" Truax peered into the closet, which had swallowed up Zeke as well as Burr.

Burr then tripped over the box of missing Christmas tree ornaments on which he then stepped, crushing them. "Zeke, out," he said. The dog backed out and into Truax, shedding on Truax's navy slacks.

"Damn it all," Truax said. He tried to brush off the dog hair, but it attached nicely to his wool trousers. "I have never been treated so rudely in my life," he said. Truax retreated to a wing-backed chair where he planted himself. He plucked off the dog hairs one by one.

Burr emerged from the closet carrying two pole lamps with snake necks. "Eve said they were in the basement, but I knew they were in here. For once, I was right about where something was," he said.

What on earth are you talking about?" asked Truax.

"Never mind," Burr said. The lamps stood shoulder high. He plugged them in behind his desk chair and sat underneath them as if he were sitting under two hair dryers at a beauty parlor. The light streamed down on him. "That's better," he said. "The full spectrum of natural sunlight." Burr did not immediately feel his depression fade.

"Look here, Lafayette. On your desk is a warrant for the arrest of your client, Frank Tavohnen. Various police departments, including Petoskey and Grosse Pointe Park, cannot locate him. You are his attorney. He was released into your custody. Surely, you must have known we would issue another warrant." Truax slid the warrant over to Burr.

"Not so soon, I didn't." Burr pushed the warrant back across his desk

"Well, where is he?" Truax said.

"I don't know." Burr remembered that it took at least two weeks for the lights to work. This further depressed him.

"I give you credit," Truax said. "You got him out of the courthouse in a big hurry, with that madwoman tree hugger of a lawyer."

"Do not, I repeat, do not, insult my aunt," Burr said. "Mr. Tavohnen was not released in my custody."

"You faxed that order up to her before we could turn around," Truax said. The vein in Truax's temple pulsed again. "You are subverting justice."

"I'm the appellate lawyer," Burr said. "He's not my client any longer."

"You are the attorney of record. And you'll be in jail tomorrow if you don't produce him," Truax said.

Between the bobbing Adam's apple, the throbbing temple, and the pointing finger, Burr thought Truax had the makings of a rhythm section. "Can't you just wait until after Christmas?" Burr asked.

"No. And you know where he is. You must have known we'd issue another warrant. It was a technicality," Truax said. "Why did you even bother with the appeal?"

"Because you cheated him, that's why," Burr said.

"Out of what?" Truax said.

"You jerked him out of his house. You hauled him across the state for four days. Did it occur to you to call him up and tell him to turn himself in? Instead you have a bunch of cops beat him up and take him away. The man is not exactly a menace," Burr said.

"He is wanted for murder," Truax said.

"What's in this for you, anyway?" Burr said. "Who cares what happened way back then?"

Truax picked one final dog hair off his pants then stood up. "One of you will be spending Christmas in jail. You decide who it's going to be."

Truax slammed the door behind him. Burr waited until he heard the stairway door slam shut. He wished that Truax had taken the broken elevator. The city had made him spend one hundred twenty-five thousand dollars to have that elevator installed. He wished that it would have stopped with Truax in it.

DECEMBER 25, 1988 – CHRISTMAS DAY

Deputy Brubaker, apparently the same deputy who had ferried Frank to Petoskey, arrested Burr at 1:00 p.m. on Christmas Day. The good, but tubby, deputy had parked in front of Grace's house, the house Burr still made payments on, and waited for him. Burr didn't even have a chance to get out of his car. Burr wondered how Truax knew where to find him, but apparently Burr had been easier to find than Frank.

"That warrant's no good," Burr said.

"Looks good to me," said the deputy.

Burr decided not to pursue that line of thought any further. "What about my dog?"

"What about him?" Deputy Brubaker said.

"I can't just leave him here," Burr said.

"Bring him with you, then. If we go right away, I can be home for Christmas dinner and still get my holiday pay."

As it turned out, Zeke-the-dog did not make the trip. Before they could leave, Zeke-the-boy had run out. He had hugged the dog. Burr wished both Zekes a Merry Christmas and said he had to go with the policeman.

"To arrest somebody?" Zeke-the-boy asked.

"Yes," Burr said, not saying they were arresting he, himself. Deputy Brubaker, full of the Christmas spirit, had been kind enough not to say anything.

"Can Zeke stay here with me?" Zeke-the-boy asked.

After a short conference with Grace (who liked dogs but not dog hair), and a hand signal from Burr, the two Zekes trotted up the sidewalk and into the house. A minor Christmas miracle, he thought.

Burr persuaded the affable (and jolly) Officer Brubaker that he wasn't a risk to flee and followed him in the Jeep for six hours to the Emmet County Jail, his anger growing with each mile.

Burr then found himself (according to Deputy Brubaker) in the same cell from which he had rescued Frank, the irony not lost on Burr, the prisoner.

Jacob arrived at eight that evening, festive in a subdued way, wine-colored crew neck sweater, tan corduroys. He had called Frank on Walpole who said he would drive up and surrender himself tomorrow, the day after Christmas.

As soon as Jacob left, Burr fell asleep. The next thing he heard was the jail door swinging open. Jacob and Frank met him in the hall.

"Thank you for Christmas with my family," Frank said.

"You're welcome," Burr said. He thought Frank looked much better rested. "Jacob, where is my suit and tie?"

MONDAY DECEMBER 26, 1988

Burr and Jacob stood at the defense table, Truax across the aisle. "I trust you had a pleasant Christmas," Truax smiled at him.

"Quiet. It was very quiet." Burr said.

The accommodations were to your liking, then?"

"A little Spartan, but the price was right." Burr saw the vein at Truax's forehead pulse.

"Highly illegal. And you know it," Jacob hissed at Truax.

"And who might you be?" Judge Gillis peered down at Jacob over the top of his reading glass.

"Co-counsel, Your Honor. Jacob Wertheim."

"Effective though, wouldn't you say?" Truax sneered at Burr, using only the left side of his mouth.

"It is false arrest. Actionable against you individually, Prosecutor. Definitely an ethics violation," Jacob said, who could have a very indignant manner when he felt it necessary.

Truax turned red.

"Enough," Gillis said. Burr thought Gillis looked like a black olive stuffed with a slivered almond, his bald head stuck out of his robe. "Gentlemen, I note that Mr. Tavohnen is present. Do we finally have agreement that, after all this, he may be properly charged?"

"No, Your Honor," Burr said.

"And why not?" said the Judge.

"There is no probable cause that Mr. Tavohnen murdered his wife," Burr said.

"There is," Truax said.

"I already decided there is," Gillis said.

"It's not enough," Burr said.

"Listen to me, counselor. I say there is probable cause, so there is. You don't like it, show up at the preliminary exam. Now, sit down, all of you," Gillis said.

"Frank X. Tavohnen," Gillis said, "you are charged with open murder in the death of Claudia Marie Tavohnen on December 18, 1982. How do you plead?"

"Not guilty, Your Honor," Frank said.

"Enter a plea of not guilty," Gillis said.

"Bail?" Burr asked.

"One million," Gillis said.

"Too high," Burr said.

"Who do you think you are?" Gillis said.

"I spent Christmas in jail at your pleasure, totally illegally. You can charge him now, but if the bail is more than one hundred thousand dollar, which means we post ten thousand now, I'm filing an ethics charge."

Judge Gillis shifted his glare from Burr to Truax, whose forehead continued to throb. "Bail is set at One hundred thousand dollars," Gillis said. "The preliminary exam will be February 6, 1989." Down came the gavel. Burr saw Frank jump at the bang. Burr, Jacob and the rest of the courtroom rose, now standing along with Frank. Judge Gillis disappeared out the back.

The three of them, Frank, Burr, and Jacob followed Truax down the aisle between the rows of seats —pews really —but dedicated to a wholly different religion. Burr heard the floor creak underneath his feet.

At the double doors, Truax turned left. Burr caught up with him. "Could I speak with you for a moment?" Burr said.

Truax stopped short. "Why?"

"A procedural issue. For the preliminary exam," Burr said.

Truax shifted from foot to foot. "Like what?"

"Could we talk in your office?" Burr asked.

"You may have one minute," Truax said.

He started down the hall. Burr followed him. Up a flight of stairs, down a hall, around a corner. Truax unlocked the door and held it open for Burr who walked in. Truax stood. He did not offer Burr a chair. Burr looked around the room. He thought Truax must have his walls filled with every diploma and award he had ever earned. In the confines of Truax's office, Burr again smelled the sweet smell of Old Spice.

"This happened six years ago," Burr said. "Why now? What's in this for you?"

"Justice, Mr. Lafayette. There is new evidence."

Burr shook his head, stared down at his dress shoes which needed polishing.

"I imagine you'll be turning this over to a trial lawyer now," Truax said.

"I am a trial lawyer," Burr said.

"In light of the circumstances," Truax said.

"Circumstances?" Burr asked.

"Since you've been so thoroughly humiliated," Truax said.

"Humiliated? By whom?" Burr asked.

"Well, actually, by the judge and by me. Frankly, I've thoroughly thrashed you on this," Truax said.

"I see," Burr said. Burr had completed his survey of Truax's office and trophy room. From his vantage point he looked right up the bony slope of Truax's nose. Truax literally looked down his nose at Burr. The prosecutor's chin disappeared somewhere under his nose. He looked like a weasel. Burr shook his head, but he couldn't shake off the weasel image, a weasel standing in a doorway.

Burr exhaled slowly. He felt all the air empty from his lungs. Then he hit Truax in the face, on the left cheekbone, being careful not to risk breaking Truax' nose, which he found interesting. Truax fell straight back into the hallway. "That's for Christmas. I'll see you at the preliminary exam." Burr stepped over him on his way out.

CHAPTER SEVEN

MONDAY, FEBRUARY 6, 1989

Swede, the lispy bailiff, announced the arrival of Gillis. Burr sat at the defense table between Frank on his right, Jacob to his left. Suzanne and Sarah sat in the first row of the gallery behind them.

Truax called his first witness, Roland Gustafson, a policeman and the first to arrive at Frank's house on the night of the accident. Gustafson was about sixty-five, oily hair, combed straight back, mostly black, a red puffy face, neck bulging over his collar.

Truax first established Gustafson's qualifications, then led the cop through a narrative account of the evening. "Thank you, Officer Gustafson," Truax said. "Just a few more questions." Truax paused. "Going back to the beginning, do you recall what Mr. Tavohnen's first words were when you asked him what had occurred at the crime scene?"

"Objection," Burr said. "There is no evidence that a crime was committed."

"I note, Mr. Lafayette," Gillis said, "that there is no jury present who might be prejudiced by that statement, and I am slightly offended that you might think I would be affected by such a comment."

"Your Honor, I apologize if I offended you," Burr said. "Still, I ask that the prosecutor's statement be stricken from the record."

"Granted," Gillis said. "Please proceed, Mr. Truax."

"Yes, Your Honor," Truax said. "Let me repeat the question. Mr. Gustafson, do you recall Mr. Tavohnen's first words when you arrived at the, at the, at Mr. and Mrs. Tavohnen's home on the night of the murder. Strike that," Truax said, turning and smiling ever so slightly at Burr, "on the night in question."

"He said, 'I killed her.' "

"He said that?" Truax asked.

"Yes," Gustafson said.

"And then what did you do?"

"Well, I went down to the basement and there she was," Gustafson said. "Dead all right. I should say so."

"Did you examine the body?" Truax said.

"Sure did," said the policeman.

"What did you find?"

"Bullet holes," Gustafson said.

"More than one?" Truax asked.

"Yes, sir," Gustafson said.

"How many?" Truax asked.

The man raised two fingers on his left hand. Stubby fingers, pink flesh and a wedding ring that looked to Burr like it choked off the circulation above the finger. "Two," he said.

"No further questions, Your Honor," Truax said.

Burr, still seated, leaned over to Frank. "Two bullet holes? I thought you said the gun only went off once. How do you shoot somebody accidentally two times?

"Mr. Lafayette, do you wish to question this witness?" The bald judge peered down over his reading glasses. "If not, I will excuse him."

No matter what happened today, this would be the last of Gillis. If Frank were bound over for trial, it would go up to the circuit court and that would be the last time Burr or anyone else would have to deal with this fat, bald district judge. Burr leaned over to Frank.

"Did you shoot her two times?" he asked.

"No," Frank said.

"Mr. Lafayette, are you listening to me?" asked Gillis.

"Yes, Your Honor. May I have a moment with my client?"

"No, you may not," Gillis said. "When this hearing is over, you may have all the time you wish with your client."

Burr walked to the witness box. "Would you like to loosen your collar, Officer Gustafson? Did I pronounce your name correctly?"

"Yes, you did, and I think I will." He unbuttoned the top button on his shirt and his neck sagged down onto his chest, like he'd been punctured and all the air rushed out. "That's better," Gustafson said.

"Mr. Gustafson, are you a police officer?"

"Yes, Gustafson said. "Well, no."

"I note that you're not in uniform," Burr said. "Are you a detective?"

"No," Gustafson said.

"But you're a police officer," Burr said.

"Not any more," Gustafson said. "I'm retired."

"I see." Burr knew very well he was retired. "But you were the first one to arrive at the house on the night of the accident."

"Yes, I was."

"Mr. Gustafson, how long have you been retired?"

"Five years," Gustafson said.

"And this accident, shooting, occurred six years ago," Burr said. "Just before you retired. Is that right?"

"Yes," Gustafson said.

"That's a long time to remember, isn't it?" Burr asked.

"Objection," Truax said. "Calls for an opinion."

"Sustained," Gillis said.

"Mr. Gustafson, how many times had Mrs. Tavohnen been shot?" Burr asked.

"Once," Gustafson said.

"Once," Burr said. "Then why were there two bullet holes?"

"Once where it went in. Once where it went out," Gustafson said.

"I see," Burr said. "One shot. Is that right?"

"Yes," Gustafson said.

"Thank you," Burr said. "Mr. Gustafson, did Mr. Tavohnen say anything else?"

"What's that?" Gustafson asked.

"When you arrived, Mr. Tavohnen let you in," Burr said. "Is that right?"

"Yes," Gustafson said.

"And did he say anything right away?" Burr asked.

"Well, no, not right away," Gustafson said.

"What was he doing?"

The cop looked away. Then over at Truax who was turning red.

"Officer Gustafson, what was Mr. Tavohnen doing when he opened the door?" Burr asked.

"Crying," Gustafson said.

"What did you say?" Burr asked.

"He was crying," Gustafson said.

"And when he did say something, do you recall what he said first?" Burr asked.

"He said, 'she's dead, Rollie The gun went off'."

"Anything else?" Burr asked.

"No, I don't think so," Gustafson said.

"Did he say it was an accident?" Burr asked.

Truax, showing more color now, rose. "I object. Counsel is putting words in his mouth."

"Your Honor," Burr said. "I'm merely asking the witness if my client said it was an accident."

"I'll allow it," Gillis said. "Answer the question."

"I think so," Gustafson said.

"Did he or didn't he?" Burr asked.

"He did," Gustafson said.

"So when you arrived, you found Mr. Tavohnen crying," Burr said. "His first words were, 'she's dead.' Then he said, 'it was an accident.' Is that right?"

"Yes," Gustafson said.

"I thought you said the first thing Mr. Tavohnen said was 'I killed her'," Burr said.

"No," Gustafson said.

"That's what you said earlier," Burr said.

"Well, I might have said that, but that's not when he said it," Gustafson said.

"When exactly did Mr. Tavohnen say it?" Burr asked.

"Well, down in the basement, I guess," Gustafson said. "I had to look at her. Frank said the gun went off and it killed her."

"It killed her," Burr repeated. "Earlier you said, 'I killed her.' What exactly did Mr. Tavohnen say?"

"'I killed her', no, 'it'." The retired cop wrapped his lower lip over his upper lip like a frog, a sweating frog.

"He said 'it', didn't he?" Burr said.

"Objection," Truax said. "Leading the witness."

"I am simply asking a question," Burr said.

"Overruled," Gillis said.

"What did he say, 'it' or 'I'?" Burr asked.

"He said 'I.' No, he said 'it'." Gustafson's shoulders sagged. "I guess I don't remember," he said.

"No further questions, Your Honor," Burr said.

The policeman heaved himself off the witness stand and shuffled between Truax and Burr. Burr saw Truax scowl at the fat cop who refused to look in his direction. As Gustafson passed the two tables, he whispered, "Long time ago, Frank. Long time."

Truax said, "The people call Lawrence Van Arkel," who the bailiff managed to swear in.

Truax had tried to use Gustafson to mislead Gillis. Burr knew it and he was sure Gillis knew it. Van Arkel, though, might be a different story. Burr had read the autopsy and this guy was no fool. Van Arkel wore a gray suit that fit him. A dark red tie. Funereal. Burr couldn't see the pattern. About sixty, bags under his eyes. Ears that looked like they were taped to his head. Sincere. He looked sincere, except that his chest had sunk to his waist which made him look like he might have something to hide.

Truax began by qualifying Van Arkel as an expert. He was a licensed physician and a mortician. Then he launched into the autopsy.

"Dr. Van Arkel, you were the county coroner at the time of Mrs. Tavohnen's death. Is that right?" Truax said.

"Still am," Van Arkel said.

"Answer the question, please," Truax said.

"Yes," Van Arkel said.

"Thank you," Truax said.

"And you performed the autopsy," Truax said. "Is that right?"

"Yes."

"And what was the cause of death?" Truax said.

"Gunshot," Van Arkel said.

"Can you elaborate?"

"The bullet entered here." Van Arkel touched his left side at his armpit, "It passed through the left lung, the heart, the right lung, and exited here," he said, touching his right side, just above his hip. It's in the autopsy."

"I am aware of that, Dr. Van Arkel," Truax said.

Burr pushed his hair back off his forehead. That concludes the two bullet hole question. No harm there, he thought.

"What actually killed Mrs. Tavohnen?" Truax said.

"The bullet, as it passed through the heart and lungs," said the coroner.

"Thank you. Now, Dr. Van Arkel, is it consistent with your findings that Mr. Tavohnen could have picked up the gun and shot Mrs. Tavohnen?"

"Yes, I suppose so," Van Arkel said.

"You suppose so," Truax said. "Can you be more definite? Is it consistent with your findings that the gun could have been picked up and fired from the shoulder?"

"Yes, it is," Van Arkel said.

"Objection, Your Honor," Burr said. "That's not what the autopsy says."

"The autopsy does not speak to that issue," Truax said.

Burr was on his feet now. "The autopsy does not say that Frank Tavohnen picked up the rifle and fired it from his shoulder."

"Your Honor," Truax said, "It also does not say he didn't."

'Overruled," Gillis said. "I will let the testimony stand."

"Thank you, Your Honor," Truax said. "No further questions."

Burr approached the coroner. He saw the pattern in the coroner's tie. Red with little blue diamonds. The smallest blue diamonds he'd ever seen.

"Dr. Van Arkel. It is doctor, isn't it?" Burr asked.

"Yes," Van Arkel said.

"Thank you. Doctor, when you did the autopsy, did you think the shooting was accidental?"

"I did," Van Arkel said.

Burr glanced at Suzanne who gave him a resolute smile, which lifted his spirits. "Was there anything in your examination that caused you to think that the shooting might have been intentional?" he asked.

"No," Van Arkel said.

"Did the police ask you to determine if the shooting was intentional?" Burr asked.

"No," Van Arkel said.

"But you thought it was accidental?" Burr said.

"Yes," Van Arkel said.

"Then why did you say that your report was consistent with picking up the gun and firing it?" Burr asked.

"It could have happened that way," Van Arkel said.

"Your report says the gun went off while lying flat on the workbench. Doesn't it say that?" Burr demanded.

"Yes. Yes, it does," Van Arkel said, who seemed to be getting a bit flustered, which was just fine with Burr.

"Then why did you testify to Mr. Truax that the gun could have been picked up and fired?" Burr asked, not really asking.

"I suppose it could have," Van Arkel said.

"You suppose," Burr said.

"Objection," Truax said. "Counsel is badgering the witness."

"I assumed it was lying on the workbench. I didn't think Frank picked it up. I supposed it could have been. They told me it was an accident. I had no reason to . . ."

Burr raised his palm to Van Arkel. "Stop," he said. This wasn't going the way Burr wanted it.

"I registered an objection, Your Honor," Truax said.

"Let the witness finish, Mr. Lafayette," Gillis said.

"I withdraw the question," Burr said.

"Very well, then." Gillis said.

Burr thought he had refuted Truax's claim but he wanted to press. He knew it could backfire, but he thought it worth the risk.

"Dr. Van Arkel. You are a doctor, correct?"

"Yes," Van Arkel said.

"Do you practice medicine?" Burr asked.

"No," Van Arkel said.

"Are you a full-time coroner?"

"No," Van Arkel said. "There's not enough work for a full-time coroner."

"I see," Burr said. "You are employed though full time?"

"Yes," Van Arkel said.

"You're an undertaker aren't you?" Burr asked.

"A mortician," Van Arkel said.

"You embalm dead people, sell caskets, and do funerals," Burr said. "Isn't that right?"

"I have my own funeral home," Van Arkel said.

"Why aren't you a practicing physician?" Burr asked.

"Objection, Your Honor," Truax said. "Irrelevant."

"Mr. Lafayette, where is this going?" Gillis asked.

"Your Honor," Burr said. "I am speaking to the qualifications of the witness."

"Mr. Lafayette, Mr. Truax, approach the bench." Judge Gillis did not look at all pleased.

"Your Honor," Burr said. "I'm trying . . ."

Gillis waved him off. "Mr. Lafayette, as I hope you are aware, there is no jury present." Gillis pointed to an empty jury box. "It is empty. All we're here to do is determine whether or not there is probable cause, I repeat, probable cause to determine if a murder has been committed. And I will decide that. As I hope you are aware, the rules of evidence are not as strict as they would be in a trial and I repeat, probable cause is the standard for binding over for trial. The standard is not beyond a reasonable doubt." The portly judge sighed and folded his hands.

"Your Honor, my point is that this was an accidental shooting," Burr said. "The investigating officer thought so. The coroner, if you want to call him that, thinks so, too.

Gillis peered down at him over his reading glasses. "Mr. Lafayette. I think you thought he was well qualified when he agreed with you."

"Your Honor," Burr said.

"Mr. Lafayette, in high school, Dr. Van Arkel played tackle and I played halfback. He blocked for me," Gillis said. "His qualifications are impeccable. Any more questions?"

"No," Burr said. He sulked back to the defense table and sat down.

CHAPTER EIGHT

After Gillis adjourned for lunch, Burr herded his clients down Mitchell Street to the City Park Grill. The wind blew across them and swirled the snow around their feet. Suzanne cut through the snow in her black boots, which disappeared in her fur coat. Jacob had on rubbers over his dress shoes which Burr knew to be practical but absolutely refused to do himself. He had his dress shoes resoled when the leather rotted. Long ago, Burr had promised Eve lunch at the City Park Grill, supposedly a haunt of Hemingway's, and Burr decided today might as well be the day to make good on his promise to a fellow Hemingway fan. (Burr feared this might be all that he would accomplish today.)

When Burr's eyes adjusted to the half light inside, he saw the cherry paneling which curved into a tin ceiling, the original, with a raised Victorian pattern. The original carved wooden bar stuck out from the corner. The City Park Grill smelled of smoke and stale beer. Burr watched Eve take it all in.

The waitress arrived.

"So this is where Hemingway ate his lunch," Eve said to the waitress. "What do you think he might have had for lunch?"

"I wasn't here then," the waitress said. She looked around the table hoping that someone would order something.

"Hamburger and fries," Jacob said. The rest of the table ordered, all except Sarah who said she couldn't possibly eat.

"Mr. Lafayette," Sarah said, "One more witness. Then this awful business will be over, and we can all go home."

"Assuming, Gillis finds there's no probable cause," Jacob said.

"How can there be?" Sarah asked. "Frank didn't murder anyone."

Jacob cleared his throat. "All Gillis has to do is find it is more likely than not that a crime was committed," Jacob said. "If he finds that, then Frank will be bound over for trial."

"But he didn't do it," Sarah said.

Jacob ignored her. "At a trial, the jury can only find Frank guilty if they believe beyond a reasonable doubt that the crime was committed. It's a much higher standard at a trial."

"I don't care about your standards," Sarah said, not quite hysterical. "I want our life back." Turning to Burr, "Mr. Lafayette, what about you? What do you think?"

"I don't think Truax did much damage this morning. He had to show that Frank killed Claudia, which he did, but he also had to show that Frank did it on purpose, which he didn't."

"Well, then," Sarah said, with waning hysteria, "There's just one more witness. Then we're done."

"Yes," Jacob said, "but this witness is the expert on lasers. We don't know what she's going to say," Burr said.

"We don't?" Sarah asked. "Why don't we?"

"Sarah," Burr said, "Gillis is going to allow almost anything. And he won't allow the experts to be discredited. I tried it with the coroner, and it backfired."

"What's our defense then?" Sarah asked.

"You didn't pay for a defense," Eve said.

Burr cringed.

Suzanne lashed out at Eve. "Shut up, Eve," she said.

"Sarah, there is no discovery prior to a preliminary examination," Jacob said. "The expert is going to testify, and Gillis is going to allow everything in. His job is to determine if there is probable cause. If he finds there is, he sends it up to the circuit judge and the jury."

"Let Frank testify this afternoon. Let him tell what really happened," Sarah said.

Jacob cleared his throat again. Then he straightened his tie, a club, red and yellow diamonds on a blue background. With his blue shirt and white collar, Jacob looked every bit the New York City lawyer, which is what he had been before Detroit. "Mrs. Tavohnen," Jacob said, "if at this point your husband tells his version…"

"It's not a version," Sarah said. "It's the truth."

"Yes, of course it is, but Frank will be telling what happened to the judge. With no corroborating witnesses, it's really not that useful in this type of hearing," Jacob said. He cleared his throat again. (It's all that marijuana, Burr thought.) "Whatever he says can be used against him in the trial," Jacob said.

"You two have given up, haven't you?" Sarah said. "Suzanne, why did I hire him? You said he knew what he was doing."

The lunch arrived. Burr stabbed a forkful of the planked whitefish. Finally, he said, "Sarah, if I put Frank on and he says the wrong thing or if Truax twists it around somehow, it will hurt us later. And if I put Frank on and he has to take the Fifth Amendment when Truax questions him, that hurts, too. Right now we need to lay back and see what they have."

"Then what are you going to do?" Sarah asked, truly hysterical now.

"I'm going to listen," Burr said. He stabbed another forkful of whitefish.

Back in the Courtroom of the Honorable Judge Gillis

Truax called Anne Gannon, a prim woman in her late thirties. She had a fair complexion, complete with an upturned nose, brown hair with auburn highlights, and a pageboy, perhaps the most fetching pageboy Burr had ever seen. Lispy swore her in and she sat down. She pulled the skirt of her suit down to her knees and crossed her legs. She rocked her leg a bit. Burr watched the heel of her black pump slip off her heel and bob up and down. He found it slightly erotic. Once again Truax led his witness through her (impeccable) qualifications.

"Ms. Gannon," continued Truax, "you work in the criminal laboratory division for the Michigan State Police. Is that correct?"

"Yes, sir," she said.

"What is your educational background?"

"I have a Ph.D. in applied physics," she said.

"Do you have a specialty?" Truax asked.

"Yes, sir," Gannon said. "Laser technology."

"I see," Truax said. "And how does that relate to this case?"

"I studied the path of the bullet that killed the deceased," said the witness.

"Just a moment, Mr. Truax." The judge took off his reading glasses, looked through them and then stuck them over the edge of the raised desk. As if on cue, the court stenographer, who sat below and to the right of the judge, reached up with her left hand. She had long thin fingers like those of a piano player, reduced to a keyboard of a different sort. She took the glasses from his hand and looked through them herself. Then, in a practiced way, Miss Longfingers breathed on each lens front and back and scrubbed them on the hem of her skirt. Back up went the fingers holding the glasses. Out reached the plump fingers of the judge and back on the end of his nose went the glasses. The whole performance lasted barely half a minute, a ritual that must have been accomplished hundreds of times. At least he didn't thump his forehead, Burr thought.

"As I was about to say," Gillis said. "Mr. Truax, in the interest of time, you might ask the witness to tell us what she did in a narrative fashion."

"Your Honor?" Somehow Truax didn't follow.

"No more twenty questions," said the judge.

"Ah, yes. I see." Truax said. "Of course." A throat cleaning noise from Truax whose Adam's apple bobbed. "Ms. Gannon, would you please tell the court what you did and what you found. In a narrative fashion."

"The State Police, me actually, in conjunction with the Physics Department at Michigan State University developed a new technology to determine the path of a projectile. In layman's terms, a bullet."

Burr raised his eyebrows, surprised she hadn't said lay person.

"Actually, I work backwards," Gannon said. "In this case, I found where the bullet struck the basement wall. Then I studied the coroner's report to determine where the bullet entered and exited the body."

"And what did you find?" Truax asked.

"I found that the bullet entered the deceased about four inches below the shoulder and pierced the heart and lungs and exited the right side three and a half inches above the hip. From there it stuck in the basement wall, approximately thirty inches above the floor."

"Ms. Gannon, please tell us the significance of determining the path of the bullet," Truax said.

"Based on the bullet's trajectory, path, I can, with the use of a laser, determine where the gun was fired and at what angle it was pointed," she said.

"Objection, Your Honor." Burr stood up. He heard his vertebrae crack as he straightened. "The witness stated the gun was fired. The inquest determined that the gun went off accidentally. Firing connotes a purposeful activity."

"Mr. Lafayette, the shooting was purposeful," said Ms. Gannon.

"Ms. Gannon," Gillis said, "while I take heart at your strong opinion, please do not respond to defense counsel's question directly until he questions you." He turned to Truax. "Counselor, I'm sure you have a response."

"Yes, Your Honor," Truax said. "The witness is expressing her opinion based on her scientific analysis of the evidence. I do not agree with Mr. Lafayette that the inquest found the shooting to be an accident. But that, Your Honor, is the very reason we are here today. To show that the shooting was not an accident. In fact, Your Honor, if I may proceed, I will demonstrate the factual nature of the witnesses' statement."

"Mr. Truax," Gillis said, "you may proceed, but may I remind you, too, that there is no jury present." Once again he swept his left arm —the black robe sweeping behind his arm in a grand gesture —past the empty jury box. "I will decide if there is enough evidence to bind over the defendant. Spare me the theatrics I'm sure you will lavish on the jurors, if indeed we get that far."

"Yes, Your Honor." Truax walked back to the prosecution table and picked up a thick, bound report. He opened it to a paper clipped page and returned to the witness. Ms. Gannon stopped bobbing her foot.

"Ms. Gannon, I have here the report issued following the inquest, which counselor," Truax turned toward Burr, "you may recall has already been entered into evidence. On Page 41 of the inquest, the following was found to have occurred: on the night of

December 18, 1982, while Frank Tavohnen was cleaning his deer rifle on his workbench in the basement of his home, the rifle went off and the bullet struck and killed his wife. Now, Ms. Gannon, what is your opinion of that finding of fact?"

"According to my analysis," Gannon said, "that statement is factually incorrect."

"Objection," Burr said. "The statement is exactly what is made in the report. The statement is factually correct."

Burr saw the vein on Truax's forehead pulse, but he knew what Truax would do. Burr couldn't yet see where this was going, but he hoped to rattle Truax. So far Gillis didn't seem too impressed with the laser hocus pocus. Maybe he could distract him enough to muddle the testimony.

"Let me rephrase the question," Truax said. "Do you believe that the findings of the inquest to be factually correct?"

"No," Gannon said.

"Objection," Burr said.

"I get the point, Mr. Lafayette," Gillis said. "Overruled. "Proceed, Mr. Truax,"

"Ms. Gannon, what did your research show?" Truax asked.

Here it comes, thought Burr. Ann Gannon might be about to hurt him more than he thought she would.

"According to my measurements," she said, " the workbench in question stands three and one half feet off the floor. If the rifle went off while being cleaned on the workbench, I would expect the bullet to have a trajectory virtually parallel to the floor. That is, the bullet should enter and exit the body at roughly forty-two inches, and it should strike the wall at forty two inches."

"And what happened in this case?" Truax asked.

"In this case the bullet had a downward trajectory. The path went from high to low," Gannon said.

"Objection, Your Honor," Burr said. "This whole line of questioning, while moderately interesting, does not prove, does not even hint at anything suggesting a crime. Let alone murder."

The Judge took off his glasses again, looked through them and passed them down again to Miss Longfingers. Burr couldn't see how they could have smudged so soon "Mr. Truax," Gillis said, "unlike Mr. Lafayette, I don't find this even moderately interesting. Do you have a point to make here?"

Truax reddened and his Adam's apple bulged in and out. "Your Honor, I apologize for the lengthy testimony, but it is necessary to supply a foundation for the factual conclusions of the witness. If I may have just a few more minutes, it will become obvious that a murder was indeed committed."

"I wait with bated breath," Gillis said. He realigned his glasses and thumped his forehead.

"Now, Ms. Gannon," Truax said, "please tell us once more what you found in layman's terms." Burr didn't think he'd rattled Truax at all.

"Backing up a bit," she said, "I was able to establish the path of the bullet because I knew where it struck the wall, where it exited the deceased and where it entered the deceased.

"And how did you know this?" Truax asked.

"Because I knew the height of the deceased and where she was standing in the basement."

"And how did you know this?" Truax asked.

"From the coroner's report and from a physical examination of the basement. I then set up my laser and fixed the bullet's path. From there I was able to determine the location of the rifle when it was fired."

"Objection," Burr said.

"Overruled," Gillis said.

Truax nodded at the judge. "Again, and what did you find?"

"I found that the rifle could not have gone off from the workbench," Gannon said. "The angle determined by the laser makes that impossible."

"How then do you believe the gun was fired," Truax said. "Strike that. Discharged."

"According to the path of the bullet, there is only one way for the entry and exit wounds to occur the way they did and for the bullet to strike the wall the way it did," Gannon said.

"And how would that be?" Truax asked.

"The defendant would have to raise the rifle to his shoulder, aim it, and pull the trigger," she said.

"Objection, Your Honor," Burr said. "This is speculation. Total speculation. Based on unfounded technology."

Frank wrung his hands. Burr turned to Jacob, under his breath, "Are you following this?"

"Yes," Jacob said, "are you?"

"I am now," Burr said. "Now what do we do?" Burr pulled his shirt cuffs down well past his suitcoat. He favored a blue pinpoint oxford shirt with his gray pinstripe suit, although at the moment his clothes weren't helping much. "Frank," he whispered, "did you pick up the gun and shoot her?" Frank gave him a blank look.

"Your Honor," Truax said, "before you rule may I demonstrate what the witness has said?"

"I will allow anything that will further the cause of clarity," Gillis said.

"Objection," Burr said.

"Noted," Gillis said. "Proceed, Mr. Truax."

Truax reached under his table and picked up a wooden rifle. He introduced the facsimile of a deer rifle into evidence, over Burr's fervent but futile objection. Truax then walked over the witness box with the pretend rifle.

"Now, Ms. Gannon, assume the railing is the workbench and place the gun the way the inquest reported the position of the gun."

She took the toy from Truax and placed it flat on the railing.

"Is this how your findings show that the gun went off?"

"No," answered the prim expert.

"Please show us how, according to your study, the gun was discharged."

Burr watched her uncross her legs. She stood and smoothed her skirt. She reached for the wooden rifle. She was enjoying herself, he thought.

"The only way it could have happened was like this," Gannon said. She picked up the toy gun and raised it to her shoulder. "There is only one way to explain the path of the bullet." Anne Gannon looked down the barrel of the rifle and aimed it at Burr's chest. "Bang," she said.

"No further questions, Your Honor, "Truax said.

Burr walked to the witness stand. "Ms. Gannon, you have testified that you determined the trajectory of the bullet by a connect the dot method," Burr said. "Is that right?

"Objection," Truax said. "Defense counsel is ridiculing proven technology."

"Sustained," Gillis said.

Burr continued. "Ms. Gannon, assuming that this technology is scientifically sound, and I for one have always been suspicious of the foundations underlying the laws of physics..."

"Objection," Truax said.

"Please don't prattle, Mr. Lafayette," Gillis said.

"Assuming your straight line theory, couldn't a bullet be deflected and strike a bone and essentially go off in another direction?" Burr asked.

"I suppose it could," she said.

"And couldn't the bullet's course, trajectory if you will, have veered enough to change the path of the bullet?" Burr asked.

"What?" she said.

Burr thought the prim Ms. Gannon looked a bit unsettled. "A bone," he said. "If the bullet hit a bone, couldn't that change the path of the bullet?

"What?" she said.

"Ms. Gannon, please don't be coy," Burr said. "Could the course of a bullet be changed if it struck a bone?"

"Yes, it could, but it didn't here," she said.

"And why is that?"

"Because the gun was fired..."

"You mean discharged," Burr said.

"At such close range, the force of a 30:06 rifle is so strong that if the bullet did strike a bone, the bullet's trajectory would not be changed," Gannon said.

"But it could happen," Burr said.

"It could, but it didn't. Not here," she said.

"Ms. Gannon, your findings were made by your knowledge of the location of the wounds and the location of the bullet in the basement wall. Is that right?

"Yes," she said. Her foot begin to bob.

"And how did you obtain this information?" Burr asked

"From the coroner's report," she said.

"The undertaker?" Burr asked.

"Objection," Truax said.

"I withdraw the question," Burr said. "Any other sources? "The inquest," Gannon said. "Yes, the written report from the inquest."

"And did either of those reports, particularly the coroner's report, mention whether or not the bullet had struck a bone?" Burr asked.

"I don't remember," she said.

"I see," Burr said. "Well, let me refresh your memory. The coroner's report does not mention whether or not the bullet struck a bone. It is silent on the matter."

Ms. Gannon, too, was silent.

"Now as to the documents," Burr said. "These two documents contained all of the information necessary for your findings?"

Burr saw her eyes dart to Truax then back. If he hadn't been staring at her he would have missed it.

"Ms. Gannon, to determine the angle of the bullet, wouldn't you have to know the height of the deceased? Yes, of course you would," he said. "Correct me if I'm wrong, but I don't recall the height of the deceased discussed anywhere in either report."

"I'm sure it's in there," she said.

"Perhaps you could find it for me." Burr handed her the two reports. For the first time he smelled her perfume, a flowery fragrance he couldn't identify. She shuffled through the report.

"I'm sorry, I can't find it," Gannon said. But I know it's in there."

"I assure you, it's not," Burr said.

"Objection, Your Honor," Truax said. "This is irrelevant."

Gillis peered over his glasses again. "Mr. Lafayette, where is this going?"

"Your Honor, the prosecution's theory is based on establishing the trajectory of the bullet. To do that, they have to know the victim's height. I believe it is eminently relevant to learn how the witness determined the height of the deceased, or if in fact she ever knew her height."

Gillis sighed, and his robe sagged. "Continue Mr. Lafayette."

"Ms. Gannon, how did you determine the deceased's height?"

"I don't remember," she said.

"Surely something this critical ..."

She interrupted. "I know, yes, now I remember. I got it from her driver's license.

"Thank you," Burr said, who wasn't at all thankful. "And what about her shoes?"

"Her shoes?"

"Yes, her shoes," Burr said. "Most people wear shoes, especially in the winter."

"Oh, yes. Her shoes," Gannon said. "We added an inch," she said.

"An inch. Why an inch?" he asked.

"Because that's the average heel height," Gannon said.

"But if she were wearing dress shoes," Burr paused. "Say pumps, sensible pumps like yours. That's a two inch heel you have, isn't it?" Gannon stopped in mid-bob.

"Yes, but she wasn't," Gannon said.

"How do you know that?" Burr asked.

"Because she just came in from cutting a Christmas tree," Gannon said.

"What if she took her boots off when she came in," Burr said. "Then she'd just be in her stocking feet. No shoes. I often do that. Don't you?"

"Objection," Truax said.

"Mr. Lafayette, I tire of this," Gillis said.

"Your Honor. I tire of this also. But my client is accused of murder. And the prosecution has based its entire case on this laser technology which, if it is accurate, which believe me will be a subject for debate if there ever is a trial, is worthless if the data is shoddy. And I submit the data is shoddy. Yes, and one more thing. How do we know that the information on the deceased's driver's license is valid? It's my understanding that we all shrink over time. We get shorter as gravity slowly pulls us down. For instance, I report my height as six feet. Indeed, once I was. I know I'm not that height now, but I've never changed my height on my driver's license."

"Then, you're lying," Truax said.

"Judge Gillis, how about you?" Burr asked.

The judge jumped in his seat. "Who me? It doesn't matter what I say my height is."

"Your Honor," Burr said, "My point is that the prosecution, in trying to establish probable cause, relies on precise scientific measure. Yet it is not clear that their data is at all precise. They don't have any first hand evidence. It is all second hand. Hearsay. Admissible hearsay but no first hand knowledge. They have not examined the body. They have not visited the site of the accident."

"That's not true," Gannon said. "I did visit it."

"Even the location of the bullet is the result of reading a report," Burr said.

"No, that's not true. I was there."

Burr spun toward Gannon. "What did you say?"

"I said, I was there in the basement. I measured precisely where the bullet hit the wall."

"You were in the house?" Burr asked.

"Yes," she said.

"How did you get in?" Burr asked.

"The realtor gave me the key," Gannon said.

"The realtor," Burr said.

"Yes," Gannon said.

"Were you interested in purchasing the house?" Burr asked.

"No," she said.

"I take it you weren't going to lease it either."

"No," she said.

"So you entered the house for the purpose of finding information for your study," Burr said.

"That's right," Gannon said.

"Who suggested you do this?" Burr asked.

"Mr. Truax," she said.

"I see," Burr said. "Your Honor, my client was illegally arrested in Detroit. Now it appears that his home has been illegally searched. Is the prosecution required to abide by the Constitution?"

Burr thought he had something. All this fumbling around and now he tripped over this. He had lit up Truax who showed every sign of exploding —pulsing forehead, gulping Adam's apple, and crimson face.

"Objection," Truax said. "The house was for sale. It has been for sale for six years. The house was available for the public to enter. Ms. Gannon gained access legally."

Burr stepped toward Judge Gillis. "Your Honor," Burr said, "I move that the testimony of this witness be stricken from the record."

"I'll do nothing of the kind. Mr. Lafayette, I am tired of your procedural niff naws. I am going to allow Ms. Gannon's testimony. If you don't like it, you may take exception to my ruling and appeal it."

"Your Honor," Burr said, "Does not the protection of the Bill of Rights extend this far north?"

Truax popped up. "Objection, Your Honor."

"Sit down, both of you," Judge Gillis roared at them. "This is a preliminary exam, and I intend to be done with it." This time Gillis tore off his glasses and whipped them at the visibly shaken Miss Longfingers. He rubbed his eyes. "If the defense has no witnesses, we'll take a ten-minute recess and then I will hear closing arguments. "My glasses, please," he said. Gillis placed them on the bridge of his nose, gavelled his gavel and stomped out.

Burr didn't believe Truax's closing argument had gone particularly well. Truax had a dead wife and an expert witness who said that the rifle could not have been lying flat on the workbench when it went off. The gun had to have been shouldered, aimed, and fired. Gillis seemed attentive until the radiator, the old steam kind, silver with rust, started to hiss. Somehow this seemed to agitate the Judge, and Truax, sensing this, had charged through the conclusion of his argument.

For his part, Burr felt keeping Frank away from the witness stand had clearly been strategically correct. He didn't know Frank that well, but so far Frank didn't seem either particularly strong or particularly bright.

Burr had done his best to discredit Gannon's laser study and to batter Truax and his methods. Burr thought the Judge sufficiently unimpressed with Truax, and he intended to finish off the overzealous prosecutor right now.

Burr paced back and forth on the front of the bench, and he knew the judge had followed him with his eyes. Now he stood in front of the judge, close, about three feet, but gave Gillis a clear view of both Frank and Truax.

"Your Honor, if just for the sake of argument, we assume that the prosecution obtained its evidence legally and that the findings of the laser study are accurate, then I submit the evidence is still not sufficient to bind Mr. Tavohnen over for trial. Even if we assume that Mr. Tavohnen picked up the rifle, there is still something missing."

Burr paused, swept his hair back behind his ears and pulled his cuffs down past the sleeves of his jacket. Then he turned to Truax. "We have here a killing, a tragic killing. But murder?" Burr said. "It was an accident just the way Mr. Tavohnen's statement at the inquest said it happened, the way the investigating officer determined, the way the coroner said it happened, and the way the inquest concluded."

"What about motive? The prosecution doesn't even mention motive. In the State of Michigan, Mr. Truax, there is no murder without motive. And you," Burr pointed straight at Truax, "have done nothing, nothing whatsoever to show any type of motive. All you have done is continually trample the rights of my client over a tragic accident that happened six years ago."

"Keep to the legal arguments, Mr. Lafayette," Gillis said.

"Yes, Your Honor," Burr said. Further, if the prosecution claims, as it must, that there must be a motive because the gun was shouldered, and therefore the shooting intentional, I object. Rather, I submit this theory. If, in fact, the rifle was shouldered, is it not possible that Mr. Tavohnen picked up the gun and looked down the barrel while he cleaned it, and it went off in that position? That

I submit is a reasonable explanation even if you believe everything the prosecution alleges. And that is not murder."

"Your Honor, failing the introduction of a motive, the prosecution has nothing more than the ephemera of intangible evidence. It is a shadowy line of reasoning, built on questionable scientific principles, questionably applied," Burr said. "If the prosecution cannot demonstrate a reason why Mr. Tavohnen killed his wife of almost twenty years, then I submit there is no likelihood, no probable cause that a crime was committed. Even with the lower legal threshold for determining whether Mr. Tavohnen should stand trial, the prosecution has simply not met the threshold for murder." Burr paused again. He could feel his shirt clinging to his back. Gillis stared at him, head cocked, like Zeke-the-dog when he didn't quite understand. "In sum, Your Honor, no motive, no murder."

Gillis straightened his head and arched his eyebrows. "Hmm," he said. "What do you say to that, Mr. Truax?"

"At this point, Your Honor, nothing," Truax said. "The people believe the facts speak for themselves."

"Anything else, Mr. Lafayette?" Gillis asked.

"Your Honor," Burr said still standing, "The defense repeats its objection to the laser evidence. There is no scientific foundation, nor precedent, for its use in this matter.

"Overruled, Mr. Lafayette. This is an evidentiary hearing, and the court intends to take notice of all potential evidence.

"Your Honor, the defense ...."

Gillis interrupted him. "Mr. Lafayette, please approach the bench." Once more Gillis passed his glasses down to the stenographer. (Burr did not think this a good sign, but at least Gillis hadn't thumped his forehead.) Gillis' eyes tunneled back in his head and peered out at him, shrunken without his glasses to magnify them.

"Mr. Lafayette. I will note this objection as I have noted the nineteen prior to this one. This is my goddamn courtroom, and I will do as I see fit. I'm allowing the testimony and if you don't like it you can appeal. Again." Gillis grabbed his glasses and stuffed them back on his face. His eyes appeared. "Is that clear?"

Burr turned on his heel and returned to his chair and sat down. He sucked deliberately on four Altoids.

"Mr. Lafayette, if you have no further comments, I will rule from the bench, although the court notes your uncharacteristic silence, after such a heretofore bellicose defense."

"Your Honor, the defense believes that God himself could not dissuade you, much less the feeble rebuttal we might offer," Burr said.

"Mr. Lafayette, my statement did not invite a reply." Gillis cast his eyes to the gallery (mostly empty) like an actor on a stage. "The court finds that the state has presented sufficient evidence to conclude that probable cause exists that the defendant, Frank X. Tavohnen, did murder Claudia Tavohnen on December 18, 1982. Therefore, the district court hereby remands this case over to the circuit court for the County of Emmet where Mr. Tavohnen will be tried for murder. Bail will remain at one hundred thousand dollars. The defendant is further ordered to remain in Emmet County until after the conclusion of the trial." Gillis raised his gavel.

"Your Honor," Burr said, standing.

Gillis stopped, the gavel suspended. "Mr. Lafayette, in case you hadn't noticed, I am about to adjourn. What is it this time?" Gillis said.

"Your Honor," Burr said. "Mr. Tavohnen has a home and a business in Grosse Pointe. I respectfully ask that he be permitted to return to Wayne County."

"Mr. Lafayette, the court notes that, based on Mr. Tavohnen's recent behavior, he could be considered a flight risk. The court further notes that the defendant has a home here in Emmet County. My order stands. We are adjourned." Gillis crashed the gavel and left the courtroom.

Burr looked down at Frank, seated to his right. Sarah rushed to him, hugged him, didn't say a word.

Truax grinned and Burr saw his mouth spread to his ears. Truax's lower jaw receded into his neck. His Adam's apple hung down his neck, like a tumor. He offered his hand to Burr who didn't take it. "A battle well fought, counselor," he said. Truax thrust his hand out further, almost in Burr's face now. "Of course, you could have saved us all a lot of bother if you'd have just cooperated from the beginning."

Burr snarled at him. "You're talking about a man's life." Burr turned on his heel and left Truax standing there with his hand out. Finally, Jacob, having stuffed the last of the documents into his briefcase, reached across the table and shook the hand of Truax who had left it hanging there.

Burr chewed the olive, slowly. It had been marinating nicely, along with the other three, in his very dry, very dirty martini. Bombay Sapphire on the rocks. He sat at the bar of the Resorter, the restaurant housed in the Harbour Inn. (He thought the "u" an affect.) It was 5:30 p.m. and perfectly dark outside, not much more light inside, but a perfect place to consider the day's debacle.

The Harbour Inn rested comfortably on the beach of Little Traverse Bay, just outside Harbor Springs and on the way to Petoskey. It housed the Resorter on the main floor, one of Northern Michigan's finest restaurants. Stewart the Innkeeper, one of Burr's oldest and most difficult friends, sat down next to him. Burr, in light of his cash position, had taken a room at the Harbour Inn, knowing that Stewart wouldn't charge him.

"I'll have what he's having, but hold all the olive paraphernalia," Stewart said to the bartender. "I see she's back," this said to Burr.

"It's business," Burr said. He took a rather large swallow of his martini.

"Monkey business," Stewart said.

"This time it is business," Burr said, but he did quite like seeing Suzanne again, even if it was at arm's length.

"So it's just business plus sex, right?" asked Stewart.

"No, not this time," Burr said.

"Not yet," Stewart said. He had dark hair, a big nose and a mustache that grew out from inside his nose. Stewart sipped at his martini. He reached into a pocked of his blazer—blue with the family crest on the breast pocket—and produced a brass ring with at least thirty keys. "You know," he said, "there are no dogs allowed."

"Zeke has been a guest here before," Burr said.

"We have to protect our four-star rating," Stewart said. He always let Zeke stay at the Inn, but he always complained about it.

Stewart's great grandfather had founded the Harbour Inn at the turn of the century when the two-hundred foot passenger liners steamed in from Chicago and Detroit to the deep water port at Harbor Springs. The resorters, as Stewart still called them, came for the pollen-free air of Northern Michigan, the clear, blue water of Little Traverse Bay, and the artesian springs. Stewart the First built the four-story, wood frame hotel for them on the shores of Little Traverse Bay. Burr thought the elegance had slipped to a genteel shabbiness.

"I say we adjourn to the dining room and have the veal morel," Stewart said, standing. Stewart, all six and a half feet of him, stood and looked down over his nose at Burr. A rough hewn walking stick with a big nose. "I suppose you'll be wanting to stay here for the trial."

"I thought I'd live on the boat," Burr said.

Stewart thudded to his chair. "My God, the Kismet?"

Burr traded the use of his boat, the Kismet, for a room at the Inn, complete with food and drink at the Resorter. In turn, Stewart sailed the boat when Burr wasn't there, which was most of the time. Apparently, a little more Burr would cramp Stewart's yachting style.

"Married women don't like boats," Stewart said.

"Where did that come from?" Burr asked. "I don't have a wife."

"Something about marriage," Stewart said. "Girlfriends always love boats. But you marry them and all of a sudden, poof, they hate boats." Stewart touched the fingertips of his left hand with those of his right, and, at the poof, he flashed them apart like a magician. "Poof," he poofed again.

"Suzanne likes the boat," Burr said.

"Righto. That's because you're not married," Stewart said, in his irritating faux English innkeeper dialect. "My wife doesn't like them, and she was brought up on the water. Long Island Sound."

Stewart led him into the dining room—a great high-ceilinged room with wall to wall windows on the bay side—to a table just off the fireplace, a fieldstone column built from the rocks marooned on the site millions of years ago by the retreating glacier.

"We'll start with the whitefish pate," Stewart said to the waiter. "Now, as I was saying, married women do not like boats, particularly sailboats, and, to reiterate, neither my wife, nor your former wife for that matter, liked Kismet after we married them."

"You're right," Burr said. "Grace didn't like the boat."

"And if you were to marry Suzanne, she will then not like the boat, even though she purports to like it now," Stewart said. He picked up his cocktail napkin and began folding it.

"Suzanne loves sailing," Burr said. "While I agree with your theory generally, I think Suzanne would be an exception. I am also certain it will not be put to the test."

"We'll see about that," Stewart said. "We'll see." With that, he dropped the cocktail napkin, now folded into the shape of a rudimentary boat, in Burr's martini where it floated for a moment then sank.

~

The next day, evening actually, Burr lay on the couch in his office. He stretched his toes and brushed against the leather arm. The couch had to measure seventy-three inches —inside arm to inside arm —so he could nap fully stretched out, and it did. How long had he slept? No idea. Apparently, the phone hadn't rung. Strange for such a thriving practice, he thought.

Suzanne had finally told him about Frank and Sarah. Sarah had followed Suzanne to college at Vanderbilt. During college, Sarah had worked summers at Bay View in Petoskey, a grand collection of Victorian cottages, originally a Methodist retreat and now a cottagers' association whose bylaws required that all the cottages be closed from November until May. After graduation and on a lark, she moved to Petoskey where she met Frank. They fell in love after Claudia's death (This part sounded a bit fishy to Burr), married, moved to Grosse Pointe, and had a child.

But what about Truax? Burr didn't think Truax had much of a case. Just the laser. And what about motive? The possibility of hanky panky notwithstanding, there was no mention of motive at the preliminary exam, but then Burr didn't think Gillis knew enough about the legal definition of murder to know what was required.

Across the room, a silhouette filled one of the chairs in front of his desk. The shadow sat there with its back to him, looking out the window. It stood and walked to the window, back still to Burr. It turned to him.

"Frank, what are you doing here?" Burr asked. These unannounced visitors were too much. First Truax. Now Frank. And then there was Suzanne whose unannounced visit at Walpole Marsh had started it all. "What in God's name are you doing here?" he asked. Burr, feeling he needed a little more authority, got up from the couch and sat at his desk. He stretched his legs into the kneehole of the desk and accidentally kicked Zeke who had been sleeping there. The dog yelped. "Sorry, Zeke." Burr ducked under the desk and scratched the dog behind his ears.

"Nice watchdog," Frank said.

"Frank, what are you doing here?"

"I was a dentist for almost twenty years, and I coached baseball at the high school. I liked being a dentist. I liked coaching. I liked deer hunting. I love my son. "Actually," he said, "I loved coaching baseball. I knew how to do it. I was good at it."

"Your son?" Burr asked. "Where is he now?"

"He's in the Navy, "Frank said. "After Claudia died, Jason hated me. He enlisted in the Navy.

"My practice fell apart after Claudia died. I fell in love with Sarah, and we got married. We moved to Grosse Pointe, and I bought a practice from a dentist who wanted to retire. But it didn't work out, so I took what was left of my savings and Sarah and I opened a greeting card store. Sarah's Cards and Candles. It's on the hill. You must know where it is. .

Burr nodded.

"I sell greeting cards, knick-knacks, and perfumed candles. The cards are okay, but, my God, the smell of those damn candles.

"And now we have a little girl. She's five and I'm fifty. And I killed my first wife. It was an accident and I'll never be over it. I lost my son and my practice, but I love Sarah." Frank stopped abruptly "I lost my life once," he said. "And I'm not going to lose it again."

"You will go back to jail if you don't go back to Petoskey," Burr said.

"What do you mean?" Frank said.

"We went over this," Burr said. "You were not to leave Emmet County."

"I have to run my business," Frank said.

"You heard what the judge said," Burr said.

"I have no choice," Frank said.

Burr tried a different tack. "What about Truax? Why's he doing this?"

"I have no idea," Frank said.

"I guess it's time to hear what happened that day," Burr said. He turned his back to Frank and looked out the window at the Christmas tree below. Its lights twinkled at him.

CHAPTER NINE

SATURDAY, DECEMBER 18, 1982

The Christmas tree bounced up and down in the truck bed as the pickup bounced out of the woods on the frozen two track.

"Frank, slow down," Claudia said. "You'll shake all the needles off before we get home."

Frank had seen her looking at the bouncing tree through the outside mirror. He'd seen the bouncing, too, but hadn't paid any attention to it.

Claudia had been rounder and softer when they had met, attractive in a mousy sort of way, with shoulder-length black hair that she wore in a ponytail. But now it was salt and pepper, mostly, salt. He wished she would color it. Claudia had thin lips and no eyebrows to speak of. She rubbed them when she was anxious, which was most of the time.

"We could have just bought a tree in town," Claudia said.

"No, we couldn't," Jason said. "We've always cut our own tree." He sat in the middle between the two of them. Black hair stuck out underneath his stocking cap. He looked like a taller, leaner version of Frank, except for his hair, which was like his mother's used to be.

"Yes, we could have honey, but I thought you had outgrown it," Claudia said. She leaned forward and bore down on Frank. "The tradition need not have taken us to the most remote spot in Emmet County and your father racing to get out of the woods."

Two hours earlier, they had slipped into the woods on a two track, north of Harbor Springs, just east of Lark's Lake Road, near the prison. It had been started snowing just as they entered the woods.

Frank had had his eye on the tree all deer season. The tree, a white pine, grew at the edge of a clearing created by a downed hemlock, a big, old tree hit by lightning. It grew in the sun and had thick, bushy branches. It stood about eight feet. He would have to trim it, cut off the bottom to set the angel on its crown. Jason had seen the tree, too, and had insisted on coming way out here for it.

The tree grew on state land which, of course, made the proposed chopping, sawing actually, highly illegal except that around here nobody thought very much about cutting down your own Christmas tree on state land which, after all, was public.

Before they cut down the tree, Jason, as was the custom, had built a fire and sharpened sticks. They roasted hot dogs and marshmallows and drank hot chocolate from snow, melted and then boiled. Frank had seasoned his with peppermint schnapps which had not gone unnoticed by Claudia who, Frank thought, grew skinnier each day, despite the fact that she ate like a horse. In fact, the more she ate, the skinnier she got, and the fatter he got. It was almost as if what she lost he gained. Meaner, too. Skinnier and meaner.

Jason then recited the druid-like prayer (made up in years past by Frank and generally frowned upon by Claudia). "Oh Great Spirit, the season of darkness is upon us. Our earth is without life. Give us your gift of life through the eternal green of this tree. We accept this gift mindful that as we take the life of this tree, we take it into our home so that its greenness reminds us of past summers and gives us hope for the new life of Spring. For your gift of life we give our thanks. Amen."

Jason summarily disposed of the tree. Frank smothered the fire with snow. The steam from the doused fire carried the smell of the ashes. They hoisted the tree into the bed of the pickup and skidded their way out of the woods.

Frank parked the truck in the driveway. The snow had stopped. He hoisted the tree out of the pickup and dropped it down to Jason who dragged the tree across the snow and into the garage through the side door. He saw his deer rifle leaning up against the wall. Frank sawed off the bottom foot of the tree and then another foot of branches, which Claudia would weave into a wreath. He pounded the prongs in the bottom of the Christmas tree stand into the butt end of the trunk. Sap oozed out of the trunk. He stood the tree up and Jason twisted the screws into the trunk. The sap bled there, too.

Frank carried the tree into the house and was greeted by that infernal Christmas record. Somehow Jason had found Mitch Miller, and he and his singers scratched away on the record player they used once a year and only when they trimmed the tree, another of their Christmas rituals.

"Frank, you're dragging snow across the floor and soaking the carpet," Claudia said.

"It's just water," he said.

"No, it's not," she said. "There's mud all over that tree and it's on your boots, too."

He looked down at his boots and then at his tracks back to the door. He started off to the door.

"Stop. Stop right there," Claudia said. "There's just more mud if you go back. Stand right there and take them off."

Frank felt his face flush. He knew his ears were turning red, and he felt them get hot. "Claudia, just how am I supposed to do that?"

"On one foot. Sit down. I don't care, but I will not have my carpet ruined over a Christmas tree."

Frank stood on his left foot and raised his right foot. He tried to untie the boot but lost his balance. He hopped on his left foot while he tried to extract his right "For Christ sake, Claudia, this isn't going to work," he said.

"Don't talk to me like that," she said.

Frank got the other boot off. Jason buzzed in with three glasses of spiced wine on a tray. Each glass said Merry Christmas in a flourish of red and green letters.

"You're too young to drink," Claudia said. She took a glass from the tray.

"Claudia, we do this every year," Frank said. As he reached for a glass he tripped over his boots, stumbling into Claudia who dropped her glass on the carpet. Jason ran for a towel.

"Claudia," Frank said, "don't say a word. Not a word. I'm sorry. We'll clean it up."

Jason dashed back in with a bucket of cold water and rinsed most of the wine out. Frank hoped it was enough to avoid buying her a new carpet. Claudia left in a huff.

Frank and Jason decorated the tree without Claudia. The tree had to be trimmed just the way they always did it. First, Frank spiraled the lights around the tree, top to bottom. Then Jason strung gold (Frank thought ugly) garland around the tree. Frank observed this through the bottom of the Merry Christmas glass. He had just about finished his fourth class of spiced wine, which had more kick than he thought. He spied Jason through the thick glass bottom, bending the edges of his vision. Then they hung the ornaments. The colored balls. This, too, sans Claudia.

"Now we just need to put the angel on the top," Jason said.

Claudia huffed back in. "My God, that garland is ugly," Claudia said. "Take it off."

"We always put this garland on, Mom."

"It's so old and faded," she said.

"Let's put the angel on now," Frank said. "Then we're done."

"Take off the garland," Claudia said.

"Claudia, we always put this garland on."

"It's ugly," Claudia said.

"I'll take it off," Jason said.

"Let's put the angel on," Frank said.

"Take off the garland, Jason," she said. "Frank, put that stupid glass down. Are you drunk?"

"Hey, Claudia. I've got an idea," Frank said looking at her through the bottom of his glass. "You be the angel this year. I'll shove the tree up your ass, and you can sit up there for two weeks."

Frank left in his own huff. He retrieved his deer rifle from the garage and stomped down the basement stairs. He thought he was safe there. Since he had moved the washer and dryer upstairs into the little room off the kitchen, Claudia never came down here. Fieldstone walls. He touched one of the rocks, granite, pink granite, with gold flecks. He sat down on a stool at his workbench, facing the stairs. He laid the rifle on the workbench.

The gun was dirty and had started to rust, and the clip was still in it. He pushed the catch that held the clip in the gun and pulled it out. The clip looked full, but it was springloaded, so he couldn't tell for sure. At least the safety was on. Then he racked the bolt to make there was no bullet in the chamber. No bullet ejected.

He wiped off the stock with a damp towel, and then he worked Linseed oil into the stock with his fingers. A drop oozed onto his shirt, spreading with the texture of the weave. Claudia will play hell with that too, he thought.

He poured the gun oil, Hoppes Number 9, on a rag. The smell of the gun oil reminded him of the electric train his father had given him when he was nine. Frank ran the rag up and down the barrel, rubbing off the rust.

Jason bent his head down the stairs. "Mom wants to see you," he said.

"Tell her I'm busy," Frank said.

"She said she wants to see you," Jason said

"Tell her I'm busy," Frank said again.

Jason left. Frank went back to wiping the rust off the barrel.

Claudia thundered down the stairs. "Goddamn it, Frank. I said I wanted to talk to you."

"So talk," he said.

"Not here," Claudia said. "Upstairs."

"Say what you've got to say and leave," Frank said, still wiping the gun.

"How dare you," Claudia said. She stood across the room at the foot of the stairs. "Come upstairs now."

"For Christ's sake, Claudia," Frank said, "give it a rest."

"You will not talk to me that way," she said. "You will not."

"Leave me alone," he said.

"Frank Tavohnen, you will come upstairs. Now."

Frank started cleaning around the trigger. "Claudia, listen to yourself. You're a bitch, a raving bitch."

"I hate you," she said. "You know that, don't you. Goddamn it, how I hate you!"

Frank was rubbing the trigger with the rag when the gun went off. The crash deafened him. He fell off his stool. The rifle spun on the workbench and kicked backwards onto the floor, falling behind him. His ears rang. He picked up the rifle and set it back on the workbench.

Then he saw Claudia. The bullet had ripped through her and thrown her against the wall. Blood dripped off the fieldstone, and she lay in a pool of blood at the foot of the stairs. She stared at him, eyes fixed.

PART TWO
THE INVESTIGATION

IF ONLY THERE WERE WORLD ENOUGH AND
TIME ENOUGH LADY, THIS COYNESS BE NO CRIME.

To His Coy Mistress
— *Andrew Marvel*

CHAPTER TEN

April Fool's Day, 1989

Burr spent the rest of February and all of March with clients who could actually pay their bills. If he was careful, he just might have enough money to work on Frank's little problem, even if he didn't get paid right away (or ever).

Having no idea where to begin, Burr decided that the best place might be the scene of the crime, or rather, what he hoped to prove, the scene of the accident. He would start where it started and see where it led. He had met Suzanne here who was, at best, reluctant to see where Claudia had been killed.

Burr slipped on the first step of the basement stairs at Frank's house and grabbed at the railing, but it wrenched from the wall. He bumped down the stairs feet first, bumping over each step. He sprawled on the concrete floor at the bottom of the stairs with his face to the wall. An edge of one of the fieldstones scratched his nose. He felt the cold and the damp of the fieldstone against his face, and he traced the mortar between two of them with his finger.

"Are you all right?" Suzanne asked.

"Yes," Burr said.

"You could have killed yourself," she said.

"Yes," he said.

"What happened?"

"I slipped," he said.

"I can see that," Suzanne said. She stepped over the railing and put her hands on his shoulders. She turned his head, and he kissed her on the cheek.

"Would you please be careful," she said, ignoring his kiss.

He got to his feet and put his arms around her waist.

"Not here, Burr." He pulled her a little closer, remembered her small waist.

"Burr, of all places, not here," she said.

He had been feeling slightly amorous ever since Suzanne had suddenly reentered his life but had restrained himself until now, partly because of the way it had ended between them, partly because he was not quite sure it was a good idea to relight the fire, but mostly because Suzanne had given him no inkling that her interest was in anything other than his lawyering, such as it was.

He let go of her and made his way over to Frank's workbench. Frank's tools still hung on the pegboard. There was a small room off to his left with just a hint of daylight filtering through the cobwebs. Standing at the workbench, he looked back at Suzanne on the stairs. "This must be where he shot her," Burr said.

"Where she was killed," Suzanne said.

"That's what I meant," he said.

Suzanne glared at him. Burr found a broom against the wall and pointed it, handle first toward the base of the stairs, where Frank said Claudia had been standing.

"Go stand over there," Burr said.

"I will not," Suzanne said.

"I need to understand what happened. That's why we're here. Whether what Frank told me was true."

"Why wouldn't it be true?"

Burr pointed to the far wall about twenty feet. "That must be where it happened. Right about there. Go stand there so I can line it up," Burr said.

"I will not," she said again.

"I need to see what happened. From where the gun went off," he said.

"It's bad luck," Suzanne said.

"What is?"

"To stand where someone died," Suzanne said. "In their shadow."

Burr walked to the spot himself. The floor didn't look any different here than anywhere else. The stones didn't either. He felt the wall. Here, maybe here, a chip out of this stone. But the stone mason could have done it. He couldn't see any blood on the stones or on the floor.

"All right then, you go over to the workbench and be Frank."

"No," she said.

"Suzanne, I need to see how it happened."

"Why?"

"Truax has a laser and we've got a broom," Burr said. "Go over there and point it at me."

Suzanne backed up the stairs, a step at a time, then turned and ran up the rest of the way. He heard the door at the top of the stairs slam.

Back at the workbench, Burr laid the broom on the workbench and pointed it toward the wall again. If the gun had gone off, lying on the bench, while Frank cleaned it, the bullet would have struck Claudia at the level of the workbench, which was just below his chest but higher on Claudia who was only five foot 4 inches. It could have happened the way Frank said. But the laser lady said the bullet entered her near the shoulder and exited through her right kidney, on a downward trajectory. Maybe the laser lady was right. But it was possible that Frank could have picked up the gun and it still have been an accident. The way Burr had (brilliantly, he thought) argued in the preliminary exam.

He picked up the broom and aimed it again. He swung it around, banging it on a pair of cross country skis leaning against the wall, the old wooden ones with the cable bindings. They slipped to the floor. For the first time Burr noticed that the basement was still full, like someone still lived there, like Frank had never moved out. Frank had his screwdrivers in rings on the pegboard, lined up in a row, little ones to big ones. They all had red handles. There were cardboard moving boxes stacked up behind him as if someone had started to pack. He reached underneath the workbench and pulled on the handle of a paint roller. When he tried to lift it out of the roller pan, the roller stuck. He jerked on it and the pan stuck to the floor. Burr then yanked with both hands and the pan let go of the floor. He hoisted the roller, still stuck in the pan, to the workbench, below the work light. In the blue of the fluorescent light, the battleship gray paint looked like putty. Burr pushed his finger in it and the smell of paint—sweet, thick oil based paint—oozed up at him. He walked back over to the stairs. His shadow cast across the floor where Claudia must have fallen. The light faded at the wall, but now, in front of him, he thought he could see the uneven edges where the roller had stopped rolling. He ran his fingertips along the edge of the roller marks and felt the ridge where the paint ended. Burr didn't know why fresh paint on the floor would surprise him. How fresh could it be though? He had no way of knowing when it was done—right away or later when Frank had tried to sell the house. Who wouldn't want to wash the blood away, cover it up. No blood stains on the wall that he could see. Maybe those scrubbed up. She must have been shot right here, right where he crouched. Burr stood up and looked over at the workbench.

"Bang," he said. He crumpled to the floor, surrounded by the new paint. He laid there, shot by his own word. "Bang," he said again, sprawled on the floor.

"Bang yourself," said a voice, from somewhere.

Burr saw a pair of legs on the stairs, legs in black tights that disappeared in a wine colored skirt that ended slightly above the knee. The legs bent at the waist and the arms above the waist pointed a pistol straight at him.

"Bang," said the woman, now a corporeal voice, and stepped down far enough to stand straight up. The tights disappeared into a camel coat, a thick one belted at the waist.

"You missed me," she said.

"What?" Burr said.

"You missed. You know, bang, bang."

"Oh," Burr said.

"I only fired a warning shot," she said.

"Good," Burr said, confused.

"Usually I just point this thing and get some answers." The woman waved the gun at Burr, a shiny automatic. Nine millimeter, thought Burr. "I have a permit, but I don't really need a gun to sell houses," she said. "But you never know who you might run into in this business. You, however, do not look menacing."

"She died right there, right where you're standing," said the woman. "They couldn't get the blood off the floor so I painted it. I can't rent a house with blood on the floor, much less sell one."

Burr took two steps away from the wall. Maybe if he escaped the kill zone, he could get his wits back.

The woman had blond hair, streaked very tastefully, in a pageboy, a pageboy not unlike Anne Gannon. He couldn't tell if the pageboy made her look younger, older, or both. She had the beginnings of crow's feet (not unlike Eve's), probably too much sun, Burr thought. Dark red lips. Almost fifty, like Eve.

"Do you have a name?" she asked.

"Yes," he said. "Yes, I do."

"That's encouraging," she said. "Now I suppose there's a good reason you broke into my listing."

"Your listing?"

"I'm the realtor," she said. "Have we met?"

"No, I wouldn't forget someone like you, especially if you're in the habit of introducing yourself with a pistol," Burr said. "Would you mind putting it away?"

"You can't be too careful, and this house does have some notoriety. But it's priced to sell. I can have the boxes out in a jiffy. And the furniture upstairs. Or you could take it with the furniture. Up to you," she said.

She put the pistol in her purse, a large black shoulder bag, and marched right up to him, a head shorter than Burr, thin from what he could see with her coat on, but certainly no waif. She had a narrow face. Blue eyes framed with eye shadow and eyeliner. Slightly dramatic. Very white teeth inside bright red lips. She is at least my age, he thought, and she looks good.

"What exactly did happen here?" Burr asked.

"Oh. I thought you knew," she said. "What with the bang bang and all. You mean you don't know?" She sighed and her shoulders sagged suddenly, not so perky and her wrinkles showed.

"No," Burr said. "I saw the sign outside and the door was open."

"The door was definitely not open," she said. The woman twirled a strand of hair around her trigger finger. "You mean you didn't know?" Then she glanced down at the floor where Claudia had been shot. Then she brightened. "The house was owned by an elderly lady and she had a heart attack and died over there." The realtor pointed.

"What about the blood?" Burr asked.

"The blood?" she said.

"I didn't know there was blood with a heart attack," Burr said.

"The blood. Oh, the blood. Well, she fell and hit her head. And the blood wouldn't come off. People don't like blood on the floor. A house where someone died. So it's priced to sell." She smiled sweetly at him, hoping he believed her.

"I see," Burr said. "How long has it been for sale?"

"Not too long."

"What's this little room over there?" he asked. "The one with just a bit of light."

"That's the old coal room. The light must be from the coal chute. I'm sure it's boarded up," she said. "Or at least it's supposed to be."

"What about these boxes?" he said.

"They belong to the owner. He lives in Detroit. Grosse Pointe, actually. Although I don't think he can afford it. And I know he can't afford two house payments. But the furniture upstairs comes with it if you like. It's a beautiful old house, Victorian. Turn of the century."

She started up the stairs. Burr followed her. At the top of the stairs, she looked over her shoulder. "It's a nice basement. Stone walls, the stones from right around here. Fieldstone. Very cool in the summer. Not damp at all. It breathes somehow."

Burr hadn't seen the rest of the house when he'd come with Suzanne. They had come in through the garage, then through the side door which opened on a mudroom and gone right down into the basement. Burr and the realtor climbed to the top of the basement stairs. The mudroom also opened onto the kitchen, ten-foot ceilings with hardwood moldings and windows facing east. The linoleum underfoot felt like long swells on the lake, wavy and uneven. Straight-backed spindle chairs ringed a maple table. What he took for a bathroom turned out to be a walk in pantry, floor to ceiling shelves and a pull string on a light bulb. He saw two cans of stewed tomatoes on the shelf.

From the foyer, she directed traffic with her arms. "This, of course, is the dining room," she said. "And through here the parlor. That's what they had then you know—and then the living room."

An oak staircase ran up from the foyer. "You'll want to see the upstairs of course." She started up the stairs. "Four bedrooms, small ones, and a bath. One bath. That's a problem, I know, but you could make the pantry off the kitchen into a half bath. And the furniture comes with it, if you like. I already said that, didn't I?"

"Are you listening to me?" She gave Burr a pointed look from the top of the stairs.

"Not really," Burr said.

"I didn't think so. My name's Kaye. Kaye Collins. And you are?"

"Burr Lafayette."

"I like your name," she said, warming up again. "And what do you do?"

"I'm a lawyer."

"Good," Kaye said. "Are you're looking for a summer home?"

"No, not really."

"You're moving up here?"

"No," he said.

"Well, what then?" she said, irritated.

"I'm Frank Tavohnen's lawyer."

"Oh. So this is all a put on, is it? Why didn't you tell me? I knew you knew. What with the bang, bang and all." She sat down on the top step and looked down the stairs at Burr who was halfway down. "And don't look up my skirt."

"I wanted a tour," Burr said.

"Well, you got one. Now get out."

"How long have you had this listing?"

"I knew I should have asked your name at the beginning. I always do that." She blinked three or four times and extracted an eyelash from her left eye. "But, you gave me the eye, and I was being vain. Of course, that still doesn't explain how you got in here in the first place." She stood up and stared down at him from the landing.

Burr wondered, worried, how he was going to get out of this one. Suzanne had the key and he hadn't thought to ask where she got it.

"Of course, the thought of a sale revved me up. Stupid though, really stupid," she said. "Even if you are Frank's lawyer, which I doubt. So let's just forget about this silly tour, shall we, Mr.

Peepers?" She looked down at him from the landing and started down the stairs.

"I'm sorry, Ms. Collins," he said. "I thought you knew."

"You did not," she said.

"Really, I did." Burr said this in his most I'm-sorry-I-threw-the-baseball-through-the-window-it-was-an-accident voice.

"You did not," Kaye said. "So, what do you want me to do? Pull the listing? He doesn't need a lawyer to yank it. You can have it back. I can't sell it anyway."

"I represent Frank on the murder charge."

"You look too prosperous to be a criminal lawyer." She came back down the stairs and looked him straight in the eye. "Unless you're a drug lawyer."

Burr was getting hot. Even with the heat low he was sweating. He started to take off his coat.

"Nice coat but leave it on, " Kaye said. "We're not staying."

Burr did like this coat. It was a Barbour. Waxed cotton. It smelled like the tent he had camped in when he was twelve.

"I think it's a crime. I do," Kaye said. "I really do."

"Apparently that's what the prosecutor thinks," Burr said.

"It's a crime that Frank was arrested," he said. "After all this time. It was an accident. Of course it was."

If I can get her on the jury, that's one vote, he thought.

She sat down in the parlor on the upholstered cushions in the bay window, a flowered Victorian print with a faded yellow background.

"Do you have any idea why the prosecutor would do this?" Burr asked.

"No," she said. "Not really. He's a law and order guy, though. Very conservative."

"Do you know him?"

"A little. Just to say hello," she said. "He's got a decent reputation. I think he's smart. Tough on crime."

"Something doesn't seem right to me," Burr said. Notwithstanding Kaye's admonition, he took off his coat.

"No one wants this house," she said. "Believe me, I sell a lot of houses."

"I'm sure you do."

"Mostly in Harbor Springs. To the rich people. From Grosse Pointe or Bloomfield. This is my only listing in Petoskey. It's a favor to Frank. He taught my son how to play baseball. His father couldn't hit a baseball if his life depended on it. But nobody wants this house. You know. A murder. Not a murder but a...."

Kaye's mouth hung open. She had lost her way. Burr saw the sun shine on the gold crowns in the back of her mouth.

"A death," he said.

"That's right. Who wants to live in a house where someone died?" she said. "An accident. A tragic accident. But nobody will buy this house. Once they find out. The realtors here won't touch it. Anyway, no one wants it, and I was hoping you didn't know."

"That's honest of you," he said.

"I would have told you," she said. "Eventually."

What about Frank and Sarah?" Burr asked.

"He married her and they left. Six months after his wife died. Just like that." Kaye snapped her fingers. "That turned some heads, but they seemed really happy. They moved to Detroit, Grosse Pointe, actually. I lived in Bloomfield Hills before I moved up here and divorced Maury. Actually, it was the other way around."

"What?" Burr asked.

"Maury. First I divorced him and then I moved up here."

"I see," he said. "But Frank and Sarah could have stayed."

"I suppose, but it was pretty ugly." Kaye studied the wallpaper. An edge had separated at the baseboard and flipped up. She licked her fingers and pushed the edge back down and held it there. "It's dry in here. But what do you expect. Nobody lives here." She took her finger off and the wallpaper poked back again. "It's a shame" She cocked her head at him. Her pageboy fell away from her head and Burr saw a gold earring, dangling.

Burr crossed his chest with his arms. He did it when he was anxious. Sort of holding himself, but he liked to think it gave him a thoughtful look.

"Are you cold?"

"No," he said.

"You look like you're cold."

Burr drummed his fingers against his ribs, his arms still wrapped across his chest. He took his coat off the banister and put it back on. The smell, waxed canvas, drifted by again.

"Well, then, I guess we're done," Kaye said. Burr opened the door for her. She walked straight down the stairs, looked back at him over her shoulder. "You don't know much about your client, do you," Kaye said, not asking a question. Eyes front, she walked away.

~

Burr was close to the high school, so he decided he might as well see where Frank coached. He took Mitchell to Petoskey High School, a mile east of downtown and half a mile east of Frank's (for sale) house. When he got there, school had recessed for the day. He saw the baseball diamond and proceeded in that direction.

Once there, he saw a man he thought to be about sixty-five, standing on home plate, hands in his pockets. The boys were warming up, playing catch on the diamond.

"I don't think I saw you at the parents' meeting," said the man.

"I wasn't there," Burr said.

"Who are you, then?"

"I'm Frank Tavohnen's lawyer," Burr said.

"Stahl. Dallas Stahl." The man pulled his right hand out of his pocket and plowed it at Burr. Stahl shook Burr's hand with vigor.

"Are you the coach?"

"No, I'm just freezing my ass off out here because I like kids who don't listen and can't hit a curve ball."

"Didn't Frank Tavohnen coach baseball here?" Burr asked.

"My assistant," Stahl said. "He would've been head coach by now and I'd be trolling for browns in the Bay. If the ice was out."

"Wasn't he kind of old to be an assistant?" Burr asked.

"I was grooming him," Stahl said. There were snow banks around the backstop. Burr decided that the first step in Spring baseball in Petoskey was shoveling the field. The coach walked towards the pitcher's mound, leading with his left leg and then pulling his right leg through without bending it, as if it were wooden with no joint at the knee. He pulled off his hat and scratched the top of his head. His hair was cropped short, more gray than black. Stahl sent the boys to the outfield to run laps. He took a cigarette from his jacket and hid behind Burr. "Don't let them kids see this," Stahl said.

"Do you think it was an accident?" Burr asked.

"Yeah, it was an accident all right. Frank couldn't kill no one." Stahl cupped the cigarette in his hand, like this wasn't the first cigarette he'd sneaked

"Why did a dentist coach baseball?" Burr asked, trying another tack.

"This is a small town," Stahl said. "It's hard to find somebody who knows baseball."

"It's been six years," Burr said.

"I had a guy but he didn't work out. And I couldn't just quit without a new coach. We got good baseball here." He dropped the cigarette into the snowdrift. 'I don't like the boys to see me smoke. But they probably know. On my breath, I guess." Stahl limped around the fence to where Burr stood and then leaned against it. He pointed over the parking lot. "If you was to go through the parking lot and down the hill, it would take you right to Frank's house, which he still can't sell. But you probably know that. "Anyway," said the coach, "I did wonder after it was all over with, if they just didn't sneak over there, during the day, for a quickie. I mean, I never thought Frank had it in him. Maybe he didn't. But shit, Claudia was always off at church doing something or other."

"Do you think Frank and Sarah were having an affair?" Burr asked.

"Sarah. That was her name. Can't for the life of me remember her last name," Stahl said. "She was a pretty thing. Probably still is, I bet. But hell, he's just about old enough to be her father."

"They have a child," Burr said.

"Hell, they do," Stahl said. "They do?" Stahl spat "So maybe they did. Maybe. Well, it cost him his practice and his job here. But maybe she was worth it. Sweet, I thought, but bossy. Frank needed that. Henpecked by Claudia. Couldn't make up his mind. Except in baseball. He always knew what to do there."

"What happened?" Burr asked.

"You know, just between us, Frank wasn't that great a dentist. Nobody went to him for anything complicated. Just simple stuff. But he was a hometown boy." Stahl kicked at the snow. A chunk broke off, and he crushed it with his foot. "Killing his wife, even if it was an accident, sure didn't help his practice."

Burr kicked at his own snow bank, but his foot bounced off the icy remains of winter.

"Why?" Burr asked, fearing that he knew the answer.

"How'd you like somebody poking around in your mouth who can't even figure out how to keep from pulling a trigger on a gun that ends up being loaded?"

Burr nodded.

"It don't exactly inspire confidence, what with dentistry being all about fine motor control.

"I guess not," Burr said.

"And the School Board don't renew his coaching deal. That just about broke his heart," Stahl said. "But that ain't what really did it."

Burr looked at Stahl. A blank look.

"Well, if you ain't gonna ask, I'll tell you anyway." Stahl said. "Sarah worked for him. Office manager or, some such thing. Well, that's no big deal, but he takes up with her right after Claudia died. Nobody much liked it, I guess."

"And?"

"It's not what they do. It's what they don't do.

"And, what's that?" Burr asked. He feared that if Stahl told him anything else, he would truly not understand where Stahl was headed.

"People just stop coming in. They stop making appointments. His practice falls off. Then he makes it even worse."

"How?"

"He marries her," Stahl said. "And that's like turning off a faucet. Shuts his practice right off. This shames Sarah. So she makes Frank move. Not like they probably had much choice." He paused. "Maybe if they'd waited awhile," said the coach. "But that's how it all went down." Stahl dropped the now smoked cigarette in the dirt and crushed it with his foot, like he had done with the snow.

Then he picked up the butt and stuck it in his pocket. He whistled the running baseball players over and turned his attention to them, which ended the interview.

CHAPTER ELEVEN

Burr drove back to the Harbour Inn on the Harbour-Petoskey Road, turning left on Beach Road. The road twisted through a climax forest, the only green from the hemlocks, a tea stained green. The road emptied onto the beach and ran along the shore to the Inn and then into Harbor Springs. He skirted the bay, the sun still well above the horizon. He thought it an odd time of year up north. There was light in the evening sky, and it was spring downstate, but here there was snow in the woods and ice on the bay.

Suzanne had left him a note at the Inn saying she was sorry she had run out, but the basement had been too upsetting. She was going to be with Sarah in Grosse Pointe, and he could reach her there. He passed an uneventful, alcohol-free night, waking up once to the tapping of rain on Stewart's tarnished copper roof.

The next morning Burr and Zeke-the-dog drove back to Petoskey. The rain had turned to partly cloudy. At US-131, the fast food restaurants sprung up in earnest. The Petoskey city fathers did not display the same aversion to serial franchise commerce as did their Harbor Springs counterparts.

At the crest of the Mitchell Street hill, Burr u-turned and pulled up to the curb. He parked the Jeep under a leafless maple tree, cracked the windows for Zeke, and strode purposefully up the sidewalk to the Van Arkel Funeral Home. Lawrence Van Arkel, Director. The funeral home had once been a real home, a three-story Victorian.

Burr let himself in. An appropriately somber man, roughly ageless, in a dark and altogether funereal suit was immediately upon him.

"Pruett or Mothershead, sir?"

"What?" Burr asked.

"The Pruett visitation is in here," said the man. He pointed into what must have been the dining room, where Burr could see a nose—male or female he couldn't tell—sticking out of a casket. "Mothershead is underway down there." The living room, no doubt, thought Burr.

"Actually, I'm here to see Mr. Van Arkel," Burr said.

"I'm afraid Dr. Van Arkel is with the Mothersheads. Do you have an appointment?"

"Mothershead it is," Burr said. He left the funereal, funeral director, mouth agape, and trod silently on the navy herringbone carpet to the Mothershead Funeral. He slipped in the chapel, nee living room, and slid into a pew.

Burr quite enjoyed the eulogy, thought he would have liked the deceased Mr. Mothershead (if the eulogy were accurate). When the service and the mourners departed with the now departed, all save Burr and Van Arkel, who now stood over him.

"I came to ask you a few questions," Burr said.

"I thought you came for the service," Van Arkel said. "If you have questions, you may subpoena me."

The undertaker put on reading glasses, then unfolded his handkerchief. Someone had pressed it. He attacked a smudge on the pew. At least he hadn't left, Burr thought. "I'm sorry I upset you, but I'm trying to save a man's life," he said.

"You know perfectly well that Michigan doesn't allow capital punishment," said the undertaker.

"Dr. Van Arkel, I am defending a man on a charge of first degree murder. A charge brought years later. For God knows what reason. My client has a wife and child ..."

Van Arkel interrupted him. "Two children," he said. "You ridiculed me. That's what you did. You ridiculed me."

Burr was glad to know what he had done. "I'm very sorry. That was not my intention at all," he said.

"Well, you did, and it could hurt my business," Van Arkel said.

So it's about money, Burr thought. "I'm very, very sorry," he said. "Is there anything I can do to make this right?"

"No," Van Arkel said.

Burr walked over to a bay window on the street side of the funeral home. Zeke still had his nose poked out of the window. "There you are, Zeke," Burr said.

"Who?" Van Arkel said.

"My dog," Burr said

"What kind of dog is it, and why did you leave it in a car?" Van Arkel asked.

"He's a yellow lab, and I didn't think you'd want a dog in here," Burr said.

"Your dog is more welcome here than you." Van Arkel peered out the window over his reading glasses. "Do you hunt your dog, Mr. Lafayette?"

"Ducks and geese mostly. Some pheasants, but arthritis has slowed him down on the pheasants."

"I have two German Shorthairs," Van Arkel said.

"Grouse and woodcock," Burr suggested.

"Indeed," Van Arkel said. "I prefer pointing dogs. They have a preciseness about them that flushing dogs do not. But a Labrador Retriever is useful in the water." Van Arkel tilted his head back and stared at Burr through his reading glasses, which provided Burr a most unwelcome view of the inside of the undertaker's nose.

"I arrived after Officer Gustafson," Van Arkel said. "I had no idea what had occurred or where. Then I saw Officer Gustafson at the head of the basement stairs. I examined the body and took pictures."

"Excuse me," Burr said, "but shouldn't the detectives or the crime scene cops take the pictures?"

"This is a small town, Mr. Lafayette. Petoskey isn't big enough for all that. In a murder, the chief would call in the state police. But not for an accident." Van Arkel looked him square in the eyes. "There was a great deal of blood. I had forgotten how much really. I never really see it because I drain it into . . ."

"Dr. Van Arkel, I appreciate your . . ."

"A touch queasy, are we? Of course. Sometimes I forget," Van Arkel said. "I asked Officer Gustafson if he had moved the body, and he said no, he hadn't, well only to check for a pulse which there wasn't, of course. No one could survive a gun shot from a 30:06 at that range."

"First, I took pictures—an entire roll. Then I examined the wound. The entry bullet left a small hole of course, no bigger than a nickel. The exit wound was much bigger—about two and a half inches across. Normally, a 30:06 tumbles inside the flesh and leaves a gaping hole, but at this range, it pierced the body, like a rapier.

"Where did the bullet enter?" Burr asked.

"As I testified, just below the left armpit, slightly to the rear of the arm. It then exited between the right armpit and the hip, just on the abdomen side of the right side, slightly below the point it entered. Like this." The undertaker drew a line through himself marking the bullet's path.

"Did you see anything that struck you as odd?"

"No, I did not. It appeared to be what it was. Accidental death by gunshot," said the undertaker.

"Why an accident?" Burr asked.

"Who would be so stupid as to shoot one's wife in the basement with one's son upstairs?" Van Arkel said.

"Unless one was very clever," Burr said.

"I assure you, Frank Tavohnen is not that clever," Van Arkel said.

"What about the difference in the height of the entry and exit hole? Doesn't that seem like the gun was fired from the shoulder at an angle?"

"It does," Van Arkel said. "But the angle was not acute."

"But Frank said he was cleaning the gun on the workbench. Wouldn't that mean it was flat, horizontal, so the bullet would have traveled parallel to the floor and entered and exited at the same point?" Burr rubbed his nose. "But that's not what the laser showed."

"No, it is not," said Van Arkel.

"But your autopsy said it was an accident," Burr said.

"That's correct," Van Arkel said.

"Did you see where the bullet struck the wall?"

"I did," Van Arkel said.

"Then, how can the laser study be reconciled with your autopsy?" Burr asked.

Van Arkel stiffened again. Then he pulled his glasses down to the end of his nose. "The facts are that the entry height and exit height of the bullet differed by seven inches. The laser was obviously more precise than my examination, but a variety of other reasons could explain the difference."

"Such as," Burr said.

"What if she weren't standing up straight. That would explain the angle, wouldn't it?"

"Yes, but not where the bullet hit the wall," Burr said. Van Arkel bit his lip. Burr could see that he did not like his opinions being questioned. "I'm just trying to understand the angle of the bullet," Burr said.

Van Arkel chewed on his lip. Burr let him chew. Finally, he smacked his lips. "If the bullet skimmed, no, let me be slightly more precise. If the bullet glanced off a rib, that would do it. Not enough to shatter the bone, but just enough to deflect the bullet."

"Gannon testified that the force of the bullet would be too strong, even if it struck a bone," Burr said.

"She said if it struck a bone, not if it glanced off a bone," Van Arkel said.

"I asked her that question at the preliminary exam," Burr said.

"No, you didn't," Van Arkel said. "You asked her if it struck a bone."

"She misled me," Burr said.

"Mr. Lafayette, you did not ask the right question," Van Arkel said.

Burr considered this. He hadn't asked precisely that question, but he was close. Science has failed me again, he thought. "Dr. Van Arkel, did the bullet glance off a rib?"

"I don't know," he said, but I can assure you, there was no shattered bone. The other issue is problematical."

"But it could have happened," Burr said.

"It could," Van Arkel said.

"So, Dr. Van Arkel, how could we find out what happened?

"You cannot determine from the autopsy if the path of the bullet was altered when it entered the body."

"Well, then, are we euchred?"

"Not we, Mr. Lafayette. You." Van Arkel looked down his nose again. "There is a way."

"There is?"

"Yes," Van Arkel said.

"And ..."

"Exhume the body," said the undertaker

CHAPTER TWELVE

Burr, moderately excited about the prospect of refuting the laser lady's theory, drove around the west side of Crooked Lake, to the address he had for Rollie Gustafson. A woman in her late sixties who he assumed to be Gustafson's wife, opened the door.

"Well, he ain't here. But I know where he is. Come on in and I'll show you," she said.

Burr stepped in. He saw five, maybe six, cats duck underneath the furniture. The house was dark and it smelled musty, like it was never aired out.

"If you look out the dining room window, you can see his shanty." She pointed to the northeast, the flesh on her upper arm flapping.

"Isn't it a little late for ice fishing?" Burr said.

"The old fool don't know when to quit. Says this is the best fishing. Just before ice out. He'll drown one of these days. But that's where he is all right."

Burr saw the shanty, half a mile out on the ice, tilting. He thought it must have settled during last night's rain. Smoke steamed through a chimney pipe and blew off to the northwest.

Burr followed Mrs. Gastafson's directions, parked the Jeep, once again leaving Zeke. He trudged through the slushy ice to Gustafson's shanty.

Burr knocked on the door of the shanty. No answer. He looked around. He saw a snowmobile behind the shanty. "How did he get that thing out here?" he said to himself.

"What? What's that? Who's out there?" said a voice from inside.

"It's Burr Lafayette," he said. "Your wife said I'd find you here."

"She did, did she?"

"She did," Burr said.

"That figures," said the voice.

Silence. Burr looked at the snow machine. The back end had started to sink in the ice. Finally, a head, disembodied peaked out of the shanty door, its eyes squinting in the sunlight.

"Mr. Gustafson?"

"Who wants to know?"

"Could I ask you a few questions?" Burr asked.

"You from the DNR?" Gustafson said.

"What?"

"The DNR. You know, the Department of Natural Resources," Gustafson said.

"No, I'm not," Burr said.

'How would I know that?"

"I'm a lawyer. Frank Tavohnen's lawyer. From the preliminary exam."

"You do look a bit familiar," Gustafson said.

"How did you get that snow machine out here?" Burr asked.

The shoulders of the head appeared at the door. They wore a tee shirt only. "I drove it," Gustafson said.

"Isn't the ice getting a little thin out here for this?" Burr said.

"Yup, it is. She's starting to rot. One more rain and some wind and she'll be gone. But now's when the fishing's best."

The head and shoulders stepped out of the shanty. They had on gray work pants, the waistband folded over by the belly. Gustafson pulled at his left ear. "Well, get in then," he said.

Coming in from the glare of the sun, Burr was blinded by the darkness, and tripped on the threshold of the shanty.

"Watch your step you don't fall into the hole." Gustafson shut the door. "The light spooks the fish," he said, "Especially the walleye. Just stand there 'til your eyes adjust.

Burr felt a small bottle pressed into his hand. He took a pull. The liquid, sweet and syrupy, stuck to the sides of his mouth, oozed down his throat, burned in his stomach. He handed the bottle back. "Thank you," he said. If there was anything sweeter than what he had just swallowed, Burr had no idea what it could possibly be.

"Good, ain't it?"

"It is," Burr said, though it wasn't.

"Betcha can't guess what it is."

Burr did know. Or was afraid he did. "Schnapps. I'll say butterscotch Schnapps," he said.

"By God, that's right. Used to drink peppermint, but it got to taste too much like toothpaste," Rollie said. He sucked on the pint again.

"So what happened to Frank after I left?"

"He's been charged with first degree murder," Burr said "Since you were the first one there, I was hoping you'd tell me what happened."

"I don't know what happened," Rollie said. "I wasn't there when it happened."

If Gustafson was an example of Petoskey's former finest, Burr thought there might be a number of unsolved crimes within the city limits.

"Would you tell me what happened after you arrived?"

"I suppose I could," Rollie said. "Course you could read all the paperwork.

"I did that," Burr said.

"I suppose you did," Rollie said.

Burr's eyes had adjusted to the twilight of the shanty. He watched the retired cop stumble over to what Burr could now make out as a lawn chair, with green and dirty white plastic straps woven over and under each other and around a bent aluminum frame. Gustafson stationed himself in front of the chair and sat. He reached into a bucket, caught a minnow and baited his hook. Then he dropped the minnow in a hole at his feet and started jigging.

"I only have this one chair," Rollie said. "You can sit on the cooler. There's cold beer in there. Course we don't need a cooler to keep it cold, now do we." Burr took a Labatt. The blue can exhaled when he pulled the tab. He sat on the cooler. "Why don't I join you?" Rollie said.

Burr stood, fished out a can and passed it to Rollie who seemed to be readying himself to hold court, a slightly drunken Santa. "Mr. Gustafson, would you please tell me what happened, what you remember."

Rollie leaned back in his chair and took a pull on the Labatt. "I was on duty that night, of course. Saturday it was. The Saturday before Christmas, which was on a Saturday that year," he said. "Anyway, I'm cruising downtown by the Perry Davis, the hotel. You know the one? By the old train station. Lookin' for drunk skiers coming out from the bars. I haven't seen any, but then it's only eight, maybe eight thirty. All of a sudden the dispatcher comes on, says there's been a shooting, no that's not what he said, an accident with a gun over on Waukazoo. Well, I'm only seven or eight blocks away, so I respond. I was going to turn my flashers on, but hell, I was so close and there wasn't much traffic. I didn't really see the need. I just drove over there, quick as I could. Couldn't have taken me more than two minutes. I go up to the door and rung the bell. Nobody answered. But I heard all this hollering inside. I turned the knob and went right in. There's old Frank and he's holding his boy, Jason. He must have been seventeen or eighteen. Frank's got him in a bear hug, got his arms around the boy's chest, got his arms pinned to his chest. You know like this." Rollie reached out his arms, in a hug.

"There's blood all over the boy's shirt so I think he's the one that did whatever it was. Then I start to pick out the words. He's hollering and crying at the same time. 'You killed her. You killed her.' Over and over. Over and over. Frank, he's not saying anything but his face is real red and I can see he's crying. Well, they're standing right by the basement door. I can see the stairs. So I put two and two together and I run down the stairs. There's blood everywhere on the way down—on the walls, the railing. Anyway, there she was all crumpled up next to the wall, about ten feet from the stairs, lying there in a puddle of blood. A big puddle. She was dead all right. No pulse, but she was still warm. So I looked around a little, not too much because that yelling was still going on and I didn't want that to get out of hand. First, though, I called for help, that's just the procedure when something like this happens. Called for an ambulance, too. For the body. Old Claudia was dead all right."

"Well, I saw this deer rifle on the workbench. I went over and looked at it. Didn't touch it. It was pointed in the general direction of Claudia. I smelled the barrel. You could tell it had been fired. Gone off I guess is more like it. So then I go over and look at Claudia. I can see where the bullet went in and where it came out.

Rollie stopped talking and bent down to the hole. He jigged his line twice, then once more. He took another long draught on the Labatt. "I can't think of anything else to do down there, so I start up the stairs. I'm not in too big a hurry because I don't know what I'm going to do when I get up there, and I can see I've got to call the station and tell them Claudia is dead. So that'll mean Van Arkel will have to come. I'm hoping the ambulance gets there pretty quick. And I'm going to have to get a statement from Frank which I don't want to do and won't be able to do until that boy quiets down. And I can see I'll have to get a statement from the boy, too, but I don't see how that's gonna happen tonight. All in all, I was wishing I hadn't been so Johnny-on-the-spot when the call came in."

"That's what you remember?"

"Yup," Rollie said. "And all before I got to the top step."

"Is that right?" This could well be a colossal waste of time, Burr thought.

"So I go up there. And old Frank's still got his boy bearhugged. By now the boy's just sobbing. Not saying anything. Just crying. I ask Frank if there's anything I can do. He says no. I start to take my pad out but then I think better of it. So I go to the phone and call the station. Tell them Claudia is dead. Then I just go sit down in old Frank's Lazy Boy. Dark blue, nice one, too. Wishing that ambulance would hurry up. Then I see it."

"See what?"

"The Christmas tree," Rollie said.

"The Christmas tree?" Burr asked.

"'Don't you see? Rollie asked.

"Yes," said Burr, who didn't.

"Who the hell would kill their wife in the basement with a deer rifle while they was decorating the tree. Especially with a kid around. Don't make sense."

"What if that's what Frank thought?" Burr said. "Did it that way on purpose. For just the reason you said."

"I thought about that. Truly, I did. But you know what? Frank's not that smart. Oh, he's smart all right. I mean he's a dentist after all. Pretty fair baseball coach, too. But he's not devious smart. Not like a lawyer. No offense."

"None taken," Burr said.

Rollie stopped for a moment, then, "you getting all this? I don't see no notes being taken."

"I'm getting it," Burr said. "I just want you to tell it.

"Well, right about now Van Arkel shows up and off we go downstairs. He only needs to look at her once to know she's dead. Asks me what happened. I point to the deer rifle on the workbench. That's the gun killed her."

"Accident?" he says."

"I haven't talked to Frank yet, I said, but I'd say so. Van Arkel looks at me, looks at the gun, looks at her. Then he yawns. He stays down in the basement to give Claudia a more thorough going over."

"The ambulance guys have now showed up, and I point downstairs. The neighbor lady is there, old Mrs. Larson. She's holding the boy. Asks me if she can take him next door. I saw yes."

"Frank walks out the front door with them, but he walks across the street. Turns around and stands there, looking back at his house. In his shirtsleeves."

"I go outside, turn the lights off on my cruiser. Frank's still standing there so I motion for him to come back in. By this time, they got Claudia in a body bag on a stretcher. They start to take her out. On the way, they knock over the Christmas tree. Damndest thing. Frank comes in. I go sit on the couch. He plops himself down in the Lazy Boy now. It is his chair after all."

Burr nodded.

"So now it's just me and him. Neither of us saying anything. Finally, I say, 'Frank, you feel like talking about this.' 'Not really,' he says. 'Well, you want me to come back tomorrow? Or you want to come down to the station?' 'No,' he says. Well, I got up then. No use wearing out my welcome. I figured it could wait. Started for the door."

"You just left?"

"Wait now, let me finish." Rollie shifted in his chair. "If you're not careful, this chair will make your butt look like a tic tac toe game. So anyway, I'm about at the door and Frank says, 'No, let me do it now.' I go and sit down and get out my notebook. Boy, does Frank look bad. Eyes all puffy. Red, too. I just sit there waiting for him. He tells me what happened, and I got to get it all down because somebody died and this is one report that's going to get read."

"What did you think?" Burr asked.

"I thought it was an accident," Rollie said. "Any fool could see that. Don't know why anybody would go to all that trouble to murder someone that way. Too much to go wrong," Rollie said.

"What if he just got mad and picked up the gun and shot her?"

"I thought about that. But it don't make sense. How does he know she's coming down? He didn't call her. The boy said he didn't. It could have been on purpose, but I think it was an accident. Bad luck. Very bad luck." The old man shook his head back and forth. Then he took another pull on the butterscotch Schnapps.

Hey, look out!" The fishing pole bent down towards the hole. The line ran off the reel. "Damn. Now that's a fish." Rollie let the line play out. When it stopped, he lifted the pole slightly. Burr watched him mouth 1-2-3 then he jerked hard on the pole. The line ran off the reel again. "Gotcha now, you bastard." The old man tightened the drag two turns and began reel in. The fish took off again. "It's a pike, see. The way he took that minnow. They grab it and run but he can't swallow it until he's got it head first in his mouth. So he stops and turns that minnow around head first—then he swallows it. When he stops, I count to three than I let him have it.. This is one big pike and we are gonna dance until I get him in."

Five minutes later Rollie nosed the fish to the hole, and with one quick move, he stuck his free hand in one of the gills and jerked the fish out of the water and onto the ice. The fish looked to be at least two feet long. It flopped on the ice until Rollie held it down with his boot. "Well, I'll be damned. You know what this is?"

Burr saw the bulging bug eyes and the two back fins. "Walleye," he said.

"Sure as shit is. This ain't no pike. I could of sworn it was a pike. Bit just like one. Too bad though," Rollie said.

Burr arched his eyebrows.

"Best eating fish there is. Eight pounds if he's an ounce." Rollie looked down at the fish. Then sideways at Burr. "Too bad the season's closed," Rollie said. The old man opened the door and stepped out, carrying the fish by the gill. Burr followed him, blinded by the glare of the ice. He saw a dozen perch lying on the ice in the shade of the shanty. He hadn't noticed them when he first got there. "All right, then," Rollie said. "This here will be our little secret." Rollie walked out of the shadows and kicked at the snow until he found the corner of a board. He kicked the board away uncovering a hole gouged into the ice. He dropped the walleye in the hole where it flopped next to the other five.

CHAPTER THIRTEEN

Leaving Rollie Gustafson to his own devices (namely poaching), Burr made peace with Zeke, who sulked at being left behind. (Zeke forgave him.) On his way back to the Inn for what he assumed would be another uneventful evening, Burr detoured to the north. He thought he had the makings of a defense and decided to take a drive and think things over. After talking to Van Arkel and Gustafson, Burr thought he might need his own laser expert.

Three miles north he stopped at a gas station across from Boyne Highlands and next to Nub's Nob. (There were still a few skiers.) He called the ever resourceful Suzanne and asked her to find a laser expert.

Burr climbed back in the Jeep and drove on. He believed he could use both Van Arkel and Gustafson to his advantage. The question was what to do about the laser. Lost in his musings, he realized he had taken Frank's route on the afternoon of the Christmas tree cutting. He passed three two tracks on Lark's Lake Road, wondered which one Frank had taken, decided there was no point in following the accident (was it an accident?) to its origin. At Robinson Road he turned left, passed the minimum-security prison, not where Frank would go if convicted, and followed it west to the stop sign at M-119, which ran along a bluff a hundred feet above Lake Michigan. A right turn here would take him to Cross Village via the Tunnel of Trees. He turned the other way, south, which would take him on a twisting road through Good Hart and then back to Harbor Springs. The twilight settled through the trees, second growth hardwood. To his left, away from the lake, the snow had a yellow cast from the failing light. A black Cadillac (an Eldorado, he thought) roared up from behind, slowed, there being no room to pass. Through his rearview mirror, Burr saw the Cadillac, perhaps a bit too close. This was no road on which to hurry, the road so narrow there was no centerline and no real shoulder, just a white line on each edge of the pavement.

Below him to his right, the bluff dropped to the beach, no ice here. The trees rose at an acute angle to the cliff, stacked next to each other, mostly saplings, ending just before the missing guardrail. That's what the trees are for, he thought.

The road untwisted here a bit. Burr judged he was about two miles north of Watson's grade, a mile-long hill. The Cadillac pulled out in the left lane. Though the road was straighter here, Burr thought it still a poor excuse for a two-lane road and no place to pass. Annoyed by the Cadillac, Burr sped up to prevent its passing. Probably another middle-aged man with too much testosterone, he thought. He heard the Cadillac downshift, undeterred, and accelerate. The moderate curves yielded to more hairpins. Burr did not slow down, for an instant considered speeding up himself. The Jeep swayed on the curves, its suspension not built for this type of driving. The Cadillac was now alongside him. Burr tried to look at the driver, but the tinted window kept him hidden. Burr gave up on his own testosterone and eased on the gas pedal to let the Cadillac pass, but it slowed with him. Burr sped up a little, but the car stayed next to him. I might have deserved this, he thought.

The Jeep and the Cadillac simply could not drive side by side and stay on the road. It was just too narrow. They swerved around the corners together like horses hitched to a wagon. Burr had to run the right tires off the edge of the road on what little shoulder there was.

He saw a sign marking another hairpin curve, knew that on this road, a sign marking a curve meant something. He had had enough and slowed down, but the curve came on him too fast, the Cadillac still on his left. Then it was too late.

At the hairpin, the Cadillac kept going straight for an instant too long. By the time it cut to the left, Burr ran off the road. He crushed his foot on the brake. The Jeep skidded as the right rear tire scraped across the shoulder. Then the Jeep was in the air, floating over the bluff. Burr saw the Cadillac race on, apparently unaware of the airborne Jeep. Zeke, to his right, seemed blissfully unaware that they were flying, at least for the moment. Burr heard the engine race, no friction from the road. He watched them sail over the bluff, noticed the shadow of the Jeep on the ground below. Then the Jeep struck the trees, saplings really, crashing into them, which broke their fall. Burr pulled Zeke to his lap and covered him with his chest just as the Jeep struck the next of the trees, these smaller than the first. The Jeep rolled once, completely over, righted itself. Burr felt the Jeep drop through the trees. He sat up, and looked out the driver's side window. He saw the branches scrape the Jeep as it fell, ducked as one smashed his window. The Jeep caromed off tree trunks on its way down, then stopped, a broken trunk jammed through the floorboards on the passenger side, impaling the Jeep. The Jeep slid slowly down the broken trunk until it struck the roof. The skewered Jeep stopped its descent and came to rest fifty feet below the road bed, ten feet above the ground, wedged between the hardwood saplings and impaled by the bottom fifteen feet of a beech tree.

Zeke sat up, reassumed his position as shotgun, and on the whole seemed fairly relaxed about what had just happened. Burr, on the other hand, could not stop shaking.

There remained the problem of actually getting out of the Jeep, which had become a treehouse with no ladder. He couldn't open the doors and the electric windows had no electricity. The smashed driver-side window had a branch poking into the Jeep that made escape impossible. The only thing he could think of was to break the rear window. He hated to break it, even though he was sure the Jeep was a total loss. Climbing into the back upset the balance of the tree house. The back of the Jeep dropped and (mercifully) settled three feet off the ground, Burr kicked out the back window, extricated himself and then Zeke.

The two of them dodged through the trees, then started to climb the bluff. Burr stopped halfway and waited for Zeke to catch up. At his feet, here on the southwest slope where the spring sun was the strongest, he saw a bloodroot. The eight-petaled flower with a yellow center had a single leaf that wrapped around the blossom like the hood of a cobra. Burr considered the bloodroot the first wildflower of spring, which lifted his spirits despite the tragic loss of his Jeep. He climbed to the road with renewed vigor, walked side by side with Zeke, to the nearest occupied house (a mile away).

Burr called his Aunt Kitty first, but there was no answer. He thought about calling Kaye, the realtor, but he didn't think he knew her well enough. (That and the fact that he didn't have her phone number.) He had been left with Stewart who he knew would be available and who he knew would be his harshest critic and who, in fact, was.

Stewart retrieved Burr and Zeke with the Harbour Inn's luggage vehicle, a brown Oldsmobile Vista Cruiser, the last of the station wagons, circa 1977. Burr allowed that it was fortunate that the Vista Cruiser was brown since the color blended nicely with the rust. Stewart failed to see the humor and lectured Burr on his reckless driving (which Burr knew he would).

After yet another uneventful (but welcome) night at the Inn, Stewart had indeed had the last laugh as Burr, without wheels (the Jeep was indeed hopelessly wrecked) had to borrow the Vista Cruiser. The lone blessing had been another night rain and the ensuing east wind, which had dispatched the ice on Little Traverse Bay. Buoyed by open water, clearing skies and the conclusive arrival of spring (at last), Burr made his way back to East Lansing in the Vista Cruiser.

~

It snowed while he slept, a heavy, wet, cottage-cheesy snow, eight inches, a late and discouraging snow, even for Michigan. That evening he dined by himself at Michelangelo's where he continued to eat (and drink) down the back rent. Suzanne caught up with him during his third glass of a remarkably unremarkable Old Vine Zinfandel. Burr stood and pulled out a chair for her.

"Burr, are you all right? You could have been killed," she said, again wearing her fur coat, which must surely be its last outing of the season. The waitress brought a wine glass for Suzanne.

"No, thank you," she said to the waitress. "Burr, you're awfully calm for someone who flew off a cliff."

"I've had two days to deal with it," he said.

"Who was it?"

"I have no idea," he said. "The driver passed me before I went over the edge. I'm sure it wasn't intentional."

"I wouldn't be so sure," Suzanne said.

"Thank you for your concern, Suzanne," Burr said. He took a small sip of the wine. Still unremarkable, he thought. "Did you have any luck?"

"I found us an expert," she said. "We can see him tomorrow. He's in Ann Arbor."

Burr looked at her, admiring the full lips that framed her mouth, and her big smile, almost too big. She is not beautiful he thought, not at all beautiful, but she is stunning.

It was the fur coat that had finally started their affair. Burr had done his best to woo her. He had long ago given up on the pretext of the lawsuit and the pretense of client relations. Not only had he offended the firm's sense of propriety, worse, he had courted Suzanne right under Grace's nose, had been courting her for six months. Burr was sure Suzanne enjoyed his company, liked him, found him amusing. He was more smitten each day. She was very bright, quick with a word, perhaps a bit too cynical. Very well read. Clever in a naughty way. Of course, there was the fact that he had virtually lost his mind in her physicality. Her legs, her smell, and of course, her lips.

But until that particular evening, wearing her fur coat, she had parried his every advance. He did have two fairly private box seats—the firm's seats—for the Red Wings at the Joe—the Joe Louis Arena. He had a stainless steel thermos of very dry martinis with olive juice and no expectations. Suzanne had worn her fur coat again and not much else.

The Red Wings were getting the better of the Toronto Maple Leafs; the martinis, the better of Burr. Suzanne, apparently a student of the game, ignored him, kept her coat on, refused to take it off, although with the ice, it was a bit chilly at the Joe.

She wore black heels that night which was too formal for hockey, her legs disappearing into her coat. Just after the first intermission, he watched her as she uncrossed her legs. Her coat parted and Burr saw the top of her stockings and a slice of bare thigh above them. He was instantly aroused and befuddled for the rest of the game. They ended up in the bar at the Pontchatrain and then her apartment. He kissed her as soon as he closed the door, his hands on her shoulders inside her coat. He brushed it off her shoulders, and it fell to the floor.

That was how it finally began. He had chased her until she caught him. Burr had fallen in a complete and absolute swoon.

~

"Burr," Suzanne said. "Burr, are you listening to me?

"Yes, of course, I am," he said, jarred back to the moment.

"We'll go to Ann Arbor first thing in the morning."

The next day, Burr looped into the circle drive of the University Marriott promptly at 8:20 a.m., precisely twenty minutes late. The hotel stood right next to Burr's building. It had upped the value of his building (also his taxes) but blocked most of his view of the campus. All in all, Burr preferred life pre-hotel.

Suzanne opened the door of the Vista Cruiser. Zeke, in the passenger seat, tried to kiss her. Burr thought that it seemed like a pretty fair idea on Zeke's part, even considering all that had gone on.

"Zeke, back seat," Burr said, pointing to the back seat. The dog turned toward Burr, then climbed into the back seat, slowly.

"Thank you," she said.

An hour and a half later, Burr parked in the faculty lot at the law school.

"You don't have a permit to park here," Suzanne said.

"I didn't have one thirty years ago either," he said.

They walked through the law quad, Elizabethan architecture, built in the thirties. Cut granite, four buildings all in a quadrangle. The leaves on the oaks were just now coming out.

Then they cut through the main campus, across the "diag", the commons where sidewalks entered from all directions, at all angles, to the Physics Building, on the east side of the main campus.

They took the stairs to the fourth floor and followed the room numbers to 434. Henry R. Pattengill, Ph.D. Suzanne knocked.

The door opened. "Yes," said the voice, which belonged to a tall, thin, sixtyish man, with very little hair except that which grew out of his nose and ears and more or less erupted from his eyebrows. Burr wondered if any of it could be transplanted to his head. They sat across from him in two university-issue side chairs, early indestructible.

"My colleague tells me that you are an expert in the field of lasers and that you would be willing to testify that the prosecution's laser study was defective."

"I did not say that."

"Suzanne, you told me that ..."

Professor Pattengill raised his hand like a traffic cop. "Stop," he said. "That's not what I said. What I said was, I am an expert in the area of lasers and I was sure I could find an irregularity in whatever it was."

"And what did you find?" Burr said.

"Nothing," said Pattengill.

"Suzanne, I thought you said you sent Professor Pattengill the study."

"I did," she said,

"I have the study," said Pattengill. "I have not read the study."

"Why would that be?" This guy annoyed Burr.

"Because I have not received my fee."

"Your fee," Burr said. He decided to try a different tack. "Professor Pattengill, we are most impressed with your vitae" (which Burr had not seen), "and I'm sure we would be equally impressed with your lab."

"My lab," Pattengill repeated.

"Yes," Burr said. "May we see it?"

"Mr. Lafollette," said Pattengill.

"Lafayette," Burr said.

Pattengill ignored this. "This," he said, holding up an 8 ½" by 11" yellow pad, "is my lab."

"You have no lab," Burr said.

"I do indeed and this is it," he said, waving the yellow pad in the air. "I am a theoretical physicist. I have no need for a lab."

Burr realized he had taken the wrong tack. "Then how do you know you can help us if you haven't read the study?"

"I can find something wrong with anything," Pattengill said.

That, Burr believed. "Then you'll help us?" he said.

"I will need my fee," Pattengill said.

"Of course," Burr said.

"Twenty-five thousand," said Pattengill. "Half now and half the day before I testify. Plus expenses."

"That seems a little high," Burr said.

"I have many projects," said Pattengill.

"How many yellow pads do you think you'll need?" Burr said under his breath.

"We'll take it," Suzanne said.

Outside on the "diag", Suzanne fumed at him. "Why were you taunting him? He is an expert on lasers," Suzanne said.

"Suzanne, where are you going to get the money?"

"We'll get it," Suzanne said.

"Does he get paid before or after I do?"

"Burr, please."

"Suzanne, even if you get the money, that guy is not going to be able to help us."

"Why not?" she said.

"He's not exactly Mr. Personality," Burr said.

"He's the best there is, and he's the only one who said he would help," she said.

Burr angled back to the law quad, Suzanne on his heels. "I don't think you should give up on Pattengill so soon," she said.

"I'm not giving up," Burr said.

"What are you going to do then?"

"At the moment, I don't know," Burr said.

"I think we should do what Van Arkel said."

"Which was?" Burr asked.

"Exhume Claudia," Suzanne said.

Burr shuddered. "We need a court order."

"So, get one," Suzanne said.

They arrived at the Jeep. Zeke woofed at them. Burr saw a familiar brown envelope under the windshield wiper. "If we go to the trouble of getting a court order and we're wrong, it will be a disaster."

"Why?"

"If there's no broken or chipped bone, then we're worse off than we are now," Burr said. "Right now, we can rely on what Van Arkel said could have happened. If we know for sure, and we're wrong, Truax wins."

"Why doesn't Truax exhume the body?" Suzanne asked.

"My dear Suzanne" (Burr knew it irritated her when he spoke to her this way), "Truax doesn't want to know either. He's got Gannon."

Burr pulled the envelope off the windshield. Another parking ticket. "Twenty five bucks," he said. "Prices have gone up."

"I thought you said you parked here in law school."

"I got tickets then, too," Burr said. He crumpled the ticket and stuck it in his pocket.

~

Two weeks later, Burr had two bilge pumps going but they weren't keeping up. He had one more pump, a hand pump. He had poked the end of the intake hose into the bilge and duct taped the hose itself to the mast where it came out of the floorboards. Then he ran the exhaust hose out into the cockpit and cleaned out the self-bailers. Now he sat on the starboard berth and began to pump. "If the two electrics won't stop it, I don't really see how this one more will turn the tide," Burr said. Zeke looked back at him from the quarterberth next to the nav station. "Don't just sit there," Burr said. "Do something." The dog looked at him then started grooming himself.

Kismet was a forty-one foot, cutter-rigged yawl, circa 1937 (sleeps six, lays twelve as Stewart said), still in good shape for a fifty-year-old boat, but not like she was when Burr had the money to write checks. The planking had soaked up; squeezing the caulking and sealing the hull (mostly). But somewhere (Burr thought it was starboard side midships) there was a leak and Little Traverse Bay poured in.

Footsteps on the dock. Zeke barked.

"Permission to come aboard?" Suzanne peered at him from the companionway. Burr kept pumping. "Need any help? She asked.

"No," he said. He stopped the up and down of the hand pump. The companionway framed her, not quite a profile, silhouetted her pointy nose and her ponytail. He remembered what it had been like when they were together. After they had made love that first time, Burr absolutely had to see her every day, which of course, proved to be impossible, particularly since he hadn't (quite) left Grace. He saw Suzanne whenever he could, loved her or at least thought he did. He took her to dinner, to the Tigers', to the movies (he loved movies and they were dark and clandestine). He took her sailing. Looking back on it, Burr knew he had been a fool. Suzanne had never said she loved him. He should have believed what she didn't say.

"Can I get you another pump?" Suzanne said, jolting Burr back into the reality of his leaky boat.

"No, I've got three," he said. He stopped pumping. Suzanne climbed down the companionway. No one looked better in blue jeans. Her running shoes squished on the floorboards.

"My, but it's wet in here," she said.

"Once again you demonstrate a remarkable grasp of the obvious," he said, annoyed at the leak and taking it out on Suzanne. Burr started with the hand pump again.

"Why exactly have you picked this particular time to launch Kismet?"

"I need a place to live," he said.

"While you're working on Frank's case," she said.

"Yes," he said.

Suzanne kissed him lightly on the cheek, which invigorated him. "Why don't you stay at the Inn," she said, not really asking.

"Stewart won't let me stay there," Burr said. "He's coming into his high season."

"He has at least one room."

"Stewart says I abuse room service," Burr said.

"And dogs are not allowed," Suzanne said.

"That, too," Burr said, relieved that Suzanne hadn't brought up Aunt Kitty's cottage, enormous, but not big enough for the both of them.

"I'm going to have a phone and fax here. I'm going back to East Lansing as soon as Kismet soaks up. I have three or four cases to finish before the summer recess, then I'm going to live here until the trial is over.

"I'm not sure this is the best way to help Frank," Suzanne said.

He pried up one of the aft floorboards. The pumps were gaining now, but only if he kept pumping with the hand pump. Kismet was still taking on water.

"Did you check all the through hulls?" Suzanne asked.

"Yes," he said.

"Of course you did." She opened the locker under the galley sink and stuck her head in. "These are closed," she said. "Pardon me," She squeezed by him and made her way into the head. "These are closed," she said. Suzanne emerged from the head. "Kindly stand up."

"I'm pumping," Burr said.

"I noticed," Suzanne said. "Pump over there."

Burr knew from experience it was easier to move than argue. He shifted his pumping operation to the port bunk. Suzanne took off the cushion on the starboard bunk where he had been sitting and put it on the pipe berth and lifted the cover. She reached inside.

"There it is," she said.

"There's what?"

"The open through hull," Suzanne said.

"There's no through hull there," Burr said.

"It's the old water intake for the head," she said.

"How did you know?" Burr asked.

"I was here when the holding tank was put in." Suzanne reached into the locker and turned the valve clockwise until it locked down against the fitting.

"Apparently, I forgot," Burr said.

"Apparently," Suzanne said.

"Thank you, Suzanne," Burr said. The electric pumps took hold. He stopped pumping.

CHAPTER FOURTEEN

May 20, 1989 – Mother's Day

Burr had second thoughts about meeting Kaye. Somehow he felt he was cheating on Suzanne, although he didn't quite see how he could be cheating on someone with whom he had a relationship in the historical sense only. Besides, he thought, he was really here with Kaye to find out more about Truax, Burr being of the opinion that residential realtors knew more about what was actually going on then perhaps any other group of people. As a further besides, Suzanne had left for East Lansing yesterday, so she wasn't even here anymore. As these lines of thought confused him, he decided to think about these particular subtleties and nuances at a later date.

Burr had arranged to meet Kaye at Marina Villa, her condominium in Harbor Springs, a long white building, fronting on Little Traverse Bay. That morning he had hunted (successfully) black morels in a secret spot north of Harbor Springs, and now he was cooking them for Kaye. Burr thought Kaye looked frisky in a red turtleneck and a blue jean skirt that ended well above her knees.

"I've always had morels with steak," Kaye said.

"Steak ruins the flavor," Burr said. "Just try them this way. I'll buy you a steak afterwards."

"I don't really like steak anyway," she said.

Burr clarified the butter and slid the morels, whole, into the saucepan. He uncorked a red Burgundy, a supple Pinot. He poured the wine into tow glasses. "We'll let this breathe while I sauté the mushrooms," Burr said.

"Cheers," he said.

"Fruity," Kaye said. "But thin."

"Yes, but try it with this." He fed her a mushroom.

"The wine is much better with the mushroom," she said. "And the mushroom is..."

"Nutty," Burr said. "In a word, nutty." Burr took a swallow of his wine. "Why do you think Truax is doing this?" he asked.

"What?"

"Prosecuting Frank, after all this time," Burr said.

"I don't know why," she said. "He must believe Frank did it."

"I think there's more to it than that," Burr said.

"Ambitious. He's ambitious," Kaye said. "And political. He's smart, and he's political. Politically correct."

"Is he married? Kids?" Burr asked. He filled her glass.

"Yes. And three," Kaye said. "Catholic. Anti-abortion. Republican. Law and order. Business. Pro business, I think. He wants to see Northern Michigan grow. I'm sure the real estate developers love him.

"Interests?" Burr asked.

"Ties flies. Doesn't fish," Kaye said.

"Shoots. Doesn't hunt," Burr said.

"How do you know that?"

"A lucky guess," he said.

"I see," she said.

"Would you say he is Puritanical?"

"Puritanical?"

"Of or relating to Puritans," Burr said.

"I know what it means. It's an old fashioned word. She licked her lips. "Puritanical would be good. Proper might be better."

"Proper," he said. "That would work."

"Why aren't you with your family? It's Mother's Day, you know," Kaye said.

"Why aren't you?"

"I canceled it for this," she said.

"I see," Burr said.

"Actually we celebrated last week," Kaye said.

This relieved Burr. "It's not my week," he said. "With my son."

"What about your mother?"

"Dead," Burr said. "My father, too."

"I'm sorry." Kaye looked up at him. "So, why today?"

"I wanted to find something out. It's morel season. And I wanted to see you."

"Do you want to stay?" Kaye asked.

"Stay?"

"Yes, stay."

She turned to face him and looked straight at him. Burr saw the black flecks in the blue of her iris. She pushed the hair back off his brow.

He kissed her on the cheek, then on the lips. Then he left.

Late the next afternoon, the day after the mushrooms and the kiss, Burr stopped the Vista Cruiser at Harbor Point security, a small white building marking the entrance to Harbor Point.

"I'm sorry, Mr. Lafayette," said the security guard. "I didn't recognize you in the Vista Cruiser."

"That's all right, Norbert," Burr said. He absolutely had to find a different car to drive, but he was a bit short at the moment.

"We're on the summer schedule now," said Norbert, who was sixtyish, in a pencil-like way, but he still had a full head of black, like midnight, hair, neatly parted.

Burr backed up and pulled around to the garages behind the tennis courts. He parked in the stall next to his Aunt Kitty's silver Mercedes, vintage 1965 and climbed on a bicycle, a red Huffy with a basket on the front, and a bell on the handlebars, no gears, no hand brakes. He started pedaling to the cottage. Harbor Point, founded in 1896, had been one of Michigan's first gated communities. It was accessible only by bicycle and horse during the season, which, he had forgotten, began May 1st. Passing the gate, Burr ding-a-linged at Norbert as he pedalled by. Burr cycled past a wooded nature preserve on his right, turn of the century cottages to his left. At the end of the point, the cottages fronted on both Lake Michigan and Little Traverse Bay, these the cottages of the top drawer.

He dismounted at the cottage, yet another three-story Victorian, white with forest green trim. A turret on the Lake Michigan side. Three cottages from the end of the point and the lighthouse. He smelled the lake blowing across the point, wet and sandy, walked up the porch, twenty feet deep, its ceiling painted a baby blue.

The cottage, built in the early 1900's by his great grandfather, had been his father's, and now belonged to Aunt Kitty, his father's younger sister, a maiden lady who had become a lawyer long before it was fashionable.

The family trust specified that the cottage pass by age and blood. Burr was next in line if he outlived his aunt, a feudal manner of passing title but one designed to prevent dilution, and the only thing left in the trust, the Lafayette's not what they once were, financially speaking.

Burr believed he had been the perfect gentleman with Kaye the previous evening. After the kiss with Kaye, he had retreated to the secure but monkish confines of his new home afloat. He didn't know what to do about either Kaye or Suzanne.

Aunt Kitty, a tall, erect woman with silver hair pulled back in a ponytail, opened the leaded glass door, led him through a hardwood foyer which in turn led into a hall with varnished oak hardwood underneath oriental throws. Her ponytail gave her an air of defiance. She continued through the servants' quarters to the kitchen. At the refrigerator, Aunt Kitty filled two tumblers with ice. "I have an olive for you, but I will not allow olive juice. It ruins the gin," she said. Burr rolled his eyes.

"Don't you look at me like that," Aunt Kitty said.

"How long have you had that Vermouth?"

"It can't be more than a year old. I buy a new one every year," she said.

"As long as it's fresh," Burr said.

"Don't be smart with me. I keep it in the refrigerator. Gin in the freezer." She handed him his drink, and they made their way to the fireplace back in the parlor. It covered almost half the interior wall, pieced together with rock from the point, eight feet at the floor then up six feet to the mantle, birds-eye maple, then narrowing to four feet.

Aunt Kitty sat in a wingback chair next to the fireplace where she could see the big lake. Burr sat next to her on its mate. "What can you tell me about Truax?" he asked.

"What do you want with him?" Aunt Kitty asked. "As if I didn't know. You should not be trying a murder case. You know nothing about it."

"I'm a litigator," he said.

"Commercial. And a damn good one. Until you started that appellate work. Probably lost your touch by now."

"A trial is a trial," Burr said.

"It's not and you know it. Criminal law is about as much like civil law as dating sex is like married sex."

Burr ignored this. "Truax?"

She took a rather large gulp of her martini. "Why is he doing this?"

"He's got new evidence," Burr said.

"The state police didn't come up with this on their own. This case was closed seven years ago. Somebody wanted it reopened," Aunt Kitty said. "Maybe it was Claudia's family. Or the boy, what's his name?"

"Jason," Burr said. His martini tasted like jet fuel. It was all gin. "I don't think so. I can't even find him."

"So you think Calvin wanted this looked at?"

"He's the only one," Burr said.

'That man is ambitious. I'll say that for him. No one gave him a chance when he ran for prosecutor," she said. "Light that fire, will you." she said. "I have a chill."

"It's May," Burr said.

"And it can get damn cold here in May."

Burr lit the fire. Aunt Kitty edged her chair towards it, the firelight flickering. "Does he have a case?" she asked.

"No motive," Burr said.

"There's a new young wife. That's your motive."

"It's not in any of the pleadings," he said.

"Not yet," she said.

"All he's got is the laser," Burr said.

"And a dead woman," said Aunt Kitty. "And a house that hasn't sold in seven years."

"Six," Burr said.

"Nobody likes to see a house empty for six years," said Aunt Kitty. "Not anywhere, but really not in a small town like Petoskey. Especially a tourist town."

"So he brings a charge of first degree murder to get the house sold," Burr said.

"That smart attitude is what gets you in trouble," said Aunt Kitty.

"And?"

"Care for another?" she said.

"I think I'll wait," Burr said.

"Make me a dividend," she said. "No. Help me up. You'll ruin it." Burr followed her to the kitchen. She poured gin on what was left of the ice. "I know it's off the subject," she said, "but how is Suzanne?"

"She's fine," Burr said.

"Fine," Aunt Kitty said. "Just fine. After all that you went through to get her and then spoiled. That's all you have to say. Fine."

"She's fine," Burr said, this not being the time to talk about, particularly since he didn't quite know how he felt. Burr followed Aunt Kitty back to the parlor where she sank into the wing-back chair. Burr followed suit. The fire blazed at them, which Burr thought had been a good idea after all.

"Well then, as to Truax, I think he may want to run for office," Aunt Kitty said.

"He already did," Burr said.

"No. The House or Senate," Aunt Kitty said.

"Congress?" Burr said.

"I doubt it. Is anybody quitting down in Lansing?" she said.

"I don't know," Burr said.

"Term limits," Aunt Kitty said. "I'll bet somebody can't run again. Term limits are a bad idea." She stirred her martini with her finger.

"That doesn't make any sense," Burr said.

"Then why do you think he's doing it?" Aunt Kitty took her finger out of the glass and licked it.

"For the publicity?" Burr asked.

"That's right," she said.

"Because it's the best advertising he can get," Burr said.

"When is the trial?"

"October," Burr said.

"Bingo," said Aunt Kitty. "A month before the election."

"What if he loses?" Burr asked.

"Loses what?"

"The case," he said.

"It doesn't matter," she said. Aunt Kitty drained her glass "Because if he wins, it's justice. If he doesn't, the people have spoken," she said. "And he has the publicity either way."

"He just did his job," Burr said

"He has to file by July 1st," Aunt Kitty said.

"Frank is his advertising campaign," Burr said.

Aunt Kitty threw the remains of her martini onto the fire. The ice hissed and was no more.

In the end, Burr hadn't really been surprised that the always affable Deputy Brubaker had shown up at Frank's store in Grosse Pointe. With yet another warrant drafted by Truax and signed by Gillis. If Burr hadn't been surprised about Deputy Brubaker, he shouldn't have been surprised to find Frank back where he'd started. Gillis had told Frank not to leave the county. So had Burr, but Burr would have been even more surprised if Frank had stayed in Emmet County.

Burr, Truax and Gillis concluded yet another bail hearing. Truax asked that Frank be held without bail because he was obviously a flight risk. Burr argued that Mr. Tavohnen had a business to run (what else would he say) and that he, Burr, would be personally responsible. Gillis said that with Lafayette's affinity for jails, he wouldn't take that chance. Gillis upped the bail to a million dollars, which meant that Frank would be in jail at least until the trial was over. Gillis said the trial would begin Monday, October 16th, and from here on, this case would be under the jurisdiction of the Emmet County Circuit Court Judge, Samuel J. Dykehouse presiding.

CHAPTER FIFTEEN

Burr drove home to East Lansing that evening. He spent the next three weeks working on what was left of his other cases, collecting as much in fees as the decorum of his rarefied practice would allow, and driving back and forth to Grosse Pointe to see Zeke-the-boy. He moved on board Kismet the day after both the Michigan Appellate Court and the Michigan Supreme Court recessed for the summer and brought what little work he had left with him.

The day after he moved on board, Burr parked in front of the courthouse and climbed three flights of stairs, turned left down the second hall, knocked twice on the door bearing the name Truax. Hearing no response, Burr let himself in. Truax was not in residence.

Burr found himself staring into Truax's gun case and an imposing trophy case which stood next to it. He looked at himself in the reflection of one very large, shiny, yellow, metal trophy. The trophy distorted his visage, bending his head like a banana, but he could see where his ear had winged up the hair on the left side of his head. Regrettably, he had forgotten his comb. He spit in his palm and ran it from front to back. Then he pushed it back with his fingers as Truax entered.

"There is a mirror in the men's room," Truax said. "What is it that you want?"

"I was hoping we could work things out," Burr said. He looked out the west window of Truax's office to Lake Michigan. The office had a view worth condominiumizing. Burr wondered if a developer had propositioned the county for its courthouse yet.

"So far you have done very little to smooth out anything, including your hair," Truax said.

"Not true," Burr said, although it was true.

"You have contested each step in the process," Truax said.

"Would you like to plead this?" Burr asked.

Truax, on his way to the chair behind his desk, stopped. His Adam's apple bobbed.

That got his attention, Burr thought. "I mean, really, what have you got? He said. "No witnesses, no motive. A dead woman. That's it. Let's plead this and be done with it."

The prosecutor sat down at his desk. Now, he looked like he was really in charge. "I do not plead capital crimes," Truax said. His tie bobbed up and down every time he swallowed, more so when he spoke. "There was a murder committed and I intend to prove it," Truax said.

"You don't happen to drive a black Cadillac, do you?"

"Who me? No. I drive a Buick. A beige Buick. Why do you ask?"

"No reason." Burr retrieved the tin of Altoids from his pocket, offered them to Truax who declined, took four for himself. "Actually, I'd like to be the first one to sign your petition," Burr said.

"What petition?" Burr saw his Adam's apple bob again. "What petition?"

"You know which one. Your nominating petition for the senate. State senate. Not the real senate. The state senate. The amateur senate."

"How dare you," Truax said.

"Let me be the first to sign it. You do need signatures, don't you? Frankly, I can't imagine that you would possibly have enough family or friends to get there."

"How dare you," Truax said.

"How dare I? What do you think you're doing? Bringing this case. For your own free advertising campaign. Frank didn't murder Claudia and you know it. You trumped this up with some voodoo technology."

"I will prove this case," Truax said.

"You've got a laser and nothing more," Burr said.

"There is more," Truax said.

"Your Adam's apple is bobbing again. Did you know that? Did you know that every time you get nervous or put on the spot, your Adam's apple bobs? Did you know that?" Burr pointed at his throat. "There it goes again," he said.

Truax covered his throat with his left hand. "The next step is the witness list which I will provide at the appropriate time," he said.

"You sorry bastard," Burr said. "You sorry, lying bastard."

Truax stood, walked to the gun case, puled out a sporty looking Berretta over and under. "Get out," he said. He then shouldered the gun and pointed it at Burr's nose.

~

After the abortive settlement meeting with Truax, Barr drove back to Harbor Springs. He and Jacob sat across from each other in a window booth with red vinyl cushions at Juilerettes. Founded in 1898, Juilerettes had the best whitefish in Michigan. They trucked it in fresh every day from Lake Superior, that and the fact the cooks spread butter on it before they broiled it, which was not common knowledge. It was common knowledge that Juilerettes was the noisiest restaurant in the entire state. The ceiling, the original tin, painted white, bounced every sound back to the original creaky hardwood floor. The families with young children produced most of the din, but there was also a jukebox, whose records had not been changed for at least thirty years. Burr rarely ate at Juilerettes, however, as it had no liquor license, but believing it wise to dry out just a bit, picked Juilerettes for that very reason.

"We simply cannot conduct this matter from a diner. Especially with the roar of all these jabbering children," Jacob said. "This place is worse than your boat."

"Not really," Burr said. "It's dry in here." It had been raining again, and while Burr had most of the underwater leaks more or less under control, Kismet needed a new cabin top.

The waitress, a college-age girl with red shorts and a white polo shirt that said Juilerettes, took their order, whitefish sandwiches with coleslaw and freshly squeezed lemonade.

"Now then," Burr said. "I think we need to find the boy."

"Boy?"

"The son. Jason," Burr said.

"He's hardly a boy now. It's been six years. He must be at least twenty-three," Jacob said.

"Frank hasn't seen much of him since Claudia died," Burr said.

"Eve and I haven't been able to find him," Jacob said. "He's in the Navy somewhere."

"Then Truax can't find him either," Burr said.

"Don't be so sure," Jacob said.

"I think we need to find him," Burr said.

"Do we?"

"He was there," Burr said. "He could help us."

"He could also hurt us," Jacob said.

"I guess we'll find out if Truax knows where Jason is when we get his witness list. I can't figure out what else he might have," Burr said.

"How about a motive?" Jacob said.

"As in?"

"As in affair," Jacob said.

Burr looked away from Jacob. The rain ran down the windows in ever so many tiny rivers.

The next evening Burr and Jacob took the reliable but rusty Vista Cruise, north on US-31 from Petoskey, past Crooked Lake. They turned east on Brutus Road, then north on a two-track about a quarter of a mile. Burr pulled off at a wide spot, rolled down the window and turned off the engine. He could hear the Maple River to his right. Burr thought it sounded like whispering.

They wiggled into their waders. Burr wrapped his fishing vest around him, clipping a pencil light to his vest, then clipping another to the bill of his hat

They walked to the river, carrying their rods by the butt with the business end pointing behind them. The hatch was on, the Hexagenia Limbata, the giant mayfly, the fly that made fools of the trout, even the smart, old trout. The truly big ones. After dark, the big fish came out after the giant mayflies. Browns. Big brown trout. They would get greedy and careless. Jacob's dream was to fish a Hex hatch. Burr said he could make Jacob's dream come true, but Burr wanted something for it.

"We fish the slurps," Burr said. "You probably won't be able to see where you're fishing. Where you hear a fish rise, they make a big drinking noise, a slurp. These are big fish and big bugs. You'll hear them. And you don't have to be too precise with your casts.

The hatch, if there was a hatch, came off at night, only at night, only after 10 p.m., sometimes as late as 1 a.m. You had to wait for the hatch. Sometimes it came. Sometimes it didn't. There were better rivers for Hex than the Maple. The Au Sable, the Manistee, the Pere Marquette. The Maple was marginal, but it was close to Harbor Springs and hardly anybody knew about it. But there was a Hex hatch here on the Maple.

Jacob was a master of legal research and appellate briefs, but Burr didn't need legal research now, he needed some work out of the office, an investigation.

They reached thebank of the river.

"So Jacob, I take you Hex fishing, and you check the motels in Petoskey. See if Frank and Sarah had an affair before Claudia died. Because if they did and Truax knows, we're in trouble," Burr said.

"I'm not doing it," Jacob said.

"I already talked with the hygienist who worked for Frank. She wouldn't say much other than she didn't see any monkey business," Burr said. "I saw Frank this afternoon, and he says he wasn't romantically involved with Sarah until after Claudia died. But he wasn't all that convincing."

In the dark, Burr heard Jacob suck on a joint, then hiss as he exhaled. "If you can't trust your client, you have no chance," Jacob said.

"No motel, no Hex hatch," Burr said.

"We're here now," Jacob said.

"We're at the river, not the hex hatch," Burr said. He stood up and started back to the Vista Cruiser.

Two days after the highly successful night fishing (Jacob agreed to Burr's request), Burr met Jacob at Pirate Golf which was nestled on US-31, just outside Petoskey. It straddled Tannery Creek, which once had a fine run of steelhead in the spring. Predictably and unfortunately, the accoutrements of the miniature golf course had pretty much ruined the steelhead run.

"Sleuthing is a waste of my time, as is this silly miniature golf." Jacob said.

"It's good to do something while we talk," Burr said. He had just scored a hole in one on the tenth hole, a tricky affair that was best played through a tunnel of flowing water. He thought better of boasting about his (minor) triumph and satisfied himself by tossing and catching his golf ball repeatedly.

"I am not a private detective,' Jacob said.

Burr had just finished meeting with Mrs. Larsen, a particularly unbecoming woman who had the distinction of being Frank's neighbor on the driveway side of his house. Mrs. Larsen was vague, in a troubling way. Burr didn't think she had told all she knew, but he couldn't get anything definite out of her. "I can't find anybody or anything that points to an affair," he said. "I was hoping you'd turn something up."

"What I turned up is nothing," Jacob said. "I checked all the motels within twenty miles of Petoskey. Why don't we try to get Truax thrown out? For assault with a deadly weapon."

"There were no witnesses," Burr said, "and all he did was point it at me."

"Frank didn't have a witness either," Jacob said. "Actually he did, but she's dead. And his fingerprints were all over the gun."

"The gun?" Burr said.

"They must have been all over it," Jacob said.

"The gun." Burr aimed the putter, now an imaginary deer rifle, at Jacob. He pointed it right at his nose.

"I suppose I could check some more," Jacob said. "Stop pointing that silly putter at me."

"The gun." Burr kept it pointed at Jacob's nose. Burr pulled the imaginary trigger on the putter. "Bang," he said.

"Stop it. All I said was it might be worth a try. He did point it at you after all," Jacob said. "Truax, that is."

"Where's the gun?" Burr asked.

"I presume it's still in his office, back in the gun cabinet," Jacob said.

"Not that gun," Burr said. "The gun that killed Claudia. Where's that gun?" He twirled the putter like a baton.

CHAPTER SIXTEEN

Burr ended the round after the tenth hole (heartily endorsed by Jacob) and drove directly to the jail.

"Where's the gun that killed Claudia?" he asked.

"I don't know," Frank said.

"My point exactly," Burr said, pacing, circling clockwise, around and around the table where Frank sat. Burr stopped behind Frank who swiveled his whole body to look at him, like an owl with a stiff neck. "Where is the gun?" Burr said. "There's no murder weapon. Who's to say the gun wasn't defective, broken?" Burr resumed his pacing, still clockwise.

"It wasn't," Frank said.

"How do you know? It might have been," Burr said.

"I was careless," Frank said.

"Were you?" Burr asked. What if the safety was broken? Or the extractors? Or the trigger?"

"The gun was fine," Frank said.

"How do you know?"

"It was fine when Trevor borrowed it," Frank said.

"Trevor?"

"I lent it to him," Frank said.

"You lent it to whom?"

"Trevor. Trevor Farr," Frank said. "That's why I was cleaning it. He brought it back and I was cleaning it. Deer season was over."

"When did you lend it to him?

"I don't remember," Frank said. "I shot my deer a week into the season. Trevor said his rifle wasn't working right, so I lent him mine."

"You never told me any of this," Burr said. He stopped pacing.

"I didn't think it was important," Frank said.

"You lent it to Trevor Farr," Burr said.

"I already said that," Frank said.

"Well, that's it, then," Burr said.

"What?"

"Was that the rifle that killed Claudia?"

"Yes," Frank said.

"So where is it?"

"I don't know." Frank said. "I already said I don't know. I never saw it after the night Claudia died."

Burr started pacing again. "Frank, if you killed a deer seven days into gun season, which would be the 22nd of November, why did you wait until the 18th of December, which is almost three weeks later, to clean your gun?"

"I already told you," Frank said. "Because Trevor borrowed it from me."

Burr stopped pacing. "And?"

"And then he brought it back," Frank said. "It was dirty, and there was rust on the barrel. Trevor doesn't really take very good care of things. So I figured I better clean it."

"So you took the gun downstairs?"

"No, Trevor brought it back after Thanksgiving, and he left it in the garage. I went out to the garage and got it."

"You left it in the garage all that time?" Burr asked.

"Yes," Frank said.

"Why would you do that?"

"I don't know. I didn't think about it. I guess I left it there to remind me to clean it. If it was in the basement, I thought I might forget. It was a busy time of year."

"Did you check to see if it was empty?" Burr asked.

"No," Frank said. "I didn't pay attention to it."

"So, it could have been loaded?"

"I suppose," Frank said.

"What about the clip?"

"The clip was still in the gun. But I took it out in the basement," Frank said. "That's when I racked the gun."

"Start at the begginning," Burr said.

"We were decorating the tree, and Claudia was bitching at me. So I thought I'd go clean the gun. Anything to get away from her."

"So you got the gun out of the garage and went downstairs," Burr said. "And then she came to get you."

"Yes," Frank said.

"You didn't tell me you lent the gun to someone," Burr said.

"I didn't think it was important," Frank said again.

"What happened to the gun?" Burr asked. He started pacing again, this time counterclockwise.

"I don't know," Frank said. "I never saw it again."

"What kind of gun was it?" Burr asked.

"A Field and Jones. Bolt," Frank said.

"What model?" Burr asked.

"Model?" Frank asked. I think it was a Model 92. Would you stop that pacing?"

Burr stopped squarely in front of Frank. He opened his mouth as if to speak, thought better of it, and walked (paced, actually) out the door.

Rollie told Burr to meet him at the boat launch at Waukaushaunce Point at dawn the next day. Twenty miles north of Petoskey and just west of the Straits of Mackinac.

When Burr arrived, Rollie was already sitting in his boat. In the first light, Burr saw the abandoned lighthouse at Wankanshaunce Point, its silhouette, and the new light at White Shoal. to the north. Zeke immediately waded into Lake Michigan, actually Sturgeon Bay, took a drink and went for a swim.

"Well, come on then, let's go," Rollie said.

"I can't go with you," Burr said.

"Damned if you can't," Rollie said.

I just want to ask a few questions," Burr said.

"About what?"

"The gun," Burr said.

"What gun?" Rollie said. He pulled on the starting cord and the outboard began to putt in a ragged fashion. Burr smelled the sweetness of the gasoline and the smoke from the exhaust.

"Look, if you come, I can fish four poles," Rollie said. "So if you want to ask me something, you better hop in." Rollie had an old sea nymph, a sixteen footer with a two-cycle, fifteen horse

Evinrude that smoked. Burr thought Rollie had probably put in too much oil in the gas, but the motor looked almost as old as the boat, which looked almost as old as Rollie. At least the lake wasn't rough.

"You can bring your dog," Rollie said. "I'll have you back before lunch." He handed Burr a Labatt from the cooler, the same cooler he had in the shanty. "Have a beer. I like to think of it as liquid grain." Rollie took one and took a long drink. "These bass here, the smallmouth, are in to spawn," he said. "We'll just troll some Rapalas along the shore and see what happens."

Burr popped the Labatt. It had a crisp bite, crisp and hoppy, especially at five in the morning. The sun had broken the horizon now, over the shore and the lake had an orange cast on the gray water, the lake flat.

"Rollie, I really can't go."

"All right, then," said the old man, deflated. "So what gun are we talking about?"

"The gun that killed Claudia, the rifle," Burr said.

"Oh," Rollie said. "That gun. That was a deer rifle, a 30:06."

"Right," Burr said.

"What about it?"

"Why didn't you tell me Trevor Farr borrowed it?" Burr asked.

"You didn't ask," Rollie said.

"Wouldn't you think that was something I might want to know?" Burr asked. "That it might be important."

"I never thought about it," Rollie said. "I can't sit here with this motor running much longer. She'll stall out."

"What about Truax?" he asked.

"He knew about Trevor," Rollie said. The outboard stalled. "Damn," he said. "I told you that was going to happen."

"How do you know that Truax knows Trevor borrowed the gun?" Burr asked.

"He asked me about it," Rollie said.

"He didn't ask you at the preliminary exam," Burr said.

"That's right. He asked me before the preliminary exam. When he interviewed me," Rollie said.

Truax knew but didn't want me to know, Burr thought. He didn't remember seeing anything about it in the police report. Just that Frank had brought the gun in from the garage. "What happened to the gun?" Burr asked.

"The gun? Damned if I know," Rollie said again. "What's your point anyway?"

"What if the gun was broken?" Burr asked.

"What if it was? It's still an accident," Rollie said. "Only more so."

"What did you do with the gun?"

"Nothing," Rollie said.

"Do you know what happened to it?"

"Never saw it again," Rollie said.

"Where do you think it is?"

"Damned if I know," Rollie said. He pulled the starting cord again. The outboard staggered back to life. "If I was you, I'd get in this boat. I've got these binoculars here. If the fishing's no good, we'll just run on down and check things out at the nude beach on Sturgeon Bay. Ever been there?"

"No," Burr said.

"Me neither, but you can see real good from the lake," Rollie said. He looked at Burr, pulled on his beer again, then said, "If I was you, I'd have another beer. Beyond that, I'd talk to George Maples. He's the only one I can think of who might know." He shifted the outboard into reverse and motored backwards into the lake.

After leaving the soon-to-be besotted Rollie, Burr made his way to the basement of the Petoskey police station (situated in the bowels of the courthouse), then down a hall with tan cement block walls and a shiny waxed floor. The end of the hall opened on a room that ran at least twenty feet back with a wire mesh cage across the front, fifty feet across. A small, wiry man sat at a metal desk inside the cage, with thick glasses and a flat top.

"I know what's here," Sergeant Maples said. "And that's not here."

"How can you be so sure?" Burr said, standing outside he cage, looking in.

"Because it's my job to be sure," said the policeman.

"Have you ever been wrong?"

"No," said the policeman.

"Not that you know of," Burr said.

"What?"

Nothing," Burr said.

"I don't remember if it was here, but I know it's not here now," said the policeman.

"How can you be so sure?"

"Because, I told you already, it's my job to know what's here," Sergeant Maples said.

"Can I look at your inventory?" Burr said. The good Sergeant was already irritated with him.

"No, you can't," said the policeman. "And even if you could, that's not as important as what's here." The wiry man tapped his temple with his forefinger.

"I see," Burr said. "Sergeant Maples, can I look around?"

"No, you can't. This is all evidence. And no one can touch it but me."

Burr did not have much time to waste. Zeke was in the car, and it was getting hot. "Can you at least tell me how it works?" he asked.

"That I can do," Maples sad. "Say we get some evidence or we confiscate something—like drugs maybe or a gun—it comes to me. I tag it with the case number, make a file for it, put the shelf number in the file and go put it in the shelf. It's on computer now."

"How long?"

"Three years," the Sergeant said.

"Before that," Burr said.

"A log book and index cards."

"Then what happens?"

Sergeant Maples stood up. He began to circle his desk. "Then, when the evidence is called for, the detective, prosecutor, or whoever checks it out. When they're done with it, they bring it back."

"Then what?" Burr said.

"Then what, what?"

"When the case is over," Burr said.

"After two years, say, after all the appeals, if any, maybe shorter, whose ever it was can come claim it. Unless it's drugs, of course," Sergeant Maples said.

"Of course," Burr said. "And if they don't?"

"Then it goes to auction," Maples said.

"Then what?"

"Then it sells or I throw it away. Or I might keep it. If it's any good. You never know. I got this grandfather clock in my den. I still don't know why it didn't go at the auction." The man winked at him.

"And what happened with the gun?"

"That was a long time ago," Maples said.

" How long, would you say?"

"I don't remember that far back anymore," Sergeant Maples said.

"I thought you remembered everything," Burr said.

"That's not what I said," the Sergeant said.

"Oh, I thought it was," Burr said.

"No, what I said was, I know everything that's here. I don't know what was here. I forget about it when it leaves."

"I see," Burr said, who, again, didn't.

"I only have room for so much in my head. That's how I keep from getting confused," Maples said.

"Do you remember about the gun?"

Sergeant Maples opened the wire door, and stood face to face to Burr. "Now what did I just say?" Sergeant Maples said.

"Would there be a record?"

"There would be, but the old ones were paper and they got ruined in the flood," Sergeant Maples said.

"The flood?"

"Well, not exactly a flood, but it got pretty wet when the sprinklers turned on," Maples said.

Burr closed his eyes, took a step back, and exhaled. "Sergeant Maples, it would be very helpful if I could locate the gun that killed Mrs. Tavohnen. Do you have any idea where it might be?"

"No," the Sergeant said.

"What probably happened?" Burr asked.

"Probably?" Maples' eyebrows peered over the top of his glasses. Burr saw that they were steely, like the cage. "Well, somebody probably brought it in here. Then it would have gone out for the inquest, if they'd wanted it. Then it would have come back here. After that, it would have gone to Frank, and if he didn't get it, we'd auction it."

"Is that what happened?"

"You know, I don't know," Maples said. "See, we all thought it was an accident, so we didn't pay any attention to it."

"Frank says he never saw it again," Burr said.

"That don't surprise me. Who would want the gun that killed their wife? It probably went to auction."

"How can I find out?"

"You can't," Sergeant Maples said. He walked past Burr with nary a look.

CHAPTER SEVENTEEN

After meeting with George Maples, Burr called Eve in East Lansing and asked her to find someone who was an expert on Field and Jones firearms. Three weeks later she did. Burr drove down from Harbor Springs to Ionia, about two hundred miles south. At one time Ionia had been a boomtown, but when the timber played out and the freeway bypassed Ionia, the little town stayed little. Except for the prison, the county courthouse, and Deutsch Arms, Ionia was past tense. Deutsch Arms was the biggest gun store in the state, which Burr thought was somewhat out of place with the proximity to the prison.

A large woman led him through the gun shop, actually an old house on Main Street near the Grand River. She led him past the shotguns and the rifles, all of which could be touched, picked up and aimed, not a gun lock anywhere, the pistols also out in the open. She turned to him and stuck her hand at him. It was chubby and her fingernails were dirty. Her hand felt mushy. "I'm Frieda. Frieda Deutsch," she said.

"My name is Burr Lafayette."

"Ooh, a Frenchman," she said.

"Yes," he said, embarrassed, which was unusual for Burr. He looked down at his feet.

"Is there something I can help you with?" she asked.

"My assistant said you were an expert on Field and Jones firearms," he said to his feet.

"I've worked in this gun shop for thirty-three years," she said. "Owned it for the last five. Since my father died."

"So you're familiar with the Field and Jones 30:06. The Model 92 bolt action," Burr said, still looking at his feet. He thought it best not to address the loss of her father.

"I've been the gunsmith here for the last seventeen years. Smithette, actually." She paused. "That's a joke."

"Of course it is," Burr said, looking up from his feet, having decided that if he was going to find out anything about the gun, he would have to make eye contact.

Frieda smiled at him through her tan, tan with rings where the fat had blocked out the sun. Reading glasses hung around her neck on a silver chain. "You're awfully cute," she said.

Burr blushed and once more abandoned eye contact.

"Don't be shy," she said, "I'm too fat for the likes of you."

Burr struggled to get on point. "Does the Model 92 ever malfunction?" He looked up, once and for all, and followed the bloated gunsmith, who had set off on foot. They passed through a curtain and entered the workshop. She turned sideways, brushed both sides as she passed through. He didn't think she was any thinner sideways than front-to-back. She turned on the lights, four single bulbs, all bare.

"I hate fluorescent," she said. "It makes the guns look sick."

Off to the right, a firing range, like a single lane in a bowling alley, had been added on to the back of the house.

Frieda Deutsch rummaged around in a closet. At last, she came out with a rifle. She laid the rifle on a workbench and sat before it on a stool. Her brown stretch pants covered the seat of the stool, and, to Burr, it looked like she was sitting directly on its legs. Burr smelled metal shavings and the sweet smell of gun oil.

"This is it. The Model 92," Frieda said. "Are you familiar with it?"

"No," Burr said.

"I'm going to keep this simple and not fool around with the clip," she said. "Now, watch this." Frieda Deutsch pulled the bolt back and opened the chamber. She loaded a shell in the chamber and closed it. Then she pulled the bolt back ever so slightly. "See how the extractors work. They're like fingers. They grab the rim of the shell casing and pull it out."

Burr looked down at the top of the gun. He saw the jaws of the extractors on the rim of the shell casing. She pulled the bolt all the way back. The shell flipped out of the gun and rang against the floor.

"If the extractors don't work right, they don't grab the shell." She put on her reading glasses and worked on the gun with the tiniest of screwdrivers. She put another shell in the chamber and racked the gun. The shell didn't come out. She racked it again. No shell. "The chamber is supposed to be empty, but it's not."

Burr, feeling encouraged in a dark sort of way, said, "Has this ever happened?"

"Once in a great while," said the gunsmith.

"Have you ever seen it happen?" Burr asked.

"Once," she said. "Maybe twice. That's why I quit selling them." Frieda Deutsch shouldered the rifle and aimed at a target at the far end of the firing range. "I racked this gun twice, so it's supposed to be empty. Move over so I don't ring your ears." She fired at the target, a man's head, which she pierced through the left eye.

Burr drove back to Harbor Springs in Stewart's Vista Cruiser, which he feared he was getting used to. He arrived just ahead of the rain, resolved to pursue the missing and (hopefully) defective gun issue the next morning.

Burr woke up at 3 a.m. The rain tapped on the deck above his head. He watched a drop form on the overhead, above his eye. The drip ran down the curve of the desk and fell into the saucepan underneath the leak.

Suzanne lay next to him in the bunk in the aft cabin. She had appeared after midnight. They had made love, slowly, then fallen asleep.

The bunk, though double, was narrower than a queen-size bed. Suzanne slept as she always slept after they had made love, separate and apart from him, not touching. She slept with her jaw clenched, her mouth cast and her lips set together. She always slept this way, at least with him. He didn't know if he loved her. He didn't know if she loved him. He didn't know if she loved him last time. He had loved her the last time, or thought he had, which of course, had been the problem.

Another drop formed over Burr's head. He watched it run its course, and, finding this comforting, he fell asleep.

A blue pickup perched on a lift, and a man, who Burr assumed to be Trevor Farr, stood under it, cutting off a muffler with a torch. Burr stood in the sun on the concrete driveway, just outside the garage. The rain had blown though in the night followed by clear skies and seventy degrees. Burr saw that the man was tall enough that, underneath the truck, even with the lift all the way up, a shiny steel tube rising erect from the concrete floor, he had to stoop at the shoulders. He wore safety goggles but no mask. He had cut his shirt off at the shoulders, showing muscled arms. His shirt did not quite reach his waist. No belt. No fat.

When Farr saw Burr, he stood upright and bumped his head on the bumper. "Damn," Farr said.

He dropped the torch which flamed orange on the floor, the hose writhing like a snake held by its neck. He picked up the torch, still lit, and turned it off. Burr saw that Farr had one eyebrow that stretched across his forehead and his ears stuck out. He rubbed his head, bald on top, looked at his fingers. They were smeared with blood. "Damn," he said again. .He bent from the waist, bowing his head to Burr who stepped back. "Do I need stitches?"

"I don't think so," Burr said, "but it's pretty bloody."

"That's all right," Farr said. He wiped his head with an oily rag. "What do you want?"

"I'm trying to find out about the gun you borrowed from Frank Tavohnen," Burr said. "The deer rifle."

"30:06," Farr said.

"You borrowed it from Frank?" Burr asked.

"Right," Farr said.

"Can you tell me about it?"

"What's this got to do with me?" Farr said. He rubbed the top of his head. With the safety glasses on his forehead, he looked like he had four eyes.

"I'm trying to help Frank," Burr said. "I'm his lawyer," Burr said.

The big man, at least six foot seven, looked at the rag and pushed his left index finger into the bloody part. "Well, see, my rifle broke. The firing pin. I had this big buck, maybe ten points, coming to my bait pile. I shot, but nothing happened. I was really pissed off. I knew Frank had already got his, so I asked him if I could borrow his gun."

"And?"

"So I borrowed it and then I took it back," Farr said.

Burr smelled the sweetness of the acetylene, underneath the smell of the oil and burned metal. Farr sniffed. "Damn, it all, if I didn't leave that gas on at the tank. Shit, don't smoke or nothin' until I get this gas out of here." He walked to a green tank, next to the wall, and turned the faucet clockwise. Then he flipped a switch and a floor fan started to whine,

"When did you take the gun back?" Burr asked.

"Couple days later," Farr said.

"When exactly?"

"I don't know," Farr said. He shifted his weight from one leg to the other. "Couple days later. What difference does it make? I don't know. Less than a week later. I know that."

"What did Frank say?"

"Nothin'," Farr said. "He wasn't there."

"What did you do?"

"Left it in the garage, next to the snowblower," he said.

"Did you clear the chamber?"

"'Course I did. You think I'm stupid?" Farr said. "Hey, you trying to incriminate me? You think it was me?" Farr shifted his weight again.

"No, no, of course not," Burr said. "What was the weather like that day? The last day you went hunting."

"Rain, then snow. I remember that. 'Cause this snowflake got in my eye. That's how I missed."

"Did you clean the gun?"

"'Course I did," Farr said.

"At home?"

"Hell, no. I wiped her down good, soon as I got back to the truck," Farr said.

"Did the gun work all right?"

"Work? Worked fine," Farr said. "Except the scope might be off."

"Did you clear the chamber?"

"I already said I did," Farr said.

"Where did you get the bullets?" Burr asked.

"Frank gave me the bullets and the clip," Farr said.

"What time was it, when you quit hunting that day?"

"I don't know," Farr said. "Dark thirty. That late in the season, those deer don't move until dark."

"Did you drop the gun?"

"No," Farr said.

"Get it wet?"

"Yeah, but I wiped it off," Farr said.

"Was it muddy?"

"Damn straight, it was muddy with all that rain and snow and the ground not frozen."

"No, I mean the gun," Burr said. He needed to find out all he could without pushing Farr too far. "Was the gun muddy?"

"Yeah, but like I said, I wiped it off," Farr said.

"What about the clip?"

"The clip?" Farr asked.

"Did you take it out?"

"You know, I'm done talking with you. 'Cause I got to deliver this truck in one half hour, and I am not going to make it if I talk one minute more."

"Yes, well, I appreciate that Mr. Farr, but Frank has a lot at stake." Burr pushed the dirt on the concrete floor into a pile. "The rest of his life."

"Well, he should have thought about that before that gun went off," Farr said.

"You must have been pretty good friends," Burr said. "He did lend you his deer rifle."

"I haven't heard from him since he left. So we can't be that good of friends," Farr said, turning back to the truck.

"I am trying to help Frank," Burr said. "Is there anything you remember? Anything wrong with that rifle?"

"I suspect the scope was off. He told me he had it sighted in, but I don't know," Farr said.

"Anything else? Did it stick when you racked it?"

"No, not really," Farr said. "Maybe a little."

"Did you drop it?"

"No," Farr said. "I already said I didn't."

"What did you do with the shell in the chamber?"

"I racked it out," Farr said, shifting his weight again.

"What about the next one?" Burr asked, trying to be a bit careful with Farr.

"What next one?"

"The next shell," Burr said.

The big man looked at him. "I took the clip off. Because the next shell would rack in when the empty racked out. That's what bolt actions do."

"What then?" Burr asked.

"What do you mean, what then?"

"With the gun and the clip," Burr said.

"I took it back to Frank's," Farr said.

"What did you do with the clip?" Burr asked.

"How should I know? It's been seven, eight years," Farr said.

"Almost seven," Burr said. "Did you put the clip back in the gun when you returned it?"

"What do I want with the clip? It won't fit my gun," Farr said.

"What about the shell, the shell you racked out?" Burr asked.

Farr turned his back on Burr, turned the tank back on, then lit the torch. Burr saw the blue flame with the orange at the edge and watched Farr pull his safety goggles back down and cut the metal with the torch.

That evening Burr sat in Kismet's galley sipping a glass of Cabernet, alone again, except for Zeke, snoring on the quarter berth across from him. The alcohol stove flamed blue underneath the baked beans in the saucepan. He always enjoyed a hearty Cabernet with his baked beans.

Burr didn't believe Farr's story, not all of it. He didn't really believe that Farr remembered exactly what happened, and if he did remember, Burr didn't think Farr had told him everything. If he could prove that Farr had returned the gun with a shell in the chamber and that the extractors didn't work right, then he could prove it was an accident. A careless friend. A defective gun. But a very poor witness.

~

Jacob met Burr at Kismet the next morning. Jacob stepped aboard and sat down in the cockpit under a bright morning sun. Burr thought his friend looked a bit queasy.

As much as Jacob loved flyfishing, which involved standing in the water, he hated all boats. Burr had seen him seasick at the dock.

"I have decided that we should stop looking for the gun," Burr said.

"Why?" Jacob said.

"Because we don't need it," Burr said.

"Why?"

"Because if we find the gun," Burr said, "there might not be anything wrong with it. This way no one knows for sure."

"What if Truax finds it?" Jacob asked. He had gone pale but probably not because of their discussion about the gun.

"He doesn't want to find it either."

"Why not?" Jacob asked.

"Because it might be defective," Burr said.

Jacob leaned over the side and threw up.

CHAPTER EIGHTEEN

One week later Truax presented Burr with the prosecution's witness list. The cop, the undertaker and the laser lady. No surprises there. Friends, neighbors, assorted co-workers, including the baseball coach. Mrs. Larsen, the neighbor. Burr had interviewed them all and thought none of them particularly damning, with the possible exception of the evidentiary nature of the laser lady's testimony.

There was no one on the witness list that could be remotely connected with the missing and (hopefully) misfiring gun and, more importantly, no one who Burr thought could persuasively testify to motive-—an affair—what Burr considered to be the critical weakness in the charge against Frank.

Burr then retreated to East Lansing and Detroit, failing miserably in his attempt to persuade Pattengill to reduce his fee, succeeding wildly with Zeke-the-boy at a Tiger's game, the caramel corn and Fudgesicles being the chief attraction.

As to his own witness list, Farr was easy to leave off. He included Sergeant Maples, the less than helpful keeper of the evidence cage, as well as Pattengill (to confound Truax), agonized over the inclusion of Frieda Deutsch, the heavy-set gunsmith. Suzanne wanted to leave Frieda Deutsch off the witness list and call her as a surprise witness. Despite Suzanne's exhortations to the contrary, Burr decided to play it straight up.

Just before dawn on September 1st, the two of them, Burr and Zeke-the-dog, hid in corn stubble two miles from Cross Village in a field he had found two days before. Chopped corn for dairy cattle. He smelled the sweet smell of the manure where the cows had been let in to graze. He didn't think he had laid in any, but it was hard to tell in the dark.

Burr had laid cornstalks over Zeke, not enough to cover him, but enough to break up his profile. Burr had covered himself as well, facing west, downwind, just outside the decoys. He heard the geese in the distance, like dogs barking, getting up off Wycamp Lake. Then he saw them in the distance, seven or eight, a family group. Then he heard a voice.

"Burr, Burr," Jacob said, "Where are you?"

"What? Get down and be quiet," Burr said.

'I've got to talk to you," Jacob said.

"Not now," Burr said.

"Now," Jacob said.

Jacob, clearly overdressed for goose hunting, found him. He looked down at him in the chopped corn. Burr smelled the manure again. Jacob waved his arms up and down from his sides.

"Damn it, Jacob. You'll scare the birds."

"That was my intention," he said.

"Whatever it is, it could have waited," Burr said.

"No, it couldn't," Jacob said.

"You have not only confused and annoyed me, but I might add, you have disappointed Zeke mightily," Burr said.

"I found them out," Jacob said.

"What?"

"I found them out," he said again.

"Who?"

"What is this?" Jacob lifted his left foot. He had brown leather loafers. Italian. Burr admired Jacob's taste in shoes.

"That is cow shit," Burr said.

"Damn it all," Jacob said. "You are hunting in the midst of cow droppings."

"The geese like the chopped corn. They like the cow shit, too."

"Damn it, Burr," Jacob said, picking up a cornstalk.

"Damn what?"

"Damn you and all your follies. Damn your client. And damn Suzanne," Jacob said. He began waving his arms again, cornstalk in one hand.

"Suzanne?"

"She must have known all along," Jacob said.

"Known what?"

Burr saw the geese as they cleared the tree line, watched them set their wings and glide in, despite the man waving his arms. Jacob now waved on one foot. He stopped and began scraping his shoe with a cornstalk. "Sensible Rates. I found them at Sensible Rates," he said.

"What?"

"That's what the sign says on the road, underneath the name, Indian River Cabins," Jacob said.

Burr lifted his shotgun, pointed it at the lead bird. Jacob had stopped waving, and the birds were still coming in. They got within thirty-five yards, wings set, then veered to the south. He swung through the lead bird but didn't fire. Zeke had held as long as he could and ran after them.

"You may as well have shot," Jacob said.

"I didn't want to kill one that badly," Burr said, lighting a cigarette, the first of the new season.

Jacob threw away the cornstalk. "They were clever. Clever as they could be. Just outside the village of Indian River," Jacob said. "They trysted there. For almost a year."

Burr understood now. He felt his ears blaze, turning red. He spit out the cigarette and ground it in under his boot heel. "Goddamn it," he said. "Zeke, come."

Burr was mad. No, he was furious. Shocked, but not surprised, not really. Maybe that's what those other names were all about. Maybe Truax knew, too. He should have known. He had suspected it. He sighed and let all his air out. When he took a breath, he smelled the silage and the manure, green and sweet. Damn it, he thought. I should have known. I did know. "How many?" he asked.

"What?"

"How many did you check? Motels," Burr said.

"One hundred and sixty two," Jacob said.

"How did you find out?"

"I was having lunch in Indian River, at Vivios. The manicotti is quite good. I was thinking, if they were having an affair, they would be smart enough not to stay in Petoskey. Plus I had already checked all of the motels in Petoskey and Harbor Springs. So they'd go out of town. But not too far. I'd already tried Pellston, and I thought Charlevoix would be too expensive for a dentist who wasn't doing so well. Indian River is only half an hour from Petoskey, so why not?"

"I tried three other motels, then I saw the sign," Jacob said. " 'Sensible Rates.' So I turned left, followed the sign. Cabins, six of them. Old ones. Square. Wood siding, white with blue trim."

"Are you sure?"

"Quite," Jacob said.

"How?"

"The motelier," Jacob said. "If you could call him that."

"Motelier?"

"Actually it was his wife," Jacob said. "She didn't remember Frank specifically. She remembered an older, middle-aged man and a younger woman. Not that they hadn't ever seen that before. She remembered two cars. That always gives them away. That's what she said. That plus cash. The motelier kept trying to silence her, his wife. I think he liked the idea. She would have none of it. She said it went on for almost a year, once, twice a week. Not for very long. No overnights. Then it stopped."

"Stopped?"

"Just like that," Jacob said. He snapped his fingers, but they didn't snap. He looked at them like a lighter that doesn't light.

"When?"

"The summer after Claudia was killed," Jacob said.

Just before they moved," Burr said.

"Exactly," Jacob said.

"How do you know for sure?"

"I looked in one of the rooms," Jacob said. "Perfect for an affair on a shoestring budget. Vintage 1960. Perfect. One room with a bathroom. No tub. A shower stall, stained with rust. Iron from the water, I presume. Bedspread with fringe. Kitchenette. Hot plate. No microwave."

"Mini bar?" Burr said.

"The mini bar concept has not come to Sensible Rates," Jacob said.

"Did they have records?"

"Mercifully, no. Something about the IRS, I expect," Jacob said.

"That doesn't prove anything," Burr said.

"The old girl followed Frank home," Jacob said.

"She what?"

"She followed him home one night," Jacob said.

"She didn't," Burr said.

"She did. She was going to tell Claudia, but her husband wouldn't let her."

"What's her name?"

"Her name? Her name is Zolkowski. Berdette Zolkowski," Jacob said.

"She's not on Truax's witness list," Burr said. "Do you think he has finally connected the dots?"

"Not unless that's what those other names are about," Jacob said.

Burr paid a visit to Frank as soon as the jail opened, an odd choice of words he thought as jails were quite obviously very closed.

"It's none of your business," Frank said.

"It is now," Burr said.

"How did you find out?"

"Does it matter?" Burr asked.

"I guess not," Frank said.

"I asked you, Frank," Burr said. "I pleaded with you. You lied to me. How can I help you if you lie to me?"

"I don't know," Frank said.

Burr saw Frank sweat, saw his wet armpits, the orange jumpsuit sticking to him.

"That doesn't mean I killed her," Frank said.

"You did kill her," Burr said.

"Not on purpose," Frank said.

Burr opened his tin of Altoids and took four. He didn't offer any to Frank.

"It was an accident. I swear it was," Frank said.

"Right." Burr sneezed.

"Bless you," Frank said. "I love Sarah. I stopped loving Claudia years ago. Our marriage was dead. That doesn't mean I murdered her."

"No," Burr said. "It just looks like it."

"It doesn't if nobody knows," Frank said.

"If I know, Truax either knows or he can find out," Burr said. "Why didn't you tell me?"

"Sarah said you wouldn't help us if you knew."

"Does Suzanne know?" Burr said.

"No," Frank said.

Burr sneezed again.

Harbor Springs, the next afternoon. The Saturday of Labor Day Weekend. Seventy-five and sunny. A high-pressure system and a brisk fifteen-knot wind from the north. Burr thought it a perfect day for a sail. The Fourth of July mob was long gone, victims of the teachers union who, for their own reasons, insisted on starting school the last week of August. Burr and Suzanne were going for a sail as soon as they finished their project, and as soon as Burr had the answer to one question.

A cormorant had perched on *Kismet*'s wind vane since July. Daily. Nothing Burr had done could keep it off. He had hoisted a plastic owl to the top of the mast. He shot at it with a BB gun until he had been threatened with arrest for harassing a federally protected bird. Finally, the wind vane sheered, which caused the cormorant to relocate but spoiled locating the wind direction. Suzanne stood on the deck in the bosun's chair about to be on her way to the top of the mast.

"Is this a safe thing to do?" Suzanne said, standing on the deck of *Kismet*.

"Perfectly," Burr said.

"It is not safe," Suzanne said. "It would be safe if you had someone to tail the halyard."

"I've got it through the jam cleat. Nothing will go wrong. The jib halyard is your safety line." Burr wound the main halyard around the winch, snapped in the winch handle and began grinding. He turned the winch handle two more cranks and Suzanne was off her feet.

Burr had clipped a safety line around her waist and tied it to the jib halyard, which he hauled up without tension, along with her dead weight on the main halyard. She crossed her legs at the ankles around the mast until Burr pulled her to the first spreaders. She let go with her legs and he hauled her up farther. *Kismet* had a wooden spar, laminated fir, with three sets of spreaders. Wispy at the top, the mast would only hold a woman, child, or perhaps a jockey, someone who weighed less than one-hundred thirty pounds.

He ground the winch until she was shoulder high with the top of the mast. He cleated off the halyard and sent up the new wind vane and the tools in a canvas bag on the spinnaker halyard. Suzanne unbolted the old vane and bolted the new one on.

Burr lifted the jam cleat and let the halyard play through his hands around the winch, keeping four turns on it. She slid slowly down the mast, past the top spreaders. She dangled there reaching for the mast with her shoes. Burr locked down the jam cleat and tied off the halyard. Suzanne dangled thirty feet above the deck, looked down at Burr.

"Suzanne, I was wondering," Burr said.

"Don't wonder about anything until I'm on the deck," she said.

Suzanne, I was wondering," Burr said.

"Yes," she said. "What is it?"

"I was wondering how long you had known about Frank and Sarah."

"Known what?"

"Oh, you know," he said. "Their affair."

"What affair?"

"Suzanne, you are in no position to be cute."

"Let me down, please," she said.

"Suzanne, you are perfectly safe up there." The wind had blown her hair into her mouth and she didn't dare let go of the halyard to take it out. He looked up at her as she tried to spit the hair out of her mouth. This was the first time Burr had ever seen Suzanne lose her composure.

"Suzanne, I am greatly disappointed in you," he said.

"In me?"

"Yes," he said.

"What for?"

"Yesterday I learned what I suspected all along," Burr said.

"What? For God's sake, what?"

"That Frank and Sarah were having an affair," Burr said. "Before Claudia was killed."

"Please let me down," she said, begging really.

"You're her sister," Burr said. "She never told you? You never found out?"

"No, she never told me," Suzanne said.

"You're her sister," Burr said. "You must have known."

"If I'd known, I'd have told you," she said. "You'd have to know that to defend Frank."

"Would I?" Burr asked. "Or is that why you hired me?" Burr said.

"What do you mean?"

"Because I wouldn't know? Because I'm not from here. Because I can be a bit gullible around you," Burr said.

"Burr, I love you."

"Right," he said.

"Burr, I didn't know. I swear."

"Jacob found out. Sensible Rates in Indian River," he said.

"I don't believe it," Suzanne said.

"Believe it," he said.

"How can you be sure?"

"Frank admitted it," he said.

"We'll just have to figure out what to do," Suzanne said.

"We?"

"Yes, we. I swear I didn't know," Suzanne said.

"Promise?"

"Yes," she said.

"Cross your heart," Burr said.

Suzanne crossed her heart. Burr lowered her to the deck. She climbed out of the bosun's chair, disappeared down below, and emerged with her carry-on bag. She slapped him and left.

After Suzanne's abrupt but not unexpected departure, Burr decided to go for a sail anyway, himself and Zeke. He motored past the moored boats then turned back to the harbor into the wind. He set the staysail and mizzen, came back around, killed the engine and made for Harbor Point on a broad reach. The wind had freshened to about twenty knots, whitecaps on the bay. At Harbor Point, Burr hardened up, and headed out into Lake Michigan now on a beam reach, *Kismet* making six knots due west. Burr thought she seemed a bit sluggish, but then he hadn't put up the main, preferring to sail on staysail and mizzen when single handing.

Perhaps, he thought, Suzanne hadn't known. It was possible. Sarah might not have told Suzanne everything, especially if she thought Suzanne wouldn't ask for Burr's help if Suzanne had known there had been an affair. But it did seem a bit farfetched that Suzanne would not know, even to Burr, who, though smitten, was doing his best to remain objective.

Five miles out, Burr tried to come about, but *Kismet* would not respond. She was dead in the water. He looked down below. The cabin was full of water, over the floorboards and halfway up the bunks. "That's why there's no steerage, Zeke. We're sinking." Burr turned on the bilge pump, but it couldn't keep up. He climbed down below, water up to his shins, and reached for the VHF radio. "Charlevoix Coast Guard. Charlevoix Coast Guard. Charlevoix Coast Guard. This is the sailing vessel *Kismet*. WT 6948. Five miles north of Harbor Point. We are taking on water and require immediate assistance." No response. Burr waited one minute. "Charlevoix Coast Guard. Charlevoix Coast Guard. This is the sailing vessel *Kismet*. WT 6948. Five miles north of Harbor Point. We are taking on water and require immediate assistance." Still no response. He waited another minute. He would have to get off *Kismet* soon, figure out what to do with Zeke, who surely could swim, but for how long? "Charlevoix Coast Guard. Charlevoix Coast Guard. Charlevoix…"

"Sailing vessel *Kismet*. This is the Charlevoix Coast Guard."

"Thank God," Burr said into the microphone. "Charlevoix Coast Guard, this is the sailing vessel *Kismet*. We are taking on water and require immediate assistance."

No response. Then static. *Kismet* was settling. Burr climbed out into the cockpit, stretched the cord from the radio.

"*Kismet*. What is the condition of your vessel?"

"Charlevoix Coast Guard, we are sinking. Estimate twenty minutes."

"*Kismet*. How many are in your party?"

"Charlevoix Coast Guard. One person. One dog."

"*Kismet*. Stand by on Channel 68. We will . . ."

The radio went dead. "Damn it, Zeke," Burr said. He thought the water must have shorted out the electrical system. Burr looked over the side and saw that *Kismet* had about a foot of freeboard left. Then she would sink. Gone forever in two hundred feet of water. How could this have happened? Did she blow a seam?

Burr pulled the inflatable life raft from the lazerette. He attached the CO_2 cartridge and the raft inflated. "At least we won't drown," he said. Burr reached back down into the cabin and turned off the power. Then he climbed down into the cabin, now safe from electrocution. He sloshed in waist-deep water, retrieved his files. In spite of Burr's protestations, Eve had insisted on storing them in plastic bags. Then he pried up the floorboards and took out what was left of his wine—eleven bottles. He deposited the files, the wine, and all of the life jackets he could find in the raft and slipped it over the side. He climbed in, called Zeke, who had little interest in the raft. He pulled the dog over the side and into the raft. Burr cast off, paddled fifty feet off the stern, far enough away to avoid fouling on *Kismet* when she sank. The wind had blown a bit of a chop on the lake, just enough to make the raft uncomfortable. Here in the deep water, the waves would lengthen out before long, become rollers. If it blew hard enough, they would break, probably over the raft. He hoped he wouldn't be here long enough find out.

Burr rummaged through the bottles and found a bottle of Veuve Cliquot. He decided the champagne was too good to waste. It wasn't chilled, but the water in the bilge wasn't much more than sixty degrees. He thought they'd be here about an hour before the Coast Guard showed up, less if a boat close by had heard his transmission. He thought me might as well pass the time pleasantly.

He had drunk about half the bottle when he determined that the raft was sinking. "Damn it all, Zeke," he said. "Now what are we going to do?" Immediately, he wished he had not drunk the champagne. Burr gathered the files and wine and wrapped them in three of the life jackets. He put on the fourth. He released the signal dye stored in the raft.

Zeke would be the hard part. He couldn't swim for more than ten minutes. They could never make it to shore.

Burr wrestled Zeke into the fifth life jacket, a Mae West, pulling the vest over Zeke's head then tied the sides of the life jacket on Zeke's back. The dog squirmed but did not growl. He clipped on Zeke's leash and held the dog close to him. The raft filled up with water but did not sink. Zeke was clearly scared but not panicky. Burr talked to him softly. They bobbed up and down in the swamped raft. And waited.

Half an hour later, the Coast Guard rescue boat roared up from the south. The helmsman cut back on the throttle, coasted up to them, and put the engine in neutral. Burr, with one hand on Zeke's collar, grabbed the gunwale of the boat with the other. Zeke panicked and clawed at the side of the boat with his front paws. The seaman grabbed Zeke by the collar and pulled him over the side while Burr boosted him up from behind. The dog splashed into the boat, shook himself off, and sank to the cockpit sole.

Burr hooked one leg over the side and the seaman hauled him in. He sat against the hull, soaked, and like Zeke, shivered. Burr was waterlogged, but his files were not. He had managed to rescue the wine, which did amuse the U.S. Coast Guard. They radioed the Irish Boat Shop and deposited the two waterlogged boaters there. Suzanne met them with towels, handed him one, dried off Zeke with the other. Until now, no one had spoken.

"My God, Burr," she said. "What happened?"

"I don't know," he said. "*Kismet* wasn't handling right, wouldn't come about, so I checked down below, and she was filling up. I think she may have burst a seam."

"You could have drowned," she said. "Take your shirt off. You'll never warm up this way."

"I'm all right," Burr said.

"No, you're not. You'll get hypothermia," she said. "Is Zeke all right?"

"Fortunately he's a Labrador Retriever, but he was almost gone," Burr said.

"What about *Kismet*?" Suzanne asked.

"She is gone," Burr said.

Suzanne pulled his shirt over his head and wrapped him in a towel.

Three days after the sinking of *Kismet*, Burr sucked on his finger, the forefinger on his right hand, and drew out the blood. He thought it ironic to be finally, literally, skewered after all of the figurative skewering thus far. He had poked it on one of Stewart's quilting needles. Not Stewart's exactly, but Stewart had filled the Inn with a quilting clinic, and Burr had found the remains. The fall color season hadn't started yet and Stewart would do anything to fill up the Inn and pay the mortgage. The quilters had commandeered the Inn and its conference room for the quilting bee. Upon their departure, Eve booked it as Burr's trial headquarters.

The conference room, a cinder block basement paneled over with tongue and groove, varnished, knotty pine, peeled near the floor. The only sunlight, refracted from the window wells. Burr did not like his new headquarters.

He sat at a folding table, like the tables in a school lunchroom. A black phone, a rotary, rested in front of him, its cord snaking off to the wall. He heard shoes click down the stairs.

"Isn't this a nice office," Eve said.

Burr removed his finger from his mouth. "It is, isn't it," he said with as much sarcasm as he dared.

"I thought I found all the needles," Eve said.

Burr sucked on his finger again, walked to the southernmost window well, and looked up. "One good thing," he said. "At least I can see out. Into the shrubs."

"Since I know how much money we don't have," she said pulling the firm's checkbook out of her shoulder bag, the big black one with rings and the check stubs (the checkbook made Burr nervous), "I took the liberty of finding you a cheap office."

Burr raised his eyebrows, pondering the cost of renting the basement of the Harbour Inn, Stewart's friendship going only so far.

Eve, as if reading his mind, said, "You will be updating Stewart's estate plan."

"I don't know much about estate planning," Burr said.

"Stewart doesn't have much of an estate," Eve said.

"And be careful with Suzanne. It's one thing to be a fool with your personal life. Professionally, it's quite another."

Burr turned from the window. "She didn't know," Burr said.

"So she says."

"She was telling the truth," Burr said.

"Why? Because you hung her from the top of your mast in a bosun's chair."

"Would you lie up there?"

"I hate boats," Eve said.

"That is a personal shortcoming," Burr said.

"If you would not persist in keeping old things like that Jeep and that waterlogged boat, none of this would have happened," Eve said.

"Please don't talk like me," Burr said.

Eve had had enough of Burr and left without a word.

Burr sulked at his metal desk. He missed his Jeep and his boat. Jacob arrived shortly thereafter with news that could not be considered promising.

"District judges don't try murder cases," Burr said.

"That's right, they don't," Jacob said.

"So that settles that," Burr said.

"Not really," Jacob said.

"Why would that be?" Burr asked.

"Because Gillis is not a district judge anymore," Jacob said.

"Why would that be?" he said again.

"Because some ancient on the Court of Appeals had a stroke and Dykehouse, our trial judge, got appointed in his place," Jacob said.

"So Gillis has been promoted from district judge to circuit judge," Burr said. Jacob, wearing a blue pinstripe shirt and charcoal slacks, had clearly switched to his fall wardrobe.

"Now we have Gillis," Jacob said. "And Gillis hates you."

Burr looked at the knife edge crease in Jacob's slacks, then at his own rumpled khakis.

On September 25th, Burr made his annual pilgrimage to Walpole Island to hunt the Canadian duck opener with Victor. This over the protest of all the affected parties (except Zeke-the-dog).

Burr then migrated in reverse to Harbor Springs, the fall color season in full swing. The brilliant red, orange, and yellow from the maples; yellow from the aspen, birch, and beech; red and purple from the oaks. He drove through a stiff northwest wind, the wind blowing the color off the trees.

Part Three

The Trial

There are more things in heaven and earth, Horatio,
than are dreamt of in your philosophy.

Hamlet, Act I, Scene V
—*William Shakespeare*

CHAPTER NINETEEN

MONDAY, OCTOBER 16, 1989 – DAY ONE

"Sir, I refuse to accept another of your challenges," Gillis said.

"Yes, Your Honor," Burr said, "but…"

"Do not interrupt me. You may use your peremptory challenges. Let's see here… Judge Gillis looked down through his reading glasses. He eyes crossed slightly. "I see, yes, here it is. You have one left. Do you wish to use it?"

"No, your Honor," Burr said.

"Fine. Then, Mrs. Horton, you are hereby impaneled."

"Your Honor," Burr said, standing.

"Yes, Mr. Lafayette."

"May I approach the bench?"

"No," Gillis said. "Whatever it is, say it from there."

"Your Honor," Burr said. "I think it may be prejudicial."

"Prejudicial to whom?" Gillis said.

"To my client," Burr said.

"Why would that be?" Gillis said.

Burr sat, stared at the court rules on the table in front of him. He ran his hands through his hair, front to back.

"Your Honor," he said looking up. "As I know you are aware, the court rules regarding jury selection require that a juror be disqualified, if among other things, he or she is prejudiced regarding the matter at hand."

"You are quite correct, Mr. Lafayette. I am well aware of that provision."

"Well, your Honor, I submit that Mrs. Horton should be disqualified for that reason."

"For what reason?"

"That she is prejudiced and has a preconceived opinion regarding this case," Burr said.

Gillis took off his glasses, held them up to the light, the light from the windows. The October light was pale in the afternoon but not as weak as it had been in January. Burr thought about his lights, tried to remember where he had left them. Gillis then put the right lens in his mouth, licked it actually, first on one side, then the other. He rubbed the lens with the sleeve of his robe. Burr wondered why he didn't pass them down to Miss Longfingers.

"Mr. Lafayette. It is beyond me how this poor woman, poor I say because she will undoubtedly have to listen to your dither during this misbegotten trial, is by any fathomable reason prejudiced."

"Your Honor, I believe she has already made up her mind," Burr said.

"And why would that be?" Gillis said.

"Because…"

"Never mind." Gillis cut him off, pointed his forefinger at him, fist down, then turned his fist up and curled his forefinger.

"Come here, Mr. Lafayette, and I'll tell you." Burr didn't believe he was going to like this. He slipped quietly to the bench.

"This is why you want her disqualified," Gillis continued, not especially sotto voce, "because she is overweight, not particularly attractive, quite likely unhappily married, and resents the hell out of your client who she probably thinks killed his wife so he could marry a younger woman." Gillis had now turned red, out of breath, each chin darker than the next. "That is your theory of jury selection, is it not?"

"Your Honor, I object," Burr said. "I must ask that the prospective jurors here all be disqualified."

"Why?"

"You have prejudiced them," Burr said.

"They didn't hear me," Gillis said.

"Your Honor, I submit that they did."

"Mr. Lafayette. I am a simple man, naive even. Nonetheless, I have sat on the bench for thirty years. While this is my first murder trial, I have conducted a multitude of jury trials. And how many have you tried? Never mind, I don't want to know."

Gillis put his glasses back on. Thinking better of it, he took them off..

"Here's how I see this. If you had your choice the jury would be composed of men over fifty, each married to a woman under thirty. Isn't that about right, Mr. Lafayette?"

"No, Your Honor."

Gillis ignored him. "And here is the profile of the juror you are loathe to have. Female, at least fifty, divorced. Husband remarried to a younger woman. Like Mrs. Horton, right?"

"Mrs. Horton is married, your Honor."

"Well, then that's your second worst choice. Female over fifty, unhappily married. Is that right?"

"No, Your Honor," Burr said.

"Mr. Lafayette. I appreciate the type of juror you want. I also appreciate the type of juror Mr. Truax wants."

"What Your Honor?" Truax said from the prosecutor's table.

"Nothing," Gillis said. "It doesn't concern you."

"I thought I heard my name," Truax said.

"You didn't," Gillis said.

"Yes, Your Honor," Truax said.

"Here are a few facts, Mr. Lafayette," Gillis said. "I assume because of your connection to the area, however nautical it may be, you may be aware of them, but perhaps not. Forget about the fact that almost everyone here is white. There is no diversity here. It's a problem, but it doesn't matter, at least as far as Mr. Tavohnen goes.

"Mr. Lafayette, the facts are that most people here are married, most I daresay, unhappily. More than half of the prospective jurors are women because their husbands have predeceased them. So that's the universe. You have to deal with it."

Gillis put his glasses back on, and this time he left them on. "Before I forget," he said, "it's so nice to see you again. I didn't think I'd ever again have the pleasure. I applaud your efforts to impanel an all-male jury, composed of divorced men remarried to younger women. There may be twelve in the county. There probably are, but we don't have time to find them. And while I'm at it, I'm sure you would prefer no Catholics. The county, however, is over sixty percent Catholic."

"Mr. Lafayette, I have allocated five days for this trial," Gillis said. "It is now two o'clock on Monday afternoon. This trial will be over by the close of business on Friday. Jury selection will be completed by 4:30 today if I have to pick them myself. Is that clear?"

"Yes, Your Honor," Burr said.

"Well, then proceed."

"Your Honor, respectfully, I ask that you disqualify Mrs. Horton for cause and that you disqualify the jurors who heard your outburst."

"My outburst? My outburst?"

Judge Gillis adjourned for the day at 4:25 p.m. after impaneling a twelve-person jury and two alternates. There were eight women and four men. The two alternates were both men. Of the eight women, five were over fifty, three of whom were divorced. The other three were married with children at home. Five were Catholic.

Of the four men, one did have a younger second wife, but only by four years. The other three were married. Burr believed that, unfortunately, they were happily married. He didn't pay much attention to the two alternates.

They had four days left to finish the trial and meet Gillis' self-imposed deadline which, all things considered, Burr thought was interesting but not particularly compelling. He would finish when he finished and Gillis be damned.

TUESDAY, OCTOBER 17, 1989 – DAY TWO

"Ladies and Gentlemen," Truax said, at 10:15 a.m. the next morning, "Thank you for taking your responsibilities as citizens seriously. In our democracy, it is both an obligation and a privilege to serve on a jury. All of you, I know are very busy. I am aware that serving on this jury takes time from your lives, time that could be put to good use in your own lives. I assure you, however, that the time you spend here, invest here, is also very valuable. Because in our great system, each person accused of a crime is entitled to be judged by his peers."

Truax swept his right hand, left to right, across the jury, including them, and Burr thought, embracing them. He thought it was trite but from their looks, it looked like it had worked.

"In this case," Truax said, "judged by you. It is a great responsibility and one I am sure that each one of you will take seriously."

"While your responsibility is to decide if the accused is guilty of murder, it is my job, on behalf of the people of the State of Michigan, to prove that the defendant," another sweeping gesture ending with a pointed index finger at Frank, a long bony finger, "Frank X. Tavohnen, murdered his wife Claudia on December 18, 1982."

"Legally," Truax made quote signs with his fingers, "we will prove that Mr. Tavohnen committed first-degree murder, which is premeditated murder. All that means is that Mr. Tavohnen killed his wife on purpose and that he had a plan for doing it. That is all it means. It is very simple."

Truax thrust his hands in his pockets and rocked back and forth on his heels. He looked like an upside down pendulum swinging back and forth.

"You know why it's simple? Because this case has only three pieces. Three easy pieces. When each piece is proven—which they will be—there will be no choice but to convict the defendant of murdering his wife. No choice whatsoever."

Truax stopped rocking. That was fortunate as Burr thought he might tip over from the momentum of his tick-tocking.

"Three pieces. Piece one." A finger shot straight up. "Frank Tavohnen killed his wife. We know it's true. How? He admits it. Yes, I killed my wife. He said so. Over and over. I killed my wife."

"Piece two." A second finger pierced the room. "He did it on purpose. How do we know that? We have an expert, an expert from the State Police who has proven, proven that, from the way the bullet entered Claudia Tavohnen's body, it could only have done so if the gun had been picked up and aimed at poor Claudia."

Truax aimed a pretend gun at the foreman of the jury, a younger woman.

"Like this," he said. "The only way this could occur is by aiming the gun." The unlucky juror cringed.

"Third," now a hand with three erect fingers. "Mr. Tavohnen had a plan. He had a plan. That's what premeditated is. A plan. He called her down to the basement. That was his plan. He called her down and he killed her. He murdered her. And do you know why he murdered her?"

"I'll tell you why. Because he was having an affair, a sordid affair, with a woman almost twenty years his junior. With a woman who could have been his daughter. That's right, his daughter. He could be her father. Frank Tavohnen made a plan to kill his wife so he could have a younger woman."

"Damn it. Damn it to hell," Burr said under his breath. Truax knew. This was exactly what Burr had been afraid of. How did he know? We are now screwed, Burr thought.

Truax stopped there. He looked down at his shoes then at each jror, one by one.

"Three pieces. That's all. That is what we will prove. When we do that, we ask that you find the defendant, Frank Tavohnen, guilty of first-degree murder."

Burr was tiring of Truax's arm waving and finger pointing. He thought Truax looked like a windmill in a stiff wind. The prosecutor turned toward them again.

"And here," he said, aiming at Sarah, who sat primly in the front row, just behind Frank, "is the source, the reason for this heinous crime. This is the younger woman, the woman who threw herself at him."

Burr thought Truax had made a mistake here. Burr had instructed Sarah that, if she were drawn in, to look directly at Frank, then at the jury, then towards Frank, then to her lap. Not a defiant look, but a concerned and thoughtful look. At least she had done as she was told. She wore a dark dress, not professional, slightly matronly, as instructed. He had Frank in a blue suit that purposely didn't fit him too well. His tie was too wide and Burr had it tied just slightly crooked. Frank had put weight on in jail, which suited Burr just fine. The round face and too small clothes gave him a harmless look, like the bumbler Burr thought he was.

Burr thought going after Sarah could backfire on Truax, thought it probably had, especially with her demure appearance and her performance, which in her case was nothing more than an act. Burr watched Truax's Adam's apple bob, his nostrils flare.

In spite of his gaffe with Sarah, Truax sat down, looking satisfied with himself, smug Burr thought, his thin lip spreading in a line across his face.

"Mr. Lafayette, you may proceed."

"Your Honor," Burr said, half rising, "I would like to request a short recess."

"We just started. Surely your opening remarks were prepared in advance."

"They were, Your Honor."

"Then proceed," Gillis said.

"May we have thirty minutes?"

"You may have five minutes," Gillis said. "No one is to leave. Caucus right there."

Truax had caught him off guard. What did he know? Burr had worried Truax might discover Frank and Sarah's affair, but Truax's witness list didn't seem to have anyone who could speak directly to the affair. Burr had interviewed them all himself, and he didn't think there was any evidence, other than circumstantial. Certainly Berdette Zolkowski of Sensible Rates was nowhere to be found on Truax's list, but Burr had been wrong about Truax and his knowledge of the affair. Burr brushed his hair back from his eyes.

"What now?" Jacob asked.

"I don't know," Burr said. "My opening statement had a lot to do with motive. Do I leave it in?"

"I don't think so," Jacob said. "Not unless you want to make an issue out of it."

"That's the point," Burr said. "I did. Now, though, it's contested. I'm not sure I want to draw attention to it."

"First, there's no affair. Then there was, but we didn't know about it. Now Truax knows and we didn't know he knew," Jacob said.

"Counsel," Gillis said, "proceed."

"Just a few more minutes, Your Honor."

"Now," Gillis said.

"Yes, Your Honor," Burr said. "Ladies and gentlemen," he said, speaking it as he stood, speaking it to the defense table, not looking them in the eye, not yet. Now he looked at them, one by one, left to right, like he was reading a book.

"Ladies and gentlemen," he said again. "My name is Burr Lafayette. This is my partner and co-counsel Jacob Wertheim. We represent Frank Tavohnen and as a practical matter, we also represent his wife, Sarah, who has been pointed out to you, and his children, Jason and Becky, who are not here today. You may know Frank, or know of him. His family has lived here for a long time, and he has too, until recently, until the accident."

Burr slid his hands in his pockets, talked to his shoes, cordovan in color, shined until they shined. He did have on socks.

"You see, I really don't understand why we're here. Why you've been taken from your lives, what you do each day, to be here. More importantly, really, why Mr. Tavohnen has been ripped from his life. He's been in jail since last December, for almost a year (Burr exaggerated), unable to work, to provide for his family, to be with his family, his wife, his son, his daughter. His daughter who is six years old. She doesn't understand, doesn't understand why her daddy isn't home at night. She's mad at him for not being there."

"What I do know is that, no matter where you live, it would be terrible to be ripped out of your home, at gunpoint, and thrown in jail and kept there for almost a year. I do that know that would be terrible. And you know, for Frank, it has been terrible."

"Murder, of course, is terrible. If you murdered someone, you'd deserve to be in jail, you'd deserve it for what you did. I believe that. I'm sure you all do, too."

Burr paused here, squinted at the jury, who nodded collectively.

"But if all this happened, this wrenching away from your family, this jail, for an accident, not a murder, but an accident, well that would be terrible." Burr paused, looked down at his shoes. Somehow the left one had come untied. He looked at the jury. "Wouldn't it?"

Another collective nod.

"That's what happened here. An accident, a horrible, horrible accident. Would you like to know what happened?"

Of course they would. He had them now. He had them, and he knew it, and they did, too, and they were glad of it.

"Here's what happened. Frank lent his deer rifle to a friend. His friend went hunting with it. Then he brought it back and left it in Frank's garage, left it there because no one was home." Burr paused here, looked at Truax, thought he saw him flinch. "You know why no one was home?"

They didn't.

"Because Frank, his wife, and his son were out cutting their Christmas tree just like they did every year. So they get home with the tree. They take it into the garage. Frank and Matt trim the branches so it will fit in the stand. Frank sees his deer rifle. It's dirty. Frank thinks he'd better clean it, thinks it's not a good idea to leave it in the garage. They get the tree in the stand, then take it in the house. Then they decorate it, just like they always do. Frank does his part. He strings the lights. Then he tells his wife and son that he's going to clean his rifle and put it away. "I'll be right back," he says. (Another stretch). "So, he gets the rifle from the garage, takes it down to the basement and starts cleaning it. And you know what?"

No, they say with their eyes.

"He's a little upset with his friend because he thought he would have taken better care of his deer rifle. It's dirty, really dirty. And his friend left the clip in the gun. Can you imagine that? Then Claudia comes down the stairs, tells him they need him. They're ready to put the angel on top of the tree." (This, a very big stretch, but Burr believed he could get away with it in his opening statement.) "And that's Frank's job. Frank looks up, looks at his wife. The gun is on the workbench where he's cleaning it. Then, bang."

Burr clapped his hands. They all jumped: the jury, Frank, Sarah, Suzanne, Jacob, the gallery, Gillis, even Truax. They all jumped.

"The gun goes off. His wife falls. There's blood. Frank rushes over. Jason, his son, starts down the stairs. Frank stops him, won't let him come down, takes him upstairs. Then you know what Frank does? He calls the police. Jason goes next door to the neighbors. The police come. They ask Frank what happened."

"He says the gun went off. As you might imagine, he's in shock and doesn't really know what happened, but he thinks that the cleaning rag might have gotten tangled around the trigger. He thought the rifle was empty. He was careful. He took the clip out. He racked the gun, threw the bolt, but somehow there was still a shell in it. Perhaps the gun had been returned broken. Nonetheless, it was an accident. A terrible accident."

"You know what? That's what the police thought, too. They thought it was an accident. A terrible accident. But an accident. The coroner thought so, too."

"There was an inquest," Burr continued. "An inquest is an investigation to see if charges should be filed. But do you know what happened?

The jury didn't know. "The people at the inquest thought it was an accident. There were no charges filed. A terrible accident."

"And then you know what happened?"

They didn't, or if they did, if they remembered, they wanted to hear it again.

"Then Frank mourned, was sad. But then he began living again. He remarried, had another child. He got on with life. That makes sense, doesn't it? Of course it does." Burr paused. "But then do you know what happened?"

They didn't, but they wanted to.

"Then six years, almost six years, after the accident, after the evidence, the physical evidence has disappeared, and everyone's memory has faded. Six years, not six months. Six years after this terrible tragedy, an ambitious prosecutor arrests Frank for murder. Right out of the blue. Almost six years after it happened, after the police said it was an accident. After the coroner decided it was an accident. An ambitious prosecutor, this man," Burr didn't point. Rather, he nods at Truax who had reddened, "arrests Frank for murder."

"And do you know what? Until that time, Frank had never been arrested for anything. Never, in his whole life. Not once. He had no points on his driver's license. Once he got two points for going 65 on US-31, ten over, between here and Boyne Falls."

Burr saw three or four of the jury snicker.

"The points expired fifteen years ago. But Mr. Truax has him arrested for murder because a laser, a laser like Star Wars, says it couldn't be an accident."

"And you know what else?"

They didn't.

"Mr. Truax doesn't even have the gun. He doesn't know where it is. What if the gun was defective, didn't work right? Then what?"

"And you know what else?" They didn't, but they wanted to. "This man," he said, pointing to Truax, "This man has refused to let Frank out on bail. So he's spent almost a year in jail. He can't provide for his family in jail, can he? No, of course he can't." They agreed. "And do you know why? Because this man believes Frank is a threat to society and might run away. A flight risk. Frank, a flight risk. I don't think so, do you?" They didn't.

The jury was ready to let Frank go, right now, right here and now. Burr sensed it, knew it.

"To find Frank guilty do you know what you must do?" He had them and they leaned towards him, rapt. "Because to find Frank guilty, you must believe that Frank murdered his wife beyond a reasonable doubt, beyond a reasonable doubt, not a hunch, not a guess, not an I suppose so. You've really got to believe it. And, ladies and gentlemen, I just don't see it. So, why bring a case like this? Why do it? Why after all this time, when the evidence is old, what there is of it, when Frank has led an exemplary life, husband, father, breadwinner, coach. Why do it? Why, and this is important. I'll tell you why we're here."

For the first time, Burr walked toward the jury. Slowly. This intimidated them, like God approaching. He crept right next to them. His eyes in their eyes.

"I'll tell you why. I'll tell you why you're here. It's not about justice. It's not even about Frank. It's about him." He pointed at Truax. "It's about him." Then he whispered so only the jury could hear, not Truax, not Gillis, not anyone but the jury. "It's because he wants to be a state senator, that's why. He wants publicity. It has nothing to do with Frank."

Truax shot up. "What, what did he say? I object. I object. What did he say? I couldn't hear."

"Mr. Lafayette, you must speak so that we all can hear you," Gillis said.

"Yes, Your Honor," Burr said.

"Strike that from the record," Gillis said.

The court reporter turned to Judge Gillis. "Your Honor, I didn't hear what he said."

"Mr. Lafayette, please repeat what you said to the jury so that we all may hear it."

"With all due respect, Your Honor," Burr said, "if I repeat it, in order that you may hear it so that you may then strike it, wouldn't it be better not to repeat it?"

Gillis thought this over. It looked to Burr that his eyes crossed when he concentrated. Finally, over his glasses to Truax. "Counselor," Gillis said. "I must know what he said." Gillis, still looking over the top of his reading glasses, said, "What was it that you said, Mr. Lafayette?"

Burr turned counterclockwise, three-quarters of a turn from the jury to the judge to Truax, stared at Truax. "I said that the real reason for this trial was to get Truax publicity for his election to the state senate."

Truax reddened then launched himself to his feet. "I object, Your Honor. I object," he said, his Adam's apple bobbing.

"Strike that from the record," Gillis said.

After Burr finished his opening statement, Gillis recessed for thirty minutes. On Burr's way out of the courtroom, he saw Kaye sitting four rows behind Suzanne and Sarah. Kaye returned his smile with what could charitably be described as a wry look. Burr and Jacob adjourned to the Vista Cruiser. Suzanne joined them. Eve had packed Burr and Jacob a snack, peanut butter and honey for Burr. Salami for Jacob, with a joint chaser.

"Bold it was. I'll say that. Bold. And you got to say it twice," Jacob said.

"I did," Burr said, smiling at his stoned partner.

"I think you pushed Gillis as far as he'll go," Jacob said.

"Please don't get stoned," Burr said. "You'll have to finish if I get thrown out."

"That's not going to happen," Jacob said.

"You have the tongue of a serpent," Suzanne said. Burr handed her half of his sandwich

CHAPTER TWENTY

After the recess, Truax established that Frank had killed Claudia. He did this from Gustafson's police report and Van Arkel's autopsy. Truax apparently, electing not to call them as witnesses. Burr, grudgingly, thought Truax was smart, in light of Burr's cross examination at the preliminary exam. Truax then called Anne Gannon.

"Ms. Gannon, in your own words, in lay terms, please tell us how the laser method works and what you found," Truax said.

Burr thought it also smart of Truax to start with his best witness. Truax had done a good job with her so far, her credentials, the technology. He also thought the testimony of Ms. Gannon might well tell the tale.

She recrossed her legs. "It's very simple, really," she said. "A laser shoots a straight line. We can determine the path of the bullet because we know where the bullet struck the wall, where it exited the victim's body and where it entered. Because we know the victim's height, we can connect those three points. The result is a line that points to where the bullet came from. Because the murder weapon . . ."

"Objection, Your Honor," Burr said. "It is a rifle. It is up to the jury to determine if a murder was committed."

"Sustained," Gillis said. He scowled at Truax.

"Please continue, Ms. Gannon," Truax said.

"The rifle then," she said. "The gun has a long barrel. We merely place the rifle barrel on the line, and it tells us where the bullet was fired from."

"And what did it tell you?" Truax asked.

"It showed us that the gun could not have gone off from the workbench. The angles don't work."

"Where would the gun have to be?"

"May I show you?" she asked.

"Please," Truax said.

Ms. Gannon stood. She picked up her arms as if she were shouldering a rifle. She swung them, pointed at Frank. He ducked.

"Objection, Your Honor," Burr said.

"What for?"

"The witness is intimidating my client," Burr said.

"Overruled," Gillis said. "You may proceed, Mr. Truax."

"What you are saying is that when the entry, the exit, and wall points are connected, it is not possible for the gun to have been on the workbench," Truax said.

"That is correct," Gannon said.

"The way they line up, though, fits with a gun that had been shouldered and fired," Truax said.

"Exactly," Gannon said.

Burr understood, but he hoped it might be confusing to the jury.

"Now, Ms. Gannon, I think I understand this, but could you perhaps demonstrate it graphically?" Truax said.

"Damn," Burr said to himself. He had counted on Truax doing this but had hoped he wouldn't.

"Yes," she said. "I have two charts that illustrate my point. May I?"

"Please," Truax said.

Gannon rose, smoothed her skirt and walked (purposefully) to the prosecutor's table. "Here they are," she said.

"Your Honor," Truax said. "The people would like to introduce these diagrams as Exhibits One and Two."

"Let me see them," Gillis said.

They were everything Burr hoped they wouldn't be. Better than the toy rifle at the preliminary exam. Two poster boards, each with a wall and a woman and three marks: the wall, the exit wound and the entry wound. A line drawn through each one. On the first poster, the line ran up to a man aiming a rifle at the woman. A straight line connected them all. On the second poster, the gun was on a workbench. The line ran up from the entry wound just as in the first drawing. When it reached the height of the workbench, though, it angled parallel to the gun on the table, a crooked line. Clearly not possible, at least according to the laws of physics.

"Ms. Gannon," Truax said, "how could the workbench drawing occur in the real world?"

"It couldn't," she said.

"Why not?"

"Because the trajectory of a bullet is straight, especially at close range. It won't change its path unless it strikes something," Gannon said.

"I see," Truax said. "Well suppose the gun had fired, gone off, say, accidentally from the workbench. How would that look?"

"That would be the third chart," she said.

Truax marched to his table and retrieved another poster, which he introduced as Exhibit Three. This showed a line drawn from the gun on the workbench to an entry wound just below the armpit, an exit wound at the same height, and a mark on the wall at the same height.

"Now Ms. Gannon, tell us about Exhibit Three."

"Well," she said, "if the gun had indeed gone off from the workbench, the path of the bullet would be very close to parallel with the workbench and the bullet would have ended up in the wall at the same height it left the gun."

"And the wounds?"

"They would be in line with the two end points," she said. "Here and here."

"But?"

"But the bullet hit the wall substantially below the height of the table, and it entered the body above the level of the table," she said. "Both of these points are inconsistent with the gun going off from the table."

"Inconsistent?"

"Impossible," Gannon said.

"Impossible? What are you saying?" asked Truax.

"I am saying that there is no way that Mrs. Tavohnen was killed by a bullet from the workbench," Gannon said.

"It is impossible," Truax said.

"Yes," she said. "It is impossible."

"How, then, was she killed?"

"Objection," Burr said. "Calls for a statement of fact which the witness cannot know."

"I withdraw the question," Truax said. Truax gave him a peeved look. "Let me restate the question," Truax said. "In your opinion, how was she killed?"

"She was killed by someone who aimed a rifle," Gannon said.

"Objection," Burr said. "It has not been established, even by these voodoo physics, that the gun was aimed."

"Sustained," Gillis said.

"Ms. Gannon, please give us your opinion as to what occurred," Truax said.

"In my opinion," she said, "the gun could only have been fired from the shoulder."

"Which diagram is that?"

"This one," she said. She pointed to Exhibit One, the man firing the gun from his shoulder.

"Let the record show this is Exhibit One," Truax said. "Please show us once more what that would look like.

"Sir?"

"Demonstrate, like you did before," Truax said. "But don't point it at Mr. Tavohnen this time." Truax backed up. "This time aim at me."

Gannon very primly picked up an imaginary rifle, shouldered it, and aimed it at Truax.

"Now, pull the trigger," Truax said.

Burr watched as she pulled an imaginary trigger.

"Bang," she said.

Truax clapped his hands. The jury jumped as one. Burr did not object.

"No further questions, Your Honor," Truax said.

Burr began his cross-examination of the comely Ms. Gannon and immediately went to the question of her credentials.

"Objection, Your Honor," Truax said. "The qualifications of the witness have already been established, and I might add, they are impeccable."

"I agree, Your Honor," Burr said, "but as to expert witnesses, the court rules clearly allow cross examination regarding qualifications."

Gillis seemed to ponder the objection made by Truax. Burr couldn't understand why he had any hesitation. "Proceed, Mr. Lafayette," he said.

"Thank you, Your Honor." Burr walked to the witness box, next to Ms. Gannon, almost intimately. "Now, Ms. Gannon, you have testified that you hold degrees in physics. Is that correct?"

"A masters and a doctorate," she said.

"Quite right," Burr said. "Any other degrees?"

"My bachelor's degree was in astronomy."

"Oh, I see. Astronomy. Comets and meteors," Burr said, leaning on the railing, closer to her than before.

"Objection, Your Honor," Truax said. "Counsel is taunting the witness."

"Watch your manners, Mr. Lafayette."

"Yes, Your Honor. Now, Ms. Gannon. Do you have any other degrees?"

"No, I don't," she said.

"Any other course of study or specialties? For instance," Burr said, "did you ever study anatomy? Human anatomy?"

"No, I did not," she said.

"You have not studied human anatomy, but you have applied the principles of physics to the human body," Burr said.

"Yes," she said.

"Now then, Ms. Gannon," Burr said, backing away. "A laser is nothing more than a beam of light. Is that right?"

"Yes."

"And the whole point of your laser analysis is based on the premise that light travels in a straight line," Burr said. "Is that right?"

"It is," Gannon said.

"Objection, Your Honor," Truax said. "This is going nowhere."

"Your Honor, if Mr. Truax would afford me the simple courtesy of listening politely, we would be there by now."

"Proceed, Mr. Lafayette," Gillis said.

"Now, Ms. Gannon. What happens if, for example, I take this" —Burr fished around in the pocket of his suit, a navy blue chalk stripe with pleated trousers, and came out with a small pocket mirror—"a simple mirror and place it in the path of the laser? What happens to the beam of light then? What happens to its path?"

"Its path changes such that the angle of reflection equals the angle of incidence," she said.

"Spoken like a physicist," Burr said. "Now in English, is it true that when the laser, the light, hits the mirror, the path is changed? It no longer travels in a straight line."

"Yes, that's true," she said.

"Now suppose a bullet strikes a bone," Burr said. "Would that change its path?"

"No, not in this case," Gannon said.

"No? How do you know?"

"Because the shot was fired at close range," she said. "The bullet would be traveling too fast. It has too much force to alter its path."

"Have you studied anatomy, Ms. Gannon?"

"Yes, I studied it for this case," she said.

"But not formally," Burr said, pressing closer to her again.

"No, not formally."

"Would you consider yourself an expert on anatomy?"

"Objection," Truax said. "That is a legal question."

"Sustained," Gillis said.

"Very well," Burr said. "You have no training in anatomy, yet you studied it enough to know that if the bullet hit a bone, it would not bend, not like a laser striking this mirror.

"Yes, that's right," Gannon said.

Burr had just enough light from the windows to position the mirror so the light flashed into Gannon's eyes. What luck. He hadn't counted on this. She blinked then moved her hand to block the mirror.

"Objection, Your Honor. Counsel is taunting the witness again," Truax said.

"I'm so sorry, Ms. Gannon. The light must have gotten in your eyes." Burr put the mirror back in his pants pocket. "Now Ms. Gannon, your findings on the entry and exit wounds, were from where?"

"From the coroner's report," she said.

"The coroner's report," Burr repeated.

"Yes," she said.

"And did they indicate the location of the wounds?"

"They did," she said.

"And where were they?"

"The bullet entered here." She pointed to a spot on her left side just below her shoulder. "And exited approximately here," she said.

"You say approximately," Burr said.

"Yes," Gannon said. "The report is very specific. Where I am showing you on my body is only approximate."

"I see," Burr said. "And what was the size of the entry wound."

"The diameter of the bullet. Very small," Gannon said.

"The size of my little finger," Burr said. He raised the pinkie of his left hand, made sure the jury could see it.

"Yes, approximately," she said.

"Approximately," Burr said. "You are fond of that word. Now what was the size of the exit wound?"

"The exit wound?"

"That's what I said," Burr said.

"It was circular, about six centimeters, the radius," she said.

"Excuse me," Burr said. "In English, that means the hole had made almost a two and a half inch circle. Is that right?"

"Approximately," she said again.

"Come on, Ms. Gannon. That's a big hole." Burr made a circle with his thumb and forefinger, two inches in diameter and looked through it. First at Gannon, then the jury. "I'd say that's a big hole. A big hole to guess at where the actual path of the bullet was. A guess that's what I'd call it. A big guess to determine a man's fate."

"That is not the critical hole," Gannon said.

"I did not ask you a question, Ms. Gannon. Now, I'd like you to look at this chart." Burr strode to his table where Jacob handed him a poster board. "Ms. Gannon, I would ask you to tell me what you see here."

"Objection, Your Honor," Truax said. "That is speculation. An expert witness need not give credence to speculative evidence by reading it."

"Sustained," Gillis said.

"Very well, then," Burr said. "Please accept Defense Exhibit One" (which Gillis accepted). "Suppose a laser is placed on the workbench where this rifle is, as in this exhibit, and the beam of light is directed on the path of the rifle and when it gets here," he touched the entry wound, "there is a mirror, what would happen?"

"The light would deflect," she said.

"Down this line?"

"Yes," she said.

"And similarly, if the bullet hit a bone, might it not deflect down this path?"

"No," she said.

"Why not?"

"Because the bullet has too much force," she said.

"Ms. Gannon, did you examine the body?"

"No, of course not," Gannon said. "It was six years ago."

"Yes, it has been a long time, hasn't it?" Burr said.

"Objection," Truax said.

"I withdraw the question," Burr said. "The point is, Ms. Gannon, you don't know, do you? This is a fine theory except you didn't examine the body. It is certainly possible that the bullet could have glanced off a bone and changed its path. Isn't that possible?"

"No, it's not," she said.

This is nothing more than a theory," Burr said, "It's not proof."

"Objection, Your Honor," Truax said.

"Sustained," Gillis said.

Burr could see Gannon was getting angry. He pressed. "Ms. Gannon, one more question," Burr said, leaning in again. "How many times before have you used this laser analysis in a murder trial?

"This time," she said.

"Not this time, Ms. Gannon. Please don't be cute. How many times before have you used this?"

"None," she said.

"This is the only time?"

"This is the first time," she said.

"The only time," Burr said.

"Yes," Gannon said.

"No further questions, Your Honor."

"We reconvene at 1:30," Gillis said. He banged his gavel and left for lunch.

Burr reprised lunch at City Park Grill, the restaurant decidedly empty on a Tuesday in October. He thought it would fill this weekend, the fall colors peaking. With the leaves coloring and some falling, the grouse hunting should pick up along with the woodcock flight, a few days late this year. Duck season was in full swing.

Burr squeezed the lemon on his whitefish. The juice squirted on his tie. Eve dipped her napkin in her water glass and wiped it off. Suzanne watched her do it, disapprovingly, thought Burr.

"I scotch guarded it yesterday," Burr said. "Trial tie. Bulletproof." No one laughed. Burr noted his poor word choice.

"Will Truax finish this afternoon?" Sarah said.

"He might," Burr said. "Depends on how far he goes with the third finger."

Sarah cocked her head to the left. Her face looked lopsided.

"Truax told us he has three parts to his case," Burr said. "He proved Frank killed Claudia. The first part was easy. Then he tried to prove it was intentional, with the laser. That was the second part. I think I hurt him there. A little anyway." He scrubbed at his tie, didn't think the lemon broke through his scotch guard shield. Looking down at his tie, this should dry before we start this afternoon, he thought. Eve had his spare if necessary.

"Truax has proved or tried to, that Frank killed her intentionally. He's still got to prove it was premeditated, with malice aforethought. Which means he planned it. That's the third part." They all knew what Truax had to do. He said it for himself, to hear it himself, not for them.

"Now he's going to work on the motive, try to show why Frank did it," Burr said. "That he thought about it in advance, called Cladia down to the basement and shot her. It's not enough that he did it on purpose. Intentional, that's second degree. Truax has got to show that Frank thought about it in advance. That would be the affair."

Sarah looked around. "Please, let's not talk about it here," she said.

After lunch Truax began with his third finger, the motive finger. (Burr thought Truax skipped over the undertaker, because he believed Van Arkel might cause further damage to the laser theory.) Now Truax was well on his way with Dallas Stahl, the baseball coach, and, as it turned out, a math teacher. "And where did he place his hand?" Truax said.

"On her bottom," Stahl said.

"On her bottom?"

"Yes," Stahl said.

"Mr. Stahl, please go back and tell us again," Truax said.

"Objection, Your Honor," Burr said. "We've already heard this."

"Overruled," Gillis said.

"Well, at the awards ceremony, for baseball, I saw him open the door for her at the school, then she walks through," Stahl said.

"Who is she again?"

"Her," Stahl said, pointing at Sarah.

"For the record, her is the current Mrs. Tavohnen," Truax said. "And?"

"And then she starts to go in and he puts his hand on her bottom, on it and kind of underneath it, with his fingers kind of spread," Stahl said.

"Well, couldn't he have just been helping her through the door?"

"Not that way," Stahl said.

The courtroom snickered.

"Why not?"

"Well, if it was me," Stahl said, "I wouldn't touch anybody there unless I thought they'd like it. Otherwise, You could get sued."

Burr opened his tin of Altoids. Why hadn't Stahl told him this?

"No further questions," Truax said.

"You may proceed, Mr. Lafayette," Gillis said.

Burr chewed up his Altoids and swallowed them quickly. Thank God Truax hadn't thought to ask what Sarah had been doing at the awards ceremony in the first place, Burr thought. He stood. "Mr. Stahl, did you ever see Mr. Tavohnen kiss Miss Fairchild?"

"Yes," Stahl said.

"Let me rephrase that," Burr said. He had made a mistake, and he knew it. "Before Mrs.Tavohnen was killed, did you ever see Mr. Tavohnen kiss Miss Fairchild?"

"No," Stahl said.

"Did you ever see them hold hands?"

"No," Stahl said.

"Did you ever see any other public displays of affection?"

"No," Stahl said again.

"Did Mr. Tavohnen ever speak romantically about Miss Fairchild to you?"

"No," Stahl said yet again.

"Yet, you believe they were having an affair."

"I saw what I saw," Stahl said.

Burr approached Stahl. "Please answer the question, Mr. Stahl," Burr said.

"I don't know. Maybe not an affair, but he had a crush on her. I know that."

"A crush, Mr. Stahl, is not an affair," Burr said, looking at the jury.

Truax then called Elizabeth Lisecky, a diminutive fiftyish woman with a round face, like a pumpkin, and matching orange hair. She was the hygienist Burr had found, but she, like Stahl and everyone else, hadn't told him everything. Her answers weren't quite as graphic as Stahl's, but they were still damaging.

Now it was Burr's turn.

"And you were a hygienist in Frank Tavohnen's office?" Burr asked.

"Yes," she said.

"Please tell us what you told Mr. Tavohnen," Burr said.

"I told him to keep his distance from her," she said.

"From whom?" Burr said.

"Miss Fairchild," Ms. Lisecky said.

"Why did you say that?" Burr said.

"Because he was married," she said. "Isn't that pretty obvious?"

"Why did you tell him that?"

"I saw them holding hands," she said.

"Where?"

"In the office," she said. "And I saw it in his eyes. Like a puppy."

"Just answer the question, Ms. Lisecky," Burr said. "Did you ever see Mr. Tavohnen kiss Miss Fairchild?"

"No," she said.

"Touch her breast?"

"No." She blushed.

"Put his hand on her bottom?" Burr said.

"No," she said, still blushing.

"But he held her hand," Burr said.

"Yes, in the office," Ms. Lisecky said.

"When was it?" Burr asked. "I don't remember," she said.

"Ms. Lisecky. Surely you do. Could it have been at an office Christmas party?"

"I don't remember," she said.

"You remember that you saw them holding hands, but you don't remember when or where," Burr said.

"That's right," she said.

"I see," Burr said. "Well, Ms. Lisecky, isn't it possible that you are slightly overzealous in your pursuit of decorum?" Burr asked.

"I know moon eyes when I see them," she said.

"Where and when did you see them holding hands?"

"I don't remember," she said again.

Answer the question," Burr said.

Truax popped up. "Objection, Your Honor," he said. "I don't remember is an answer."

"Sustained," said Gillis. Please try to remember, Ms Lisecky."

"I don't remember," she said.

"No further questions," Burr said.

Gillis adjourned for the day.

Wednesday, October 18, 1989 – Day Three

The next morning, Truax called five more witnesses, trying to prove, at least show, an affair. Burr thought Truax hadn't gotten very far with it. Burr had called it innuendo, which Gillis had stricken from the record. Somehow Truax hadn't found the Sensible Rates lady. At least not yet. So it wasn't as bad as thought, at least not yet.

Truax called the last witness on his list, Mrs. Larsen, the neighbor. Burr didn't think she would do much damage. She hadn't told him anything of consequence when he'd questioned her in her backyard.

"Now, Mrs. Larsen, did you ever see Mr. Tavohnen and Miss Fairchild together before Claudia Tavohnen was killed?"

"Yes," she said.

"And where would that be?" asked Truax.

"In the garage," she said. "Frank's garage."

"Mr. Tavohnen's garage? And where is that garage?"

"What do you mean, where is the garage?" She stopped. Bit her lip. "Oh, I get it. Where's the garage. It's hooked onto his house which is right next to my side yard."

"And what did you see?"

"I was in my garden, my vegetable garden. There were a few tomatoes left, ones that hadn't gotten frosted. And I see Frank pull up, alone in the car or so I thought. He gets out of the car, opens the garage door, and drives in. Then he shuts the door. Well, I don't think too much about it. I got back to looking for tomatoes. But then

I don't hear the door to the house open or close. I can always hear the door because it squeaks, the hinge, I guess. So I get curious. I walk over to the garage window. Now I can hear the car running. So I wonder, is everything all right. So I go up to the window. But I can't quite see in. So I cup my hands like this." She shaded the sides of her face with her hands. Then she leaned forward. "Well, I'll tell you what I saw. I saw Frank in the car all right, but he's in there with her." She pointed at Sarah, who for the first time lost her poise, opened her mouth and turned red. "She must have ducked down when he drove up."

"What were they doing?"

'He was kissing her. Hard," she said.

"Anything else?" asked Truax.

"I don't like to say this, but since you asked, he had his hand up her skirt."

"He did? How far up?"

"Objection, Your Honor," Burr said. "This is not necessary."

"It is certainly necessary," Truax said. "It shows motive."

"Overruled," Gillis said.

"How far up her skirt was his hand?"

"Way up." She stopped. Here it comes, thought Burr. "All the way up. All the way up so you could see her underpants. They were black."

"Your witness," Truax said.

"Mrs. Larsen," Burr said, not sure where to begin, "did you tell Mr. Tavohnen that you had spied on him?"

"Objection, Your Honor," Truax said.

"Sustained," Gillis said.

"Mrs. Larsen, did you tell Mr. Tavohnen that you watched him through his garage window?"

"No," she said.

"Did you tell anyone else before today?"

"No," she said.

"What about Mr. Truax?"

"Who?"

"Him," Burr said, pointing at Truax.

"Him," she said. "Oh, him. I might have told him."

"Did you tell him?"

"I suppose I did," said Larsen.

"And do you recall when we spoke in your yard, earlier this summer?" Burr asked.

"No," she said.

"Mrs. Larsen," Burr said.

"Yes, now I do," she said.

"And do you recall that I asked you, asked you specifically, if you ever saw Mr. Tavohnen and Miss Fairchild together prior to Claudia's death?"

"No, I don't remember that," she said.

"I did ask you that, and you said you had never seen them together," Burr said. "Why did you lie to me?"

"Objection," Truax said.

"Sustained," Gillis said.

"Did Mr. Truax tell you to keep this to yourself?"

"Objection," Truax said.

"No further questions," Burr said, who tried to walk confidently back to the defense table. Once there he said, "Goddamn it, Frank. What else is there I don't know?"

Suzanne leaned over the rail of the spectator's gallery, hissed at him. "Burr, be quiet," she said. "The jury will hear."

"Who cares" Burr said. "Why didn't you tell me?" he asked Frank.

"I didn't know," Frank said.

"Didn't you see her?

"No," Frank said. He wrenched his neck around to Sarah who smiled at him, sweetly.

Truax lifted himself from his chair, uncoiled himself, stretching his fame to his full height.

"Your Honor," Truax said.

"Are you quite through, Mr. Truax?"

"Not quite, Your Honor. I have one more witness."

Burr looked at Truax's witness list. Jacob had crossed out all the names. He stood, did not uncoil, just stood. "Your Honor," he said, "the prosecution has called all of its witnesses."

"Have they now?" Gillis said.

"Your Honor," Truax said, "I have at last been able to locate Jason Tavohnen, the defendant's son."

"Damn it. Damn it to hell," Burr said it under his breath, snapped his head forward. "Your Honor, I object. This witness was not on the prosecution's list."

"Mr. Tavohnen is in the navy, Your Honor. We were unable to locate him until now," Truax said.

"Nonsense," Burr said. "The court rules require the prosecution to notify the defense in writing of all witnesses it intends to call. At least twenty-one days before trial."

"Mr. Tavohnen was at sea, Your Honor. We were unable to reach him," Truax said.

"That is patently untrue, Your Honor," Burr said. He pointed at Truax. "The prosecutor is lying."

"Mr. Lafayette," Gillis said.

"Your Honor, is Mr. Truax aware of the U.S. mail, telephones, or telegrams?

"He was at sea, Your Honor," Truax said.

"The radio was invented seventy-five years ago," Burr said.

"Be quiet, Mr. Lafayette," Gillis said.

"If you allow this witness, I will move for a mistrial," Burr said.

Gillis once more looked over his reading glasses, his left eye crossed. Rubbed the end of his nose. "Mr. Truax, you may call your witness."

"I move for a mistrial," Burr said.

"So noted," Gillis said. "Proceed, Mr. Truax."

"Your Honor," Burr said. "The defense requests a thirty-minute recess."

"Mr. Lafayette, the court will recess for the day after it hears this witness."

Burr thought that Frank was glad to see Jason, even as a witness, and even if Jason testified against him, and Truax was indeed going to come after them with Frank's own son.

Truax called Jason, asked him a few introductory questions. Then he got to the heart of the matter.

"He hated my mother," Jason said.

"Hated? Isn't that a bit strong?" Truax said.

"No, sir," Jason said. "It is not."

Truax had his man now. Jason Gordon Tavohnen—Gordon was his mother's maiden name—sat stiffly as Burr would expect a sailor, a young, zealous sailor, to sit. He looked like a sailor, hair cropped, clean shaven. Broad shoulders, square face. And he wore his uniform. Damn that Truax.

"How do you know?" Truax said.

"I lived there," Jason said. "I saw it."

"Did they argue?"

"Yes, sir," he said in a military fashion that probably meant more than what he actually said.

"Fight?"

"Yes, sir."

"They argued and they fought," Truax said.

"Yes, sir."

"Tell me, Jason, why do you think he hated her?"

"Objection," Burr said.

"Overruled," Gillis said.

"I don't know, sir. I really don't know."

"Was she a good mother?"

"Yes, sir," Jason said.

"A good wife?"

"Yes, sir."

"Objection," Burr said.

"In your opinion, was she a good wife?"

"Yes, sir."

There it was, Burr thought, the beloved mother and dutiful wife. Truax had led the boy through it. By the time Truax was done, Claudia would be up for sainthood, which was the reason Burr had left Claudia out of his defense. The living could not compete with the dead. He had wondered why Truax had left her out. He hadn't. He had merely waited. Snuck up on him.

"Now then, Mr. Tavohnen, where were you on the night your mother was killed?"

"I was in the living room," Jason said.

"What were you doing?"

"We were decorating our Christmas tree," Jason said.

"Tell us what happened."

"Mom said something to my Dad. I don't know what, but I heard him swear at her."

"What did he say?"

"I'd rather not say, sir."

"Please," Truax said. Burr knew Truax knew the answer.

"He said, 'go fuck yourself'."

The courtroom rustled, feet shuffling.

"Then what?"

"Then he went to the garage. He got his deer rifle and went downstairs to the basement. Then he told her to come down there."

"He what?"

"He told her to come down there," Jason said.

"And then?"

"She handed me the ornament she had in her hand. It was red, red with silver, silver like frost. She handed it to me, then she went downstairs. Then I heard him yell at her. And then he shot her."

"Objection, Your Honor. Calls for a conclusion," Burr said.

"Sustained," Gillis said.

"Mr. Tavohnen, you say your father called to your mother from the basement. Your mother then went down to the basement. You heard your father yelling at her and then you heard a gunshot," Truax said. "Is that what happened?"

"Yes, sir," Jason said.

"No further questions," Truax said, who looked grimly at the jury, marched to his seat, and sat. Burr sat in his chair, motionless.

"Mr. Lafayette, I believe it is your turn," Gillis said.

Burr rose from his chair, the hardwood chair. His back now hurt at his shoulder blades, Burr said, "Your Honor, may I have a ten minute recess?"

"No, you may not," Gillis said.

"Your Honor, we have had no opportunity to prepare for this surprise witness."

"Proceed, Mr. Lafayette, or you forfeit your opportunity."

"Your Honor," Burr said.

"Now," Gillis said.

"Yes, Your Honor."

Burr was in dangerous territory and he knew it. He had not believed Truax would be able to produce Frank's son. Burr had foolishly believed, Truax had provided him with a complete witness list. Burr had no reason to question it. Now he wondered if he should have put the gunsmith on his witness list, but it was too late for that. Burr had wondered why Truax hadn't tried to show that Frank and Claudia had a bad marriage. Now he knew why. Truax had planned to lull the defense, Burr actually. Why had Burr thought that Truax would base everything on a laser? Because that's what Truax wanted him to think.

"Mr. Tavohnen?" Burr said, standing near Jason. He said it as kindly as he could.

"Yes, sir?"

"How old are you?"

"Twenty-three, sir."

"And how long have you been in the navy?" Burr said, still kindly, moving to conversational.

"Four years, sir."

"And how old were you when your mother died?"

"Eighteen, sir."

"Eighteen," Burr said. "And your birthday, I believe, is in January?"

"Yes, sir."

"You'll be twenty-four in January," Burr said.

"Yes, sir."

"Well, based on that, wouldn't that make you seventeen when your Mother was killed?"

"I was almost eighteen," Jason said.

"Yes, almost, but not quite. But that was almost seven years ago. That's quite a long time, isn't it?"

"Yes, sir."

"Do you remember everything that long ago?" Burr asked, still in a conversational tone.

"Not everything," said the boy, "but I remember that night."

"Do you? Do you recall what your parents argued about that night?"

"My mom didn't like the way my dad strung the garland on the tree," Jason said.

"I see," Burr said. "And did he rearrange the garland?"

"Yes, sir."

"And then what?"

"She still didn't like it," Jason said.

"And did she say anything then?"

"I don't remember," Jason said.

"You don't remember," Burr said.

"No, sir."

"You don't remember," Burr said again. "You remember what your father said, but you don't remember what your mother said. Is that right?

"Objection," Truax said. "The witness already said he didn't remember."

"Sustained."

"Mr. Tavohnen, after your father rearranged the garland, is that when he went downstairs?"

"Yes, sir."

"I thought you said he went to the garage, got his deer rifle and then went downstairs."

"Objection," Truax said. "Counsel is trying to confuse the witness."

Burr left Jason, stood in front of Gillis, looked at the jury. "Your Honor, I am merely trying to determine the sequence of events, which is not clear. Perhaps because it was so long ago," Burr said.

"I object," Truax said. "Your Honor, counsel is stating conclusions of fact which have not been established."

"Mr. Lafayette, I see where this is going and I ask that you stop it," Gillis said.

"Yes, Your Honor." Burr felt a pen in the right pocket of his slacks. He took it out, looked at it. It was blue with a cap. The cheap kind that Eve bought because he always lost the expensive ones. He fingered it. "All right, Mr. Tavohnen. I know it's been a long time. Your father then went down to the basement."

Truax glared at him.

"Do you remember if your mother said anything to him when he went downstairs?"

"I think she said something," Jason said.

"What would that be?"

"I don't really remember." Catching himself, he said, "I remember she said something to him about the garland."

"I see," Burr said. He didn't want to ask any more questions about the garland. "Was your mother particular about the Christmas tree, about how it was decorated?"

"Yes, sir."

"She wanted it done in a particular way, a particular order."

"Yes, sir."

"When your father went downstairs, was the tree all decorated?"

"No, sir," Jason said.

"What was left?"

"Well, the angel had to go on," Jason said.

Burr had to speed up now. "Did the angel go on last?"

"Yes sir." The boy always said yes sir. This annoyed Burr.

"And where did the angel go?"

"On top of the tree," Jason said.

"Who put the angel on?"

"My father," Jason said.

"Did he put it on then?"

"No, sir," Jason said.

"Why?"

"He was in the basement," Jason said.

"And wouldn't it make sense that your mother would call to him, call him up to put on the angel?"

"I don't know," Jason said.

"Isn't it possible that she called him, told him to come upstairs and put on the angel? I mean if she was as particular as you said, might she have called him?"

"She might have," Jason said.

"Objection," Truax said. "Counsel is leading the witness."

"I simply asked a question, Your Honor," Burr said. He took his pen out of his pocket. He made sure the jury was watching him, then he pointed it at Truax who flinched.

"Overruled, but watch yourself, Mr. Lafayette," Gillis said.

"Isn't it possible that she called your father?" Burr asked. "And when he didn't come upstairs, she went down to get him?"

"No, sir," Jason said.

"Mr. Tavohnen, I remind you that you are sworn to tell the truth," Burr said. "Isn't it possible that your mother went down to get him?"

"I don't know," Jason said. "It might be."

"Is it possible that you don't really remember exactly what happened?" Burr asked.

"Objection," Truax said.

"What now, Mr. Truax?" Gillis said.

"He is badgering the witness," Truax said.

"Your Honor," Burr said, "I am trying to determine what actually took place that night, and I think we have determined that Jason Tavohnen isn't sure what happened. In fact, what Jason Tavohnen says happened is contradicted by the police report."

"This is irrelevant, Your Honor," Truax said.

Burr pointed his pen at Truax again. "It is extremely relevant. If Mrs. Tavohnen went downstairs to fetch her husband so he could put the angel on the tree, that categorically refutes the prosecutor's claim that Mr. Tavohnen, my client, called her down to the basement to shoot her, which by the way, seems preposterous with their son in the room above."

"Mr. Lafayette, save your theory for your summation," Gillis said.

"Yes, Your Honor," Burr said, but he already made his point. "Now, Mr. Tavohnen, would you say you have a close relationship with your father?"

"Close?" Jason said.

"Yes, are the two of you close?" Burr said.

"Objection," Truax said. "Too vague."

"Sustained," Gillis said.

Burr put the pen back in his pocket, edged closer to the witness stand. "Mr. Tavohnen, when, before today, was the last time you saw your father?"

"I don't remember," Jason said.

"You don't remember," Burr said.

"No, sir."

Burr leaned on the railing of the witness stand with his left arm. "You don't remember when you last saw your father, but you remember that he called your mother downstairs that night? That night, almost seven years ago?"

"Objection," Truax said. "Rhetorical question."

"Sustained," Gillis said.

"Mr. Tavohnen," Burr said, "According to your father, this is the first time he's seen you since you joined the navy, over four years ago. Is that right?"

"Yes, sir."

"But you do have leave, do you not?" Burr said.

"Yes, sir."

"How many in the past four years?" Burr said.

"I don't know," Jason said.

"Twelve?"

"I don't know," Jason said. "Probably."

"Twelve times and you haven't seen your father once," Burr said to the jury.

"No, sir."

"Would it be fair to say that you hate your father?"

"No, sir."

"Mr. Tavohnen, where did you live after your mother was killed?"

"With my grandparents," Jason said.

"Your grandparents. Here in Petoskey?" Burr said.

"Yes," Jason said.

"And why was that?"

"I don't know. I didn't want to live in that house," Jason said.

Burr looked at Jason. "And what about when your father lost his job and moved to Detroit? Did you go, too?"

"I wanted to stay by my friends," Jason said.

"And what do you think of Sarah Tavohnen?" Burr asked.

"I don't know," Jason said.

"Do you like her?"

"She's all right," Jason said.

"Mr. Tavohnen, you have been recently at sea?"

"Yes, sir."

"How long?"

"Four months," Jason said.

"That would be since May," Burr said.

"Since June," Jason said.

"Since June," Burr said. He walked towards Frank and the defense table. "And do you receive mail while you're at sea?"

"Yes, sir," Jason said.

"How often?" Burr said.

"It depends," Jason said. "Every couple weeks."

"And telephone calls," Burr said.

"Yes," Jason said.

"How often?"

"It depends," Jason said.

"Monthly, at least once a month?" Burr said.

"Yes, sir," Jason said.

"Mr. Tavohnen, your ship landed in the last few days then?" Burr said.

"No, sir."

"Really," Burr said, feigning surprise, now standing next to Frank. "When did you return?"

"I don't know," Jason said.

"How long ago would you say, a week ago, two weeks?" Burr said.

"Maybe two weeks," Jason said.

"And did Mr. Truax contact you then?"

"Yes, sir."

"And did he contact you before that?"

"Yes, sir."

"How many times?"

"I don't remember," Jason said.

"Was it more than once?"

"Yes."

"More than twice?"

"Yes."

"More than three times?"

"I don't remember."

"More than four times," Burr said.

"Objection, Your Honor," Truax said. "The witness says he doesn't remember."

"I note," said Burr, his hand on Frank's shoulder, "that Jason Tavohnen has been in contact with the prosecutor at least twice in the last two months, yet he has not seen his father in at least four years." Burr walked to Truax, stood next to where Truax sat. "And the prosecutor, the would-be state senator, said that this witness has just been discovered, that he has been totally unavailable and unreachable. Which appears to be a lie."

CHAPTER TWENTY-ONE

Burr excused himself as soon as Gillis recessed for the day. Burr, his shotgun, Zeke, and a handful of decoys, escaped to a marshy spot hidden away on Crooked Lake. He needed some quiet time to think things over. Truax had done a masterful job with Gannon, but Burr thought he had cast some doubt on the laser theory. Truax had hurt him today, though, with the affair and especially Jason. Burr had looked bad, but as Eve had pointed out, it wasn't really about him, and the trial was on schedule. Despite the surprise witness, Burr still had two days to offer his defense.

Burr thought there was still something about this case that he was missing. He didn't know what, but he did have an idea. He would enlist Jacob one more time, just before they met Sarah and company for dinner.

The Side Door Saloon (next to Pirate Golf but not quite in Petoskey) had, eponymously, no front door but did have decent sandwiches if you kept it simple. Burr ordered a Rolling Rock, the only place anywhere nearby that had it on draft. Jacob ordered a club soda with a lime. Burr had arrived just behind Jacob who was not warm to his idea.

"You should, we should, resign," Jacob said. "Your client, your client's wife, and quite possibly, your paramour, are all lying to you."

"Do you mean that Suzanne is quite possibly my paramour or that Suzanne is quite possibly lying?"

"You know very well what I mean," Jacob said.

"I am not going to resign," Burr said. "Not now."

"Why ever not?" Jacob asked.

"Because I don't believe Frank murdered Claudia," Burr said.

"Anything else?" Jacob asked.

"There is something else going on here." Burr said.

"And what else?" Jacob asked.

"I do not intend to lose to Truax," Burr said.

"And?" Jacob asked.

Burr took a long draught of his beer, set it down. "And," he said, "And, it's my ego."

"Bingo," Jacob said.

Burr ignored Jacob's punctuational comment. "There is something else beyond my ego going on here, and I intend to find out what it is," Burr said.

"Whatever it might be, I don't want to know," Jacob said.

"Do you think Becky might be a bit big for her age?" Burr asked.

"Who?" Jacob asked.

"The girl," Burr said. "Frank's daughter."

"I never thought about it," Jacob said. "I'm afraid I'm no judge of it either." He sipped on his club soda.

"I saw her at the last bail hearing, and she seems big to me," Burr said, "for her age."

"I don't see what that has to do with anything," Jacob said.

"I'd like to know how old Becky is," Burr said.

"Ask Sarah," Jacob said.

"I mean, precisely how old. Like, when is her birthday?" Burr said.

"Why do you want to know?" Jacob asked.

"I'm curious," Burr said.

"I am a writer of appellate briefs," Jacob said.

"Yes, you are," Burr said.

"I have no idea where to begin," Jacob said.

"I think we need a birth certificate," Burr said. "You could start in Detroit, at the City-County Building."

I despise downtown Detroit," Jacob said.

"We used to work downtown," Burr said. Jacob continued his protest but was cut short with the arrival of Suzanne and Sarah, followed shortly thereafter by Eve. Burr ordered another Rolling Rock.

"I hardly think it appropriate to try to catch ducks at a time like this," Sarah said. She had changed from her virgin suit to jeans and a black sweater.

"I wasn't trying to catch them," Burr said.

"What were you doing then?" she asked.

"I was trying to kill them," Burr said.

"Oh," Sarah said. "What are we going to do now? About Truax. He lied to us about Jason. Didn't he?"

"He did," Jacob said.

Burr thought Jacob would have excused himself for his after dinner joint by now. Perhaps he has stayed to defend me, thought Burr. More likely it wasn't dark enough outside to light up. Or no wind to disperse the smell.

"I don't think there's much we're going to do about it," Jacob said.

"It looks like Gillis will allow almost anything," Burr said.

"We preserved our rights for an appeal," Jacob said.

"An appeal? Do you mean you're going to lose?" Sarah asked. "All you do is ridicule Truax. And then you put everyone on the witness list, because it's the rule. And look what Truax did to us."

Burr drank from his beer again. "What exactly would you say he did to us?" Burr said.

"He snuck in Jason," Sarah said "Truax cheated and lied. That's what he did," Sarah said.

"And you are suggesting that I do the same?" Burr asked.

"I am suggesting that you win, and I don't care how you do it," Sarah said.

"Before you advise me to cheat and lie, you might consider why we're here right now," Burr said.

"And why is that?"

"Because you cheated and lied to me. That's why," Burr said. "Did it ever occur to you that I might have done things differently had I known back in February that the two of you were screwing each other's eyes out?"

Sarah reached over and slowly, every so slowly, poured the Rolling Rock in his lap. That, unsurprisingly, ended the dinner rather abruptly.

Thursday, October 19, 1989 – Day Four

Burr began his defense the next morning. He had decided to begin with Van Arkel, the physician turned mortician, because he thought Van Arkel would hurt Truax the most, the quickest. He suspected that Truax thought so too, especially since he hadn't called him as a witness for the prosecution.

Van Arkel testified that he had performed an autopsy, a standard procedure when the cause of death was a gunshot. He said that he believed Claudia's death to be accidental, which corroborated what the police believed. Then Burr took him to the heart of the matter (so to speak)."You believed that the cause of death was accidental," Burr said. "In spite of the fact that the exit wound was lower than the entry point of the bullet," Burr said, in keeping with the litigator's first rule: ask only questions to which you already know the answers.

"Yes," Van Arkel said.

Burr knew he was on safe ground here. "Let me go back a step," he said. "Would you explain what you saw and what you concluded?"

"The bullet entered here," Van Arkel said. He touched his right forefinger under his left armpit. And then it came out here," He touched a spot about four inches above his waist. The nail on Van Arkels's forefinger was black. Burr saw it but he didn't think the jury did.

"Did you think it unusual that if the gun went off parallel to the floor that the bullet exited below at a point where it entered?" Burr knew the answer.

"No," Van Arkel said.

"And why not?"

"If the bullet glanced off a bone, and it did go in through the ribs, that could change its path," Van Arkel said.

"A bullet entering on a path parallel to the floor could be deflected downward?"

"Yes," Van Arkel said.

"And the result would be wounds of the type suffered by the deceased."

"Yes," Van Arkel said.

"Thank you, Dr. Van Arkel," Burr said. "Now, please show us the size of the entry wound."

"It would be about this size, the size of the bullet." Van Arkel held up the forefinger with the blackened nail. Burr winced, as did the jury.

"And the size of the exit wound?" Van Arkel made a circle with his thumb and forefinger. Mercifully, thought Burr, the black fingernail did not show this time.

"Please tell us the size of the exit wound," Burr said, who wanted a written record.

"A circle with a diameter of approximately two inches," Van Arkel said.

"And is this consistent with a bullet that has struck something?"

"It is," Van Arkel said.

"How is that?"

"Well, when a bullet enters flesh, animal or human, if often tumbles or spins off center, particularly when it strikes bone," Van Arkel said.

"And could you pinpoint from the wound exactly where the bullet was when it left the body?" Burr asked, this the critical question of the entire examination.

"No," Van Arkel said.

"Why is that?"

"Because the exit wound was so much bigger than the diameter of the bullet," Van Arkel said.

"Then the laser would be useless to determine the path of the bullet by using the exit wound," Burr said, not asking.

"That is correct," Van Arkel said.

"Objection," Truax said.

"Sustained," Gillis said.

"Ladies and gentlemen, I submit that the testimony of Mr. Van Arkel casts grave doubt on the scientific theory of the prosecution. This is simply another example of voodoo science. And in this case, voodoo science wrongly applied. Thank you Dr. Van Arkel. No further questions."

"I object, Your Honor. Counsel is preaching to the jury."

"Strike Mr. Lafayette's last comments from the record," Gillis said. Turning to the jury, "You are to disregard Mr. Lafayette's comments regarding voodoo science." To Burr, "Mr. Lafayette, surely you know better than this."

"Yes, Your Honor," Burr said, delighted by the repetition of voodoo science by Gillis. "We have no further questions."

Van Arkel stood up, unfolded himself really. The effect of this silly stretching certainly didn't help Van Arkel's credibility.

"Dr. Van Arkel, are you quite through?" Gillis said.

"Yes," he said, still standing.

"Then please sit down," Gillis said.

Van Arkel sat. Truax stood. "Dr. Van Arkel," he said, "when you performed the autopsy on the accused's wife," head bent towards Frank as he said this, "did you follow the standard autopsy procedure for gunshot wounds?"

"I did," Van Arkel said.

"And what exactly is that procedure?"

"I take a steel rod, a stiff wire really, and insert the rod into the entry wound and push it through the body and then out the exit wound," Van Arkel said.

"And did you do this?"

"I did," Van Arkel said.

"And you were able to push the rod all the way through?"

"Yes," Van Arkel said.

"Easily?" Truax chewed on his cheek. "Did it slip through easily, Dr. Van Arkel?"

"I don't remember," Van Arkel said.

"Surely you would remember something like that," Truax scowled at him. "After all, how often do you get a case like this?"

"I really don't remember," said Van Arkel.

"Dr. Van Arkel, please," Truax said.

"Objection, Your Honor," Burr said. "He said he didn't remember. 'I don't remember' is an acceptable answer."

"Sustained," Gillis said.

"Dr. Van Arkel, you did push the rod through though?"

"Yes," Van Arkel said.

"Did the rod strike anything hard on the way through, say a bone?"

"Objection," Burr said. "Calls for speculation."

Truax had opened his mouth to speak. He left it open but no sounds came out. Finally, "It most certainly does not call for speculation, Your Honor. It calls for a factual answer."

"Answer the question," Gillis said.

Burr knew Truax was right, that Van Arkel would have to answer. He wanted to give Van Arkel time to settle himself, show the jury that Truax was a bully.

"I don't recall that the rod struck a bone," Van Arkel said. He began chewing the inside of his cheek.

Truax rescowled at the combination coroner/undertaker. "Dr. Van Arkel, this is important and there is a difference here. Is your answer, you don't remember what happened, or you don't recall that the rod struck the bone."

"The latter," Van Arkel said.

"The latter," Truax said who made no attempt to hide his disgust with the word choice. "Dr. Van Arkel, is this what you mean? 'I do not recall the rod hitting a bone'."

"Yes," Van Arkel said.

"Thank you. Now, Dr. Van Arkel, it is customary to take photographs of the body with a rod such as this in place. Is that correct?"

"Yes," Van Arkel said.

"And did you do that?"

"Yes," Van Arkel said.

Truax marched to his table and snatched a manila folder "Your Honor, the prosecution would like to introduce these photographs as People's Exhibit Four."

Burr on his feet, "Objection, Your Honor," he said. "The prosecution has presented its case. If he wanted that evidence introduced, he should have done it then."

"Your Honor," Truax said, "the court rules permit the introduction of physical evidence if it is used to rebut the proofs offered by the defense."

"This is not being introduced for that purpose," Burr said, although he knew it was. "This is being introduced to horrify and repulse the members of the jury."

"Nonsense," Truax said. "You want to talk about angles of entry, we'll show them," Truax said.

"Stop it, both of you." Gillis said it like a parent to quarrelling children. "Let me see them." Truax passed the folder to Gillis who opened it, shut his eyes and exhaled. Then he paged through them.

"I'll allow them," he said.

"Thank you, Your Honor," Truax said.

Burr knew they would be allowed. He had seen the photographs and purposely decided not to use them.

"Would these be the photographs?" Truax asked, opening the file and handing the letter-sized photographs, one after the other, to Van Arkel. Burr counted twelve.

"Yes," Van Arkel said.

"Did you take these photographs?"

"I did," Van Arkel said.

"And what do they show?"

"They show the rod going into and coming out of the body of the deceased," Van Arkel said.

"They show rather more than that, don't they?"

"No," Van Arkel said. "No, I don't think so." Van Arkel began chewing on his cheek again, from the inside of his mouth.

"Your Honor, may I show these to the jury?" Truax said.

"You may," Gillis said.

Burr started to his feet than sat back down again. He saw no point in objecting now that the pictures had been admitted.

Truax marched to the foreman and handed her the first picture. She looked at it, turned away, then back, now staring at it. The man next to her tried to look across her, but her shoulder blocked his view.

"When you're done, please pass it to your right," Truax said.

Like the potatoes on Thanksgiving, Burr thought.

Truax handed her the next photograph and so it went until they had all been passed around and their faces showed him horror, revulsion, and fascination. Truax collected them at the back row, like an usher in church with a collection plate. He took the retrieved pictures back to Van Arkel.

"Now, Dr. Van Arkel, what in fact do they show?" Truax said.

Burr knew exactly what they showed. Claudia on a stainless steel gurney, naked from the waist up, with a white rod, the diameter of a coat hanger sticking into her left armpit and out from her right side at a forty-five degree angle. She looked like she had been speared and the spear had been left in.

"Let me tell you what they show," Truax said. "These pictures taken by Dr. Van Arkel show that the bullet was fired into Mrs. Tavohnen, the deceased's wife, from a gun on a shoulder. That's what they show."

Dr. Van Arkel began to stand, hands on the railing, the black fingernail wrapped around it.

"Dr. Van Arkel, I'm not quite through," Truax said.

"Oh," he said, a bit shaken. He stood there though as if standing, he would be excused earlier.

"Dr. Van Arkel, please sit down," Gillis said.

The coroner sat.

"Dr. Van Arkel, do you have a relationship with Mr. Tavohnen?" Truax said.

"No, not really. He moved away, you know."

"I am aware of that," Truax said. "Prior to that, did you?"

"No. No, I guess not," Van Arkel said.

"You weren't friends?"

"No, we weren't friends," Van Arkel said.

"But you knew him," Truax said.

"It's a small town," Van Arkel said.

"So you knew him," Truax said.

"Yes," Van Arkel said.

"You have two sons, do you not?"

"Objection," Burr said. "Irrelevant."

"I will show the connection, your Honor," Truax said.

"Please then, Mr. Truax," Gillis said, "do connect the dots."

"Yes, Your Honor," Truax said. "Now then, didn't your boys play baseball?"

"Yes," said Van Arkel.

"And didn't Mr. Tavohnen coach them?"

"Yes," Van Arkel said.

"And were they good baseball players?"

"I thought so," Van Arkel said.

"Were they starters?" asked Truax.

"Yes," Van Arkel said.

"And you went to the games," Truax said.

"I did," Van Arkel said.

"Mr. Tavohnen coached your sons and they were good baseball players who started and you went to their games." Truax pressed.

"Yes," Van Arkel said.

"But you had no relationship," Van Arkel said.

"He coached my sons," Van Arkel said.

"I would say that that is a relationship, the father of the players who this man coached (pointing to Frank), a relationship that might at the very least predispose your findings," Truax said.

"Objection," Burr said. "I fail to see how the dots have been connected."

"Sustained," Gillis said.

"Dr. Van Arkel, please tell the court what you were asked to do by the police."

"I was asked to do an autopsy," Van Arkel said.

"And did anyone from the police say what they thought had happened?" asked Truax.

"Yes," Van Arkel said.

"And who would that be?"

"Rollie Gustafson," Van Arkel said. "It's been a long time, but I think he said that Frank shot his wife."

"Did he use the word accident?"

"He might have. Yes, I think he did," Van Arkel said.

"This, by the way, is your deposition. Mr. Gustafson said that there was an accident. Frank's deer rifle went off by mistake and Claudia is dead," Truax said.

"If you say so, "said Van Arkel.

"If I say so? This is what you said, sir. Do you wish to contradict your sworn testimony?"

"No," Van Arkel said.

"Very well, then." Truax said. "Mr. Gustafson, the officer in charge, tells you that Claudia was accidentally shot."

"Yes," Van Arkel said.

"And with that direction, and knowing Frank as your sons' coach, isn't it possible that you might have been predisposed to determine this was accidental?"

"No," Van Arkel said.

"I submit to you," Truax said this to the jury, "that Dr. Van Arkel merely confirmed what the police thought and did not independently think on his own. That he rubber stamped a sloppy investigation."

"Objection," Burr said. "We're not talking about the police here."

"Not yet," Truax said.

"Sustained," Gillis said.

"Dr. Van Arkel," Truax said. Van Arkel was clearly in pain and wanted this over, "just a few more questions. You are a licensed physician. Is that correct?"

"Yes," Van Arkel said.

"And the county coroner?"

"It's a part-time job," Van Arkel said.

Burr groaned to himself. How many times did he have to tell them to answer with yes or no. Nothing more.

"You are a physician and a part-time coroner," Truax said.

"Yes," Van Arkel said.

"Do you practice medicine for a living?"

"No," Van Arkel said.

"Really?"

"What do you do for a living, your primary income?"

"I am a mortician," Van Arkel said.

"A mortician," repeated Truax, rolling his eyes. "Oh, you mean an undertaker. You are a licensed physician, but you are an undertaker. That's odd."

"It's a family business," Van Arkel said.

Burr's spirits flagged as Truax used Burr's tactic at the preliminary exam against him.

Truax ignored this. "Now, Dr. Van Arkel, when you performed the autopsy as part of the process, I believe it is the prescribed procedure to remove certain of the internal organs and examine them. Is that correct?"

"Yes," Truax said.

"And did you do that?"

"I did," Van Arkel said.

"And what did you find?"

"The only abnormalities were in both lungs and the heart," Van Arkel said.

"And what were these abnormalities?"

"The bullet passed through both lungs and the heart," Van Arkel said.

"The heart," Truax said. "I see. And the cause of death was?"

"The cause of death was a bullet wound to the lungs and heart," Van Arkel said.

Truax dropped his head, paused. Slowly and sadly (nicely done, thought Burr), Truax looked up at the undertaker and then the jury. "Mr. Tavohnen shot his wife in the heart," Truax said.

~

At 11:00 a.m. Gillis declared a ten-minute recess, during which Burr made a pre-arranged call to Jacob at the City-County Building in Detroit.

"How old did you say Becky was?" Jacob said.

"I didn't say, but she's six. She was born in December," Burr said, telephonically.

"I checked November through January," Jacob said.

"And?"

"And nothing," Jacob said.

"Where did you check?" Burr asked.

"The City-County Building. In Detroit."

"Keep going. February, March and so on," Burr said.

"I do not like downtown Detroit," Jacob said. He hung up.

~

Rollie Gustafson, Roland officially, did not look like a policeman. He did not even look much like a former policeman.

He had on a brown suit, brown, no pattern, just brown, and what Burr took for the same white shirt he had worn at the preliminary exam, the white shirt with a collar that was still too small for his neck, which spilled over the collar. His tie, turquoise, was just that, solid and no pattern. At least he had it tied, Burr thought, but it wasn't any kind of a knot he had seen before. The knot had slipped and pulled to the right, which made the ex-cop's head look like it was on crooked.

Burr led Rollie (expertly, he thought) through the tale, that he was first on the scene, that Frank had bear hugged Jason, not letting him go down in the basement, that the gun was dirty, that Frank said he had killed her accidentally, that the findings of the inquest determined it to be an accident.

He was especially pleased with Rollie's testimony about the accident:

"Well, I was a cop for a long time, been retired for five years, five years. That's right. Five years. Anyways, I seen a lot of strange stuff, stranger than this."

"Would you please elaborate," Burr said.

"Well, first of all, Frank was crying. He was real upset. And I could tell he really was. Then, if you were going to kill your wife, there's way better places to do it than at home with your kid upstairs. Oh, I'm not saying he wasn't mad at her or she at him. More likely than not, knowing Claudia. But it sure looked like an accident to me," Gustafson said.

That was what Burr had been waiting for, what they had practiced. Say you thought it was an accident Burr had told Gustafson. That's how he'd coached him. Of course, if that's what you really thought, Burr had said.

Gustafson smiled slightly, pulled at his tie. It was now straight but he'd pulled the knot so tight the tips of his collar popped up.

Then it was Truax's turn.

"Mr. Gustafson," Truax said, straightening his own tie, which was already straight. "Did you retire from the City of Petoskey police force?"

"Objection, Your Honor. Irrelevant," Burr said.

"This goes to the question of competency, Your Honor," Truax said.

"I'll allow it," Gillis said.

"Now then, Mr. Gustafson, did you retire from the city of Petoskey police force?" repeated Truax.

"Yes," Gustafson said.

"You did?" Truax said.

"Yes," Gillis said.

"Did you retire or were you fired?"

"I retired," Gustafson said. "I'd been in law enforcement for thirty-three years."

"I see," Truax said. "Did you retire or were you asked to resign or you would be fired?"

"Objection, Your Honor. The witness already answered the question," Burr said.

"I am merely trying to give the witness the opportunity to tell the truth," Truax said.

"Proceed, Mr. Truax. But do not badger the witness," Gillis said.

"Yes, Your Honor," Truax said. Truax turned on his heel. Burr thought it looked like an about face. At his table, he opened a folder, and walked back to Gustafson. "Mr. Gustafson, I have your personnel file here. Would you care to comment on it?"

"No," Gustafson said.

"It says here," Truax turned and faced Gustafson, "that you were suspended without pay for six months, then you retired," Truax said.

"Would you care to comment on that?"

"No," Gustafson said.

"Objection, Your Honor. This is irrelevant," Burr said.

"Mr. Truax?"

"I will connect this, Your Honor," Truax said.

"All right, but you better do it soon," Gillis said.

"Mr. Gustafson, according to your file, you were suspended on three different occasions, the last time, as I said, for six months. Then just before your hearing you retired," Truax said. "Why did you retire?"

"I had enough time in for my pension," Gustafson said.

"Yes, of course," Truax said. "It also says in your file that you were suspended for drinking. No, let me be precise. You were suspended because you were drunk on the job. Is that right?"

"I was not drunk," Gustafson said.

"That's not what your file says," Truax said. Truax stepped in for the kill. "Mr. Gustafson, were you drunk that night? So drunk that you couldn't do, didn't do, a proper and complete investigation?" Truax said.

"No," Gustafson said.

"Objection," Burr said.

"Sustained," Gillis said. "That's enough, Mr. Truax."

"Your Honor, I am trying to show that the investigation may have been corrupted by Mr. Gustafson's inebriation," Truax said.

"You haven't shown it. Strike the last comment by Mr. Truax," Gillis said.

Over his glasses to the jury, Gillis said, "Ladies and gentlemen, you may consider the competency of Mr. Gustafson. You may not consider that Mr. Truax has come anywhere close to proving him intoxicated on the night of the killing."

"Mr. Gustafson, did you have a personal relationship with Mr. Tavohnen?"

"Personal relationship?" asked Gustafson.

"Did you know him prior to the killing?"

"Yes," Gustafson said.

"Were you friends?"

"No," Gustafson said.

"But you went to the same church. Immaculate Heart. Is that right?"

"Yes, but I don't think Frank went too often," Gustafson said.

"Just answer the questions, please," Truax said. "And was Mr. Tavohnen your son's baseball coach?"

"Frank coached everybody's son," Gustafson said.

"Answer the question please," Truax said.

"Yes," Gustafson said.

"Ladies and gentlemen of the jury, I submit to you that Mr. Gustafson, the officer in charge, the first one at the scene is a drunk.

He was a friend of Mr. Tavohnen's, and bent over backwards to make this out to be an accident."

"Objection, Your Honor," Burr said. "That is an outrage."

"Sustained. Strike that from the record." Gillis tore his glasses from his face. "Calvin, for once I agree with counsel for the defense. This is outrageous. If you have more of these antics, I will throw you out. Is that clear?"

"Yes, your Honor," said Truax, smugly.

"Do not be smug with me, Calvin." Gillis shook his gavel at him, like he was hammering a nail.

CHAPTER TWENTY-TWO

Burr, his timing impeccable, had arranged for Jacob to call him at his subterranean headquarters during the lunch recess. By this time Burr had a very good sense of the feeding schedule of Judge Gillis.

"Burr, you were right. And wrong," Jacob said.

"What?" Burr said.

"Becky. She was born in August," Jacob said.

"Really," Burr said. "She is young."

"Not exactly," Jacob said.

"What?"

"The prior August. August 1983. I had to go backwards. She's not five," Jacob said. "She's six."

"Hurry back," Burr said.

George Maples, of course, still had his flat top, a flat top from the early sixties, thirty years later. No sideburns. Hair cut close on the sides then where his skull rounded, a little longer, still short but long enough so that when the barber drew the electric razor across the top of his head front to back, the top of his head had no contours, flat across, straight down the sides and back, which made his head look square and his face look like it had been carved from a block of wood. He looked solid to Burr, solid the way you would expect the property manager to look.

"Sergeant Maples, was it your responsibility to keep track of all evidence?" Burr asked.

"Yes," Maples said.

"And that would include Mr. Tavohnen's deer rifle?" Burr stayed as far away as he could from "gun that killed Claudia" or "murder weapon," God forbid.

"Yes," Maples said.

"And did you take custody of the deer rifle?"

"I did."

"Please tell us the procedure," Burr said.

"Back then, before we had a computer, I would record the item on a log book, what it was, date, case number. Then I'd put it in the cage, find a place for it and then record that in the book."

"What is the cage?"

"Down in the basement of the police station, next door, there's a room, back of the shop, with wire mesh in front of it, and a chain link door. My little world is behind it."

"And it locks?"

"Yes, sir," Maples said.

"Who has the key?"

"Me," Maples said. "Me and the Chief. That's it."

"I see," Burr said. "And did you inventory the rifle?"

"I did," Maples said.

Burr stepped two steps closer to the witness. "Mr. Maples," he said, "where is the file that contains this information?"

"I don't know," said Maples.

Burr, incredulous, "You don't know?" he asked.

"That's what I said."

"How could you not know?"

"That file, along with a bunch of others, was destroyed in a flood."

"A flood?"

"Not exactly a flood, but somebody was having a smoke, and the sprinklers turned on. Ruined a bunch of files." Maples yawned. "But you already know . . ."

Burr cut him off. (It was, after all, Burr's show.) "So you have no records concerning Mr. Tavohnen's deer rifle. Is that right?"

"Yes," said Maples, who looked like he had been taken advantage of. And, of course, Burr had done just that.

"Mr. Maples, what happens to an inventory item, such as this deer rifle, when a case is closed?"

"We usually return it to the owner," Maples said.

"What if no one claims it?"

"Then we sell it at our garage sale," Maples said.

"Garage sale?"

Maples smiled. His eyebrows lifted the corners of his flattop. "Yeah, you know, where we get rid of everything we don't need."

"I see," Burr said. "And what happens when someone claims an item or it goes to the garage sale?"

"I get a signature, a release," Maples said. "Mark it gone."

"I see. And is there an entry of that type for Mr. Tavohnen's rifle?"

"No," Maples said.

"Are those the only ways, if a case has been closed, to dispose of something?"

"Yes," Maples said.

"And do you have a release for the deer rifle?"

"No," repeated Maples.

"Does the Petoskey Police Department have the rifle?"

"No," Maples said.

"You didn't release it, but you don't have it. Is that right?"

"Yes," Maples said.

"Sergeant Maples," Burr said, "what happened to Mr. Tavohnen's deer rifle?"

"I don't know," Maples said. Maples' face, not just his face, his entire head, began to turn red. He was turning red underneath his flat top.

"What happened to it?" Burr asked again.

"I don't know," Maples said. Now his ears turned red.

"Ladies and gentlemen. The prosecution has brought Mr. Tavohnen before you on a murder charge, an open murder charge, which means you could conceivably cause him to be imprisoned, in jail, for the rest of his life. Yet," Burr stopped, turned to Frank, then back to the jury, "Mr. Truax has no weapon. He doesn't know where it is. The police can't find it. They can't even file the file. And yet, Mr. Truax wants you to find Mr. Tavohnen guilty. And he can't find the gun. And we will show you why that's important. Why is it important? Because the gun may well have been defective. That's why. No further questions, Your Honor." Burr sat down at the defense table.

Truax stood. "Your Honor," Truax said. "The prosecution asks that the testimony of Sargeant Maples be stricken from the records."

"What on earth for?" Gillis asked.

"The point," said Truax, "is that somehow the police lost the gun. But the gun is not the issue. Everyone admits that the defendant killed his wife with his deer rifle. Where the gun is doesn't matter. Who has it, if anyone does, doesn't matter. What matters is Frank Tavohnen killed his wife with that gun. The gun doesn't matter."

Burr thought it did.

So did Gillis. "Counselor, I will not strike the testimony of Sargeant Maples. You may question him if you wish."

"The people have no questions," Truax said.

Gillis dismissed Maples. Burr called Frieda Deutsch who was the key to his defense. He had great hopes for her, especially since he believed he had laid a strong foundation about the missing gun with Maples.

"Mrs. Deutsch," Burr said.

"It's Miss," she said. "I'm a widow."

"Oh, I see," Burr said, who didn't. "I'm sorry."

"That's all right," Frieda Deutsch said, smiling at him.

"Miss Deutsch, what is your occupation?"

"I'm a gunsmith," she said.

"A gunsmith," Burr said. "What does a gunsmith do?"

"You know what a gunsmith does," Frieda said. "A gunsmith repairs guns."

"Do you do anything else?" Burr asked.

"I also own a gun shop," she said.

"Miss Deutsch, as you know, I've been to your gun shop. I'm not sure a gun shop is a fair description. To me it seems at least like a store, maybe a super-store."

"Objection," Truax said. "Counsel is not the witness."

"Sustained," Gillis said.

"Miss Deutsch, in addition to being a gunsmith, how many guns do you sell in your store a year?"

"About four hundred," she said.

"Four hundred," Burr said. "That's a lot of guns."

"That's right," she said.

"And how long have you been in the business?"

"I've worked there thirty-three years. I've been the gunsmith for seventeen years. My father started it fifty years ago, and I took it over when he died. She stopped there, for effect, he thought. "That would be five years ago."

"I'm sorry," Burr said.

"Yes, well it is tragic," Frieda Deutsch said.

Burr had to get her focused. "Mrs. Deutsch, how many guns do you repair per year?"

She scrunched her nose.

"About a hundred and fifty, I'd say."

"A hundred and fifty," said. "Year in and year out?"

"Yes," she said.

"For seventeen years," Burr said.

"Yes," she said.

Burr thrust his hands in his pockets and looked down at his shoes, this intended as a signal to the jury that he was done qualifying the witness. (He noted that his socks didn't quite match, almost, but not quite. He further noted that he'd have to ask Eve for a clothes check, although she usually did this without being asked.)

"Miss Deutsch, are you familiar with the Field & Jones, Model 92, 30:06?"

"I am," Frieda Deutsch said.

"And why would that be?"

"We sold them in the shop for awhile," she said.

"You sold them?"

"Yes," she said.

"How many?"

"Eleven," she said.

"Eleven," Burr said. "Miss Deutsch, you said you sell four hundred guns a year. If my math is right, that's almost twenty thousand guns in fifty years. Field & Jones is one of the most successful gun companies in the world, and I believe deer rifles are one of their specialties. And you only sold eleven Model 92's? Why is that?"

"Two reasons," Frieda Deutsch said. "They were only out for three years. And I quit selling them before Field & Jones stopped making them."

"Why was that?"

"Bad design," she said.

"Really," Burr said, feigning surprise. "Could you elaborate?"

"I could. They weren't safe. In fact, they were dangerous. So Field & Jones took them off the market. Came out with a new model."

"What about them was dangerous?"

"Sometimes they wouldn't eject a live shell," she said.

"Really?"

"The Model 92 is a bolt action rifle," Frieda Deutsch said. "You rack in a shell. Then when you shoot, you rack the bolt. Then the extractors, like fingers, grip the shell by the rim and pull it out. While that's going on, another shell gets pulled up from the clip. When you push the bolt back it pushes the bullet into the chamber. It works fine. If you shoot. But if you leave a live one in the chamber and don't fire, then pull the bolt back to eject the live shell, once in a while the shell won't eject."

"And," Burr said.

"Well, you think you emptied the gun, but you didn't," Frieda Deutsch said.

"And," Burr said again.

"And the gun you thought was empty, isn't," Frieda Deutsch said"

"Your Honor, to make this perfectly clear, may we demonstrate?"

"Objection, Your Honor," Truax said popping up. "This is sheer speculation."

"Your Honor," Burr said, "if the prosecution could produce the rifle that killed Mrs. Tavohnen, this would not be necessary."

"I'll allow it," Gillis said. "But, Mr. Lafayette. Do not endanger anyone in this courtroom."

"We won't, Your Honor. The point we will demonstrate, ladies and gentlemen, is that the rifle in question, which as you now know is missing, may have been loaded. It may then have accidentally discharged despite safety efforts."

Burr nodded at Swede, the baliff, who fetched the rifle from the storage closet.

Burr didn't want the jury wondering why Frank and Farr hadn't testified. He couldn't put Frank on the stand even if he wanted to because Truax could question him about his marriage to Claudia and his affair with Sarah. If Burr didn't call Frank, Truax couldn't. Truax couldn't call Sarah because a wife could not be required to testify against her husband. And he didn't want Farr on the stand because he was stupid and dead certain that he'd unloaded the rifle. This was the only way, and he didn't want anyone to have too much time to think about it. Truax had missed his chance to call Farr. Unless he did it in rebuttal. And Burr didn't think Gillis would give him the time. Not that Farr would be credible.

Swede handed Burr the guncase. Burr started to unzip it.

"Bring that up here," Gillis said. "Take it out of the case where I can see it."

Standing below Gillis, Burr finished unzipping the case and took the rifle out. He felt the jury recoil in the presence of an agent of death. "The defense would like to introduce this rifle as Defense Exhibit Three.

"Yes, yes," Gillis said. "Mr. Lafayette, are you sure that gun is empty?"

"I am, Your Honor," Burr said.

"Rack it for me," Gillis said.

Burr pulled back the bolt. Then closed it.

"Open it again," Gillis said. Burr slid the bolt back. "Let me look through the barrel."

Burr handed Gillis the rifle, stock first. Gillis peered through the chamber. "All right," Gillis said. "I can see daylight. Where's the clip?"

Burr reached into his pocket and pulled out the clip, a thin metal case about the size of a cigarette pack, open at top and bottom, and handed it to Gillis. He fingered it, turning it over and over in his hands.

"Where are the bullets?" Gillis asked.

Burr fished five bullets from his pocket, each three inches long, with shiny brass casings, cylindrical, flat at the base with a rim, and tipped at the business end. He laid them in his palm, tilted down, so the jury could see them.

"Are they live?"

"Yes, Your Honor," Burr said.

"How do you expect me to allow a loaded gun in my courtroom?"

"The safety is on, Your Honor," Burr said.

"Apparently that is what Mr. Tavohnen thought," Gillis said.

"I am afraid I must object, Your Honor," Burr said.

"I apologize, Counsel. Strike that from the record," Gillis said.

Burr felt the tension in the courtroom. They were all nervous with the gun and the bullets this close to them. He was sure the jury could feel its lethalness, its killing power. That alone should help him, especially if what he was about to do worked.

"All right then, Mr. Lafayette, what do you propose to do?" asked Gillis.

"I am going to ask Miss Deutsch to demonstrate how this gun might malfunction," Burr said.

"She's not going to fire it," Gillis said.

"No, Your Honor," Burr said.

"All right, then, go ahead," Gillis said. Now to the gunsmith, looking over his glasses again, "but don't point that thing at anyone." Gillis let his breath out, took off his glasses. "Here's what you do. Go stand over there." He pointed to a spot about six feet from the jurors. "Do it there. Point the gun at the back wall, and keep the barrel pointed at the floor."

She hauled herself to her feet by pulling on the railing of the jury box. The top of her pantyhose showed above the waistband. Gillis handed her the gun.

"Be careful," Gillis said.

"Your Honor," Truax said, "I must object. This purported demonstration has no bearing on what actually occurred."

"Your objection has been noted," Gillis said.

"Okay, let's see this," Gillis said. He was curious now. "Here's the clip." He handed it to Burr.

Burr hoped (prayed, actually) that Frieda Deutsch would perform the demonstration (it truly was a performance) just the way they had practiced. Practiced and practiced, ad nauseum, until she refused to practice anymore. While it was true that the Model 92 did occasionally malfunction, she said that it failed only under certain circumstances and not very often. So they had to do it just right and the extractors had to fail (which could be guaranteed with a slight adjustment to the extractors, not that Burr had asked Frieda Dentsch to make such an adjustment.)

Burr had drilled her and drilled her, told her exactly what to say when Truax cross-examined her. He had posed as the prosecutor time and again, until she had it right. Now it's showtime, he said to himself.

"Ladies and Gentlemen," Burr said. "Miss Deutsch will show you how the gun is loaded and how it malfunctions."

She passed him the gun. He handed her the clip. Then he held out the shells in his hand.

"Miss Deutsch, please tell the jury what you are doing," Burr said.

"This clip holds the bullets," she said. "There's a spring in here to force the bullet up in the chamber when the bolt is pulled back. Here's how you load it."

She pushed a bullet in the clip, took another from Burr's open hand, and pushed it in. She did this until all five bullets were in the clip.

"Hand me the gun," she said. "The clip goes here—underneath the rifle in the breech. Right here. Where it's open." She fit the clip in. "Now to put a shell in the chamber, you rack back this bolt."

"Miss Deutsch, is the safety on?" Gillis said.

"Yes," she said.

"Proceed," Gillis said.

Frieda Deutsch looked irritated at the interruption. "As I was saying, when you rack the bolt it pulls a bullet up into the breech, like this." She showed the bullet, then rammed the bolt shut. "Now it's ready to fire. Let's say that man was a buck." She stopped, shouldered the gun, pointing at the county's namesake, whose portrait hung on the back wall.

"Be careful," Gillis said.

She ignored him. "But, let's say it was a doe and you don't want to kill a doe, so you don't shoot." She dropped the gun to her waist. "And now let's say you're done for the day. So you unload the rifle. Here is where you have to watch yourself. If you take off the clip, like this," she said, snapped it off and put it in the waistband of her stretch pants. "And then you rack the gun like this." She pulled back the bolt; the extractors grabbed the bullet; and it flipped out. "You're empty. See one bullet here," she unloaded the clip, "and one, two, three, four bullets here. No problem. But watch this."

Frieda Deutsch put the bullet she had ejected back into the clip. "Five in the clip." She snapped the clip back into the rifle. "Clip in the gun. Right? Now I rack one in the chamber."

She mounted the gun to her shoulder. "Another doe. I put the gun down again. Now watch closely," she said to the jury. "This time I rack the gun first, with the clip still in." She racked the gun. The bullet ejected. "Out comes the bullet. Here it is," she said showing it to the jury. "Now I close the bolt." She slid it shut. "You know what just happened?"

The jury didn't.

"Another shell goes into the chamber when the first shell ejected. That's how a bolt action works. So when I take the clip out there's three bullets in the clip." Frieda Deutsch took the clip off the rifle and handed the rifle to Burr. She then emptied the clip. Three bullets came out.

"Now I have these three bullets, plus the one I ejected," holding the four bullets in the palm of her hand.

"Where's the fifth shell?" she asked the jury. "I'll show you." She traded Burr four bullets for the rifle. "The fifth shell is still in the chamber."

"But that shouldn't be a problem," she said. "Why? Because when I rack the gun again—and every hunter knows enough to rack the gun again just to be sure—out comes the shell. Like this."

Frieda Deutsch racked the gun. No shell.

"Let me try it again," she said.

"No, stop right there," Burr said. "You see, ladies and gentlemen, there is a shell in the chamber that did not come out."

"I was getting to that," said Miss Deutsch.

It is apparently her trial, thought Burr, but then again, it is her performance.

"Now I rack it again," Frieda Deutsch said. "Still nothing. And again. No shell." She racked the gun a third time and then a fourth. Then a fifth. This time the shell came out. "Here it is. Five tries to get out a live shell." She handed the gun back to Burr.

"Thank you, Miss Deutsch," Burr said.

She headed toward the gallery.

"Miss Deutsch, a few more questions, please," Burr said.

"I don't see why," she said.

"Please," Burr said.

She rotated to the witness stand, slowly, deliberately, like a freighter changing course, and lowered herself to her seat.

"Thank you for the demonstration, Miss Deutsch," Burr said, "What exactly does it mean?"

"It means that if you take the clip off first, the gun works fine. But if you eject the shell first, the next shell goes into the chamber, and it might not eject because sometimes the extractors don't grab it."

"How many times did it take you?"

"Five," she said.

"And what does that mean?"

"It means that you might think the gun is empty when it's not," she said.

"Have you ever seen this happen?"

"Only on this model," Frieda Deutsch said.

"Have you seen it on this model?"

"I have," she said.

"How many times?"

"Twice," Frieda Deutsch said.

"And how did you find out about this?"

"Two different guys brought this same model in," she said. "They knew how many shells they had in. Knew something was wrong."

"I see," Burr said. "And what was wrong?"

"Over time, with use, the extractors can loosen up."

"Is this dangerous?" Burr said.

"I would say so," Frieda Deutsch said.

"And what would you recommend?"

"Well, I wouldn't use a gun like this," Frieda Deutsch said.

"Did you notify the manufacturer?"

"I did," she said.

"What did they say?"

"They said it wasn't a problem. But they changed the design the next year," Frieda Deutsch said.

"How do you know?" Burr asked.

"I took one apart, a new one," she said. "They changed the action. Then they quit making them altogether."

"If someone borrowed this gun and unloaded it, then racking it, he might return a loaded gun. Is that right?"

"I object, Your Honor," Truax said. "This is speculation."

"Overruled," Gillis said. "You may answer the question, Miss Deutsch."

"Yes," she said. "Someone might return a loaded gun."

"And then if the person who got it back, racked the gun, the shell still might not come out," Burr said. "The gun might still be loaded. Is that right?"

"Yes," she said.

"So the gun could go off by accident even if you tried to make sure it was empty."

"That's right," she said.

"Did the manufacturer ever issue any warnings about this gun before the design was changed?" Burr said.

"No," Frieda Deutsch said.

"Would you say this gun is defective?"

"Yes," she said.

"Even if you exercise gun safety," Burr said.

"Yes," she said.

"If the gun were dirty," Burr said, "does it make it more likely to malfunction?"

"Yes," she said.

"Why is that?'

"The mechanism, the extractors, have a tendency to stick more often," she said.

"One more question," Burr said. "Is it conceivable that Mr. Tavohnen could have reasonably thought that the gun was unloaded, could have taken precautions to make sure it was unloaded, and still the gun could be loaded. It could have gone off and killed his wife?"

"Objection," Truax said. "Calls for a state of mind, which the witness could not know."

"Sustained," Gillis said.

Burr knew her answer would not be allowed. He wanted to ask the question anyway so the jury would understand what all this meant. He thought they did. "Thank you, Miss Deutsch," he said. "I have no further questions."

Truax uncoiled himself once more, speaking as he stood. Burr thought he could see his tongue darting in and out of his mouth. "Mrs. Deutsch."

"It's Miss," she repeated. "I'm a widow."

"Actually," Truax said, "it's Mrs. Widows are referred to as Mrs."

"Well, I'm not," Frieda Deutsch said.

"Very well, then, Miss Deutsch," Truax said. "I take it that you are an expert on the subject of guns."

"Objection," Burr said. "The credentials of Miss Deutsch have already been established."

"Overruled," Gillis said.

"Miss Deutsch," Truax unperturbed, "You have a Ph.D. in your field?"

"No," she said.

"A master's degree, then?"

"No," she said again.

"Surely, you have a college degree," Truax said.

"No," she continued.

"Yet you consider yourself an expert?"

Burr saw dark circles growing from Frieda's armpits. Not a good sign.

"Objection," Burr said. "The witnesses' qualifications have been established."

"Have they? I don't think so," Truax said.

"Counsel, there is no degree program in gunsmithing," Burr said. "Miss Deutsch has received a great deal of training and almost seventeen years of experience as a gunsmith."

"I did not ask for your opinion," Truax said.

"Enough. Mr. Truax," Gillis said. "You will not humiliate the witness. Her credentials have been established."

Burr watched Truax turn red, first his ears, then from the neck up, his face.

"Now, Miss Deutsch, you testified that the gun could malfunction and appear to be empty when in fact it was loaded," Truax said. "Is that right?"

"Yes," she said.

"But when the gun is loaded, it will not fire on its own, will it?"

"What do you mean?"

"Miss Deutsch, for the gun to fire, the safety must be off," Truax said. "Is that right?"

"Yes," Frieda Deutsch said.

"And the trigger must be pulled," Truax said. "Is that right?"

"Yes," she said again.

"So, even if the gun malfunctioned, someone still must have turned off the safety and pulled the trigger," Truax said.

"Objection," Burr said. "It is not established that the trigger was pulled."

"Sustained," Gillis said.

Truax's color barometer went off again. "Let me rephrase the question," Truax said. "For the gun to go off, even if it malfunctioned, the safety had to be off and the trigger had to be pulled. Is that right?"

"Yes," she said.

"Thank you," Truax said. "Finally, Miss Deutsch, as to the demonstration gun, did you adjust the gun in order to make it malfunction?"

"I beg your pardon," she said.

"Did you adjust the demonstration gun to make it malfunction?"

"No," she said.

Burr suspected she had adjusted the gun but didn't want to know.

"Did you rig this demonstration?" asked Truax.

"What do you mean by that?" the gunsmith asked.

Here it comes, thought Burr. Please, please, please say you didn't (even if you did).

"I mean, did you intentionally tinker with this rifle in order to make it malfunction?"

"No, definitely not," she said. Burr thought she hadn't said it too convincingly.

"Don't you think it a bit odd that you were somehow able to locate one of the very few Model 92's that doesn't work right?"

"Objection, Your Honor," Burr asked. "Asked and answered."

"Sustained," Gillis said.

Truax turned to the jury. "I must say, I do. That of the thousands of Model 92's manufactured, you so conveniently found one that didn't work right."

"Objection, Your Honor," Burr said.

"That's enough, Calvin," Gillis said.

"No further questions," Truax said.

"You may stand down," Gillis said.

Frieda pulled herself to her feet, wet circles under her arms the size of melons. She smiled at Burr as she trundled past, the waistband of her pantyhose now three inches above the elastic waistband of her pants.

"Mr. Lafayette," Gillis said.

"Yes?" he said, sitting.

"Your next witness," Gillis said.

Burr had Truax on the ropes. He stood. "We have no further witnesses. The defense rests," he said. "We're quite through, Your Honor."

Burr had decided some time ago not to call Pattengill, thought it better not to validate laser science with another expert, no matter how he might testify. That and the money. Burr had left Pattengill on the witness list, hoping Truax would spend time preparing for him. Burr thought it had worked. Truax looked surprised when Burr concluded after the testimony of Frieda Deutsch. Burr thought his cross examination of Gannon and the lost and (supposedly) defective gun would not let Truax get past reasonable doubt.

"Very well," Gillis said.

Gillis made a show of pulling up the sleeve of his robe to look at his watch. He stretched his arm out squinting over his glasses. Burr wondered why he just didn't look through his half lenses. "I see it's two-thirty. We shall adjourn for the day. Closing arguments tomorrow, gentlemen." He trundled out through the private door.

Burr rushed out of the courtroom, the first one to leave. He hurried to the beige Buick, took a one-pound bag of sugar from the pocket of his overcoat. Surreptitiously, he unscrewed the gas cap and poured the sugar into the gas tank.

CHAPTER TWENTY-THREE

FRIDAY, OCTOBER 20, 1989 – THE FIFTH DAY

The next morning, on his way into the courthouse, Burr spied a black Cadillac in the parking lot. He smiled a wicked smile and dashed up the steps. He settled into his chair just as Swede lisped the entrance of the good Judge Gillis.

"We will proceed with the closing arguments," Gillis said. "Mr. Truax."

Truax popped up like a jack-in-the-box. "Your Honor, the prosecution would like to offer a rebuttal witness."

"A what?" Gillis said, clearly upset by the request. He wanted the trial over today, and a verdict by dinner time. "The prosecution concluded the day before yesterday."

"Your Honor, the prosecution has a rebuttal witness," Truax said. "It is critical to our case."

"Who is it?" Gillis asked.

"Objection, Your Honor," Burr said. "The prosecutor has completed his case."

"Your Honor, the prosecution has one more witness," Truax said.

Gillis looked at his watch. "I thought you were finished."

"This witness just came forward, Your Honor," Truax said.

"And who might that be?" Gillis asked.

"Roman Yatchek, Your Honor, the family priest."

"Objection, Your Honor," Burr said. "The prosecutor has had ten months to prepare his case."

"Counsel?" Gillis was clearly irritated. He also looked confused.

"Your Honor, we apologize," Truax said, "but the witness has just now come forward."

"Nonsense." Burr flew to his feet. "This is part of his plan, just as the son was. The defense is entitled to notice. It is clearly stated in the court rules."

"Objection noted," Gillis said. "Go ahead, Counsel."

"The people call Roman Yatchek," Truax said.

"Damn," Burr said under his breath, watching the priest sit in the witness chair. The priest had a red face with short white hair that stuck up through his red scalp like a pincushion. He also had a very red, very bulbous nose. I'll bet he drinks, thought Burr. And the black collar of a priest. Burr snaked four Altoids into his mouth.

"Mr. Lafayette," Gillis said.

"Yes, Your Honor."

"Do not eat any more of those infernal peppermint candies in my courtroom," Gillis said.

Burr swallowed the Altoids. At this point he saw no reason to argue about Altoids. He suspected there would be issues of greater consequence about which to argue.

Burr watched Truax stride, not really stride, more like saunter, he thought, to the priest.

"Father Yatchek, how long have you been a priest?"

"He had to use 'father', didn't he?" Burr said under his breath again.

"Forty-two years," Yatchek said.

"Forty-two years," Truax said. "That's a long time. And how long at Immaculate Heart?"

"Nineteen years," said Father Yatchek.

"That's a long time," Truax said.

The priest nodded.

"And Father, how long did you minister to the Tavohnen's?"

"Eighteen years," said the priest.

"Eighteen years," Truax said. "How can you be so sure?

"I remember, Claudia came to me when she was pregnant."

"Really," Truax said. "Why would you remember that?"

"She said Frank wanted her to have an abortion," said the priest.

Burr jumped to his feet. "Objection, Your Honor. This is privileged communication between a priest and a parishioner."

"Your Honor," Truax said sneering at Burr as he spoke, "The privilege does not survive death."

"Overruled," Gillis said.

"Judge, you have no idea what the law is," Burr said.

Gillis roared at him. "Once more, Mr. Lafayette, and I will eject you. No, I will not eject you. I will throw you out by the collar of your thousand dollar suit."

Burr muttered, "It was a thousand dollars when I had a thousand dollars to spend on suits."

"What?"

"Please preserve the objection of the defense for appeal," Burr said.

"So noted, Mr. Lafayette," Gillis said.

"Along with the other fifty-two," Burr said, muttering to himself.

"Father Yatchek, you said that Mrs. Tavohnen sought counsel regarding an abortion," Truax said. "Can you elaborate?"

Burr whispered in Jacob's ear, "Now there's an open-ended question. Truax knows exactly what Yatchek is going to say because he coached him. I'm sure they practiced it. Although the son-of-a-bitch has just now came forward."

"She told me that Frank wasn't sure he wanted to get married and didn't believe that having a child was a good idea."

"And what did you advise?"

"We talked about the issue at length. She came to her own conclusions that abortion was not the right choice," Yatchek said.

"And what occurred?"

"Claudia and Frank married, and they were blessed with a son," said the priest.

"There's another thing we didn't know," Burr whispered to Jacob. "Are the secrets ever going to end?"

"Thank you, Father," Truax said. "Did you counsel with Mrs. Tavohnen at any other time?"

"I did," Yatchek said.

"Would you tell us about it?'

"Well, the marriage was trying, I would say," said the priest. "Mrs. Tavohnen worked very hard at it. I know she loved her husband, but he wanted a divorce."

"Father, what did she tell you?"

"She told me that Mr. Tavohnen wanted a divorce. Many times she told me that," said the priest.

"When was the last time?"

"Just before she was killed," Yatchek said.

"And what advice did you give her?"

"We prayed," Yatchek said. "And she believed that God wanted her to have no part in ending her marriage."

"What did you advise her?" Truax said.

"I advised her to pray, to work on the marriage," said the priest. "I tried to see them both, but he refused. I simply never thought it would come to this."

"Do you believe that Mrs. Tavohnen was afraid of her husband?"

"I do," Yatchek said.

"Why do you say that?"

"She said he had a very bad temper," Yatchek said.

"Really?" Truax feigned surprise. "Did this come up very often? Her being afraid?"

"A few times," said the priest.

"How many?"

"I don't really remember. Two or three times, I suppose."

"When was the last time?"

"In November, before she was killed," said Father Yatchek.

"And what occurred then?"

"She said he lost his temper and screamed at her."

"Father, are you saying that Mrs. Tavohnen told you that she was afraid of her husband?"

"Yes," said Father Yatchek.

"No further questions," Truax said. Truax flashed his uneven teeth at Burr, smugly, a now-you're-really-cooked smile.

Burr walked to the jury. He spoke quickly. "Ladies and gentlemen, you should know that a last minute witness, like this one, also like Jason Tavohnen, is very irregular. In fact, I've never seen it done. In fact, the court lets the prosecution do anything …."

"Stop it right there," Gillis said. "You may question the witness. You may not criticize the court. Is that clear?"

"Yes, Your Honor," Burr said.

Burr had no idea where to begin, but he didn't think the priest had hurt him much. He thought Truax was desperate. He had never even heard of Yatchek before, much less seen him.

"Your Honor," Burr said, "the defense requests an adjournment so that it may properly prepare its examination."

"Denied," Gillis said. "It's now or never."

Burr clenched his teeth, felt his molars grinding. He could stop right now and ensure that they would finish today, but he thought if just asked a few questions, he could improve his position and still finish today. "Very well," Burr said. "Father Yatchek, you were the Tavohnen family priest for how long?"

"Eighteen years," said the priest.

"Did you ever meet with Mr. Tavohnen?"

"No."

"Did you meet with their son, Jason?"

"No."

"I see," Burr said. "Well then, how could you be the family priest if you only ministered to Mrs. Tavohnen?"

"She talked to me about the family," said the priest.

"I see," Burr said. "Wouldn't it be more accurate to say you were her priest, not the family priest?"

"Objection," Truax said. "Calls for a conclusion."

"Sustained," Gillis said.

"Father Yatchek, was Mr. Tavohnen a Catholic?"

The priest grew even redder, particularly his scalp. "No."

"Did he attend mass regularly?"

"No," said the priest, turning a yet brighter shade of red.

"Did he attend at all?"

"I don't know," said the priest.

"You don't know," Burr said. "Is it possible that you bore him some, if not hostility, perhaps ill will, because he didn't attend mass. Because he wasn't Catholic?"

"No," said the priest.

Of course not," Burr said. "Father Yatchek, you testified that Mrs. Tavohnen was afraid of Mr. Tavohnen because of his temper. Is that right? I note that no other witness has testified that there was any violence in this marriage." Burr looked at the jury then back at the red-faced priest. "Well, then, what did you do?"

"What do you mean, do?" the priest said.

"About Mrs. Tavohnen being afraid of her husband," Burr said.

"What?" the priest said.

"Did you tell the police?" Burr said.

"No," the priest said.

"Did you call social services?"

"No," the priest said again.

"What exactly did you do in the face of Mrs. Tavohnen's fear?"

"I listened," the priest said.

"You listened," Burr said. "Mrs. Tavohnen was afraid of her husband and you listened. That doesn't seem very proactive, does it?" Yatchek's face turned even redder, which Burr hadn't thought possible.

"Objection," Truax said. "He is badgering the witness."

"Sustained," Gillis said. "Mr. Lafayette, what point are you trying to make?"

"Thank you for asking, Your Honor," Burr said. "I am trying to show that Father Yatchek did not like Mr. Tavohnen in part because he wasn't Catholic, in part because he did not go to mass, and I'm sure because he wanted his wife to have an abortion, and finally because he wanted a divorce."

"So far you haven't shown much." This from Truax.

"Stop it. Both of you," Gillis said.

"Any more questions, Mr. Lafayette?"

"Yes, Your Honor," Burr said. This case wasn't about what he had been told. It was about what he hadn't been told. Without knowing how the priest would answer, Burr was loathe to ask any more questions, but he was angry. "Father Yatchek, earlier you testified that Mrs. Tavohnen was afraid of her husband. Is that right?"

"Yes," said the priest.

"Did you ever see any physical marks on her that would indicate that she had ever been struck by her husband?"

"Well . . ."

"Answer the question please," Burr said.

"No," said the priest.

"No physical signs of being struck?"

"No," the priest said.

"Did she say that her husband beat her?"

"No," the priest said again.

"Did she say her husband slapped her?"

"No," the priest said again.

"Did she ever say he threatened to kill her?"

"No," the priest said again.

Now we're getting somewhere Burr thought. "So what you're saying is that Mrs. Tavohnen was afraid of her husband, but she had never been so much as slapped," Burr said. "Isn't that a bit farfetched?"

"Objection," Truax said.

"Sustained," Gillis said.

The priest's pin cushion hair pricked up even more, his face now the color of a boiled lobster. "No, it is not," he said. "She said she was afraid because she wouldn't give him a divorce, because he was having an affair with her." The priest pointed at Sarah, "and he wanted a divorce so he could marry her. That's what she was afraid of."

"Your Honor, I move to strike the witness' last answer as non-responsive," Burr said.

"Objection, Your Honor," Truax said. "Counsel asked an open-ended question. He gets what he gets."

"I will let the answer stand," Gillis said.

"Your Honor, this entire proceeding has been a sham from start to finish. It is a mockery of the court rules. A fraud on fairness. I move for a mistrial," Burr said.

"Denied," Gillis said. "Any further questions?"

"Just one," Burr said. "Which matchbook cover did you get your law degree from?"

"Get out, Mr. Lafayette. Get out of my courtroom this instant and don't come back. We will recess for the day. Closing arguments will be tomorrow morning at 10 a.m. sharp." He blasted out of the courtroom like he had been shot from a cannon.

The door to the Pacesetter Tavern stuck when he pulled on it, wouldn't open. He planted his left foot, pushed off the frame with his left hand and jerked. The door flew at him and banged his forehead just above his right temple.

"Damn," Burr said.

Inside, it was dark and he had to stand in the entry until his eyes adjusted.

"You want something?" said the bartender.

"I'll have a shot and a draft."

"What kind?"

"Jack Black and a Labatt," Burr said. Burr's head throbbed and he felt a bump erupting on his forehead.

"Bump your head?"

"Yes," Burr said.

"The door sticks when it's wet," said the bartender.

"I forgot about that," Burr said.

"Doesn't help business any," said the bartender.

"I guess not." Burr hadn't been in the Pacesetter Tavern in twenty years. It didn't look like anybody else had either, except the bartender. The cigar stuck out of the bartender's mouth, like a half-eaten hot dog without the bun. He wondered how the guy stayed in business.

Kaye had stopped him on his way down the courthouse steps after his untimely ejection. She had asked to see him, which Burr thought could not be good. He had agreed, suggesting an out of the way place, told Suzanne he would meet them all for dinner later.

The bartender delivered the beer, the shot, and a glass of water. Burr considered dropping the shot glass into the mug (a depth charge, if he remembered correctly), but decided that would waste good whiskey and good beer. Instead, he sipped on the whiskey. It tasted smokey and burned his stomach.

Burr hadn't had a chance to talk to Jacob after Gillis threw him out. After his debacle with the good priest, Burr couldn't think of anything else to do other than cause a scene, hope that the drama would make the jury forget the newly found priest and the affair. He was beyond redemption with Gillis anyway. Now the trial would go into a sixth day, in spite of what Gillis had said. Burr never considered the possibility that Gillis would throw him out and push the closing arguments to Saturday. Really, though, what difference did it make?

Frank had never mentioned anything about a priest, why he didn't go to mass. Nothing about threatening Claudia. The priest was probably lying anyway, was probably recruited by Truax. Who knew when Truax found him. Probably yesterday afternoon. Jacob would have to do the closing argument, and Jacob was not good in front of a jury.

Kaye sat down next to him, on his right.

"I didn't hear you come in," he said.

"The door was partly open. Ouch," she said, touching his forehead. "What's that on your head?"

"That's why the door was partly open," Burr said.

"You're bleeding." She reached into her purse, a black shoulder bag that Burr thought could hold two days worth of food and clothing. Somehow she came up with a handkerchief right away. She dipped it in the glass of water Burr hadn't asked for and dabbed it on his forehead. Burr smelled her scent, perfume and musk.

"There," she said.

"Thank you. Would you like a drink?" Burr said.

"A drink?" Kaye said. "Yes."

"Wine," Kaye said to the bartender. "A white wine, Chardonnay." The bartender raised his eyebrows. "From a box if you've got it," she said.

"Very funny," the bartender said. He had a round face and one eyebrow, thick like a cat's tail, running across his forehead, black, salted with white. It divided his head into two pieces. Top to bottom.

Burr looked over at Kaye. Her lips were freshly painted, her eye shadow set off the blue in her eyes. She had on black wool slacks, an ivory sweater with a wine colored blazer, dangly black earrings, a black necklace. Her jacket and her lips matched nicely.

"I have something to tell you," she said.

He hadn't been out with her since he had cooked her the morels. He'd seen her in the courtroom, in the gallery, but they hadn't spoken. He opened his mouth, thought better of it, and with his mouth open, he drank from his beer. Kaye put her left hand on his right, the hand next to the shot glass.

"You know, you really are a jerk, but you're a likable jerk. Call me if you ever straighten out your personal life," she said. "But that's not why I wanted to see you." She took her hand off Burr's, reached into her purse, and pulled out something about half as long as his little finger and set it on the bar. It was a dull brass color, cylindrical. Burr cocked his head, studied it, and then held it in his thumb and forefinger.

"A shell casing," Burr said.

"Yes," Kaye said.

Burr looked at it more closely. It had splotches of rust on it. "And?" he said.

"I found it," Kaye said.

"Really," Burr said.

Kaye looked straight at him. "Don't be a smart ass or I won't tell you," she said.

"I'm sorry," he said. "Please tell me the story of the shell casing." He set it back down on the bar.

"You know, I thought we might have something between us," Kaye said.

"We do," he said. "We could."

"The three of us?" Kaye asked.

Burr thought it best to not answer that question. "What about the shell casing?"

"I found it at Frank's house," Kaye said.

"You did?" Burr said. Now he was interested.

"About two, no three, years ago. I wasn't the first realtor. I picked up the listing after the first realtor dropped it. Who could blame her? Anyway, I went through the house, like I always do with a new listing. With a vacant house, I take a shoebox and pick up what's been left behind. You'd be surprised what you find." She sipped her wine. "Maybe you wouldn't. Earrings, rings, change. I usually keep the change. Keys, combs. Well, I put the address on the shoebox and when I see the owners, I give it to them. They always appreciate it. One time I found a guy's wedding ring. He asked me not to tell his wife I found it. Like she didn't know it was missing."

"Anyway, I went through their house," Kaye said. "Frank's house, I guess. There's more stuff for the shoebox than usual. That's because it was furnished. You know, he just moved out. Left everything—furniture, some clothes. So I found a lot of stuff.

Burr tipped up the shot, took another sip. He stared at her.

"I went downstairs, to the basement," Kaye said. "There was stuff all over. Tools mostly. But the boxes were all packed. You saw them. Like he was moving out. But then he just left. So I found a lot of loose stuff for the shoebox. Drill bits, safety glasses, screws, bolts. I only put the good stuff in."

"So I'm scrounging around the floor, on my hands and knees. I see something under the workbench. It's a fifty cent piece. I put it in my purse. While I'm on my hands and knees, I see something else, just the edge of it. It's in the floor drain where you can hardly see it. So I pry off the cover, the grate. And this is what I found." She set a shell casing on the bar.

Burr looked at it, sitting on the bar like a missile, except the business end was gone.

"I never thought about it until the gun came up. I went back and looked in Frank's shoebox. He never came back to Petoskey, so I never gave it to him. Anyway, I rummaged through it. And here it is," Kaye said. She picked up the shell casing and rolled it between her thumb and forefinger, like she was rolling a joint. "I don't know if it is worth anything, but I thought you might want to see it. It was hard to find, not that I was looking for it, but it must have been there a long time, wedged in there. Almost down the drain. So here." She flipped it up in the air.

Burr watched it tumble, slowly, over and over, in slow motion. He caught it in his left hand. He studied the casing, hollow, the powder spent, the lead fired. Open at one end, closed at the other, like a pipe with a flat disk over one end, the edges sticking out, a flange.

Except. Except there was no flange on this shell casing. None to speak of. He held the casing in his left hand at the open end. He looked at the closed end. Where was the flange? He ran his forefinger around the end of the shell. There was no edge sticking out. The edge was uneven, rough to the touch. It was not quite flush with the casing.

"How long did you say you've had this?"

"Since I got the listing. Three years. Maybe a little longer. I just forgot about it?"

"Have you got the key?"

"To what? Frank's house? I'm sure I do." She fished around inside her purse again peering inside. He saw the top of her scalp. The roots of her hair just showed a little gray. He thought she'd take care of that soon, probably already had an appointment.

"Here they are," Kaye said. She reached up with a brass ring with at least three dozen keys. "My inventory. These keys are worth about five grand in commission." Each key had a piece of masking tape with a name on it. She ran through the keys, one by one. "Is this it?" She held the key at arm's length, squinted at it. "I need longer arms. No, this is the one."

Burr threw down the rest of the whiskey.

Burr followed Kaye down the basement steps. He sucked in the damp, tasted the mildew at the back of his mouth. The corners of the basement were dark where the lights from the naked light bulbs didn't reach.

Burr had focused on the gun. It was missing and could have been defective. He hadn't given any more thought to the possibility of a defective bullet.

Why hadn't the police found the shell casing? Searching the scene of an accident or a crime was standard police procedure, but the whole thing had been sloppy, no reason for this to be any different.

He fingered the casing in his pocket. There was no reason for Truax to want this. Truax didn't need it to prove what he was trying to prove.

"We're here," Kaye said. "Now what?"

Burr found himself standing in the center of the basement, not quite sure how he'd gotten there. "Show me where you found it," he said.

"Here." She pointed at a floor drain under the workbench.

One of the legs, a two by four, stood on the edge of the grate. About a foot in diameter, cast iron, rusty, with half-inch slits running across it.

Burr got down on his knees and ran his forefinger across it. Dirt and grease came off on his finger. He tried to pull it up with his hands, but he couldn't get a purchase on it. Then there was the matter of the leg of the workbench which stood on the edge of the grate.

"Where did you find it?" he asked.

"In there," she said, pointing the lacquered fingernail of her forefinger. "Inside the drain."

"Was this leg on the grate?"

"Yes," Kaye said.

"How did you get it off?"

"I pushed the workbench off and pried up the grate with a screwdriver," Kaye said.

"Why on earth would you do that?"

"I always do. You never know what you might find in a drain," she said.

"Really," he said.

"Once I found a wedding ring. A gold band. I told you that. That's what I thought the shell casing was at first," Kaye said.

"Show me what you did," Burr said.

She pushed on the workbench, but it didn't move. Then with her hands under the top, she tried to lift it and pull it to the side. "You could help me," she said.

"I could, but I want to see how you did it," Burr said.

"I don't remember it being this heavy before." Kaye jerked up on the workbench and managed to lift the edge of the leg off the grate and slid across the floor. "There," she said. She found a flathead screwdriver in a coffee can on the workbench and pried up the edge of the drain. Then she used her other hand under the grate and lifted it up by the edge and slid it to the side. "Damn," Kaye said.

"Did you hurt yourself?" Burr said.

"I broke a nail," she said. "You could have helped me."

Burr thought it best not to answer (again). He peered into the drain which smelled faintly of sewage. He still could not understand why anyone, particularly Kaye, would go to all this trouble.

"Then what?" he said.

"Here's where I found it," Kaye said.

There was a ledge about six inches down, about two inches wide, running all the way around the drain. He touched it with his forefinger. The grease outlined the whorl of his fingerprint and stuck underneath his fingernail.

"Where was it?" Burr said.

"Here on this ledge," she said. "Why does it matter? It's just a shell casing. It's probably not even the one that killed her. And so what if it is? What does that prove?" Kaye said.

Burr fingered around in his left pants pocket for the shell, among his change and his car keys. He couldn't find it. He panicked, emptied the contents of his pocket in his right hand. The shell casing lay amidst the flotsam and jetsam. He picked it up and held it between the thumb and forefinger of his left hand. "Here's why. See this edge. See how it's uneven, worn off or something. What if ..."

"Burr, what are you doing here?" Suzanne, bent from the waist, peered at him from the top of the stairs.

Burr made a fist, closed his hand around the shell casing.

"I thought you were meeting us for dinner," she said.

Burr watched her eyes dart around the basement. They flashed at him, then fixed on the drain.

"What's going on?" Suzanne said.

"I wanted to have another look around. In case I missed something," Burr said.

Suzanne took two more steps down the stairs. "What are you doing with the drain?"

"I wanted to see if there was anything in there," he said.

"And?" Suzanne said.

Burr squeezed his fist. "We didn't find anything." He wasn't sure she believed him, wasn't sure why he didn't tell her.

"Come on. We've got to go," Suzanne said. "I've got good news."

"Let me put the grate back on," he said.

"Go ahead," Kaye said. "I'll take care of it. I've got nine left." She slid the grate back on the drain.

~

After dinner, Burr parked the Vista Cruiser in Frank's driveway. He had told Suzanne, Sarah and the others that he had left something at Frank's house, which probably hadn't been too believable, but no one had pressed him on it. He got out of the car and felt the darkness settle around him. Fog had blown in off the lake. He could almost see it ooze past him, and he felt the wetness in the air.

Suzanne's good news was, in fact, good news. After throwing Burr out, Gillis had reconsidered. He would allow Burr to make the closing argument. They had a minor (very minor) celebration at dinner, after which Burr re-returned to the scene of the accident, or was it a crime?

Frank's house was a hazy silhouette in the fog. Next door, Mrs. Larsen's lights glowed through the fog. He wasn't sure why he had come back, but there was always one more thing in this case. What was it now? Another look in the basement couldn't hurt. He walked to the side door of the garage. It faced Mrs. Larsen's house. This must be where she peeked through the window.

The knob turned in his hand. He walked across the garage to the door to the house. This was where Farr had left the gun. If only he hadn't left it here. If he hadn't borrowed it in the first place. Or, if Frank had been more careful. He slid his hand in his pants pocket, felt the shell casing, turned it over in his pocket and felt the edge where the extractors on the rifle gripped. Or should have gripped.

Or, what if Frank had been careful? What if it wasn't the gun at all? What if it was the shell? He pulled his hand out of his pocket. The shell caught on his pocket and spilled to the garage floor. It tinked as it hit. Then he heard it roll across the floor.

"Please," he said out loud, "don't let there be a drain here."

Burr dropped to his knees. He dragged his hands along the floor in the darkness. He scraped his fingers on the uneven concrete. Where was the casing? He felt himself panicking. There must be a light switch somewhere. He saw a silhouette in the window of the door, framed like a portrait. He launched himself toward the door. The shadow disappeared. He flung open the door and rushed through it. No one there. Fog shrouded the Vista Cruiser. He crouched and peered under it, looking for feet. Nothing.

In front of him, Mrs. Larsen's house, the side of her house, not too far, close actually, maybe fifteen feet. Her house had a front porch that ran the length of the house. The porch had a solid railing, a kneewall, waist high. There were steps on the side and in the front. Burr turned to his left and edged along the side of the garage to the backyard. Two trees rose and disappeared into the fog. At his feet, the remains of a garden, a vegetable garden, he thought. He tangled himself in the frosted tomato vines. This must be the sunniest patch in the yard. Who had had a garden at a house that had been empty for six years? Turning back to the street, he saw a car glide by. In the fog, the beams of the headlights' twin cylinders seemed to pull the car forward. He walked back to the Vista Cruiser, scuffing his shoes on the sidewalk, not noisy, but not quiet either. He opened the door on the driver's side and rolled down the window. Then he slammed the door shut. He leaned through the window, poked the key in the ignition and turned it. The engine fired immediately. It's falling apart, but it always starts right up.

This will either work right away or I'm euchred, Burr thought. He began counting by ones, slowly. A head popped up over the wall of the porch. It looked straight at him then dived.

"Hello, Mrs. Larsen."

Silence.

"I know you're over there," he said.

More silence. Maybe she thinks I didn't see her. Maybe she thinks I'm stupid. Maybe she doesn't think about me. He stepped off the driveway and crabbed his way to the porch. He crouched there for a moment on the other side from where she went down. Then, slowly he uncoiled himself. At his full height his head just cleared the wall. He looked down at her huddled in the corner.

"There you are, Mrs. Larsen," he said, in a most charming "I've found you," as if to a four-year old in a game of hide-and-seek. She didn't move. "I'm right here you know. Mrs. Larsen, Why were you spying on me?"

Silence.

"Mrs. Larsen. I saw your head pressed against the window on the door."

"It wasn't me," said a small voice.

"I think it was," he said.

"No, not me," she said.

"Well, if it wasn't you, then who was it?" Burr said.

"How would I know?" Mrs. Larsen said.

"Who else could it be?" Burr said.

Now she stood, perhaps sensing a way out. Now he was at eye level with the waistband of her slacks.

"Lots of people come by here," said Mrs. Larsen.

"Really. Like who?" Burr said.

"Well, you did this afternoon. With that realtor woman," Mrs. Larsen said.

"Anyone else?" Burr said.

"That lawyer. The other one," she said.

"Truax?" Burr said.

"If that's his name," she said. "You seen my cat?"

"Your cat?"

"That's why I'm out here," said Mrs. Larsen.

"I see," Burr said. "No. No, I haven't. Mrs. Larsen. Was there anybody else you saw?"

"Her. I saw her," Mrs. Larsen said.

"Her?"

"You know," said Mrs. Larsen. "The new wife."

"Sarah?"

"If that's her name," she said.

Burr knew she knew full well what her name was and what everyone else's name was as well. "Did she come here after Claudia died?"

"Plenty of times. Afterward she came to see Frank. Slunk around here like a cat hunting mice."

"How did your tomatoes turn out?"

"What?"

"Your tomatoes," Burr said. "In the vegetable patch."

'How do you know they're mine?"

"Who else's would they be?" Burr said.

"It has the best sun on the block." Said Mrs. Larsen.

"Did Frank say you could?" Burr said.

"He wasn't using it," Mrs. Larsen said.

"So you spy and you trespass," Burr said.

"I do not," said Mrs. Larsen.

Burr thought he had rattled her. "Of course not. Did Sarah ever come over by herself before Claudia died?"

"Murdered more like it," she said.

"You were friends, weren't you? With Claudia?"

"Why not?" Mrs. Larsen said.

"Did she, Sarah, come before Claudia died?"

"She did. On the day Frank killed Claudia. She was looking for him. Went in the side door like you. I forgot about it until now," said Mrs. Larsen.

"Really?"

"You seen my cat?" She said.

"I already said I didn't," Burr said.

"That's why I'm out here, looking for the cat. Orange one. Pumpkin's her name."

"No, but I'll keep my eyes open," he said.

"You do that," she said.

"Good night, Mrs. Larsen."

"Bye now," she said.

Burr turned off the engine on the Vista Cruiser, opened the side door of the garage for the second time that night, and flipped the light switch. Standing under the light from the naked bulb, he saw the shell casing at the edge of the floor drain. He picked it up, turned it over and looked at the edge where the rim should have been.

He decided he would have one last look in the basement. He unlocked the side door with the key had had borrowed from Kaye. Now inside, he decided to retrace Frank's steps on the night of the shooting. He stood on the landing at the top of the stairs, and opened the door to the garage, stepped out, and pretending he was Frank, picked up the imaginary deer rifle and took it downstairs to the workbench. He racked the imaginary gun, then he set it on the workbench and started to clean it with an imaginary rag. "Yes," he said out loud, "the gun probably would point to the foot of the stairs."

He mounted the imaginary gun to his shoulder and aimed it at the foot of the stairs. He pulled the imaginary trigger. "Bang," he said out loud. "It could have happened this way." Finished with the pretending, Burr did not place the imaginary gun back on the workbench. It simply disappeared.

At first, Burr paid no attention to the smoke. He examined the grate one more time, then, at the foot of the stairs, he ran his hands over the fieldstones, felt their cold, smooth surfaces, smooth except for the precise spot where the bullet had struck the granite after passing through Claudia.

The smoke was stronger now. Where was it coming from? He ran up the stairs. Now he could taste the smoke. It burned his eyes. He saw it leak under the door. He tried the door, but it was locked. The doorknob burned the palm of his hand. He tried the door with his shoulder, but it would not give. He could feel the heat radiating from the other side of the door.

Fire. The house was on fire. How did that happen? When did it start? He crashed into the door again, but it wouldn't budge. The smoke began to pour underneath the door. He couldn't breathe here. He retreated to the basement. His lungs burned, but at least he could breathe, for now. He heard the fire above him, hissing like a snake. The house groaned. Above him, smoke drifted down through the floor. If the smoke didn't kill him, the house would rain down on him. He had to get out. He found a hammer and a chisel on the tool rack above the workbench. He wrapped a rag around his mouth and nose and started up the stairs. He reached the top, but the smoke and the heat drove him back downstairs.

The fire department should be here by now. Mrs. Larsen or one of the other neighbors must have called. They'd see his Vista Cruiser in the driveway and come find him. If they could get in.

Smoke poured down the stairs into the basement. Burr had gotten as far away as he could from the smoke, but the basement was filling with smoke. He fell to his knees and covered his mouth and nose with his coat. He couldn't breathe. If he did not find a way out, he would die here.

The floor joists above him creaked and the floor sagged, then broke open. He saw the fire above him. The floor joints gave and the floor fell into the basement. He dodged and fell back further, tripped and fell down.

The air was sweet here. Where was it coming from? Where was he? He stood up, turned. The fire, now behind him, backlit the room. He was in the coal room, the old coal room. He rushed to the sweet air. It was coming from the boarded up coal chute. He stood underneath the chute and filled his lungs. At least he could breathe, but the fire sucked in the air from the chute and the draft stoked the fire. He could breathe, but the fresh air pulled the fire toward him. If he stayed here, he would burn while he breathed. He had to get out.

The coal chute was on the side of the wall, just above ground level. Burr pushed on the boards, but they were above his head and he couldn't get any leverage.

He crawled back to the workbench. On his hands and knees, he pushed it up against the wall below the chute. He climbed on top of the workbench, laid on his back and kicked at the boards. Nothing moved. The floor above him burst into flames. He kicked again. Nothing. Behind him, the paint in the roller pans caught fire and exploded. The flames blew into the coal room. The workbench caught fire. Burr pounded with his feet at the corner of the top board. It cracked. He kicked again and it gave. The fire sucked up the air. Burr coughed, kicked again, and the board flew away from the wall. He could see outside. He clawed at the next board with his hands, pulled it free and dragged himself out of the house.

~

The fire department arrived just after Burr moved the Vista Cruiser.

Suzanne showed up just after the fire trucks. Then Jacob, Eve, Kaye, Sarah, Truax, and Frieda. Who told Frieda? Stewart, too. Mrs. Larsen, of course. They were all there. All of them. The whole dysfunctional lot of them. Together, they watched Frank's house burn to the ground. All of them.

The fire department hosed down the neighbors' houses on each side. They hosed down the big sugar maple in the front yard. They sprayed the house, but it was too far gone. It would burn to the ground, and they all knew it. And they all watched it burn. All of them, except Frank. It was his house, but he was in jail. Maybe forever.

"I am told you were the last one seen here," Truax said.

"Really?"

"Yes, really," Truax said.

"I'm sure I can guess who told you," Burr said.

"I am going to charge you with arson," Truax said.

"Leave me alone," Burr said. "I've got some marshmallows to roast."

"When I get the warrant, shall I arrest you at the Harbour Inn? I'll have the officers be discreet. They won't disturb your roommate. Ms. Fairchild, isn't it? Although I see the whole harem is here."

"Touché," Burr said. He turned back to the fire. The fire blew a hot wind on his face. Kaye edged next to him. She wore a long black coat.

"It suits you," he said. "The coat."

"Thank you. It goes well with my nightgown," Kaye said.

"There goes your listing," Burr said.

"My listing," Kaye said. "I hadn't even thought about it." The fire roared at them. She stood on her tiptoes, spoke into his ear. "The shell. I've been thinking about the shell."

"Burr had completely forgotten about the shell. "What have you been thinking?" he asked.

"Suppose the shell is defective. It's in the gun and Frank doesn't know it. And the gun goes off by mistake."

"Yes," Burr said. "But what about the shell?"

"It's defective," Kaye said. "But why?"

"What do you mean, why?"

"How did it get that way?" Kaye said.

Burr looked at her. He swiveled his head to where his ear had been. He was about a head taller than she was. Not quite. She had put on some lipstick, a burnt red. Goes with the fire, he thought. "The shell?" he said. "I guess it was made that way. At the factory. It was defective. Deformed from the very beginning." He took the shell out of his pocket, held it between his thumb and forefinger. The light from the fire flickered against the brass.

CHAPTER TWENTY-FOUR

Burr knew where Frieda was staying because he had paid for the room with his credit card, with what was left of his limit. He hoped she'd be there. He hadn't seen her leave Frank's (former) house, but he couldn't imagine her going anywhere but back to her room. Burr couldn't put her up at the Harbour because it was the color season and Stewart wouldn't give up another room.

He turned off I-31 on the south side of Petoskey into the Wayfarer. The "ER" on the end of the neon sign had burned out. Frieda hadn't been too happy about it, but with his current financial position, it was the best he could do. There was only one car in the lot, a black Lincoln town car, which must be hers.

She had on sweats, baby blue sweats, which gave her the look of a robin's egg, a giant robin's egg. She seemed genuinely glad to see him. She filled the door, stepped back to let him in. He offered his hand. She kissed him on the cheek.

"I was wondering what I'd do after the fire," she said. "Shall we have a bite to eat?"

"I suppose we could," he said. "But that's not exactly why I'm here." This deflated her. He could feel the air going out of her, but the egg didn't get any smaller.

"Thank God you're all right," she said. "You must be exhausted. Well, then, how about a drink? I've got a fresh bottle of Crown."

"Sure," he said. Burr saw an empty glass and a half-empty fifth of Crown Royal on her nightstand, which didn't quite seem fresh to him.

"It was my father's favorite—Crown, Coke and a half a lemon. He called it a Black Dog. But I substitute Diet Coke. For my figure. I call it a Black Dogette." She laughed to herself. Frieda fetched another glass from the bathroom, scooped ice from a bucket and filled half of it with the whiskey. She poured a shot of diet Coke and squeezed half a lemon on top. "I like to go easy on the Diet Coke."

"I can see that," Burr said.

She passed the Black Dogette to him, mixed herself one. She took a long pull on the drink. "So what brings you here?"

"Do you have the gun?" he said.

"The gun?"

"From the trial," he said.

"Of course, I don't. It's evidence. You know that," Frieda said.

"I forgot," Burr said.

"You should know that," she said.

"I should," Burr said.

"Here, sit down," Frieda said.

Burr sat on the bed, a king. She started to sit down next to him, made it halfway, then let herself fall the rest of the way. He bounced up when she landed.

"That's better," she said. "Now then."

"Thank you for coming up here," he said. "You're been a great help."

"But?" Frieda said.

"What if it wasn't the gun?" Burr said.

"Not the gun?"

"What if it was the shell?" Burr said. "What if the shell was defective?"

"What do you mean?"

Burr fished the shell casing out of his pocket. "See this edge. Look how thin it is. There's not much to grab onto. What if the ejectors didn't grab it, couldn't grab it. So once it was in the chamber, the ejectors wouldn't pull it out."

"Let me see that." She took off her glasses. There were red marks on each side of her nose where the frames pressed down. Without her glasses she looked like a mole that had just burrowed out of its hole. Frieda rolled the casing between her thumb and forefinger. She brought the casing to the tip of her nose. Then she bobbed her head back and forth examining it. He thought she looked like a cobra under the spell of a snake charmer.

"There's no flange on the casing. Not much of one anyway," Frieda said. She peeked up at him,

"No," he said. "What do you make of it?"

"Stay there. I'll be right back," Frieda said. She heaved herself up and off the bed and disappeared out the door. Burr heard the trunk of the Lincoln open and close. He stayed where he was, sipped his drink and tried somehow to separate the taste of the whiskey from the diet Coke and lemon. Frieda came back in carrying a four-foot black plastic case. "You know what's in here, don't you?"

"I can guess," Burr said.

She unlocked the case and put the rifle together. She slid the bolt open.

"Hand me the shell," she said.

Burr hesitated.

"Don't worry," Frieda said. "I won't drop it." She took it from him, jammed it in the breach, and slammed the bolt shut. Then she aimed at his head and took off the safety. "Bang," she said and pulled the trigger.

Burr jerked his head to the side. He spilled his drink on his crotch.

"I'm so sorry," Frieda said. She dropped the gun to her waist. "I didn't mean to scare you." She paused. "Of course I did. Frieda, you are so naughty." To Burr. "Make yourself wet did you? This is the only fun I'm going to have with you, isn't it?"

Burr scrambled to his feet, brushed the drink off his khakis.

"Don't worry honey, it won't stain," she said. "This is what we've been waiting for."

Frieda Deutsch racked the bolt. The shell did not eject.

By the time Burr reached Jacob's room it was two a.m. Jacob was annoyed by having his sleep disturbed, and, in an effort to soothe himself, had immediately rolled a joint. Jacob was convinced that someone was trying to kill Burr. First the Jeep, then the boat. Now the fire. Burr told Jacob that the Jeep was his ego, that *Kismet* was old. He said he would think about the fire later.

Burr, standing, held the shell casing in the palm of his hand. "If the shell was bad," he said, "Frank could have racked the gun to his heart's content, and it never would have come out."

"So, how did it get in the drain?" Jacob asked.

"The shell finally ejected when the gun went off," Burr said.

"Let me see that," Jacob said.

Burr passed him the shell.

Jacob sat on the edge of the bed in a belted navy robe with white ribbing. He held the casing in the palm of his left hand and rolled it over with his right forefinger. "You've got two problems, at least two problems, with this," he said. "First, there's the evidentiary chain," which Burr hadn't wanted to hear and not being a criminal lawyer by trade, had only a vague knowledge.

"It's Tinkers to Evers to Chance," Jacob said. "Who's to say that Kaye found it, that she had it all this time, that she gave it to you. And more importantly, that she found in the basement. Truax will eat you up on that."

"Second, " Jacob said, "you did a great job with the gun. Now you're going to start over with this shell casing? You will undo all of it if you try to introduce this." He studied the shell casing, looked at it closely, his nose almost touching it. "How do you even know that this is the bullet? Did Farr have his own bullets?"

"He said Frank gave him the rifle, the clip, and the bullets. But it doesn't matter where the bullet came from if it was defective," Burr said.

"Did you hear what I said?" Jacob tapped his foot, clearly frustrated with Burr. "It's too late for that. You can't start over now."

"Look at it again," Burr said. "How did it get this way?"

Jacob peered at the shell casing in the palm of his hand. "I don't know," he said. "I guess it was made that way. At the factory."

"So the shell was defective," Burr said. "Deformed from the very beginning."

"At this point the shell doesn't matter," Jacob said.

"What if Jones and Field didn't make a defective gun?" Burr asked. "And, what if they didn't made a defective shell either?"

"Even if Gillis allowed you to introduce the shell, it would just confuse the jury," Jacob said.

"It's the truth," Burr said.

"The truth stopped mattering a long time ago," Jacob said. He tossed the shell casing to Burr.

~

Standing in front of Suzanne's door, Burr remembered the "other thing," how things had come apart. How long had it been? Three years, he thought. Tuesday. His night with Zeke. They had gone to Chuck E. Cheese in Eastland, not Burr's favorite, but at least they served beer. He may have had one more than he should have. In retrospect, he certainly did. He had intended to drop Zeke off at the front door, but Grace looked particularly fetching in a particularly tight pair of faded blue jeans. He invited himself in, ostensibly to use the bathroom, then asked to put Zeke to bed (permission granted), then dallied over a glass of wine, one thing leading to another.

They had been separated for over a year. Both of them knew better.

The next morning, when Burr walked out to his car, there was Suzanne parked in the driveway, apparently all night.

Still standing in front of Suzanne's door, Burr raised his hand to knock. Then, he looked at his hand, dropped it to his side and turned away.

~

Burr sat on the beach on Crooked Lake in the cover of a fallen spruce, his waders on over his suit, Zeke next to him. He'd only thrown out seven decoys

At least it was duck season and he could sit here in the darkness with a purpose. The creek ran through a DNR hatchery then underneath US-31, then another two hundred yards to Crooked Lake. He had set up on the north side of the creek where it emptied into the lake, twenty minutes from the courthouse. He'd have twenty minutes of legal shooting before he had to leave.

Burr had been up all night for the first time in, he couldn't remember, how long. Years. He had a headache from the fire, lack of sleep, and now the caffeine. He'd had his thermos filled at Johann's and bought a very long, cream-filled long john with chocolate frosting. He extracted the long john from the bag, careful not to rub off any of the frosting. As he brought the long john to his mouth, his hand began to shake uncontrollably. He clutched his shaking hand by the wrist with his other hand. Then both hands shook. He lost his grip on the pastry and it fell into the sand.

Burr looked out onto Crooked Lake. It was even foggier here than it had been in Petoskey and Harbor. The fog hung over him, pushing down on him. Now that he had it figured out, or at least thought he had it figured out, it was too late to do anything about it. He couldn't start over. Not now. But he couldn't let it go, knowing what he knew. He felt around for the shell casing, found it in the breast pocket of his suit cot, underneath his chest waders.

There was no wind, and the fog laid over him like a blanket. It would take a wind to blow the fog off or the sun to burn it off, but it would be at least nine before that happened. By that time, he'd have to make up his mind. Overhead he heard wing-beats and a soft call. He called back, also softly. The bird, a hen mallard, called again. He quacked back. Then he heard a flutter and a splash. He was sure she landed in his decoys, but he couldn't see her.

CHAPTER TWENTY FIVE

SATURDAY, OCTOBER 21, 1989 – DAY SIX – THE LAST DAY

"The Honorable Judge Benjamin Gillis. All rise."

Feet shuffled. Chairs scoured the floor. The bald judge appeared as if by magic.

"Be seated," said Swede.

More clothing and furniture noises. This time breath exhaling.

"Gentlemen," Gillis said. "Your closing arguments please."

"Mr. Truax," Gillis said.

"Yes, Your Honor," said Truax, standing. He strode (a bit too theatrically, Burr thought) to the jury. "Ladies and gentlemen, a life has been taken. We all know that. We all know that the defendant killed his wife. This we know. He admits this. That man," Truax said, pointing his long bony finger at Frank again (it still angered Burr, that finger), "killed his wife. But this case is not about killing. It is about murder. It is about that man luring his wife to the basement of their home and deliberately shooting his wife. With his son upstairs."

Burr thought Truax was taking too long with the details. The jury was tired. They were tired of it all, had probably already made up their minds. He thought Truax should just get it over with. Truax droned on.

Finally, Burr thought, it sounds like he's just about finished.

"Again, ladies and gentlemen, this is a very simple case," Truax said. "A man has killed his wife. The people of the State of Michigan submit to you that he did it on purpose. That it was not an accident. That the defendant planned the murder. The laser evidence proves that he picked up the gun and fired it. That he did it on purpose."

"Why did he do it? Because he was having an affair with that woman." Truax pointed his long bony finger again, this time at Sarah. Burr was tempted to bite it off. Calvin reminded him of every self-righteous zealot he'd ever met. His morality confounded him.

"Why?" Truax asked. "Because his wife would not give him a divorce as Father Yatchek told us yesterday. That's the why of it."

"And finally, Frank X. Tavohnen had a plan," Truax said. "First, he went downstairs and got the gun ready. Then he called his wife. His own son said so. Then he shot her. With his son upstairs. Can you imagine anything more terrible than a father killing his son's mother? With his son just a few feet away? Why would he do that?" Truax asked. "To make sure it appeared to be an accident. Can you imagine anything more horrible? I can't."

"Ladies and gentlemen, this is first degree murder. An intentional killing with a plan. Can there be any doubt that the defendant killed his wife? No. Can there be an any doubt he intended to do it? No. Can there be any doubt that he had a plan? No."

"Ladies and Gentlemen, the people of the State of Michigan ask that you convict the defendant . . ." Truax pointed again. Burr knew he would. " …Frank X. Tavohnen of first-degree murder."

"Thank you, Mr. Truax," Gillis said. "Mr. Lafayette?"

"May we have a moment, Your Honor?"

"You may have a moment that lasts no longer than one minute," Gillis said.

Burr reached into the pocket of his suit coat and extracted the shell casing, hiding it in his first. He stood, leaned over the railing to Sarah and Suzanne. With his back to Gillis, he showed them his fist, knuckles up. Slowly, he turned his fist over, palm up. Then he opened his fist. The shell casing lay there. Burr felt their eyes on his hand. He looked at Suzanne, looking at his hand. He tried to read her look but could find no meaning. After a lie that had gone on for almost seven years, he didn't expect to learn much from her, and he didn't.

"What's that?" Sarah said. "What's that got to do with anything?"

"What are you doing?" Suzanne hissed at him.

"Mr. Lafayette," Gillis said, "if you do not continue immediately, you will lose your opportunity."

Suzanne bolted to her feet, grabbed at Burr's hand. He snatched it away, caught her wrist with his free hand, surprised at how easily his hand fit around it.

"What are you doing?" Suzanne asked again, pleading this time.

"You will sit there and shut up," Burr said, under his breath.

"I will not," she said.

Burr pushed her back. She fell into her seat.

"Will this circus never end?" Gillis said, mostly to himself. He shook his round, bald head.

Burr put the shell casing back in his pocket, turned to Gillis and the jury. He pulled the cuffs of his shirt down his wrists, past the sleeve of his jacket. Then he tightened the knot of his tie, a red, white, and blue stripe, which did not need tightening.

"Ladies and gentlemen," Burr said, turning first to Gillis and then to the jury. "That we are here today is a travesty, an injustice in itself. My client has spent almost a year in jail. He was not allowed bail. He was deprived of his family. His wife and small child." Burr swept his hand to Sarah and to Becky, who he had made sure was here today.

Burr approached Gillis. He fished the shell casing out of his pocket one more time. Then he set it on a ledge, an ornate piece of trim, just below Gillis, where Gillis couldn't see it and where Burr himself blocked Truax from seeing it, but where Suzanne and Sarah had no choice but to see it.

"Ladies and gentlemen," Burr said. "You must decide what happened that day." Burr could feel Suzanne's eyes burning a hole in his back. "This is what happened and this is why you must find Mr. Tavohnen not guilty. Mr. Tavohnen lent his deer rifle to Mr. Farr. Mr. Farr returned it. No one was home, so he left it in the garage. Where it stayed until the night that Mr. Tavohnen, his wife, and son returned with their Christmas tree, which they chopped in the woods every year. A family tradition. Then the three of them decorated the tree, as a family, just like they always did. Then Mr. Tavohnen took the deer rifle to his workbench in the basement so he could clean it. He checked to make sure the gun was unloaded. May I demonstrate, Your Honor?"

"If you must," Gillis said.

Burr picked up the gun from the evidence table. "Mr. Tavohnen racked the gun like this." Burr pulled the bolt back and then shoved it forward. No shell came out. While he was cleaning the gun, Mrs. Tavohnen came downstairs to speak with him. He continued to clean the gun, which was shown to be extremely dirty. While he was cleaning it, the gun accidentally discharged, killing Mrs. Tavohnen. That is what occurred. It was a horrible tragedy, but a tragedy is not a murder. It was an accident."

"Why was it an accident?" Burr said.

"First, the police determined it to be an accident. The investigating officer, a man with over thirty year's experience, said so. The county coroner said so, too. An inquest was held and the judge at the inquest said it was an accident. This occurred almost seven years ago, and it was ruled an accident then. What has changed in almost seven years?" Burr paused. "Nothing," he said. "Nothing changed."

"But the prosecutor would have us believe that Mr. Tavohnen killed his wife in his son's presence. Why would he have us believe that? Well," Burr now faced Truax, "his political aspirations notwithstanding..."

"Objection," Truax said.

Burr raised his right hand in submission.

"The prosecutor claims he has new evidence from a laser, of all things, that he says proves the gun was picked up and fired. Nonsense. The evidence just isn't there."

"What else does the prosecutor say? He says Mr. Tavohnen had an affair. He says Claudia wouldn't give him a divorce so Mr. Tavohnen killed her. Why does he say this? Because there is a supposed affair. Because an upset son, and a nosy neighbor, say so. And because a priest who testifies at the last minute says Mrs. Tavohnen asked him about a divorce."

Burr turned his back to the jury, hands in his pockets, "That just doesn't add up. Why? Now he faced the jury. Because in this state if someone wants a divorce, they get it. That's why. Just get a divorce. Why kill someone? Especially with your son upstairs."

Burr looked at his shoes, then back to the jury. "I for one, and of course, I have a bias here, can't understand for the life of me, why after all this time anyone would bring a charge like this?" Burr turned his head away from Truax, as to speak to them privately. "Unless there were other reasons."

Burr paused, waited for Truax to object, who didn't. Then he arched his eyebrows, again and spoke privately to the jury. "Do you know why after all this time a murder charge should not be brought?" he asked. "Well, for one reason, evidence has a way of disappearing over time. In this case, the prosecution doesn't even have the gun. Can you imagine that? A murder case with no weapon? They cannot produce the gun that killed Mrs. Tavohnen. The only gun we have is the one introduced by the defense and the expert witness says the gun that killed Mrs. Tavohnen may have been defective."

" It's one thing to pick up a gun, aim it at someone and fire it. It's another thing if it goes off accidentally. But it's still another thing if the gun goes off because—even if you're careful—it doesn't work right. And that, ladies and gentlemen, is what we have here."

"One more thing. Frank Tavohnen was never in trouble with the law before this tragic accident or after. Not once. Never."

"And let me ask you this. Is it so unusual for a man, a widower to remarry and have a child?"

"This man," Burr said, now pointing at Frank, "lost his dental practice. He lost his life here in Petoskey. He had to move away because of this. He has now spent almost the last twelve months in jail, may now lose his business, and most of all, may spend the rest of his life in jail."

"I submit to you, ladies and gentlemen, this man is not a murderer. If anything, Frank Tavohnen is a victim. A tragic accident occurred a long time ago. An accident. It was terrible, but it was not murder. I ask you, ladies and gentlemen. Do not convict Frank Tavohnen of murder. He is not guilty."

Burr turned toward Gillis and, as casually as he could, picked up the shell casing and slipped it back into his pocket. He felt sweat run down his arm. It always happened after a closing argument. At the defense table, Jacob nodded his approval. Frank smiled at him feebly., Sarah smiled wickedly. Suzanne cut him with her eyes.

Frank tapped on his arm. "What was the thing you put in your pocket?"

'Nothing," Burr said.

"Ladies and gentlemen," Gillis said. "In spite of what these two able advocates have argued, you have more choices than guilty of first degree murder or not guilty because of accidental death. It is now my job to instruct you in the various decisions you may make. It is your job to determine guilt or innocence of three crimes of which I will now instruct you. It is not your job to determine a sentence if you find guilt. That is my job."

"Your job is to determine guilt or innocence. Is that clear?" Gillis talked to them like children, and they nodded, in unison. "Very well," he said. Gillis opened a book. Burr knew he was about to read the court approved jury instructions.

"Ladies and gentlemen, the defendant is charged with the crime of first degree premeditated murder. To prove this charge, the prosecutor must prove each of the following elements beyond a reasonable doubt."

"First, that the defendant caused the death of Claudia Tavohnen. That is that Claudia Tavohnen died as a result of a gunshot."

"Second, that the defendant intended to kill Claudia Tavohnen."

"Third, that the intent to kill was premeditated. That is, thought out beforehand. That means that the killing was deliberate, which means that the defendant considered the pros and cons of the killing, and thought about it, and chose to kill."

Burr saw the jury's eyes, their collective eyes, begin to glaze over, not an altogether bad sign. He looked to Frank, who definitely looked confused.

"What's he saying?" asked Frank.

"He's saying that to convict you of first degree murder it takes three things," Burr said. "One, that you killed Claudia; two, that you killed her on purpose; three, you planned to kill her."

"I didn't plan to kill her," Frank said.

"I know that," Burr said. "But to find you guilty of first-degree murder, that's what it takes."

"You may also consider the lesser charge of second degree murder," Gillis said. "To prove this charge . . ."

"For second degree murder," Burr said, "you have to kill someone and do it on purpose. But without a plan. An intentional killing with no premeditation. You lost your temper and killed Claudia. No plan in advance."

"I didn't do that either," Frank said.

"I know, Frank," Burr said.

"You may also consider the charge of involuntary manslaughter with a firearm," Gillis said. This crime is an accidental death caused by the careless use of a firearm. To determine guilt you must find four elements. One, the defendant caused the death of Claudia Tavohnen. Two, the death resulted from the discharge of a firearm. Three, at the time the firearm went off, the defendant was pointing it at the deceased. Four, the defendant intended to point the firearm at the deceased."

"He is saying that you intended to point it and the gun went off accidentally."

"I didn't do that either," Frank said.

This time Burr didn't answer Frank.

"Are there any questions?" Gillis said. He surveyed the jury who Burr thought looked confused but apparently had no questions. "Then the bailiff will escort you to the jury room, which I know you're familiar with. Please ask him if there is anything you need. Remember, your verdict must be unanimous."

"Now what?" Frank said.

"Now we wait," Frank said. "They'll take you back to your cell until there's a verdict."

"How long will it take?" Frank said.

"I have no idea," Burr said.

"You son of a bitch," Suzanne said. "Just who do you think you are? With that shell casing. Who exactly gave you the right to play with a man's life because of your own ego." Suzanne spit the words at him, like venom. He had never seen her this mad. Her lips were blood red.

The bailiff had given them a windowless room. Jacob, Eve, Sarah, and, of course, Suzanne, who was still screaming at him. He had known since last night that it would come to this. They all sat at a rectangular table, Burr at one end; Suzanne at the other. Burr saw the cigarette burns on the varnish, black, ran his fingertips over the blemishes. Smooth to the touch but black underneath.

"How dare you?" Suzanne said.

Burr hoped he had played it right. He had taken a chance with the shell casing, and he knew it. He had done it to shock Suzanne and Sarah, to flush them out. Had the jury, Truax, or worse yet, Gillis, seen it, there would have been hell to pay. Frank didn't know what was going on, and Burr really had no right, but he had done it anyway. Once more he reached into his jacket pocket, pulled out the shell casing. He held it between his right thumb and forefinger, top to bottom. Looked at it. He had to hold it arms' length to focus on it, to really see it. (He thought he might need reading glasses.) Then he set it down on the burn mark.

"Suzanne, how dare I? I might say, how dare you? And to you, the second Mrs. Tavohnen, I might say the same, only more so."

"I was taken in," Burr said. "Duped. Played for a fool. I admit it. There was no reason to hire me, of all people, to try this case. We all know that. I allowed myself to believe there were good reasons for it. I'm smart, a great litigator. Just a little down on my luck. So I thought I could do it. And I think I did a pretty good job. The gun was genius on my part, and I think we pulled it off." He stopped, looked straight at Suzanne. "And I thought perhaps Suzanne and I might start over."

Burr picked up the shell and tapped it on the table.

"But ladies," he nodded to Suzanne and Sarah, "the genius is truly yours. Hire a broken down lawyer, convince him there's been a terrible injustice, turn him loose. And rekindle the flame of a second chance at love."

"You sent me on a fool's errand," Burr said. "Let me have just enough rope. Don't tell me everything. Just enough. And when it looks bad, lie a little, just enough to keep me going. And never, ever, tell the whole truth."

"And, Suzanne, my dear, you spread your legs just enough and at just the right times to keep me believing. Yours is the grandest performance."

"I won't listen to another word." Suzanne stood. "I'm leaving."

"Sit down," Burr said.

She didn't.

"Sit," Burr said. He stared at her. She stood and stood, then slowly she sat, like a dog who knew what had been commanded, who didn't want to sit, but fearing the consequences, sat slowly, in an act of defiance.

"Ladies and gentlemen. Here's what really happened," Burr said. "Frank, as we all know, is a very nice man, but as we all know, he's a coward—afraid to death, no pun intended, of Claudia but too scared to do anything about it."

"Frank and Sarah have this affair. It heats up. Frank's getting laid so often he can't see straight." Burr looked at Sarah who did not flinch. "Sarah is husband hunting. What she sees in Frank, I don't know, except I guess she thinks she can be on top. Literally and figuratively, I suppose."

"The little plan was going perfectly except Claudia wouldn't say yes to a divorce. Not that she needed to. But Frank was too much of a coward to push it."

"And then Sarah, you turn up pregnant. So there you were. Pregnant and no husband to show for it. And no prospect of one because Frank can't pull the trigger with Claudia. And who wants to have a baby and no husband?"

Jacob and Eve jumped in their seats.

"The baby was going to be born too soon, wasn't she? And that's why you moved away. It wasn't that there were no patients. It was the baby. Because the birth certificate says Becky was born in August, but you've always said it was the following June. Jacob found out when he went to Detroit. I thought Becky might be a bit big for her age. She's not big for her age. She's older than you said she was. I don't know how Truax missed that." Burr ran his hands through his hair. "It just wouldn't work, would it Sarah? You pregnant and no husband. Of course, that was Claudia's problem, too. But I think we all just found out about that."

"Back to the story," Burr said. "So here's what happened. And what a dumb idea it was. And how did it go so wrong?"

"Sarah, you tell Frank, look, get Claudia downstairs. Go down and clean the rifle. When she comes down, tell her you want a divorce. Pick the gun up, aim it at her. Threaten her. Maybe even pull the trigger. Scare her into it. "

"And what did you do, Sarah? You snuck over there. I don't know exactly when, but I'm pretty sure it was the day Claudia was killed. You had to make sure he'd go through with your plan, didn't you? So you snuck over when nobody was home, but Mrs. Larsen saw you. The gun wasn't defective at all, was it? It wasn't the gun, it was the shell. You took this shell from Frank's house. I don't know when. You either cut the rim off or filed it off. I don't know which. Then you snuck over and put the shell in the chamber."

"Poor old Frank. He's really into it now, isn't he? He's playing the part because you told him you were pregnant. He'd already done that once before. Get Claudia down in the basement, you said. Demand a divorce. Threaten her. Point the rifle at her. It was your idea for him to clean the gun that night, wasn't it?"

"Frank picks up the gun, points it at Claudia, threatens her and he pulls the trigger and bang the gun goes off and she's dead."

"Nobody is more surprised than Frank. He had no idea. He racked the chamber. All you ever hoped for was that the gun would go off. You never dreamed he'd shoot her. It was a dumb idea by a scared kid who was in a panic. You'd never do it now but you did it then. And you never told him. Did you, Sarah?" Burr paused. "Bad luck. Very bad luck."

"It's a lie," Sarah said.

"I wish it were a lie," Burr said

"This is a horrible, horrible lie," Sarah screamed at him.

"You should have looked in the drain," Burr said. "Your realtor did."

"It's a lie and you know it," Sarah screamed at him again, louder this time.

"I might have some of it wrong, but I think I'm close," Burr said.

"As for the possible attempts on my life, if that's what they were ...the Jeep was my own stupidity. And Kismet was old. Let's call that an accident, for now, because you needed me for the trial. But the fire—which one of you set it? I'd like to think it was an accident, but after all this, I know better. Were you trying to destroy evidence, scare me, or kill me? Was I too close to the truth? Whatever it was, by that time, I guess you were afraid I was on to something."

"I don't think you wanted Claudia dead," Burr said. "I think it was a stupid plan by a desperate young woman. How old were you? Twenty four? Twenty five? It just went very, very wrong."

"You're lying. You made all this up," Sarah said, still screaming but close to tears.

"Suzanne. I don't know when you knew. I'd like to think it was after the fact, but I really don't know. You should have known better with Frank. He wasn't a very good liar. Even after you coached him. To your credit, you are a loyal sister. And I am a true sucker."

"How can you let this happen to Frank?" Sarah shrieked at him. This was the first time he'd seen her anywhere near hysterical. "You've got to do something."

He looked at Sarah. "All you have to do is tell the truth. That's all. Tell Truax you put the shell in the gun. Then Frank is off."

Sarah looked at her lap.

"But you can't do that, can you? Because then it's you who is guilty of murder," Burr said. And there's your daughter to think of. I think you think that it's better that Frank takes the heat. You already thought that through, didn't you?"

Swede called them back in. They were all in their places.

"Have you reached a verdict?" asked Gillis.

"We have," the foreman (actually a woman) said.

"Defendant, please rise," the Swede said. Frank stood, head down.

"On the charge of first degree murder, how do you find the defendant?" Gillis asked.

"Not guilty, Your Honor," said the forewoman.

"On the charge of second degree murder," Gillis said.

"Not guilty, Your Honor," said the forewoman.

"On the charge of involuntary manslaughter," Gillis said.

"Guilty, Your Honor," said the forewoman.

Frank looked up at the jury, then to Sarah, then his chest heaved and he sat.

"Stand up, Mr. Tavohnen," Gillis said.

Burr helped him up. Frank began to cry.

Gillis to the jury, "So say you one, so say you all."

Burr thought it sounded like a nursery rhyme. The jury said a staggered yes.

"Thank you," Gillis said. "The court finds Frank Tavohnen guilty of involuntary manslaughter with a firearm. Mr. Tavohnen, you will be held in the county jail until," Gillis flipped through his papers, "until November 19, at which time you will be sentenced." He banged his gavel and stood.

"Your Honor," Burr said.

Gillis, standing, "Yes, Mr. Lafayette."

"May I address the court? Briefly?"

"Make it quick," Gillis said.

"Your Honor," Burr said, "the statute of limitations for involuntary manslaughter is six years."

"I am aware of that," Gillis said.

"Your Honor, Mr. Tavohnen was charged after the statute had run."

Truax jumped to his feet. "That's not true, Your Honor. He was arraigned December 14th, four days before the statute ran."

"Your Honor," Burr said, "as you may recall, the first arraignment was defective. Mr. Tavohnen was not properly charged until December 26th, eight days after the statute ran.

"Your Honor, that's not true," Truax said.

Gillis sat down and looked at his papers. He thumped his forehead. He shuffled through them, then, looking over his glasses at the prosecutor, said "Mr. Truax, Claudia Tavohnen was killed on December 18, 1982. You first charged Frank X. Tavohnen with open murder on December 14, 1988. While that charge was within the statute of limitations, the Court of Appeals ruled that that charge was defective and dismissed the case. Frank X. Tavohnen was properly charged December 26, 1988, eight days after the statute ran. Mr. Truax, I am afraid Mr. Lafayette has the dates right."

"Your Honor," Truax said, "if that was the case, the defense had a duty to object to the jury instructions. He could not knowingly allow a charge that could not be carried out."

"Your Honor, the jury can convict my client of a crime," Burr said, "but there can be no sentence because the statute of limitations has run."

"Mr. Truax, I am afraid Mr. Lafayette is correct," Gillis said. He turned to Frank. "Mr. Tavohnen, you either have a very fine lawyer or you are very lucky." Gillis shook his head. "Mr. Tavohnen, you are free to go," he said. "The two of you," Gillis said, pointing first to Truax then to Burr, "approach the bench." Gillis leaned forward, spoke quietly. "Calvin, do not, I repeat, do not ever, ever bring anything like this in my courtroom again."

"Your Honor, as County Prosecutor, I have the responsibility..."

"Stop right there, Calvin," Gillis said. "I said don't ever do this again. Is that clear?"

"Yes, Your Honor," Truax said.

"And by the way, Calvin, you have lost my vote." Truax reddened, did not reply. Gillis turned to Burr. "As to you, Mr. Lafayette."

"Yes, Your Honor," Burr said.

"While I have come to appreciate your skills as a litigator, I would take it as a personal favor if you never appeared in my courtroom again."

"I am sure that can be arranged, Your Honor," Burr said.

"Very well then," Gillis said. "We are adjourned." He slammed down the gavel and left. Burr and Truax removed themselves to their respective tables.

Truax stood at the prosecutor's table, his mouth hanging open. Truax jerked his lower jaw left, then right, then left again, back and forth. Truax turned to Burr and slammed his mouth shut. Smiling at Burr, Truax marched over and shoved his hand out toward Burr who took it without thinking. The prosecutor pumped his hand with vigor.

"My condolences, Mr. Lafayette," Truax said.

"Condolences?" Burr asked.

"Your client was convicted," Truax said.

"My client is a free man," Burr said.

"A technicality," Truax said, smiling. "A technicality."

"I take comfort in the fact that your behavior has been remarkably consistent throughout this entire sham," Burr said, letting go of Truax's hand.

"My behavior?" Truax asked.

"You have been an ass throughout. An ambitious, manipulative, self-absorbed ass," Burr said, who knew something about self-absorption.

Truax did not reply.

"You were the one who ran me off the road," Burr said. "It's your black Cadillac in the parking lot."

"My wife's, actually," Truax said, giving up. "My car wouldn't start this morning."

"Really," Burr said. "Why did you run me off the road? And sink my boat? And the fire? Why were you trying to kill me?"

"I had nothing to do with your boat," Truax said. "As to your Jeep, I am sorry. I was following you. I was curious about your defense."

"So you tried to kill me?"

"No, no, no," Truax said. "I was following you, trying to find out what you were doing. Then I decided I'd had enough so I tried to pass. You were driving very slowly. And then you wouldn't let me by. So I sped up. I had no idea you crashed. Until later."

"Why didn't you tell me?"

"What good would have come of it?"

Burr looked away then back at Truax. "You may need a new engine," Burr said. "For the beige Buick."

"What? How would you know?"

Burr ignored him. "I suspect," he said, "that you got exactly what you wanted out of all this."

"I suspect I did," Truax said. "When I am elected, I will serve with the same zeal as I have prosecuted crime in Emmet County He turned, walked to the prosecution table, picked up his papers. Burr watched him walk down the aisle and leave the courtroom.

Frank, still standing, looked at Burr then sank back into his chair. When Burr looked over at him, he was wiping the tears off his cheeks with his sleeve.

"What happened?" Frank asked. "I thought I was guilty,' Frank said.

"You are," Burr said.

"What happened," Jacob said, "is that your lawyer is barely a half step short of brilliant."

Sarah ran up and hugged her husband. "Frank, Frank," she said.

"What happened?" Frank asked, again.

"The law says that for certain crimes the defendant must be charged by a certain date. In the case of involuntary manslaughter, within six years after the crime occurs," Burr said. "If not, it's just too long ago."

"What does that mean?" Frank said.

"It means that after all the delay back in December, after all the arguing and fighting, by the time Truax got you charged, it was too late for involuntary manslaughter," Jacob said. "But not for first and second degree murder," Jacob said. "Those crimes don't have a statute of limitations."

"Did you know that all along?" Frank said. Frank looked at Burr like a puppy.

Burr took the shell casing out of his jacket pocket. He opened Frank's pudgy hand. "Ask Sarah about this." He dropped it into Frank's palm.

"You played with his life," Sarah said.

"You, Madam, played with his life, not me."

"Burr Lafayette," Suzanne said, "you are a liar and an arrogant fool."

"No, Suzanne. You are the liar," Burr said. "Regrettably, I suspect your second accusation is true."

Suzanne raised her hand to slap him, but something in his look stopped her. She lowered her hand and glared at him. He turned and walked away.

Burr climbed into the Vista Cruiser and drove back to Crooked Lake with Zeke. He put his waders back on over his suit and threw out the same seven decoys he had hunted over that morning.